God Just Wanted to Play Golf

The Oceanview Trilogy: Book One

God Just Wanted To Play Golf

ISBN 13: 978-0-9909010-1-3
2nd Edition
Printed in the USA

RED CROWN publishing

for Tera and Lily for the gift of love and patience...

for Fred and George for the gift of inspiration...

CHAPTER 1

The fastest way to get under the Grim Reaper's skin was to call him the Grim Reaper. Sure, he did reap souls for a living, that part of the moniker rang true, but he was not grim. Grumpy maybe, surly, sometimes, but not grim. Likewise, no one called him the Jovial Reaper or the Chipper Reaper. There were plenty of times when he acted jovial or chipper, and on rare occasions, both. No, those names packed far less of a punch as something as morose as the Grim Reaper. He preferred to be called Death, but would settle for the Man in Black, the Angel of Dark and Light, or as his friends knew him, Steve.

The second quickest way to irritate him was a reaping in Vegas. He hated everything about the city, from the obnoxious flashing lights to the constant rattling of change, and he would find Thomas Nixon, his next customer, deep in the heart of the Strip.

Thomas was thirty-seven minutes away from being the first tiny wheel in a series of events that would flip both Heaven and Earth entirely and hopelessly on their collective asses. He was in Vegas to show Dustin, his childhood best friend, the bachelor party of a lifetime. For ten hours, they bounced from strip club to casino with eleven of their closest friends, drinking more, gambling more, and tipping incrementally better.

The group started at one end of the Strip in the early evening, and each hour they moved to another venue. Aside from lap dances and enough alcohol to drop a steer, the night passed without drama. By 4:00 a.m., most of the group had either thrown up on or thrown in the proverbial bar towel, and crawled, staggered, or barfed their way back to their respective hotels.

1

Dustin raised a middle finger as the last of the deserters stumbled out of the club. "Lightweights," he yelled at their departing backs.

Thomas and the groom-to-be, the last men standing, found themselves in a smaller strip club. As they continued to slam shots and slip hundred-dollar bills into various G-strings, two dancers permanently joined them at their table. Dustin immediately turned on the charm and started sweet-talking the girls, neither one older than nineteen. They giggled at Dustin's overused anecdotes about his last night on Earth. He withheld *'as a free and single man'*.

Thomas intended to bring the party to an end, but Dustin looked far too happy, and he did not want to ruin his night. He shrugged it off and decided to deal with the aftermath in the morning. Dustin had lied to his fiancée, Kari, for years, so one more thing made little difference. Each year something larger crept into the tangle of lies. The tears on the roof lining of his Mustang from the high heels of the woman he banged in the back seat? He blamed those on two-by-fours he claimed he picked up from Home Depot. The scratches on his back? Those were from a dog that clawed him when he bent over to tie his shoe. As his indiscretions became more substantial, his lies became more pathetic.

Eventually, Dustin decided everyone should go back to his room and that the girls needed to bring a friend for Thomas. Thomas politely declined and excused himself from the chaos, leaving the group to their upcoming drunken orgy. Shouts of *'traitor'* followed him as he stumbled through the lobby. If he so much as smelled another drink, he expected to get acquainted with the floor and stay there. Besides, the chances of getting aroused, regardless of how attractive he found the girls, were low. Thomas could barely locate his wallet. Obtaining and maintaining an erection seemed like mission impossible.

The sidewalk glistened with rain as he stepped outside, the temperature noticeably colder than when he first entered. He wished Dustin had planned the wedding for the summer. It was his first time visiting the southwest, and he expected it to be much warmer, even in the middle of December. The entire world spun as he struggled to make it to the curb. He raised his hand, and a cab stopped in front of him, splashing his shoes.

"Asshole," he slurred as he opened the door and climbed inside.

"Where to?" the gruff cabbie mumbled through the open passenger separator window.

"Huh?" Thomas struggled to focus as he fumbled with the door.

"Where to? The clock is running, douchebag."

Thomas looked at the clock. Sure enough, the driver had racked up $5.35 before moving an inch. His focus was spent on trying to avoid vomiting and closing the door rather than determining his destination. "I'm in the big building on the Strip with the flashy lights."

"I don't know if you've been paying attention, buddy, but all the hotels on the Strip are big fucking buildings with flashing fucking lights on them."

Thomas glanced out of the window. Sure enough, the entire Strip glowed with seizure-inducing flashing fucking lights and really big fucking buildings.

The cabbie grunted and rolled his eyes. "You have a room key?"

"Huh?"

"Little plastic thing you use to get into your hotel room. It'll have the hotel name on it."

"Oh, yeah." Thomas reached in his pocket and fished out a plastic credit card-shaped room key. He flipped it over to see the other side. "Belgio? Bellagria? Belagoo?" He turned the card towards the cabbie.

The driver looked up at his rear-view mirror. "Bellagio."

"Yeah, that."

"There you go, Einstein," the cabbie said as he pulled away from the curb. "Fucking tourists," he mumbled under his breath.

"Fucking cabbies," muttered Thomas.

The remainder of the ride passed by in a punctuated silence. Thomas pulled out his phone and stared at the blank screen to avoid conversing with the driver. Despite the early hour, the Strip swelled with tourists. He gazed out the window as he watched people pour through the casinos. The excited and optimistic striding in, the dejected and broke stumbling out. The driver took a few detours that Thomas felt were done simply to rack up the tab, but after fifteen minutes of kangaroo stops, weird ethnic gestures, and foreign cursing, the suicidal cabbie pulled up on the opposite side of the road of the Bellagio.

"Eighteen dollars, plus tip," he said gruffly.

"What?"

"You deaf as well as drunk? I said eighteen dollars."

Thomas sneered and handed the cabbie his debit card. He had no intention of tipping the miserable bastard for an overpriced one-and-a-half-mile cab ride.

"Declined," the cabbie said as he aggressively thrust the credit card back at Thomas.

"What? It can't be."

The cabbie spun the computer screen to show him. "Dee-clined." He tapped the screen twice for emphasis. "I want another payment."

The night had hit Thomas's bank harder than he thought, and he had no idea how he would make it through the rest of the trip. He fumbled through his wallet for cash. "All I have is a hundred."

"I don't got any change."

"Motherfucker." Thomas handed over the hundred and what amounted to an eighty-two-dollar tip. The cabbie grabbed the bill with a sizeable gap-toothed grin. It was not his first rodeo.

Thomas opened the door and stepped outside as the driver pulled away. "And it's *I don't have any*. Not *I don't got any*, you illiterate fuckwit," he shouted after the cab.

The rain had increased during the ride over and soaked him seconds after exiting the cab. Thomas cursed under his breath. An eighty-two-dollar tip did not even get him to the right side of the road. He pulled his collar up and walked over to the crowd huddled at the traffic light, waiting to cross the street. He hated Vegas, and the experience had milked him from the moment he stepped off the plane.

His phone buzzed softly in his hand. He glanced down to see a picture of Dustin's face buried between a pair of ample breasts pop up on the screen. He hoped the idiot remembered to delete it before he took the trip home. On cue, a text from Kari immediately followed, inquiring about the night's activities. Barely able to focus on the screen, let alone type, he tried to respond that they were doing well.

'*Werdoon wewel*'

Delete.

'*Wed dong weel*'

Delete.

'*Wdwel*'

Delete.

"Screw it."

He put his phone back in his pocket, unable to answer. Besides, she had violated guy code. The bride-to-be should never text the groom on his last night on earth as a bachelor.

As Thomas stepped into the crowd, a man in a long black robe appeared behind him, but Thomas paid no attention. It took all his effort to remain upright. He may have taken some comfort in that even if he quickly sobered up, he would not have seen Death. No one ever saw Death. Death's cloak was not just a simple item of clothing to promote his morbid image. It allowed him to become invisible at will. With the hood up, he could walk the Earth and reap unnoticed. With it pulled down, he became more visible, but only to those in direct communication with him. His robe also allowed him to teleport, and he appreciated avoiding mass transit. Besides the fact he found public buses to be repulsive, he enjoyed the sensation of teleporting. Although he never fully adjusted to the flips his stomach made and compared the experience to bungee jumping.

Thankfully, he possessed immunity to all known diseases except for stupidity, so when he did have to interact with people in a large setting, he never caught anything. Death liked to travel and see the world, but never considered himself much of a people person. He quickly became irritated when forced to be near too many at the same time.

The reaping process was simple. Each morning, Death's office received two lists, one from Heaven, and the other from Hell. His secretary, Susan, combined them on her computer and sent him on his way. He checked his lists, located the person, double-checked his list, and then tapped them on the shoulder. A tap on the left shoulder sent them to Heaven, and on the right to Lucifer. Read twice, tap once. Simple.

Death looked down and reviewed his list. In a few moments, a cab would hit Thomas and drag him forty feet behind it. It was going to be bloody.

The walk notification lit up, and as one, the crowd stepped into the street. Thomas stood on the edge of the group, and as he reached the halfway point, he walked dangerously close to the traffic running parallel to him. The outcome seemed clear to Death as he glanced at his pocket watch and studied the second hand.

Three.

Two.

One.

He reached out to tap Thomas on the left shoulder. Just as he had done with every soul before him, and as he would with all souls who followed. But what happened next contradicted everything Death knew about reaping. Nothing. Somehow the cab missed Thomas. Death took another swipe at him as another cab passed by. Nothing.

He looked around in confusion. In all his years of reaping, he never made a mistake. He reached into his robe and pulled out his list. It highlighted the correct place and time, and the right Thomas Nixon, but he certainly could not reap him. In the act of desperation, Death tapped him a third time as Thomas reached the opposite side of the street and disappeared into the crowd. Death stopped, unsure what to do. There were no contingency plans for a failed reaping because the process always worked. He closed his eyes and disappeared.

CHAPTER 2

Given the choice of noun, one would not describe Miley as a people person. Her detest of humanity deviated from a typical run-of-the-mill dislike, such as getting David Hasselhoff's Greatest Hits CD for Christmas. Nor did she have the odium aimed at intolerance to tomatoes on a Cobb salad, or polka dots and burlap. It was a deep guttural loathing, which started in the pit of her stomach and boiled and churned until the tips of her tightly permed hairs curled round in a unified disgust. The level of fury reserved for network television when they cancel a favorite show halfway through the season. So, naturally a perfect match for customer service.

"Ninety-six?" she screamed from behind a large counter window. Miley was a grumpy middle-aged woman, and the people seated in the waiting room irritated her sixty-three percent more than those sitting there the previous day. She made no eye contact with the packed room beyond the glass as the digital number above her window ticked over to echo her irritated announcement. "Which one of you assholes is ninety-six?"

She sported rouged cheeks, clashing orange lipstick, and an obnoxious pair of bright red spectacles. High-arched penciled eyebrows earned her the nickname Our Lady of Perpetual Surprise, and her thick makeup appeared to have been applied with a paint roller. Miley owned the personality of a banshee and spent her days stabbing at a keyboard with sausage-like fingers logging in new residents.

"He went to the bathroom," said a young man in the seat closest to the window as he pointed to the bathroom door behind him. "He said he'd be right back."

"Well, fuck him and his weak bladder. Ninety-seven."

"He said he'd be—"

"NINETY-SEVEN."

The number changed as an old lady named Rose cautiously stood from her seat, unsure if she should take the place of the absent bathroom dweller. "I'm ninety-seven." She hobbled over to Miley. "Thank Heaven," she said as she reached the counter. "I didn't think you would ever call me."

"Red ninety-seven?"

Rose looked at her blue ticket and frowned.

"Wrong color. Go sit back down and wait your turn, Grandma." Miley's personality equaled the abrasiveness of her fashion sense.

"I've been waiting for four days."

"Go sit the fuck back down."

Tears welled up behind Rose's glasses.

Miley let out an agitated sigh. She hated it when the noobs cried at her desk. "Go sit the fuck back down, please." Even her pleasant voice dripped with vitriol.

The bathroom pointer sitting in the front row waved his ticket as he stood up from his seat. "I'm red ninety-seven. She can have mine if it's okay?" he said as he crossed over to the window.

Miley was unimpressed. "Whatever you want, hero. Stop trying to get into her vintage granny panties. You're holding up the line."

"I wasn't—"

"You're holding up the line."

Rose smiled at her generous donor. "God bless you, young man. You are so kind."

He smiled as they traded tickets. "My pleasure, ma'am," he said as he returned to his seat.

Miley coughed rudely. "This little circle jerk is cute and all, but the line ain't getting any shorter. What do you want, red ninety-seven?"

Rose turned back to the window. "I'm here to see Saint Peter."

"Why?"

"I think I died."

"You think you died?"

"Yes."

"But you don't know?"

"No."

"Does it feel like you're dead?"

"I don't know. I've never died before."

"Well, I don't have all day to coddle you while you figure it out. There are others in line quite comfortable being dead."

"They are?"

"Yes, and you're still holding up the fucking line."

"Can you give me any pointers? I don't know what to do."

Miley rolled her eyes and let out another long, agitated sigh. "What's the last thing you remember?"

"I woke up with a crushing pain in my chest and heading towards a bright light. Then I'm sitting here reading a three-year-old People magazine."

"Yep, sounds as though you died."

"Oh dear, oh dear. Is there anything I can do about that?"

"Are you Hindu?"

Rose shook her head. "Heavens, no. What an awful question to ask."

"Then, no. No do-overs."

"This timing isn't very good. It's a bit inconvenient if I were to be completely honest. I have some loose ends to tie up. Can I go back for a few hours to sort them out?"

"That's not how it works," said Miley.

"I didn't get to say goodbye to Toodles."

"Toodles?"

"My cat." said Rose with a sad smile, already missing her dear feline.

Miley shrugged in dismissal. "I wouldn't worry about it. It'll pace your apartment wailing in agony until it drops dead from starvation because no one came to check on you."

"Toodles is a he, not an it."

"Whatever. You'll probably be reunited soon enough."

"Probably? Don't all cats go to Heaven?"

"Nope."

"But cats are cute," countered Rose.

"Most of them are assholes."

"Toodles is not an asshole."

"No, of course not."

Rose started to get flustered again. "I want to see Saint Peter."

"He's busy."

"I thought someone might show me what to do."

"You and everybody else." Miley nodded to the rest of the room.

"Everyone here is waiting to get checked in."

"I don't know what to do."

Miley rolled her eyes and returned to annihilating her keyboard.

Rose continued to stand at the counter and let out an exaggerated sigh. The passive-aggressive type of sigh. The sigh that screamed '*save me, I'm helpless and pathetic*'.

Miley stopped typing and turned to the irritating customer. She also hated it when they sighed. "He isn't in the office today."

"Isn't he supposed to meet me at the entrance?"

"His nine o'clock ran long."

"But it's only eight-thirty."

Miley shrugged and continued her keyboard massacre. Indifferent at being called out on an outright lie.

"Doesn't he meet everyone?"

"Urban legend."

The first tear rolled down Rose's cheek.

Miley clenched her teeth in anger. The old lady was forcing her to be helpful. "What's your name?"

She sniffed. "Rose Stanton."

The receptionist skimmed through her list. "No, no Rose Standon here."

"Did you say Standon? My name is Stanton."

"It doesn't matter. Neither one is on the list."

"I don't understand."

"Did you fill out your form?"

"Form? Which form?"

"I-96a."

"What's that?"

"Immigration documentation. No form, no name on the list."

"Immigration? I don't understand."

"If you want to come here, you're permanently leaving your previous home. Therefore, you are immigrating, and you must complete the paperwork." Miley pushed a form through the gap under the window. "That's why you're not on his list. No I-96a, no entry."

"Nobody told me about it."

"Did you read the handbook? It's all explained in there."

"No one said anything about a handbook either."

"I get that a lot."

"Can I stand here and fill it in?"

"No. You'll hold up the line. You'll need a new number."

Rose looked around the packed waiting room. "It'll take forever."

"That's not my problem. There are processes in place to make sure things go smoothly. You haven't completed your paperwork, and you haven't followed the process; therefore, things aren't going smoothly. Follow the damn procedure." She returned to her typing. "Blue ninety-eight."

"Don't you mean red ninety-eight?"

"Ma'am, I work at a soulless, life-sucking job. The only, and I mean the *only* pleasure I get is fucking with the idiots in this waiting room. Don't you dare take that from me."

Rose sighed again. She did not care for Miley's dismissive attitude. "I think there's been a mistake."

"Why?" Miley continued to focus on her screen.

"I think I might be lost." Rose leaned into the window and lowered her voice to a whisper. "I'm supposed to go to the other place."

"The other place?"

"Yes."

Miley stopped typing. "That's not something I hear every day."

Rose smiled, relieved at the miscommunication. "It's okay. Mistakes happen."

Miley reached for her phone. "I'll call Lucifer's office and tell him you're on your way down."

Rose's eyes widened. "WHAT? Did you say Lucifer? I don't want to go to Hell."

"You just said you didn't want to be here."

"I know, but—"

"Then I'll make the call."

"This isn't Hell?"

"Nope."

"So, this is—"

"Yep, surprise, Grandma. Welcome to Heaven. Ninety-nine?"

Miley topped the list of complaints from visitors when they arrived in Heaven. She possessed short hair and a shorter temper and wondered which cardinal sin she committed to be damned for eternity as a customer service representative. A regular attendee at church, Miley once considered herself a God-loving person, now she borderline loathed him. The longer she stayed at the job, the angrier she became, and the harder she assaulted her keyboard.

The disappointments came thick and fast after walking into the big bright light. As no one ever visited Heaven and returned to Earth to report their findings, all guests had to go on were assumptions, wishes, and bullshit. Heaven was like getting to Disneyland to find half of the rides closed and the masked characters walking around with their heads tucked under their arm, telling kids to *'fuck off, I'm on a smoke break'*. There were no pearly gates, and Saint Peter was nowhere to be found.

Heaven comprised of a snapshot of a person's life at their happiest. Residents were surrounded by their loved ones and arrived looking their absolute best instead of the manner in which they died. It would be unacceptable to enter after a horrific car accident and be forced to walk around for eternity with an eyeball hanging out and a face full of glass. That much everyone expected. It was the employment part that threw people for a curve. All residents worked, and everyone put in a full shift. If millions of bored people wandered the halls, they would likely get into all kinds of trouble.

Instead of matching employees against a predetermined personality matrix or assigning random jobs, they were simply given the job they were happiest at during their life. Those who enjoyed wonderful careers were blessed with a delightful eternity. However, those who eeked their way through life, jumping from one soul-sucking job to the next, found having the least shitty job in a stack of shitty jobs amounted to a somewhat dissatisfying afterlife.

As if the waiting room experience could not get any more frustrating, the music piping through the ceiling speakers would push even the mellowest tempered person over the brink. For some reason, residents expected choirs of angels to be floating through the halls, serenading them with harps and cellos, but upper management put a stop to it decades ago after too many accidents. It screwed up productivity with everyone stopping for their own personal concert. These days, the only ambient music beeped and chirped its way out of a cheap 1980's Casio keyboard.

◆ ◆ ◆ ◆

Gary O'Donnell, or as his contemporaries and followers knew him, God, for short, ignored the 8-bit angelic harmony as it played softly in the elevator. He instead focused on the increasing number above the doors as he nervously rocked back and forth on his heels, clenching his jaw tight. His dentist would be upset with the state of his molars at his next check-up.

Another misconception about Heaven centered on the layout. Segregation flourished in the kingdom of angels, but neither race nor gender, or even sexual preference separated the masses. Instead, their chosen branch of Christianity determined their location. Each offshoot held its own floor as most of the branches refused to mingle. The Catholics hated the way Jehovah's Witnesses ignored the birthday of Christ and disapproved of their cult-like recruiting methods. Most branches looked at Mormonism as a bastardized version of Christianity. Much the same as the special editions of Star Wars, blasphemy to purists, while everyone else wrote it off as cute but entirely unnecessary. And the Baptists? Well, their energy and enthusiasm could get somewhat overwhelming and was the primary reason God hoped the elevator skipped the next ten floors. His caffeine levels were insufficient to deal with their hyper energy so early in the morning.

The ground floor housed the waiting room and lobby, while levels two through seventeen held the Jehovah's Witnesses. Baptists occupied eighteen through twenty-six, and Catholics twenty-seven through thirty-nine. Lutherans, Protestants, and whatnot occupied forty through fifty-nine. The Mormons owned floors sixty-five through seventy, and the ninety-seventh floor housed God's office. There were so many spin-offs that God found it challenging to keep track on most days. The levels he vehemently avoided were sixty through sixty-four, home of the evangelists and Born Agains, or as Lucifer called it, the largest per capita ratio of assholes, douchebags, and bullshitters in the universe.

God hated using the public elevator, but the private one leading directly to his office was out of commission for a week while engineering performed annual maintenance. God preferred the early days of Heaven when just one version of Christianity existed. Now there were more branches than he cared to count. Each time someone wanted to do something the Bible forbid, they rewrote it and changed the parts they disagreed with. Everyone needed their own club, and he found the sense of individuality humans craved to be quite irritating. God felt his stomach sink as the elevator slowed to a stop and pinged.

"Goddammit. Not eighteen, not eighteen."

The elevator stopped and opened on the seventeenth floor. God let out a relieved sigh as Eric, a tall, gangly man in an ill-fitting suit, stepped in. Eric directed the Jehovah's Witness floors, and God had focused so intently on avoiding the Baptists that he completely forgot all about them.

"Good morning, sir."

God nodded with forced courtesy. "Eric."

Eric smiled as he set down his briefcase. "I'm so glad I caught you."

God's shoulders slumped. That statement never ended well. It usually involved another amendment to the Old Testament. Suddenly, the eighteenth floor seemed appealing.

"I have a wonderful surprise for you. I went through my office, and low and behold, I found a box of random back issues of Watchtower."

"Low and behold."

"Although, really, it's less of a box and more of a storage bin. And less random and more like every issue ever printed."

"That goes back to—"

"1879! I know! Impressive, huh?"

"Greatly," lied God.

"Well, I have them all digitally now. However did we manage before the internet?"

"I had a much harder time finding lesbian midget porn."

"Excuse me?"

God ignored the question, desperate to reach his floor.

"Do you want them for the archives?"

"I'm sorry, Eric. We don't have a section for fiction or propaganda," God said quickly, thinking on his feet. He despised solicitors.

Eric's eyes widened. "Wait? What?"

The elevator pinged, and the doors opened.

"This is my floor." God leaped out before Eric was able to offer a rebuttal.

It was not his floor. However, it was the eighth level of the Baptist division.

"Goddammit." God realized his mistake and quickly turned back to the elevator. He frantically stabbed at the up button and held his breath, hoping no one saw him. Especially Spencer.

"Good morning, sir," said a loud sing-songy voice behind him.

"Fuck." God sighed as Spencer, a sprightly man with a mop of bright blonde hair, bounced over to him.

"To what do we owe the marvelous pleasure of your presence?" asked Spencer

"Hello, Spencer. I just got off on the wrong floor."

"Oh, phooey, what a load of old hogwash. This is an unscheduled, but premeditated visit, if I've ever seen one."

"I assure you, it isn't."

"You haven't been here in months. You've come to check on the troops." He turned to face the sea of cubicles and offices. "Royalty on deck," he shouted as everyone snapped upright to attention.

"Please don't. I'm not—" God turned back to the closed elevator doors and jabbed at the up button again. "Come on, where are you?" he growled under his breath.

Spencer put his hand on God's shoulder. "Don't be a stranger, stay awhile. Come and see how this well-oiled machine keeps ticking."

God turned to face him. "I can't. I have a… a thing I have to do." He fumbled for the right words and brushed Spencer's hand off his shoulder.

"While we're on the topic of things, we're having an office party next Friday. We're bringing our children to sing a few hymns. Well, those of us whose kids have died. Do you have a flyer?"

"I—"

"We'll have a Bundt cake."

"No, I really—"

Spencer ignored God's disinterest, eager to make use of the unexpected visit. "Someone get me a flyer, stat."

An equally energetic man pranced over and planted a flyer firmly in Spencer's hand.

"Thank you, young man. Peace be with you."

"And with you, Brother Spencer." Fancy pants floated back the way he came.

"I call him young man as I don't remember his name. I'm terrible with names. How are you with them? Oh, what am I asking? You're the supreme Lord and creator of all. You built everything and everyone. You must have a bear of a time with names. Boy, egg on my face."

"I'm just trying to get back to my office."

The elevator pinged as Spencer offered God the flyer.

God pointed at the opening doors. "This is me. I've gotta go."

Spencer raised his voice as the doors closed. "I'll get it in the mail."

God held his hand up to his ear, pretending he could not hear. The longer he stayed in Heaven, the more he hated it.

♦ ♦ ♦ ♦

Nancy, God's elderly, and soft-spoken receptionist, quietly typed an email as the office doors swung open and her boss stormed in.

She smiled politely. "Good morning, sir."

God ignored her greeting and bee-lined for his office. "Fucking Baptists."

The door slammed shut behind him.

Nancy reached over to the phone and pushed the call button. "I have today's lists, sir."

The door opened, and God marched out.

"Fucking Jehovah's Witnesses." He snatched the lists from Nancy and stomped back into his office, his exit accentuated with another loud slam of the door.

Nancy pressed the button again. "I need your signature."

The door opened again, and God stomped out. He slammed the list on her desk and held out a hand. "Pen."

Nancy gently placed a pen in his hand as she continued to type one-handed. "Your nine o'clock will be here shortly."

"Fucking clock."

He signed the list and pushed it to Nancy as he turned to his office for the third time.

"And your Thin Mints came in."

"Fucking Girl Scouts." God stopped and turned back to Nancy. "Where?"

Nancy pulled open her top drawer, and inside sat four boxes of chocolaty, minty goodness. God reached down and grabbed a box. He looked at Nancy and paused. He picked up a second and a third. A moment later, he took the last box.

He stepped towards the door. "Nancy, take a memo. I'm moving my office."

"Where to?"

God sighed. He had nowhere else to go. "Scratch the memo. Just get the list to the Grim Reaper."

"He doesn't like it when you call him that."

God stopped and turned towards Nancy. "See this?" He drew an imaginary line around his face with a finger. "This is me all out of fucks to give. Hold my calls, I'm going off the grid and eating cookies." He walked back into his office and slammed the door behind him once again.

Nancy sighed. It was going to be one of those days.

CHAPTER 3

Oceanview had always been a somewhat unassuming town for a variety of reasons. For one, it could not be found located even remotely close to the ocean. In fact, it lay on the northern end of Arizona and faced the ass side of a mountain. A mountain which suffered a devastating wildfire in the fifties, and nothing had grown on it since. So, the view seemed rather abysmal by its namesake standards. The town was named by a wet-behind-the-ears, entrepreneurial-developer-douchebag-hipster, who thought it clever and witty, the thirty-seven tourists who purchased the equally droll '*Oceanview. No ocean! No view! No problem!*' postcard from the Main Street Post Office agreed with him. However, they were also douchebag hipsters and hold no relevance to this story.

Main Street ran through the quiet southern part of town and held a third of the traffic of Port Road, which made Port Road the actual main street. Downtown Park could be found in the north, and the central bus station operated from the east side. East Valley High School sat in the west, and twenty miles from the nearest valley.

The population varied between five thousand, seven hundred, and forty-six, and five thousand, seven hundred, and forty-seven, depending on when Mayor Beck's heart stopped because of his diet of bacon and cheddar sandwiches, a twelve-pack of Dr. Pepper, and deep-fried Twinkies. Its graveyard held more occupants than the town, and most GPS systems listed it as invalid. While everyone in Oceanview held immense pride in their small and humble community, the fact remained everything about it was a cliché, a punch line, or a bad pun.

Anyone raised outside the borders found Oceanview impossible to navigate. The town map appeared as though someone threw a pile of spaghetti on a sheet of paper and labeled the roads based on the stains. The developers named the first street Pastitsio Boulevard after Julius Pastitsio, one of the original town planners. A fitting name, as the Greek word pastitsio was derived from the Italian pasticcio, which meant hodgepodge. A fair description and far more acceptable than calling it Cluster Fuck Avenue or Fubar Street. While the town faced a mountain, there were no geographical landmarks or obstructions within its boundaries that prevented it from being laid out in the typical grid format so common amongst municipal planners with half an ounce of common sense. There were no valid reasons Oceanview required being built as though it was designed by a deaf and blind moron, other than to be awkward and trendy.

Oceanview possessed all the amenities of any other town such as bars and schools. Port Road housed a library, a butcher, a coffee shop or two, numerous restaurants, and specialized retailers. The Regal Multiplex, a single-screen movie theater, showed reasonably new movies to a half-filled auditorium.

The town fielded an adult softball team called the Wildfire. They sucked. During the previous season, the neighboring town's little league champions played them and won thirty-seven to nil. The game made national papers due to the humiliation. Their football team sat at 0 for 1,963, yet each week, the entire town came out to cheer them on, clinging to the desperate and delusional hope they may someday score a touchdown, much less win a game.

The men's soccer team performed marginally better, and at one point, was number one in their division. Although, it sounded far better of an achievement than it really was. As they could only field a team of eight players instead of the traditional eleven, they were part of a league of eight-man teams, of which there were two, so being number one could barely be considered an accomplishment as there were just two games in the season. The first game they won when the other team scored an own goal and the second game tied nil-nil. So, they won the league trophy without physically scoring a goal, but, win it they did, and the golden miniature award sat proudly on display at Town Hall in the town's trophy case. The glass cabinet provided space for over two hundred trophies and awards. The designers were a tad optimistic about the town's sporting and intellectual abilities, so for fifteen years, the prize sat alone, gathering dust while it waited for a companion.

A few residents came close to adding a second on a handful of occasions. The most opportune moment came during the 2009 state spelling bee. Sixth-grader Edward Fordham made it to the finals, and the judges asked him to spell '*Pontificating*'. The other finalist flubbed her word, and Edward verbally sprinted to the finish line. He stepped up to the microphone and spelled pontificating. The victory was all but guaranteed. If he had opted to stop talking.

"My mom says words like pontificating are spoken by pretentious assholes that use complicated vocabulary to project a false sense of superiority over the seemingly less educated, amounting to nothing more than linguistic small penis compensation. Pontificating." The judges disqualified him for saying penis.

His monologue might have won over the audience if his mother were in any role other than the elementary school's English teacher. The numerous parents who made the trip down to Phoenix to cheer him on were shocked by his announcement. The morning after the event, seven of those parents who used the word pontificating, and may or may not have been compensating for micro genitals, stopped by her office to show her how big of an asshole they could be. She quit in a flood of tears and began working for the Post Office, sparing her from having to deal with people so often.

◆ ◆ ◆ ◆

The population of Oceanview fared no better than the town. A glance at the customers scattered around the bar at Jacob's Tavern showed a community as dysfunctional as the town itself. No one by the name of Jacob ever owned the bar, and to the best knowledge of the town, its owner, Hank Salvati, knew no one called Jacob. Hank was a surly man in his late fifties and one of four families who compiled Oceanview's Little Italy. Although little considerably overstated its size. It spanned four houses on Beachfront Avenue and Pilano's Pizzeria at the corner of Beachfront and Port Road. Pilano's pizza tasted awful, but no one dared tell Mr. Pilano for fear of setting him off as he served his slices with cracked red pepper and tales of concrete shoes.

At the north end of Oceanview sat China Town, which comprised only the Yan family, which pissed off Mr. Yan as he was born in South Korea. At one end of his yard, a sign stating '*You are now entering China Town*' poked out of the ground. A sign at the opposite end advised travelers they were *'Now leaving China Town'* and to *'Have a Rice Day'*. Most lawyers would foam at the mouth at the political insensitivity, except Mr. Patrick Kent, the town's lone attorney, installed it during cultural awareness week.

In the middle of the bar sat Cam Harris, the town's barfly. She studied English language in community college for one semester and sometimes used fancy multi-syllable words to disguise the fact after one shot of Jäger, she would go home with anyone. With seven weddings under her belt, she collected marriage certificates the same way kids collected Pokémon cards. The longest lasting barely eight months. On most days, she looked pretty, but after a long day of waiting tables, she looked every day of her thirty-two years. A D-average student throughout life, her creative writing class earned her the sole A of her brief academic career. To celebrate her victory, she printed it on the front of a T-shirt. A large bright red capital A inside a circle and a smiley face. Cam proudly wore the shirt whenever she appeared at Jacob's Tavern to pick up her latest broken heart because *'men love smart chicks'*. Sure, it had nothing to do with the scarlet A resting on her ample cleavage.

She raised her empty glass to Hank. "Another beer, please, hun."

Seconds later, a foaming lager slid across the mahogany. Cam smiled and sat back down in her seat. She looked around the bar and sighed at the slim pickings. Friday night often brought one or two new faces from wayward visitors passing through, but it seemed like the regular crowd. She resigned herself to the fact she was probably going home alone.

Cam desperately wanted someone to love her back. She longed for the feeling of closeness and acceptance she believed only came from being in a relationship. She did not understand the acceptance and approval she needed the most stared back at her from the mirror. For fourteen years, she repeated the same routine and received little more than the Clap, Crabs, and Syphilis for her troubles. No stranger to a round of antibiotics, she convinced herself they were all necessary tolls to find true love. Every month, she fell in love with someone new, gave them her body, and prayed to the heavens someone might return the affection. If she threw enough shit at the wall, something might stick. So far, failure ruled the roost, and she lived knee-deep in prescription copays and rejection.

On the seat next to her perched a rather strange fellow named Keith, but the rest of the town called him Kit-Kat. He wore a mess of curly hair and black horned-rim glasses. Any fashion sense long since abandoned him, if it even existed to begin with. He moved to Oceanview after his eighteenth birthday to intern at Garrett and Son Taxidermy shop. For some strange reason, he wanted to learn how to stuff dead animals for a living. Kit-Kat's luck with pets bordered on disastrous, and his apartment showed the fruits of his professional toils. It looked creepy but offered an interesting topic of discussion for the few visitors who stopped by.

Kit-Kat constantly scribbled ideas into a notebook under the delusion one day he may become a famous screenwriter. He saved money for five years to move to Los Angeles, but perpetually found himself on the end of a bad business deal, so his dream remained forever out of reach. He did, however, own 25,000 '*My other car is the Millenium Flacon*' misspelled bumper stickers, a timeshare at the same apartment complex he lived in, and 5,000 pens with the Crystal Pepsi logo. Kit-Kat lived paycheck to meager paycheck and would remain broke until the day he died.

While a regular at Jacob's, compared to the likes of Cam, who visited daily on her lunch break and the second she left work, he was less of a permanent fixture. The majority of his social interactions revolved around playing World of Warcraft online, so his face-to-face skills suffered as a result. Kit-Kat drained the last of his beer and reached for his wallet to settle his tab. His face immediately flushed red as he realized he had left it at home once again. Even if he remembered his wallet, it contained just seventeen cents. He perpetually lived one payday away from being dumped out on his ass and often relied on the generosity of others for his drinks. Beside him, Doctor David Hewett raised his hand and flagged Hank to charge the bill to the credit card he waived in the air. Hank nodded, and David returned to his drink, grunting an acknowledgment as Kit-Kat thanked him profusely. Although it ran against every fiber of David's being to be seen buying Pabst Blue Ribbon.

David smiled. "One more round, and you'll owe me a blowjob."

Kit-Kat blushed again. "What?"

"That's the going rate, isn't it, Cam?"

Cam puffed on the cigarette she wasn't supposed to be smoking indoors. "How many rounds so far?"

"Nine," said David as he put his wallet back in his pocket.

"Ten actually," said Kit-Kat timidly.

"In that case, his pretty mouth is all yours," said Cam.

"Give me a break, guys," said Kit-Kat, his voice tinged with embarrassment

The bar cheered, and everyone drank as Kit-Kat shouted out his catchphrase to the delight of the room.

David reached for his zipper. "Pucker up, rosy cheeks."

Kit-Kat fumbled for words, and finding none, instead whimpered, fell backward off his seat, and scampered for the door. A roar of laughter heralded his exit.

David grinned as the bar settled back down. His term of endearment labeled him the town drunk, and his poison smelled an awful lot like gin. At least he set high standards about what he used to torture his liver, although he felt it was an unfair label. As the town's sole psychiatrist, most of the community cheerfully grabbed his hand and led him to drink. Day in and day out, he dealt with the inane, the insane, and the stupid. For a small town, it housed a disproportionate number of residents with serious mental issues. Were David to write a summary for Oceanview, it would be institutionalized. Not state-funded behavioral health clinic crazy, but '*One Flew Over the Cuckoo's Nest*' straight jacket, full-frontal lobotomy, out of its head, bat-shit lunacy.

David had lived in Oceanview for over ten years and arrived purely by accident. A Washington native, he passed through on his way to Rocky Point one summer and fell in love with the town. He stopped off at Rob's Diner, owned by Ben, tried one of the house omelets, and never looked back. He spent the rest of his vacation thinking of the town and the logistics of relocating. On his return, he visited again and looked for a vacant property to set up his practice. He found a charming two-story house on Lake Street overlooking the park, confirmed with the real estate agent it could be zoned for commercial use and immediately put in a bid. Upon his return to Seattle, he broke the news to his girlfriend, Karen, and they split that night. She wanted no part in moving to some '*goddamn redneck, backwoods, goddamn hick town because of his goddamn midlife crisis*'. David protested that twenty-nine was not midlife, but she ignored his objection. Within the month, he cleared up his loose ends and returned to Oceanview. His practice opened within the week, and his office had experienced an overflow of lunatics ever since.

There were days when he wondered if he made the right decision. A town the size of Oceanview naturally held gossip on the tip of its tongue, and the citizens buried their noses in everyone else's business. David did his best to maintain patient confidentiality, however, after a few too many drinks, he occasionally let a nugget or two slip out. One time he told the bar about Mrs. Barrett's desire to marry her cat and demote her husband to cleaning its litter box, and Mr. Barrett's rebuttal asking if he could kill said cat if he deemed it a threat to his marriage. At times they treated him more like a priest than a psychiatrist. A few of the confessions would easily have the residents locked up if they lived in a more functioning town. The thing with Oceanview is everyone was nuts. Their neighbors were nuts, their friends were nuts, their family was nuts, and it went without a doubt that if you lived in Oceanview, then you were completely nuts too.

Despite its idiosyncrasies and his occasional doubts about why the hell he lived there, David loved the town and enjoyed his quiet life. However, he started drinking shortly after arriving, so no one could say whether his mind or the alcohol spoke for him.

Warren Hart completed the drinking quartet. He sat at the end of the bar and plugged an electronic poker game with quarters. Warren was the thirty-one-year-old younger son of the Hart and Sons Garage, handed down to him and his brother, Greg, by their deceased father. The boys tried to follow in his footsteps, and while they struggled to be the natural mechanic of their father, they knew enough to get by. In Greg's defense, he attended college for two years and earned an associate degree. The diploma and the three-year age gap gave him an edge over Warren and allowed him to take charge of the business. Warren had no issue with Greg being the boss, as he did not want to be responsible for much more than buying a round of beers and stocking the vending machine.

Warren and Cam were married four years prior, but quickly divorced after he continued playing pool every other night with Greg, and Cam hit on most guys and the occasional girl who walked in the bar. If Warren had paid closer attention, he might have experienced a few memorable nights with her and her female dates. They tried a brief period of marriage counseling with David acting as the intermediary, but little came of it. David called Warren distant and cold, and before he could give Cam her equally damning prognosis, Warren erupted and stormed out of David's office, calling him a one-sided, backstabbing bastard. The air between the two men remained hostile ever since. Mr. Kent filed the divorce papers and served them at their respective seats at the bar. Rumors suggested Mr. Kent rushed the divorce process to make Cam available for him to date. Even though he expedited the paperwork, by the time the marriage was annulled, she hooked up with someone else and left him holding the legal fees.

Warren and Greg dated the McKenzie sisters, Ashley and Amber. Their parents were two of the five deaf, blind, and moronic municipal planners who helped design the town. In reality, they could hear and see perfectly well and were miles away from being morons. They were, in fact, well educated, but one could be forgiven for thinking otherwise. Expectations for the girls were high, so when they started dating the Hart brothers, their parents were disappointed. The dating pool in Oceanview lacked choice, and Mr. and Mrs. McKenzie wanted the girls to move to Phoenix or Salt Lake City to widen their search, instead of staying in the town and settling.

Ninety minutes into his gaming session, the poker game crackled, and the screen turned dark. Warren slumped back on his stool. "Hank, the damn game's broken again."

Hank smiled at Warren. "Do you think how infrequently you win, the game ever works?"

The bar burst into laughter, but their attention quickly diverted to the door as it whipped open. A flurry of snow blew in as Nikki and Lee Adams entered from the cold evening. Snowfall had increased the previous hour, and the patrons received a fleeting glance of the whitewashed parking lot outside.

Lee knocked snow off his boots as Nikki took off her jacket, both happy to be in the warmth.

Hank looked up from the glass he was cleaning. "Still snowing?" his voice boomed across the bar.

Lee nodded. "Hasn't stopped. It's drifting pretty badly on Main. About to close it down."

Nikki and Lee crossed to the bar. Their marriage was barely two years old, but the honeymoon had long since ended. Lee and Cam briefly dated long before Nikki appeared in the picture, but for reasons known only to her, she grasped hold of her animosity with both hands. She threw Cam her customary dirty look as she crossed the floor and took a seat at the bar.

Nikki worked at the high school teaching art, and at five-foot-ten and a hundred and twenty-five pounds, large chest, blonde, and green eyes, she found herself the subject of dozens of erotic dreams from the oversexed students.

Lee had been the town's Sheriff for twelve years, learning much on the job, and although his marriage struggled, the town liked and respected him. Sure, he handed out speeding tickets and the odd parking violation or two, but he kept everyone in line with little resistance.

He was fifteen years older than Nikki, and while he enjoyed her being physically in her prime, rumors claimed she was sleeping with a few of her students. He brushed it off as teenage exaggerations and lived his life with his blinders on. Both accepted their marriage teetered on the verge of collapse, but they remained together for the sake of public appearances and nothing more. Lee believed people held greater respect for a happily married sheriff. However, their efforts were fruitless as the entire town saw their relationship was a footstep from the brink, but no one could find the heart to tell them.

Lee smiled as he reached the bar. "You're in my spot, Warren."

"What, are you going to arrest me?"

"No, too much paperwork. I can taze you, though, and say it was an accident."

"Dick," grinned Warren.

Lee turned back to Hank. "Will you be open next Friday night?"

Hank shook his head. "Are you kidding? Forefather's Day is one of the few times a year when I get a Friday night off. I'm staying home and making the most of it."

Warren smirked. "What, you mean sitting around in your skivvies watching The Golden Girls?"

Hank nodded at Warren. "Lee, do me a favor and shoot this little prick."

"It's unwise to cross the man carrying the gun, Warren." Lee tapped his holster for emphasis.

"Come on, Lee," Warren said with a smile. "You haven't fired that thing in years. You only carry blanks since the incident. Mayor Beck won't let you carry real bullets."

Lee sighed. "Thanks for the reminder, asshole."

"Anytime," said Warren as he raised his glass in a toast.

The incident referred to an evening three years prior involving Lee accidentally shooting the mayor's cat out of the tree in front of his daughter's bedroom window. In full view of Lily Beck and her ten preteen friends. Mayor Beck required Lee to hand over his bullets in exchange for keeping his job. The town experienced no crime severe enough to warrant carrying a gun, so the punishment impacted the town little. At first, no one knew he carried blanks, but news traveled, and the threat soon weakened and eventually dissipated. Lee more so used it as a warning of habit, and no one felt intimidated by him at all. Yet, to his and the town's credit, even without bullets, he kept order, and crime was near nonexistent.

"My live rounds are locked up at the station," said Lee, trying to save face. "They're there if I need them."

Warren smiled. "A fat lot of good they'll do if someone charges in here and robs the place."

"Have you met Hank?" teased Lee. "If I were a crook, I'd be more scared of him than me."

"Damn right," said David, lifting his glass. He toasted to anything.

Laughter rippled throughout the bar as Lee lost the argument. The suspension embarrassed him greatly, but as a town employee, if the mayor told him to get rid of his bullets, he had little choice.

Warren stood and grabbed his jacket from the back of his stool. "I need to jet. If Ash comes in, none of you saw me, okay? I'm turning off my phone."

The group nodded their goodbyes as Warren bee-lined for the back door.

Cam was still hung up on having nowhere to drink on Friday night. "Where am I supposed to go once the festival's done, Hank?" she complained. "You're the only place I can get a drink that late. The library is closing at six."

Yes, the library. Jacob's shared the spoils of drinking adults with a few other establishments in town, most notably the Oceanview Public Library, which enjoyed a continuous flow of people coming through the doors. The volume increased when they provided movie rentals for free, and once again when they opened an adult section. The new service upset Mr. Hughes, who owned the Freeze Frame video store. He eventually closed shop as his customers opted for the free movies at the library. Six days after closing, he scribbled out the word 'Frame' on the sign on the front of the building and reopened it as an ice cream parlor.

A handful of the more literate and vocal library members scoffed at the movie section and became downright offended when the library opened a concession stand complete with a popcorn machine. However, this strange venture was short-lived as buttery fingers clawed at the pages of vintage and irreplaceable books and left greasy DNA prints throughout. Admission improved again when they earned their liquor license and sold booze.

While the library did a fair amount of business, Jacob's biggest competitor came from Jiggles, the strip club on the end of Bracken Road. Many complained when the club opened, but a quick informal poll showed over ninety-five percent of the town's male adult population and thirty-six percent of the under-age population visited the club. Even Reverend Ellis, one of the establishment's most prominent opponents, had been caught getting a face full of jiggle, so complaints were ignored.

Jiggles became known as the first strip club in the country to offer daycare service for single dads who needed to get out of the house and were unable to find a sitter for their little ones. Mindy, one of the lead dancers, earned her CPR certification and a correspondence school diploma to become a teacher's aide, so parents were okay leaving their offspring in her care for a couple of hours. Although her skimpy panties and pasties costumes were a little inappropriate for a preschool teacher, the dads did not appear to be too upset. For such an informal daycare, there were a disproportionate number of parent-teacher conferences each week.

"Ain't my problem, Cam," Hank said as he placed a stack of shot glasses on the shelf. "If I don't get a night off, I swear I will shoot the whole damn lot of you. I can't fathom how David does it. If I got to listen to you all whine and bitch, I'd have taken you out back and let a bullet sort you out. There ain't a single mommy issue you can't fix with a bullet. Life's a bitch, buttercup. Either let your scrotum do the talking or shut your pie hole. Your choices are limited."

A few nervous chuckles slipped out around the bar as the front doors opened, and three more shivering patrons stepped in from the cold.

"Evening, ladies," Hank shouted from the bar. "Greg."

Amber and Ashley headed to a table as Greg stopped at the bar.

Hank nodded to Greg. "The usual?"

"Please."

"Join the girls. I'll bring it over."

Greg crossed over to the booth the sisters had claimed. "Drinks are coming," he said as he sat down next to Amber and took off his jacket.

Amber smiled at him. "Thanks, love."

Ashley sneered at the display of affection. "Oh, would you two stop. You're going to make me vomit. I'm nursing a rejected heart, remember?"

"Love can blossom even through the darkest of storms," waxed Greg poetically.

"One more nugget like that, and I swear to Christ, I will shank you with a broken glass."

Greg laughed at Ashley's grumpiness. "That's why your drink is coming in a plastic cup."

"Asshole." Ashley smiled playfully. "Besides, Warren's your brother, so technically, it's your fault he didn't show up."

"How do you figure that?" asked Greg. "You're the fool who dates him. He's my brother by blood. You chose to date him. This is all on you." Greg grinned at his comeback as Ashley scowled at him.

"I don't suppose you ordered me chips, did you?" asked Amber, interrupting the banter.

He opened his mouth to reply in the negative when a bag of cheese crackers landed on the table in front of them.

"Of course he did."

Greg turned to see Hank holding their drinks. Hank knew all his customers, even the ones who were missing. "Lose someone?" he said as he placed the tray on the table and matched the drinks with their respective owners.

"What?" asked Amber.

"Master Warren. Aren't you one short?"

"Oh, he's sick," added Ashley. "He stood me up tonight."

Hank let out a snort that implied he knew otherwise. His poker face was crap.

"When did he leave, Hank?"

"About two minutes before you came in. Told me not to tell you."

Ashley rolled her eyes. "Smooth. You could lie to make me feel better."

"Do you think I'd lie for him, Princess? You know me better than that. I'd rather tell you the truth and hurt your feelings, than lie for him and have you think I'm covering for him and still end up hurting you. Either way, I hurt you, but at least I'm honest with you. Better you be pissed over truth than lies."

Ashley shrugged in agreement. It was hard to argue with Hank's logic, despite how blunt it came across. "Get him on the phone," Ashley ordered Greg. "I want to hear his excuse."

"I wouldn't bother," said Hank as Greg fished his phone out of his pocket. "He turned it off."

Greg noticed Ashley's fists clenching. "You know what? Fuck him." He said as he put his phone down on the table. "This is his loss. We shouldn't let this ruin our evening. I say let's get another round of drinks, lay claim on the pool table, and pretend the balls are his head."

The sisters raised their glasses to the shouts of '*cheers*'.

"But, before we do, we are heading to the lady's room," Amber announced as she and Ashley stood up from the booth.

Greg politely raised up out of his seat as the girls left.

"She should dump your brother," Hank said in his usual gruff voice.

"I don't understand why she puts up with his shit," said Greg as he sat back down.

"Because of you."

"Me? But, I'm about to propose to her sister. I had no idea she has feelings for me."

Hank stared at him. "Really?"

"You said it's because of me."

"She isn't in love with you, you moron. She doesn't want to break up with him because it will make things hard on you and Amber. She's trying to be considerate."

"That's ridiculous. Our relationship isn't contingent on Ashley staying with Warren."

"Does she know?"

"Of course. Hell, I've even told her she should break up with him."

"Told her how? In a jokey '*oh man, you should totally dump my brother*' way or '*sit down, we need to talk about how shitty my sibling is treating you*'?"

"Probably the former."

"How about you make an effort for it to be the latter? You want to be a good man to Amber? Treat her sister right. I'll say nothing more on the subject."

"Thanks, Hank."

"Uh huh," he grunted as he turned and headed back to the bar.

"What are you thanking Hank for?" Amber wrapped her arms around Greg's neck and kissed him on the cheek.

"For being a smarter man than I am."

Ashley smiled at Greg. "Is it about you telling me to dump your brother?"

"I guess you heard?" said Greg.

"Of course," said Ashley as the sisters slid back into the booth. "Hank's voice could raise the dead. He's not exactly a quiet person."

"I heard that," Hank griped from the bar.

"You were supposed to," shouted Ashley as she turned back to Greg.

"Look, I know Warren's no good for me, but I see how you treat Amber, and I keep holding out that maybe someday he'll change and be more like his older brother. He treats me like shit, but no one's opinion, not Hank's, not Amber's, not yours, is going to change it. Stop apologizing for him, Greg, we're all adults here. Big sis doesn't need to coddle me, and neither do you. When I'm ready to check out, I will, and you two will be the first to know."

Ashley raised her arm to get the bar owner's attention. "Hank, Jack will be our fourth."

Hank carried over a half bottle of whiskey and three shot glasses. He pulled out the stopper and poured the first round.

Ashley raised her glass. "To the assholes we love, to the assholes we hate, we drink to our health, and hell if I remember the rest."

The three glasses clinked amid more shouts of '*cheers.*'

CHAPTER 4

"**E**ven though I walk through the darkest valley, I will fear no evil, for you are with me, your rod and your staff, they comfort me. You prepare a table before me in the presence of my enemies. You anoint my head with oil, my cup overflows. Surely your goodness and love will follow me all the days of my life, and I will dwell in the house of the Lord forever."

Reverend Ellis closed his Bible and looked up at his congregation. Psalm 23:4 always tugged at his heartstrings.

"I don't expect to see many of you next Sunday due to Forefather's Day," he said as he finished his weekly sermon. "So, while the doors will always be open, there will be no service."

"Thank God," Warren muttered under his breath from the sixth row

Annette Andrews, sitting on the pew behind, dealt him a swift smack with her Bible on the back of his head. "You will use manners while in the Lord's house," she said with hushed venom.

Reverend Ellis smiled. "The Lord has ears everywhere, Mr. Hart. Always be aware of it."

"Sorry, Father," said Warren, his head hung in penance.

"Nevertheless, despite the lack of a sermon, I expect there will be a few of you with a crushing urge to cleanse from a weekend of drunken debauchery and mayhem, so I will be available Monday evening for confession. I encourage you to make use of it."

While he avoided singling anyone out, his gaze never left Warren, who kept his head lowered in shame.

Warren loved going to church, but he held little understanding of most of it. Only that he needed to go for his soul to be saved. His parents dragged him and Greg every Sunday morning from birth to their father's passing. For two hours each week, he sat and listened to Reverend Ellis harp on about everyone being sinners and being born into sin, and needing to be forgiven for future sins, and sins never committed, and a bunch of other stuff about sin. From what he could gather, God punished him for sins committed hundreds of years before he was born and sins he may or may not commit when he gets older. For his part, he committed most of the sins Reverend Ellis accused him of, but he felt if he were to be convicted of the crime, he might as well have the fun to go along with it. Being punished in advance seemed unfair. How could anyone predict what he planned to do tomorrow? He compared it to refusing to tip the paperboy because a different paperboy ten years later may throw his newspaper on the sprinkler head, and it becomes a soggy mess. Regardless of his questions and a potential resentment of his future paperboy, he continued to go to church, and if anyone spoke ill of his God, he quickly jumped to his defense.

Greg, however, hated church. Whereas Warren attended out of habit and enjoyed the sermons, Greg made an appearance only to support Amber. His faith took a severe hit after their father passed. He had far more questions than the church could answer, and he doubted the existence of an almighty entity that could not be bothered to save his dad. Were Amber to stop going, he would never set foot in the building again.

As Reverend Ellis continued, the collection plate started doing the rounds, and various denominations were tossed in as it made its way up and down each row, sometimes twice. If the previous day experienced extra wickedness, a third round often occurred.

On cue, his sin diatribe commenced. "We are all born into sin. Every one of us is a sinner in one form or another. We lie, we cheat, we steal, we suppress, we oppress, we tease, we torment, we skip the collection plate."

Busted.

Judy Deacon, sitting to Greg's right, held the plate while he fished out his wallet and placed a five in it. Judy kept the plate in front of him. He grabbed his five back and put in a ten. Judy held the plate still, and Greg dropped the five back in. She smiled, and the plate continued across the row.

"Cheap bastard," said Warren from a few rows behind.

Mrs. Andrews reintroduced the back of his head to the Bible.

"Let us pray," Reverend Ellis said with a smile as the congregation lowered their collective heads.

"Dear Lord, watch over our small and humble town. Keep us safe from harm, free from temptation, and void of distress. May the fruits of our labors be bountiful, and the toils of our fingers be honest. May you lead us through times of darkness and moments of despair and stand beside us during moments of victory and joy. May our hearts soar, and our heads be grounded. Amen."

Whispers of '*amen*' floated around the church as the congregation rose and filtered outside into the cold morning air.

♦ ♦ ♦ ♦

Warren stood by his car fumbling with his phone when Greg came up behind him, crunching through the fresh layer of snow.

"Always good to see you in your Sunday best," said Greg with a smile.

Warren's Sunday best comprised his pair of jeans without the holes in the knees and a collared shirt. "I'll wear a suit when I'm dead," he said as he turned around.

"I tried to save you a seat."

"It's all right. I thought I should stay further back."

"Figured as much. Where the hell were you last night? You pissed off Ashley big time."

"I stayed in. I wasn't feeling good."

"Wanna try that again?" said Greg.

"What? I stopped and grabbed something to eat and went to bed."

Greg stared at his brother. "So, Hank's lying, is he?"

"That backstabbing bastard," protested Warren. "I told him not to say anything."

"You want to say that to his face?" asked Greg.

"Probably not," said Warren with a grin.

"You're on borrowed time, you know that, right?"

"Oh, I'm fine. She won't dump me," said Warren.

"What makes you so sure?"

Warren shrugged. "I'll propose on Christmas like we planned. She isn't going anywhere. Pool?"

"Way to avoid the question. Later, but you're buying."

"How'd you figure?"

"As you were late to church, I gave up your seat and sat next to Mrs. Deacon for two hours."

Warren screwed up his nose in disgust. "Oh, dude, I'm sorry. Now you mention it, I can detect the aroma of cod liver oil and moth balls. Did she grab your leg again?"

"Four times." Warren laughed.

"It isn't funny. Amber saw her doing it."

"Doghouse?"

"Pretty damned close."

"Well, at least one of us is getting action."

"Get in your car, asshole," said Greg with a smile. Playful ribbing was standard communication for the two brothers. "And drive safely. They still haven't salted most of the streets yet. I hit a patch of ice heading over."

Warren climbed in his car, and Greg banged on the roof as it pulled away.

"Your loud music kept me up again last night," said a shrill voice from behind Greg as he turned around.

"And good morning to you, Mrs. Andrews," he said with an exaggerated smile.

Mrs. Andrews was a miserable old cow who lived four houses up from Greg. She acted sweet but used an underlying tone of hostility and menace. At every opportunity, she camped out on her front porch, ready to pounce on anything out of place in the neighborhood. Greg wished he had known about her when he purchased the house. However, it explained why the previous owner sold and moved out so quickly. He tried to sue the appraisal company for failure to disclose a hostile environment, but the case never made it to court. Whenever Greg needed to walk to his destination, he intentionally walked two blocks south and circled back to avoid going past her house. The only place he failed to stay out of her presence was church, and once more, she found him.

"Do I need to call the police again?"

"Probably," he mumbled.

"Excuse me?"

"I said no. But I wasn't listening to music past seven."

"And there are those of us who like to retire early to get our beauty sleep."

"You should go back to bed then," he said under his breath.

"Excuse me?"

"I said I will turn it down."

"Make sure you do. And your car is leaking oil on the street."

"I know."

"You need to fix it. How can you expect our street to be respectful when your clapped-out piece of trash—"

"Hold that thought." Greg held a finger up to silence Mrs. Andrews as Amber came up behind her.

Amber kissed Greg on the lips and lingered a second past typical social etiquette. She knew public displays of affection made Mrs. Andrews uncomfortable. "Ready to go, hun?"

"Please." He turned back to Mrs. Andrews. "As much as I'd like to continue this lovely exchange of pleasantries, I must go."

Before she could respond, Amber led Greg away.

"Is Warren okay?" asked Amber.

"Yeah, he was running late."

"Any comment on last night?"

"The usual blow-off," said Greg.

"She needs to dump him. She deserves better."

"Yes, dear," said Greg as they reached his car.

"You're not helping matters. You know, right?"

"Yes, dear," said Greg with a grin.

"I'm not putting out tonight. You know, right?"

"You're a cold woman, Amber."

They both laughed as Greg opened the passenger door and let her inside.

"You're lucky you're a gentleman," she said as he closed the door.

Greg crossed around to the driver's side and climbed in. "Chivalry trumps douchery," he said with a broad grin.

"For now," joked Amber.

"How about sushi for lunch?" he said as he sat down and pulled on his seat belt.

"You know the way to my heart. I think I'll keep you. I thought you were playing pool with Warren. Is he okay being dumped?"

"Oh, I didn't dump him. I just texted him. He's coming too."

"Goddammit, Greg." Amber protested as her voice jumped up an octave. "Can we get one date without a third tagging along?"

Greg smiled. "I'm kidding. It's just the two of us."

She slugged him playfully on the arm. "Have you told him yet?"

Greg's mind raced with excuses, but the silence dragged on longer than he anticipated, and his answer became obvious before he could utter a word. The ensuing argument continued all the way to the restaurant and followed the usual skirmish.

"Greg, why haven't you told him?"

"I don't know how."

"Find a way."

"I'll tell him."

"When?"

"Soon, I promise."

"You keep saying that."

"I know."

"It won't get any easier."

"I know."

"Do it, or I will."

Silence.

They ordered their food and were halfway through their Dragon Roll when Amber finally spoke again. "You have to tell him sometime."

"The news will kill him," said Greg with a mouthful of food. "He'll have to sell the shop."

"You don't know that. He might surprise you."

"I doubt it."

"I don't want to put a wedge between you two, but you can't live your life around your brother. Maybe he'll step up and keep the place running."

"He won't have much left here when I go."

"He'll still have Ashley if he doesn't screw it up, and he's well-liked around town. He'll be fine. We're moving in six months. This won't get any easier. Every day you bail on telling him is another day closer we get to leaving."

"I don't think either one of us expected to move out of town."

"People change. Situations change. I'm going through the same emotions with Ashley."

"You are?"

"Of course I am. We haven't been apart since she was born. You'd have known if you'd bothered to ask me."

Greg fell silent. He had been so wrapped up with his own situation that he overlooked anything she may be going through. "I'll tell him tonight, I promise." After weeks of avoidance, he finally meant it.

"Thanks, hun," she said with a smile.

"How is Ashley taking it?"

"As well as can be expected. She cried, she yelled, she gave me the silent treatment. She called me a stuck-up bitch who acts like I'm too good for this town."

"Oh, so you mean exactly the same things Warren will say to me tonight?"

"Pretty much."

They both laughed, and the mood immediately lightened.

"The quicker we tell him, the quicker you can propose to me," she said with a smile as she reached across for Greg's hand. "I'm already getting crow's feet around my eyes."

"But it's such a beautiful face."

"You're biased."

"Of course I am."

Amber slugged him on the arm again. "You weren't supposed to agree with me."

"Ow," Greg protested weakly. "If this keeps up, I may be reporting spousal abuse."

"You are so sweet," said Amber as she picked a piece of Unagi with her chopsticks. "You called me your spouse."

Greg smiled at the unintentional slip, but he liked the sound of it. He raised his glass. "A toast."

Amber picked up her glass of wine. "To what?"

"To spousal abuse and a lifetime of being stuck with each other."

CHAPTER 5

God's golf clubs had seen better days. He stared at the numerous bent and broken irons, putters, and woods scattered on the floor of his office and frowned. Each one a victim of his unsportsmanlike fury of hitting well over his handicap. His options were few as he casually picked through the stark remains of his caddy, hoping to find a putter he could use to practice in his office. While he rarely visited the course as often as he planned, he liked to practice putting whenever possible.

The last club standing was a scuffed and dented single wood and utterly inappropriate for putting, but it needed to suffice. He pulled it from the bag and walked over to his desk, swinging it as he walked.

"*Sir?*" Nancy's timid voice crackled through the phone on his desk. "Hello?"

God pressed a button to answer the call and put her on speakerphone. "Yes, Nancy?"

"*Do you have a minute?*"

"No, I really don't right now. I'm kinda busy."

"*Oh. Well, I…*"

Nancy stammered to complete her thought. She obviously needed to tell him something urgent that he was not going to like. He paused momentarily in the hopes of delaying the inevitable bad news, news he had no interest in hearing. Nancy cleared her throat with a soft cough.

God sighed. "What is it, Nancy?"

"*I've checked today's list, and something doesn't seem right. Can you ask Gabriel to double—*"

"Nancy, can I putt with a driver?" God inspected the head of the club as he waited for a response.

Nancy took a moment to respond. *"I'm sorry, I don't know, sir. Golf really isn't my thing."*

God continued to stare at his driver. "Really? It's not your thing? When I hired you, didn't the job description say golfing knowledge required?"

"No."

"Are you sure? I'm pretty certain it did. Did you lie on your application, Nancy? You know we frown on that kind of thing."

"I never lied. It just said Wordperfect experience required. It said nothing at all about golf. I wouldn't have applied if it did."

"Weird." He put down the club on the desk next to him.

"I know," Nancy agreed. *"No one uses Wordperfect these days. I wish you'd switch to Word. Everyone else is using it."*

"Well, everyone else is wrong, Nancy. You don't fuck with the classics. Regardless, I'm going to need you to brush up on your golfing knowledge."

"My golfing knowledge?"

"Did I stutter?"

"I'm just a secretary."

"Personal assistant, and I need you to personally assist me."

"I wouldn't know where to start."

"Google it. The Google knows everything."

"Can't you Google it?" asked Nancy.

"I'm busy."

"Golfing?"

"Don't judge me, Nancy, I have a very stressful job. I need an outlet, or I'm going to snap, and we all know what happens when I snap."

"Fire and brimstone?"

God points an approving finger at her. "Bingo. The biggest chunks of brimstone people have ever seen."

Nancy sighed. *"Sir, I really need you to look at the lists. I think there is a problem."*

"Of course there's a problem with the lists. They are preventing me from golfing."

"But—"

"What's the number one rule on work?" asked God.

"It's okay as long as it doesn't interrupt course time."

"And is it interrupting course time?"

"Well, technically, you're not at the course yet."

"It's called prep work, Nancy. My handicap won't lower itself. Just send the damn lists out to the Grim Reaper."

"He doesn't like that name."

"I don't care. I'm sure everything is fine, it always is. We've been doing this long enough. Please have faith in the system, Nancy."

"But—"

"Faith in the system." He hung up the call and walked over to the door, grabbing his caddy on the way out.

Nancy looked up as the door opened, and God stepped out and crossed over to her. He sat on the edge of her desk.

"Nancy, did you move my balls?"

"You never gave me your balls."

God shook his head. "No, I definitely gave you my balls. I remember seeing them in your hands."

"Sir, I never touched your balls."

"I distinctly remember handing them to you."

Nancy stood firm in her denial. She did not like being called a liar. "Your balls were never in my hands."

God started to smile as Nancy fell for the bait.

Nancy glowered at God and quickly sat down as she tried to resume her work. "You are so immature."

God held up his caddy and grinned. "Yeah, I know. Would you rather hold my club instead?"

Nancy shook her head. "No. I—" She let the thought hang. "I'm pretty sure this is considered sexual harassment."

"It's not sexual harassment if you're smiling."

Nancy turned to face her monitor and resumed her typing. "That's not how it works, and I'm not smiling."

"You will." God grinned and turned towards the exit door. "You'll find it funny about thirty seconds after I leave, and then you'll feel bad for not laughing."

Nancy stood, surprised at his sudden departure. "Wait, where are you going? You can't leave."

God held up his caddy and gestured towards the door. "I'm heading off to the course, Nancy. I thought that was obvious. You know, with me carrying my bags and all. Anything you need from me can wait until I'm done. I'll be back this afternoon."

"You can't go," protested Nancy. "You have an all-division meeting in fifteen minutes. The managers are already assembling in the conference room."

"What?"

"You're meeting with the managers. It's the quarterly review. It's been on your calendar for eleven months. I sent out the meeting schedule at the beginning of the year like I do every year."

"I never read my email."

"Well now, that's not my fault, is it?

"But I have my golf pants on," whined God.

Nancy stared to smirk.

"Oh, now you smile," said God.

"Did you not say it would take about thirty seconds?" asked Nancy with an innocent grin.

CHAPTER 6

Monday morning in Oceanview chugged along much like any other. The issues Death experienced in Vegas mattered little to the happenings on Port Road. People milled around delivering papers and food, and prepared for another day of mundane. Routine firmly grabbed the town in a chokehold and squeezed the spontaneity out of it until it turned a sickly shade of pale blue.

Judy Deacon prepared to open her coffee shop, and a few minutes before flipping the sign in the window, she struggled to pull plastic chairs out onto the sidewalk, as she did each morning.

"Here, let me help," interrupted David as he came up behind her and grabbed the chair.

"Oh, thank you, my dear, don't forget the tables."

"I know the drill," he said with a smile.

Damn right he did, and so did Judy. She started to set up two minutes before David usually walked by and made sure she pulled out the first chair as he passed. She could easily move them herself, but why exert the effort when someone else could do it for her? After all, it only cost a cup of coffee.

David dragged the last of the tables out into the street and pushed open the umbrellas. "It's supposed to snow again today. Are you sure you even want these outside?"

"Of course, Doctor Hewett. We can't be changing our ways on the off chance of inclement weather, can we?"

"God forbid we should ever change our routine," said David quietly to himself. He raised his volume. "Are we brewing yet?"

"About to start pouring," she shouted over her shoulder as she stepped inside.

"Perfect," said David, rubbing his hands together in exaggerated excitement.

"You're late today," said Mrs. Deacon as David followed her inside.

"Yeah, I overslept."

"Perhaps it's time you invest in an alarm clock?" she said as she handed David a steaming cup of coffee.

"Perhaps it's time you kept your beak out of other people's affairs," he said to himself a bit louder than he intended.

"Did you say something, dear?"

"I said I can't stay too long. I have an early appointment."

"Oh, who is it this time?"

"You know I can't tell you that," said David.

"Not even for a pastry?" She handed him a fresh apple Danish.

"It's Nick," he said as he took a bite out of his newly acquired food.

"Oh, I don't like him, he's so neurotic, and he sticks his nose everywhere it isn't wanted. What's his problem now?"

David smiled. "Judy, I definitely can't tell you that."

"Not even for one of my breakfast sandwiches?"

"Okay, fine. Ham on Asiago. He's having an issue where he can't stop asking about things which don't concern him."

"I can't stand people like that," she said as she placed his food in a bag. She paused. A moment later, she took the sandwich out. "That'll be two dollars ninety-seven for the pastry," she said.

David started to laugh. "You know I love you, Judy." He leaned over the counter and planted a kiss on her cheek.

"Doctor Hewett" she gasped.

"I'll see you tomorrow." He grinned as he left, taking another large bite of his Danish.

♦ ♦ ♦ ♦

Nick paced frantically back and forth by the front door when David returned to his house. David sighed as he crossed the driveway to greet him.

"You're early, Nick. I haven't finished my coffee yet." He raised his half-full cup for emphasis.

"I'm sorry, Doctor Hewett, but it's an emergency."

"Come on, Nick. Isn't it always?"

"Yes, but this time, it really is."

David unlocked the door and gestured for Nick to enter. Nick headed to the third door on the right and flopped onto the leather couch in David's office.

"What seems to be the problem today, Nick?" David pulled out Nick's overstuffed folder from a filing cabinet and slumped back in his chair.

"Everyone hates me."

"Why do you think that?" he said as he flipped through Nick's notes. Instead of a doctor's diagnosis, there were doodles of cuckoos and people in straitjackets.

"I don't think. I know."

"Okay, how do you know it? Has someone told you?"

"Not specifically."

David nodded and doodled lazily in his notebook, but his mind wandered elsewhere. Nick visited his office weekly with a new conspiracy about the world being after him. The notes in his folder might be enough to kill him.

"No one listens to me."

David stayed silent, his thoughts elsewhere. Nick rambled for another minute as David's mind continued to wander, and Nick's voice became white noise.

"I said no one listens to me." He paused waiting for a response that would not arrive. "I SAID, NO ONE LISTENS TO ME," shouted Nick.

"Huh?" asked David as his mind snapped back to the present. "What was that?"

"Did you hear anything I said?"

"You were talking about—" he paused. "Nick, I'll be honest with you. I have no idea what you were saying."

Nick's eyes widened. "Excuse me?"

"I can't help you. Each week you come in here, sit on my couch, and tell me how much the world hates you. I can't make the world like you."

"Why not?"

"I'm not that good of a doctor, and I haven't brushed up on my mass hypnosis skills."

"But, you're the only shrink in town. You have to help me."

"Nick, the way I see it, you have two options."

"And they are?"

"Suicide."

"DOCTOR HEWETT," Nick squeaked, half yelling, half shocked. "I'm not committing—"

"I haven't finished talking," said David. "You have suicide, or you get the hell out of town."

"What kind of options are those?" he said with a whimper. "They both suck."

"Nick, you need a change. Obviously, the path you're on now isn't working, is it?"

"No, I guess not."

"Then make a change. Do you hate it here?" asked David.

"Yes."

"Do you want to kill yourself?"

"No," said Nick.

"Well, you've told me you want to enough times."

"Yeah, but I'd never do it."

"Then how do you expect me to help you if you can't be honest with me? I can only fix you if you tell me the truth. What do you want out of life?"

"I want to be happy."

David placed the folder on his desk. "Nick, the only person who can make you happy is you. If you can't find happiness here, go somewhere else. Otherwise, you'll end up dying here."

"Are you telling me to run away?"

"I suppose I am, yes."

"That's not very good advice, is it?"

"Are you kidding? It's great advice. If this place makes you unhappy, leave. It isn't rocket science."

Nick sat back on the couch. "Doctor Hewett, if you could leave this town, would you?"

David paused for a second, uncertain of how to answer the question. "This isn't about me."

"Where should I go? I don't know anyone who doesn't live in Oceanview."

"Only you can decide that. But, if it's a decision you're going to make, do it soon. If you wait, a week becomes a month, becomes a year, becomes fifty. You'll be dead before you know it. Leave while you still can." He leaned back in his chair and raised an eyebrow as he waited for Nick's response.

"It seems an awful lot like avoidance. Won't all my problems follow me?"

"Probably," said David as he checked his watch. "Okay, Nick, time's up."

Nick reached in his pocket and pulled out a fifty.

David shook his head. "Keep it."

Nick looked surprised as he cautiously paced the bill back in his pocket. "Are you sure?"

"Are you going to follow my advice?" asked David.

"Yes. Same time next week?" asked Nick, clearly showing he was unable or unwilling to follow David's advice.

"I hope not," said David with a smile.

CHAPTER 7

Owen Warner laid unconscious on the living room floor of his dingy one-bedroom apartment. Ketchupy fast-food wrappers, empty beer bottles, and various drug paraphernalia littered the stained beige carpet. A half-empty bag of heroin had spilled across the coffee table, and the electricity long since turned off. The money for the utility bill replaced by the tiny mound of white powder.

"Gross," Death muttered under his breath with thinly veiled disgust. He looked down at his list to see where he would be sending the man. "Hmm," said Death. Somehow, Owen appeared on his good list and would, therefore, be going to Heaven. Contrary to the scene surrounding him, he had previously lived a respectable life. That was until he lost his job, and everything in his world snowballed. Apparently, his eternal judgment focused on the person he used to be before his addiction. It highlighted the exact reason Death did not question the criteria, it made little sense to him. Born Agains could get in at zero hour, while others were allowed major infractions and still earned a place in the clouds.

Passed out in a pile next to Owen lay his fiancée, Jess. Vomit and either red Kool-Aid or blood pooled around her mouth. Her mascara danced chaotically down her cheeks from the flow of former tears. Death stared at her for a moment. If she gave half a shit, she looked quite attractive. At least she used to be. Two years of hard living took its toll on her. Drug cases and the homeless always hit Death the hardest. They were children, brothers, sisters, uncles, friends, and parents. Most were not born into it, they fell on difficult times, and everyone else moved on. He usually removed himself emotionally from most reapings, but these tugged at him. It seemed such a waste of life.

Her breathing labored and shallow, she somehow clung to life. The end approached, but her time was another day. However, Owen's clock had expired. Death reached over to touch Owen's left shoulder. With a soft gasp, the last glimmer of life slipped from his body. Death looked at Jess, reached down, and grabbed a letter she held in her hand. In no sweet terms, her parents told her she was dead to them and to stay the hell away from her siblings. Those were some of the nicer comments peppered throughout. Death figured she made life hard for them, but the letter did nothing to help get things moving in the right direction. They were her parents How could they give up on her? With a sigh, he reached into his robe and pulled out a red card.

Blood Cards were one of the little-known perks of his job. On the first of the month, he received a small black envelope which contained ten red cards. They allowed him to bypass the standard reaping lists and send people on their way based on his own judgment. They permitted him to play judge, jury, and executioner ten times a month. If he saw someone who needed a way out, then he pulled a card and either sent them to Heaven or Hell at his discretion, but their proverbial blood covered his hands.

When he first received the Blood Cards, he used them on people who were being complete twats. He handed the first card to a thug who snapped cartwheels off wagons in the early days of London, and the second he passed to a serial graffiti artist with a penchant for drawing super-sized penises on the walls of schools. While he enjoyed the looks on their faces as they died, the novelty quickly subsided, and as time ticked by, he found a more humane use. Every once in a while, he stumbled across a soul not on his list, someone so broken and damaged, that waiting for their number to come up seemed cruel and heartless. He called these select few 'The Lost'.

While he once wished for dozens of cards to hand out to douchebags on impulse, he soon found himself playing the Samaritan and studied the people he gave the cards to. He looked at photos and other evidence to determine if the Blood Card was the answer. Those reapings were a lot harder on him, and the faceless numbers he usually dealt with suddenly became real people. He never handed out a Blood Card without considering all viable options.

Over the years, he handed out the cards a lot more sparingly, and amassed an extensive collection in his bottom desk drawer. It was not that he did not want to use them, there were just so many people who deserved them, he found it difficult to decide who should take priority. In the early days, they were depleted by the first day of the month. As the years passed, he reached the last day and still had all ten cards. Months turned to years and years to decades, and only the most broken received one.

Death looked up at a row of shelves filled with various photographs of Jess and her family from better times. Their smiling faces were a stark contrast to the scene he faced. She looked only a few years younger in the pictures, and Death wondered how things had gone wrong so quickly.

As he leaned in and kissed her gently on the forehead, he noticed the track marks on her arm. At best, she had a few hours left. The Blood Card simply sped up the inevitable. It was the right thing to do. "It'll all go away now."

Jess did not respond.

Jess could not respond.

Death carefully placed the card next to her cheek and touched her left shoulder. Her last breath escaped her lips, and she finally found something that resembled a state of peace. Death sat by her side for a few minutes to ensure she passed. Certain she was gone, he stood and walked over to the shelves and picked up one of the pictures of Jess with her family. They were decked out in winter garb on a skiing trip, and Owen's arm wrapped proudly around Jess. Death noticed she wore an engagement ring as broad as her grin. He stepped back over to Jess and placed the picture in her hand and removed the letter. Her next journey should start with a snapshot of a smile, instead of the note she grasped. He looked at her left hand and noticed the ring missing, likely a pawn shop victim of the addiction.

Death had been so preoccupied with taking care of Jess and moving her on to the next world, that he forgot about the issue with Thomas. Owen moved on to the next world with no problems, and for the meantime, everything worked as it was supposed to. However, his delayed stay with the drug couple had put him slightly behind schedule. He would need to focus if he was going to get his day back on track. Thankfully, his cloak not only allowed teleportation and invisibility, but it also included a stopwatch that gifted him minor time manipulation. He could freeze and subtly rewind time to allow himself an adequate schedule to travel and perform his reapings. Without it, the job bordered on impossible.

He surveyed the room one last time to ensure there were no loose ends, closed his eyes, and disappeared.

◆ ◆ ◆ ◆

For reaping number two-hundred and thirty-seven of the day, Death reappeared in a tiny fishing village on the outskirts of Rio de Janeiro. Thankfully, the Christ the Redeemer statue was blocked from view and allowed him to work in peace. He found it a tad creepy having the son of one of his bosses staring over his shoulder while he was trying to work. While Brazil was a beautiful country to visit, it certainly had its unique drawbacks.

He saw an old man sitting on a dock with his feet in the river and his head hung low. Milo Santano's wife had passed three weeks earlier after eighty-one years of marriage. Their sole child died of old age three years before that, and his only grandson of cancer the previous summer, so he welcomed death. All his friends were gone, and for the first time in his life, he found himself alone. Everyone he had ever loved had been taken and left him little to live for. Even Alzheimer's skipped over him to help numb the pain. Each second that ticked by felt like a vice crushing his heart.

Death walked up behind him and pulled out his list. According to the reaping details, the poor man was moments away from a major coronary, and would spend his final seconds dying alone on the wooden dock. Still saddened by Jess, Death smiled and reached over to touch the old man on his left shoulder, happy to reunite him with his family in Heaven. "Safe travels, Mr. Santano."

Nothing happened. Death touched the old man again, and still nothing occurred. He exhaled in frustration, and knowing it was a wasted effort, touched him a third time.

The victim looked up as if aware something was amiss. Death reached out and touched him one more time. He failed to understand how the old man could still be alive. Days away from his one-hundredth birthday and his heart shattered, he had every reason to die. Death opened his list and teleported again.

The next dozen reapings were a mixed bag of varying results. They worked in both Adelaide and Moscow, but they failed again in Montenegro and Nepal.

"What the—" started Death. He clenched his teeth as he rolled up his list and tucked it under his robe. His mind raced as he tried to determine what was going on. The system had always worked. He closed his eyes and disappeared.

Something had gone very, very wrong.

CHAPTER 8

David sat at the bar in Jacob's and sipped his gin in silence. He watched Hank pour Mr. Yan a beer with a politically incorrect Asian face on the foam.

Mr. Yan beamed when he saw the foam caricature with almond-shaped eyes. "Looks like my mother-in-law," he said with a face-spanning grin. "But prettier."

Hank smiled and looked up as Warren entered from the cold mid-morning air.

Warren stopped when he saw David and contemplated leaving, but he had already been spotted. "I thought Cam was here."

"She's in the bathroom," said David. "Come and join me for a drink. What'll you have?"

Warren eyed David suspiciously. "My usual."

Hank nodded at Warren and grabbed a glass.

"What are you doing here on a Sunday morning? Don't you normally have patients to see?" asked Warren.

"Just the one today, so I get the rest of the day to myself. Now I get to spend it with you. Can we talk?"

"What about?"

"The six-year cold front."

"I'm over it," said Warren.

"So, you're not upset about what happened with Cam in my office?"

"It was six years ago," said Warren.

"And you still blame me."

"You sided with her."

"I didn't side with anyone. You stormed out before I could finish."

"That's how it looked to me."

"I respect your perspective, but you have it wrong. As a therapist, my job isn't to take—"

"Why don't you go to church?" asked Warren, interrupting him sharply.

David frowned. "Excuse me?"

"Why don't you go to church?"

"I don't see how this applies to the current topic."

Warren shifted on his seat. "If I'm taking advice from someone, I must be able to trust them."

"What do trust and church have to do with each other?" asked David.

"Everything. Why don't you go?"

David shrugged. "I don't do church."

"Why not? There's plenty of room."

David laughed. "I don't doubt it. It just isn't my thing."

Hank pushed a glass of beer over to Warren.

"Thanks, Hank." He grabbed his drink and took a long sip. "You too good for us common folk?" he asked David.

David laughed. "I gave it up for Lent twenty years ago and never went back."

"So, what are you now? Lutheran, Baptist, Jew, Mormon?"

"Subtly isn't in your range, is it?" said David as he took a sip of gin.

"What do you mean?"

"Nothing. I mean, I'm an atheist."

Warren's eyes widened as if someone had just shot his puppy. "That means you believe in nothing." It was not a question.

"Yes. I am sans religion."

"Oh, my God, you're a heathen. I am so sorry."

David took another sip of his gin. "Why? I'm perfectly happy with my life."

"Hank, want to chime in here?" asked Warren, looking for backup.

"Nope, I don't comment on Godless infidels."

"Okay, rough crowd tonight," said David.

"But, as long as you're drinking, your money is good here," said Hank with a hint of a smile.

"Surely you believe in something?" asked Warren.

"I believe in science and the tangible."

"But no God?"

"Nope."

"I don't think I've ever met a man without faith. I'm really sorry for you," said Warren with genuine sadness in his voice.

"Don't be."

Warren frowned as his mind put the pieces together. "That's why I don't like you."

"I thought you didn't like me because you think I screwed you on marriage counseling?"

"Yeah, well now I have two reasons. I don't trust a man who doesn't put his faith in the almighty."

"It's okay. I don't trust a man who puts his faith in something he has never seen."

"Just because you haven't seen something, it doesn't mean it isn't real. I've never seen a rhino, warthog, or unicorn, but I know they exist."

"You don't even like going," countered David. "You're always complaining about how boring it is and how it makes you feel guilty."

"At least I go."

"But you don't like it."

"At least I go. No one cares if I enjoy it. The important thing is I'm there."

"That's ridiculous. It all seems rather pointless to me," said David, as he took another sip of his gin. "Surely, if there's a God, he sees what all of us are doing, and if we're good people, does it matter if we spend our Sundays at the church or on the couch watching football? If I don't cheat, lie, steal, or murder, does it make any difference?"

"Of course it makes a difference. If it didn't, we wouldn't have churches, would we?"

David was unsure of how to respond.

Hank spared him the task. "Don't argue with an idiot. You won't win, and it just brings you down to his level."

"Thanks," both David and Warren said at the same time. They looked at each other, and then Hank, neither sure to whom he referred.

David turned to the booth behind him, where a lone man sat staring into his beer. "Donald doesn't go to church either. Why don't you give him a hard time?"

"Because he isn't my shrink. Isn't that right, Donald?"

Donald didn't answer. Out of all the strange people in town, Donald Fletcher was by far the most unusual. Well into his sixties, he lived next door to his aging aunt. He never married, and his last date ended decades ago. He spent the first part of his life in Maine and moved to Oceanview a few months after the town formed. He remained one of the few who could call themselves an original resident. As with David, he discovered the town purely by accident. While on vacation to the Grand Canyon, he planned to fly into Vegas and head east on I-40. Engine trouble forced the flight to be rerouted through Phoenix, and he took a rental car north to the Grand Canyon. The rental company delivered the car half empty, and he needed to get gas a few miles north of the town of Williams. He stopped at Oceanview and decided one day he would like to move there. He loved the small-town feel. It reeked of routine and serenity.

A series of personal tragedies and matriarchal guilt prevented him from spreading his wings and leaving. A few months after his trip to the Grand Canyon, his mother, May, fell severely ill, and her doctor recommended she move out west for the warmer climate. Donald suggested moving to Oceanview. So, the family packed up their belongings and headed towards the Pacific. Unfortunately, May never made it to Arizona. It would have been a tragic death, had she passed in the Grand Canyon state, instead of a few miles from the city limits of Biddeford, Maine. Donald and his aunt drove with her for almost three thousand miles before arriving in Oceanview to discover she was dead, instead of just sleeping for the previous two days. She held a family record for sleeping thirty-six hours straight, so to believe she fell asleep and the hypnotic hum of the freeway kept her sedated, seemed reasonable.

Donald's first order of business in Oceanview involved planning her funeral. The second required getting rid of the car. He posted an ad in the local paper, and after a month of people running like hell after the post test-drive confession, he visited the mall and left the keys in the ignition. He returned two hours later to find the car moved to a different spot. Defeated and a little confused, he climbed back in and discovered a note taped to the steering wheel. '*Dude, tried to steal your car. Feels like someone died in here. May want to get it detailed before offering it up*'. So instead, he took the pseudo thief's advice, detailed the car, and continued to drive it, although none of his few passengers ever sat in the back.

After this devastating loss, his life never regained direction, and thirty-six years came and went. He took a job with a security company and planted his roots, never living to his fullest potential. His mother crushed any spirit he possessed, and her ghost would haunt him to his final days. Those who looked close saw something else behind his eyes, a man who lived through a tremendous and devastating heartbreak, an event far beyond a parent dying. Something far ahead of his time, but he kept that part of his life secret, so no one ever saw the real Donald.

He was a fantastic artist but lacked any kind of confidence to pursue it past casual breakfast table doodles. Paralyzed by fear of failure or success, he never granted himself the opportunity to succeed and became a background character in the truest sense of the word. He loved to read classic literature and should anyone have given him the time for a chat, they would discover someone well-read and quite charming. His job as a security guard bored him. The most excitement came from chasing away kids tagging the side of Mr. Hughes' ice cream shop. However, the universe had bigger plans for Donald, and it involved the death of his aunt.

Two weeks had passed since her funeral, and it underlined one crushing fact; he found himself absolutely and unequivocally alone. There were no brothers or sisters, and he heard his father died years ago. There were no children, or cousins, or grandparents. When he became one with the ground, his bloodline ended. Hundreds of years of history stopped dead in its tracks.

With this depressing thought, he sat alone for three hours, his eyes focused on the dissipating head of his beer as it slowly turned flat.

The door to the lady's bathroom swung open, and Cam stepped out. "Stop looking at my ass, Donald," she said as she walked back to the bar.

He looked up at her. "I wasn't," he said weakly.

"It's okay hun, I wore this skirt for you. Figured you could use cheering up after the week you've had."

"I appreciate the consideration, but I wasn't looking at your ass, I was—" He paused. "Somewhere else."

Cam looked confused. "No? Then what were you staring at?" Guys always stared at her ass.

"Nothing. I'm just thinking."

"What about?"

"It's time for me to move on from here."

David promptly spat out a mouthful of gin. "What?"

"I'm moving on. There's nothing left for me here."

"Where are you going? You don't have anyone. You've laid on my couch and told me a thousand times." For a psychiatrist, David possessed the sensitivity of a freight train.

"Thanks for reminding me, Dr. Hewitt. I turned in my notice to Pete two weeks ago. I asked him to keep it quiet."

"You can't leave," said David. "You're a permanent fixture like the rest of us sorry bastards."

"I don't want to be a sorry bastard anymore. It's time for me to find someone, and I won't do it sitting in this town rotting in my La-Z-Boy. I've got, what, ten, twenty, thirty years left if I'm lucky. I have a list of things I wanted to see and do, and I've done none of it."

His announcement intrigued Cam. "What's on your list? No, let me guess. Bungee jumping, skydiving, and alligator wrestling?"

Donald laughed. "No, nothing that exciting."

"Then tell us," said Cam. "We want to know."

"It sounds stupid," said Donald.

"Try."

"I want what most take for granted. I want to sit on the beach and watch the sunrise. I want to go to the ocean and eat sushi. Real sushi, not the shit you get here. I want to look up from my coffee and see someone who sees me for the first time. Someone I can get a clean slate with. They don't care who I am or where I have come from, and they won't judge me. I won't be the sad old man who lived with his mom and aunt until they died. The man who went nowhere with his life. I want them to see the side of me none of you ever have found or wanted to find."

David could barely mask his excitement. "Go Donald." He raised his glass in the air. "Ten years of sitting on my couch hasn't been able to do that for you. What changed?"

Donald smiled slightly. "Maybe you're a shitty shrink."

"Touché, you socially inept bastard." David swallowed a mouthful of gin and slammed the empty glass onto the counter. "Hank, another for me, and a drink for my smart-ass friend over here." David patted the seat next to him. "Come join us, Donald. I say we propose a toast."

As Donald stood from his seat and crossed over to the bar, Hank placed a beer in front of him and, for the first time in thirty-five years, sat with someone at Jacob's and enjoyed a drink.

David put a hand on Donald's shoulder and pulled him in for a hug. "To Donald, one of the most awkward, strange, and honest people I have ever known. May you cram seventy years of living into the next twenty."

Shouts of '*cheers*' reverberated around the bar.

"You know why I love you, Donald?" David continued.

"I have no idea."

"It's because even though life handed you a complete shit stick, you grabbed it with both hands and never gave up."

Donald looked around the bar. "You call this never giving up? You are the first person I've had a drink with in years. You all say hi, but you never really acknowledge me. The booth over there has an imprint of my ass in it, and you see what's next to it?"

David craned his neck to glance over at the booth. "I don't see anything."

"Exactly. Nothing. My ass print and no one else's. I've been alone almost my entire life. I gave up a long time ago. It's why I must go. I don't want to live out what's left of my life staring at your asses while you sit at the bar with your backs to me."

Cam grinned victoriously. "So, you were staring at my ass then?"

"Hey, he said asses," David quickly added. "That's plural. He stares at mine too." He laughed as he looked over at Cam. "Credit where credit's due." He turned back to Donald. "Well, whatever you call it, I'm glad you're leaving."

"Thanks?" said Donald with an ounce of uncertainty.

"You know what I mean. The rest of these pathetic old fuckers don't have the guts to leave."

A few protests echoed around the bar at the cheap shot.

David turned to face his hecklers. "Oh, you know I'm right. You're hanging on to the desperate notion that something will change, and let's face it, it won't. People come to this town to die, and it happily obliges."

A few more patrons protested at the insults.

David dismissed them with a wave of his hand. "Don't even pretend otherwise. I hit the nail right on the head."

As Donald looked at the group, a tidal wave of regret washed over him. He suddenly felt at home in the bar and wished the last four decades could have been like this. Maybe he would be less inclined to leave.

Cam still beamed about Donald staring at her ass. "Donald, do you want to be my date for Forefather's Day next Friday?"

Donald shook his head. "I can't, I'm sorry. I'm leaving Saturday, and I need to finish packing."

"You're refusing my offer?" asked Cam with mock distress.

"I'd love to, but the sooner I pack, the sooner I can get out of here."

"It'll be your last Forefather's Day in Oceanview. We should celebrate."

"I can't, I'm sorry."

Cam looked at Donald, trying to get a read on him. "You're really unhappy here, aren't you?"

"It's more than that. There's nothing for me here."

"What are you talking about? You still have me," said David.

Donald smiled again. "Exactly."

David pretended to be shocked at Donald's bravado. "You ballsy motherfucker. Where did you get those clankers from?"

"Is that your professional prognosis?"

David laughed. "Damn right it is. Promise you'll do one thing for me, okay? When you run, you don't even give us a second look."

"I'm not running, I'm leaving. Big difference."

"Call it whatever, but promise me you won't look back?"

"Okay, why?"

"No one gets out of this damned town alive."

CHAPTER 9

"**Y**ou can't quit on me, Don," said Pete Mead, the owner of Premier Security, as he looked up at Donald from his desk.

"I'm not quitting, Pete. I'm retiring."

"Same result. You're still leaving me without a security guard. Where will I find someone with your experience?"

"I won't be hard to replace. Open the phone book and throw a dart."

Pete laughed. "You don't give yourself enough credit. You've always talked about retirement. I didn't think you meant it this time."

"Well, that's not my fault, is it? When have I ever lied to you?"

"You haven't. I just never thought you'd leave."

"Neither did I, but I gave you my two weeks." Donald sighed. "I'm a sixty-three-year-old career security guard. It's my time."

"There's no shame in security."

"I wasn't saying there is. I'm just not as young as I used to be. I can't be chasing down kids a quarter my age."

"I'll give you a gun. You can shoot, right?"

Donald laughed. "As tempting as it sounds, this isn't a bartering conversation. Even if it was, I don't even use the pepper spray and nightstick. A gun is an accident waiting to happen. This is a safe and boring job."

"So why does it matter if you can't run?"

"I'm supposed to be a security guard. There will be a time where someone will be where they're not supposed to, and I won't be able to chase them."

"But it's a quiet job," countered Pete.

"It is. I'm not arguing that."

"Then why wouldn't you spend your golden years doing something safe and boring?"

"It's why I can't. I haven't done anything with my life. I want to see what's out there."

"We're old men, Don. The game is for the youngsters. There's nothing for us out there anymore. We find a safe and quiet place, make it comfortable, and see it through to the end. It isn't a bad way to go out."

"No, but it's something I have to do. It's what she'd have wanted. Hell, she'd be crushed that I didn't do this years ago."

Pete could see the sincerity in his eyes. "I know, Don. Are you doing it for her or for you?"

"For both of us." Donald unclipped his badge and handed it over to Pete. "I need to do this. I've owed it to myself for a long time."

Pete looked at the metal emblem. "This was the first badge we ever made for the company."

"You should frame it for prosperity."

It was Pete's turn to laugh. "You keep it. A memento." He handed it back to Donald. "Premier Security won't be the same without you, you've been here since the beginning. I hope you find what you're looking for."

Donald sighed. "So do I."

"Are you okay for money?"

Donald shrugged. "I've been saving. I should be okay for a little while." He extended his hand as Pete stood and grasped it firmly.

"It's been an absolute pleasure, Don."

"Likewise." Donald started towards the door.

"Don?"

Donald stopped and turned around.

"One last thing." Pete reached into his top desk drawer. He pulled out an envelope and offered it to Donald.

"What's this?"

"A thank you."

Donald opened the envelope and pulled out a check with a lot of zeroes. He stared at it for a moment and looked up at Pete. "Is this a joke?"

Pete shook his head.

"Pete? What the hell is this?"

"It's yours."

"Three hundred and seventy-five thousand dollars?"

Pete nodded. "Actually, it's three-hundred and seventy-six-thousand, four-hundred-and-sixty-three-dollars and some odd cents."

"Christ, Pete. I can't take this."

"It's yours. You've earned it."

"How do you figure that?"

"You've been with me for nearly thirty-five years. We offered you no pension, no retirement plan. I put two hundred and fifty a month aside for you each month and planned to give it to you when you left. I never thought you'd stay this long. It's earned good money."

"I don't know what to say." Donald's face flooded with a canvas of emotions.

Pete smiled. "Thank you is always a good place to start."

Donald's eyes widened as he realized he had not shown his appreciation, and he quickly composed himself. "Of course, of course, thank you. I'm just in a bit of shock at the moment." He paused. "Can the company afford it?"

"The company never even saw the money. Most of it is compound interest anyway. You gave everything to this company. You walked the properties, trained the new recruits, and brought in new accounts. We wouldn't be where we are today without you. You're a good man, Don. You deserve this."

"You're no fob, yourself."

Donald extended his hand for a second time. "If you didn't think I was quitting, why did you have this ready?"

Pete shrugged as he grabbed Donald's hand. "I guess you could call it one-part wishful thinking and another part denial of the inevitable." He smiled again. "I knew this day would come eventually, I just didn't want to face it. Safe travels, Donald."

Donald pulled him in for a hug, and the two friends said their goodbyes in silence.

◆ ◆ ◆ ◆

The front door to Premiere Security swung upon, and Donald stepped outside for the last time. The overcast sky and cold chill clashed with the warmth running through his chest. He felt like he had been holding his breath and exhaled a long heavy sigh. His breath formed a billowing cloud in the winter air. He glanced down at the check in his hand, and his heart pumped in the back of his throat. Over the past few years, he only managed to save a few thousand and expected to need part-time work wherever he eventually settled down. The check meant he could spend the rest of his days living the life he had neglected for so long.

♦ ♦ ♦ ♦

The bank was busier than Donald expected for a Monday morning. He grabbed a deposit slip from the counter by the door and filled it out as he waited.

"Don't spend it all at once," a voice suggested from behind. Donald turned around to see David in line behind him.

"Hello, Doctor Hewett," said Donald.

"That's a lot of zeroes."

Donald looked at the slip. "More than I've ever seen."

"Are you kidding? It's more than I've ever seen," said David. "Pete's a good man."

"How did you know it was from Pete?" asked Donald.

David smiled and tapped his nose. "Priest. Well, as much as an atheist can be, I suppose."

"Right." Donald returned to filling out the slip. "Isn't you telling me someone told you a breach of your vows or whatever you shrinks call it?"

"Nah, it's only a breach if I told you who told me."

"Pete?"

"Nope."

Donald wondered who else it could be. Then it hit him. "Maria?"

"Yep. Crazy old bitch can't keep her mouth shut about anything. She's pretty pissed he gave you the money. She felt it should have gone to their retirement instead of yours."

"She's right."

"Bullshit. If it makes you feel any better, she gets mad when Pete tips the paperboy."

Donald smiled. "I've no idea how they made it forty years. I'd have left a long time ago."

"No, you wouldn't. Look how long you've stayed in Oceanview. This town is no different from a nagging spouse. Just more people under your roof."

"I almost didn't take it. It feels wrong."

"That's understandable. It's a lot of money. But he'd be hurt if you didn't. He's been saving for years, and he's waited for this day for a long time."

"I don't deserve it."

"Bullshit. You're a good man, Donald, you deserve your happily ever after."

"That may be, but I don't want to cause an issue with him and his wife."

"You won't. If it weren't this, it'd be something else. If you give the money back, you will be hurting Pete more than if you try to repair his marriage. He's been with her long enough, he knows how to pick his battles."

Donald looked back at the half-completed deposit slip and put down his pen. "Am I doing the right thing, Doctor Hewett? Is this the right choice?"

"I think at this point, you can call me David."

"Okay, David. My question stands."

"I see life this way. If I can go to bed with tired hands, a busy mind, a full heart, and a clean conscience, then I am doing the right thing."

Donald stepped forward as the line moved towards the tellers. "This changes everything."

"How so?"

"I figured I'd be tied to a job somewhere. This allows me to be completely free."

"That's a good thing, right?"

"I don't know." said Donald. "This freedom makes it an even bigger leap of faith."

"So, what you're saying is, you are leaving the stability and routine of Oceanview, and replacing it with possible stability and routine elsewhere? It doesn't seem like much of a trade."

"I'm an old man, David. What if I fail?"

"What if you don't?" countered David.

Donald shrugged. "Fair enough," he said. It was difficult to argue with that point of view.

"Donald, you said it yourself, you don't have a lifetime. Get out there and cram as much as you can into the time you have left." He paused for a second. "Are you dying?"

"Excuse me?"

"It's a simple question."

"No, I've never been in better health."

"So, then you answer to no one but yourself," said David. "There's a huge world out there, Donald. Go out there and leave your footprint on its ass."

Donald inadvertently looked down at his shoes. "I wish——" He let the sentence hang. "Please don't tell anyone about this." He looked at the check as he tried to change topics. "I don't need a line of people at my doorstep begging me for money while I try to pack. I don't want people thinking I'm only leaving because of this."

David mimicked sealing his lips and threw away an imaginary key. "Why couldn't you have gotten the check while you were still a patient? I'd have doubled my rates."

Donald smiled. "You'd still be a shitty shrink."

"Maybe you're a tough nut to crack."

"Maybe you didn't ask the right questions."

David smiled. "Yeah, I think I might be getting a bit rusty in my old age."

"Old age? You're half my age, and you've accomplished ten times as much."

"You mean the job?"

Donald nodded. "Part of it, yeah."

"Appearances can be deceiving. Being a shrink isn't all it's hyped up to be. I am the keeper of half the town's deepest, darkest secrets. I swear there are people here who could be locked up for the things they've told me. But, I took the oath. If I give people the right advice, they become dependent on me and keep coming back. If I give the wrong advice, I get threatened and in a few cases, sued. Yet they keep coming back until they get an answer they are happy with. They don't want my professional opinion, they've already made their mind up long before setting foot in my office. They want to hear their self-diagnosis repeated back to them in my voice."

"At least you get to meet people."

"True. But, it's also the reason I spend most of my free time at the bottom of a glass of gin. Come to think of it, I'm pretty sure you are the only person who has made any progress."

"You call this progress?"

"You're moving forward. It's the perfect definition of progress. Where are you heading?"

"East."

"Just east?"

"Seems like a good start."

David glimpsed at his cell phone and grimaced. "Shit, I have an appointment I have to get to. Donald, I'm so sorry, I hate to cut this short." He extended his hand. "I'm really happy for you. This is a big opportunity. Make the most of it, not everyone gets this chance."

Donald nodded as he reciprocated the handshake. "Yeah, you're probably right."

"Until our paths cross again."

"Hopefully they won't, as it means something has gone horribly wrong."

CHAPTER 10

Loud music blared from Greg and Warren's garage and masked the sound of Amber's heels clicking across the concrete. She crossed over to a yellow school bus jacked up in the center of the workshop. She gently kicked at the pair of legs lying under the vehicle, and Greg rolled out, covered in oil and grease.

"Hey, sweetheart," he said with a smile. He stood and crossed over to the stereo and turned down the music. "What are you doing here? Shouldn't you be at work?" he said as he wiped his dirty hands on the sides of his overalls.

"Early lunch," she said and leaned in to kiss him. "Is Warren around?"

"No, he's out towing Mrs. Lewis. Her transmission blew. I don't know why she won't put the damn thing out to pasture. It's in here every other week with one problem or another. She has to see how much she is investing in the piece of crap. A new car is cheaper."

"You're wandering," said Amber with a smile.

"Sorry."

"I brought you lunch," she said as she produced a brown paper bag from her oversized purse.

"Thanks, hun." He dug inside and pulled out a sandwich. "I haven't told him yet. If it's what you are here for."

Amber shook her head. "No, it's something else. I needed to make sure he wasn't here."

"Okay. Well, he isn't. He should be gone at least another hour."

"Ashley is dumping him tonight."

"Shit." He bit into his sandwich.

"Yeah, shit. So now he's going to get two big pieces of bad news. I told you to tell him."

Greg rubbed his temples in frustration. "I know, I know. What was the final straw?"

"She's got a laundry list. He isn't going to take it well."

"Warren doesn't take anything well. If he gets a hangnail, it's the end of the world. This is the exact reason I've stalled telling him. I'm surprised she lasted this long."

"If you don't start eating with your mouth closed, we won't last much longer either," she said with a smile.

Greg promptly swallowed his food. "Sorry."

"Can you talk to him?"

"Yeah, I'll take him to Jacob's, and he'll drink his way through. I wish I'd listened to you. Now I'm going to be the uber bad guy."

"I won't say I told you so."

"But you will anyway," said Greg with a smile.

"Of course, dear. Spousal privilege." There was that S-word again.

"We'll get to chaperone him at the Forefather's event," said Greg.

"I didn't even think about that," said Amber.

"You've seen how he gets over it. Not a chance he'll miss it. Is Ashley still going?"

"I don't think so."

"That makes things easier, at least. We'll humor him for a night, and then he can come back to ours and sleep it off while she packs. I take it she is moving out?"

"Yeah. She's moving back in with our parents for a bit while she gets back on her feet."

"Probably for the best."

She looked up at the clock. "I need to get back to the office. You promise you'll talk to him tonight?"

"You have my word."

Greg sighed. He anticipated a long evening as he lay down on the cart and disappeared back under the bus.

Thirty seconds later, his feet were kicked again.

"I thought you needed to be back at the office?" he said as he slid back out from under the truck.

"What?" said Warren.

"Oh, hey. You're back quick, you tow it?" He pushed himself under the car again.

"No. It wasn't the damn transmission. The old coot locked her keys in the car and was too cheap to hire a locksmith."

"I assume you broke the window?" asked Greg, knowing Warren's expected actions would cost the shop more money to repair.

"Of course I did."

"Of course you did. When am I going out to replace it?"

"Tomorrow at one," said Warren.

Greg rolled his eyes and sighed. "How much is this going to cost?"

"Negative two."

"How much?" asked Greg.

"Negative two hundred."

Greg tried to process the number. "Wait, she paid us?" he said as he rolled back out from beneath the vehicle.

Warren smiled and dropped a stack of twenties on Greg's chest.

Greg picked them up and flicked through them. "Maybe you're not so useless after all."

"Thanks, you condescending prick," said Warren.

"Anytime."

"I'm breaking up with Ash tonight," Warren casually announced.

"Okay." Greg pushed himself back under the car so Warren could not see his grimace.

"Okay? That's all you've got to say? You're not going to talk me out of this?"

"Sounds like you've made your decision."

"Well, I hadn't. I expected you to tell me it was a bad idea."

"You're a big boy," said Greg. "I'm sure you know what you're doing."

"Yeah, I guess. So, you think I should break up with her then?"

"All I'm saying is if you're unhappy, call it quits. Else, figure a way to make it work."

"I'd miss her and all, but I like my guy time. What should I do?" asked Warren.

"This is your decision."

"Man, you're no help. You were supposed to make me feel better. I should end it though, I'd been cheating on her anyway."

Greg rolled back out from under the car. "You're doing what? With who?"

"Jill."

Greg stood up. "Her best friend? Have you lost your fucking mind?"

Warren shrugged.

"Goddammit, Warren." said Greg in frustration. "What is your fucking problem?" He did not wait for his brother to respond. "Yes, you need to break up with Ashley. Right now. She'll kick your ass if she finds out."

"Well, unless you tell her, she won't," countered Warren. "I can keep a secret."

"Don't put this on me," said Greg. "I want nothing to do with it. This is completely one hundred percent, grade-A uncool. I like Ashley, she doesn't deserve this bullshit."

"I didn't do it on purpose," said Warren. "It just kinda happened." He paused as he ran a quick number through his head. "Seventeen times," he added.

"No, Warren, it didn't. Falling asleep just kinda happens. A flat tire just kinda happens. Adultery doesn't just kinda happen. I don't fucking believe you," said Greg.

"It's okay, I broke it off with Jill yesterday. That counts for something, right?"

"No," said Greg as he sighed in anger. "It really doesn't. So, when are you dropping the bomb?"

"I guess I'll go over after work. It's going to suck, she isn't going to take this well."

"You may be surprised," said Greg.

"What do you mean?"

"Nothing. How about you grab a wrench and help me with this engine?"

"Grab Bob, I'm going to go get lunch."

Greg rolled his eyes in frustration. Bob had worked at the garage since the beginning. Their father's best friend, he came with the business when they inherited it. He was half-blind, mostly deaf and utterly useless, but neither could muster the nerve to let him go.

"Can you at least pass me a seven-sixteenths?" asked Greg.

"No, I'm busy." Warren smiled as he headed to the door. "I'll catch you later."

"Thanks for nothing, dick." Greg walked over to the bench and grabbed a wrench. "Be faster to do the damn thing myself."

"Hey, you're the bleeding-heart liberal. Toughen up and fire the old bastard." Warren pressed the button on his car key remote as he walked outside to his vehicle.

"I can't fire an old man," said Greg.

"Then stop complaining." Warren pushed the button again. On the third try, the car chirped. "I think my remote battery's dying." He opened the car door and climbed in.

"Speaking of which, can you at least pick up a battery for the bay door remote while you're out?" asked Greg.

"Yeah." Warren slammed the door closed and started the engine. He forgot the request before he left the parking lot.

Greg headed back to the bus. "Oh, I'm moving out of town with Amber in June," he shouted as Warren's car pulled away. "And Ashley is dumping your ass." Greg shrugged his shoulders. At least he tried to tell him.

CHAPTER 11

"What the hell do you mean Death is here?" screamed God into the telephone. "He isn't on my calendar today. Did he make an appointment, Nancy?"

He paused for an answer from his secretary. "No, that's right, he didn't, did he? It must mean he's winging it. Do I like it when people wing it, Nancy? Do I?" God paused for another response. "No, I don't." He paused. "Yes, it does irritate me." Pause. "Yes, it gives me heartburn. Do I like heartburn, Nancy?" He waited for yet another answer he already anticipated. "Well, of course I don't. What do I hate more than anything in this world?" He paused. "No, aside from him. And her. And them. Especially them, I fucking hate them." He rolled his eyes and cursed under his breath. "Impromptu, Nancy. I hate impromptu. You should know this by now. For one, it's a silly word, and two, it upsets me. Have I ever liked impromptu, Nancy?" He paused. "Important, is it? Isn't it always important?"

He bashed the handset onto the table in anger. After a second, he composed himself and picked up the phone. "I have a golf tournament in fifteen minutes. Did you not read my calendar?" He paused again. "What do you mean it's not on there? I can see it." He listened to Nancy again. "No, of course it isn't marked as private again." He looked at the calendar entry on his computer, and sure enough, the event was marked private. He quickly clicked on the event and changed its visibility. "Try it again." A moment later, Nancy returned to the line. "It's not my fault you don't know how to read my calendar. I guess it looks like I am done with my tea then, aren't I?"

As Nancy replied, he picked up his mug and crossed to the kitchenette to the left of his desk. Slowly, he poured the brown liquid into the sink. "Nope, it's too late. I've dumped it out." He stared intently as it circled the drain. "No, Nancy, it's wasted now. Listen. Can you hear that splashing sound? It's my ten minutes of serenity going down the drain and sucking my soul down with it. I trashed my plate of thin mints too," he said as he flipped his plate of cookies in the trash. "The only ten minutes of peace and quiet I get a day, and it's gone." Another pause. "Well, yes, you might as well send him in then. It's not like I am doing anything else now, am I?" He hung up the phone and sighed. "I'm certainly not drinking my tea," he grumbled to himself. "Or playing golf."

God rinsed out his cup and put it on the counter. He looked at the trash can and paused. A second later, he reached down and picked it up. He plucked out a cookie and popped it in his mouth. With a satisfied moan, he carried the can back to his desk and flopped into his chair. His graying temples started to throb as a light tapping echoed from the office door. The door slowly opened, and Nancy meekly poked her head in.

"Sir, Death is here to see you."

The headache careening through his skull migrated south to become a pain in his ass. "Thank you, Nancy," he said through gritted teeth and a car salesman smile. "Send him in."

God took a deep breath and stood from behind his desk as Death confidently strode into the room, a large manila folder tucked under his left arm. Nancy pulled the door closed.

With a forced smile, God extended his hand. "Hello, Steve, to what do I owe?"

Death kept his arms firmly at his sides. He hated God's smile. It was fake and arrogant, and it set his teeth on edge. He wanted to punch the smug out of him. "Only my friends call me Steve."

"Okay, Steve. Same question."

"Let's dispense with the pleasantries, Gary, and get down to business."

"People call me God."

"You're not my god."

God lowered his hand. "Okay, this sounds formal." Death irritated him. He always acted as though someone had rammed a stick firmly up his butt. God gestured to the empty chair across from him. "Please, take a stick. Seat, take a seat," he quickly corrected himself. "Cookie?" he asked as he offered Death the trash can.

Death continued to stand and looked at the trash can with an air of suspicion. "No. This isn't a social visit. I don't want you to assume because we are standing opposite each other, I'm interested in exchanging small talk, or I actually care about trivial chit-chat."

"I wouldn't assume at all," God interrupted.

"Yes, you do, you always do. Every time I come here, it's the same damn thing. Your harpy of a waiting room receptionist is a colossal pain in my butt and makes me teleport into a closet and use the public elevator. I come in here, and you offer me a cup of tea, and I spend the next forty-five minutes hearing about your damned son. It's tiresome. I just want to get to the point about why I'm here, as I'm sure you have absolutely no clue."

God started to become flustered and barely managed a response. "I happen to be rather proud of my son."

"We are all proud of our children, Gary. Do I plague you with stories of how my children are doing? Do you care if Ronny has learned to ride his bike, or Kate has cut her first tooth? No, you don't. So, if it's all the same, I'd rather stand and skip the meaningless banter."

"I didn't know you had any kids."

"Exactly, I don't. I'm not your friend. I'm not your acquaintance. I am the unfortunate sap who gets to come to visit you when something is wrong, and dammit, Gary, something is wrong."

God sat down and leaned back in his chair, trying to remain calm. He was annoyed at Death gaining the upper hand so quickly in the conversation. "So, what do you want?"

"What can you tell me about Thomas Matthew Nixon?"

"Date and time of birth?"

"July 29th, 1982, at 11:22 a.m."

God turned to the computer on his desk and typed in the details. "Of Madison, Wisconsin?"

"That's him."

"Let me see. He's an African American male, he's six-foot-one tall, about one-eighty-two, black hair, brown eyes, single. Graduated Ohio State with an undergrad in civil engineering with a 3.9 GPA. Dropped out halfway through his master's degree as his life supposedly lacked direction. He now works for a software company testing code, and he hates it. Never been married, although engaged once for fifteen minutes before flirting with the waitress serving him the night he proposed."

"What else?"

"His favorite movie is Return of the Jedi."

"And?"

"What else is there? I just rattled off the guy's entire life in less than thirty seconds."

"Is he dead?" asked Death.

"Of course he isn't dead. He is alive and kicking in Vegas at a bachelor party."

"Are you sure?"

"Yes, I'm sure, Steve. It's my job to be sure."

Death placed the folder on the table and stared straight at God. He flipped it open and stabbed a finger at the page. "Then why he is on my reaping list?"

"He is?" God picked up the folder. Sure enough, the third name on the page displayed Thomas Nixon. "Oh, look at that, he is. Huh. That's weird."

"Two days ago, I had a reaping in Las Vegas," said Death.

"I love Vegas."

"Of course you do."

"It's the best place on Earth to pick up new recruits. I'm quite popular there, actually. Did I ever tell you about the time—"

Death continued. "Not interested."

"The story has a monkey in it," said God in a sing-songy tone. "Everyone loves monkeys."

"I don't care. I hate monkeys, they're stupid and they smell."

God's jaw dropped. "They are not. Take it back."

Death ignored the request. "I reach out to reap him, and you know what happened? Guess what happened, Gary?"

God opened his mouth to speak, but Death had more to say.

"Nothing. Nothing happened," said Death.

"Impossible," God countered.

"One would think so, right? So, I try again. Nothing. I assumed my watch is broken and the time's wrong. I tap his shoulder a third time and still nothing. He should have been a skid mark, but he had no idea I existed. At first, I thought I found the wrong Thomas Nixon, so I checked my list. Twice."

"Did you find out if he'd been naughty or—"

Death stabbed a finger towards God. "Zip it. Not another peep from you. I called my office, and Susan double-checked the original."

"How is Susan these days? Lovely wom—"

"If you say another word, I swear I will slap you. We never double check our lists. Do you know why? Because we're always right, and low and behold, I have the right Thomas Nixon. The next batch of reapings go by okay, and I don't put any more thought into it. Until Milo Santano this morning. He won't reap. Neither does the next person, or the two people after that."

God shifts uncomfortably in his chair as Death continued his rant.

"I then decide to go to jump out of order and go to a random name on the list. Michael Eric Bauer. Sound familiar?"

"Maybe."

"When I find him, he's stumbling down the center divider of a freeway, drunk as an Irishman on Tuesday. The center of a freeway, Gary. I'm convinced he is on his way out, and I touch his shoulder. Nothing. How the hell is a raging drunk walking in the middle of ten lanes of high-speed traffic staying alive? I tap him again. I throw a rock at him. I think it's me. I go to my therapist and tell her I feel I'm losing my abilities."

"You have a therapist?"

"Employee benefit. After three hours of intense therapy and finding out I have mother issues, she advises me to check if the same thing is happening anywhere else. I'd already sent people down, so Luc hadn't sent one person to me in error. This is all you."

"Must be good to be Lucifer then."

"At least he does his job right." Death gestured towards the list. "This ended up on my desk, and it's full of people who aren't supposed to be within an elephant's genitals length of this list. Can you tell me why I am being given lists of people who aren't supposed to die?"

"I—" stammered God.

"I'm only one person, Gary. There's an order to things, and when that order gets messed up, things go wrong. And what happens when things go wrong? I get irate. And you know what happens when I get irate? I come here. You've messed up before, but nothing like this."

"Did you triple check it?"

"Did you seriously ask me that?" asked Death.

"I can't believe it's only me having these issues," argued God.

"Well, it is. Lucifer isn't having any problems at all."

"Lucifer isn't having any problems at all," God repeated in a mock tone similar to that of a five-year-old having a tantrum. "Well, good for him."

"Hate on him all you like, but he is doing his job, which is a lot more than I can say for you. How are you going to fix this?" Death stopped mid-thought. "You know what, don't answer that. I don't care how, just fix it."

"It's not easy."

"Then make it easy. I shouldn't have to take time out of my day to come here and sort this mess out. Contrary to what you may believe, I'm busy. I have places to go and people to service. I'm already late on today's reapings."

"It isn't my fault," proclaimed God weakly.

"No? Then whose fault is it?" Death countered. "Your signature is on the bottom of this list. You signed off on it."

"I can't have."

Death flipped to the last page of the folder and showed God his hand-signed name. "Is this yours?"

God stayed quiet.

"I'll take your silence as an acknowledgment."

"You know how it is. I get a hundred things thrown across my desk daily needing my signature. You can't expect me to read all of it. I'd never get anything done."

"Just because you sign things without reading them, it doesn't make it my problem."

"It was my secretary," said God.

"You're going to blame Nancy?" Death said in disbelief. "Don't blame the hired help."

"You're making matters worse, and making me less inclined to assist you."

"You're welcome to take that stance, but if you do, there will be repercussions."

"Repercussions?"

"I could get part of Lucifer's list mixed in with yours and you'd get all kinds of unsavory characters coming in through your pearly gates. Not that you don't already."

"What's that supposed to mean?" asked God, offended that Death was calling out his flock.

"Come on, Born Again's? Do you honestly think you're fooling anyone? We know the scum who sneak in with that clause. Murderers, rapists, and all the dregs of society who spin on a dime and you welcome with open arms. You have people here who make Lucifer blush."

"Everyone deserves a second chance," said God proudly.

"Maybe, but not everyone earns it. Luc calls it the douche clause."

"The what?"

"The douche clause. You live your life like a complete a-hole, repent, and all is forgiven."

"I guess I'm a bit more understanding of humanity's potential than you and Lucifer are," said God defiantly.

"I act as your buffer. All I have to do is tap someone on the wrong shoulder. Have I ever sent someone your way who shouldn't be there? I'm even considerate when I use my Blood Cards. If you don't sort this out, you're on your own."

"I'll look into it, but I can't make any guarantees. I'm swamped these days."

"Fine. If one more name lands on my desk which isn't supposed to be reaped, and I skip the next legitimate name."

God's jaw fell open. "What?"

"I skip a reaping," said Death.

God gasped. "You wouldn't?"

"Oh, I most certainly would."

"But that goes against everything."

"Yes, it does."

"It would be extremely bad."

Death nodded.

"No one has ever gone unreaped before. The results would be—" God paused. "We don't know what will happen. It could be nothing."

"Or it could be something, a very big something. Are you prepared to take the risk?"

God stayed silent.

"Perhaps now, you see the gravity of the situation, Gary. If one more name comes my way that I can't reap, someone gets put in limbo."

God points to the folder. "How many names are here?"

"Thousands."

"Why does this always happen to me?" God whined as he leaned back in his chair.

"Stop with the passive-aggressive malarkey, it doesn't fly with me. I'm leaving this in your court to sort out. I have places to be."

"I don't have the manpower to give this the attention it deserves," protested God.

"And I do?" asked Death. "I'm the only person reaping your entire religion, sort it out, or I will. I don't want to hear another peep from you unless it's a solution. I am not fixing your mess."

"So, what do you want from me?"

"I expect a list on my desk first thing tomorrow morning, which isn't full of errors. So that I can do my job like I'm supposed to. Do I make myself clear?"

"Yes. Is that all?"

"I've already stayed longer than planned." He turned and headed for the door. As he reached for the handle, he stopped and looked back at God. "Most of the time I can deal with your crap. It's usually trivial, mundane nonsense. This is different. This affects everything. If you let this escalate, it is all on you, and I won't be responsible for the consequences. Do you understand?"

God nodded.

"This isn't a game, Gary. Unfuck this situation."

God sighed. Death seldom cursed and only did so at his angriest of moments. God had no choice but to address the situation. It appeared that he would not be getting a round of golf in after all.

♦ ♦ ♦ ♦

Overdose Owen sat in the waiting room as Death stormed out of the door. "Excuse me?" he said, raising his hand.

Death ignored him and kept walking. He had no time for Owen's after-death crisis and pushed past.

"Hey. Stop goddammit. Don't ignore me."

Death stopped and turned to face Owen. "What?"

"Am I dead?"

"Yes, you're quit dead. Your pathetic ass overdosed, and because you were unconscious on the floor, you failed to save your girlfriend from choking on her own vomit." He embellished the last part. "Somehow, you still managed to make it to the man upstairs. So, I'm guessing you saved a group of nuns from a burning building or something else equally altruistic. To be honest, I don't care. I have far bigger issues to sort out at the moment. Take a seat and wait. You aren't going anywhere."

Owen quietly sat back down as Death stormed to the exit and left, leaving the waiting room in a stunned silence.

CHAPTER 12

"**a**nother beer, Hank." Warren had hit the bottle hard and showed no signs of stopping.

"This is a lot, even for you," said Hank as he put down the glass he was drying and picked up another. "Problems with Ashley, huh?"

Warren nodded sadly.

"Sorry you were dumped," said Hank.

Warren's head slammed against the bar. "Who told you?"

"I'm a bartender, son. It's my job to know everything. Think of me as a priest with a liquor license. I just have connections with a different set of spirits."

"I feel like an asshole. Everyone knew except for me."

"Did she at least do it in person? She'd originally talked about texting you, but figured it would be too cruel."

Warren groaned and held up his phone. '*HV 2 BRK UP W/U. SRY, NT U ME. good luck*'.

"Tough break, son," said Hank shaking his head.

"Who says good luck to someone they just dumped?"

"Some people aren't good at goodbyes."

"And why write good luck in lower case?" griped Warren.

"Cheer up, cupcake. There are plenty more fish in the sea."

"But I loved my fish."

Hank sighed. It was going to be a long night. "You need another drink." He placed the glass he was holding under the nearest tap and carefully rolled it as he crafted a perfect head. Hank may have been a grumpy old bastard, but he could treat a keg like a magician. He carefully flicked the glass one last time and shut the tap off.

Warren looked up as Hank placed the piece of liquid art in front of him. Hank's latest creation comprised of a smiley face etched in the head with another layer of foam.

Warren rolled his eyes. "You're not helping, Hank."

"Do you prefer a noose? I can draw a really good noose," Hank said gruffly.

"I don't doubt it." Warren grabbed his beer. "A smiley face will do fine."

Behind him, the front door swung open, and Greg quietly entered. He gave Hank a thumbs up and waited for a response. Hank shook his head slightly. Greg turned to leave, but Warren noticed Hank's motion and turned to see the recipient of the gesture.

"Hey, Greg. Over here, man," said Warren with a drunken slur. "I guess you heard?"

"Heard what?"

"Ashley dumped me, man."

Greg feigned ignorance. "Aw, sorry little bro." He flagged Hank down as he crossed over to his brother. "Beer, please." He sat on the stool next to Warren. "Tell me what happened."

"So, Ashley is at her parent's house, and I'm heading over there to break the news. I figured she could use the support when she'd start to cry. I'm almost there when I get this." He showed Greg his phone.

"Didn't she save you the job of being the bad guy?"

"Yeah."

"Isn't this easy, all things considered?"

"No."

"Let me recap for you, in case some part of this isn't clear. The girl you were driving to break up with dumps you, and you're upset?"

"But I wanted to be the one who broke up with her. I always get dumped. I never get to do the dumping."

"This is where I'm supposed to tell you it isn't you it's her, isn't it?"

"Yup."

"Well, I hate to break it to you, little brother, but it is you. It's you, big time."

"Oh, come on, I wasn't that bad."

"No? Tell Hank what you said last Tuesday as we were leaving here."

"Ah, come on, man." pleaded Warren. "Don't do this."

"Say it."

"Fine. I said, damn girl, I hope you have pet insurance, because I am going to destroy your pussy when we get home."

David, who had been quietly sitting at the bar listening to the conversation promptly spat out his gin once again.

Greg nodded a greeting. "Oh, hey, David."

David smiled as he wiped his chin on a napkin. "Jesus, Warren."

"A real gem, huh?" said Greg.

"It made my panties wet," said David.

Warren had endured enough grief for one day. He did not need it from an atheist. "Fuck you, David. Stay out of my business." He turned to his brother. "Why don't you tell them I'd been cheating on her with her best friend too?"

David looked genuinely shocked. "You were?"

"Yup. May as well tell the world now."

Hank finished drying the glass and put it down. He slowly placed both hands flat on the bar and turned to Warren. Warren gulped. He knew that look all too well. The lecture was imminent.

Hank let out a heavy sigh. "Warren, I've known you since you were a skid mark in your daddy's briefs, rest his soul."

A few shouts of 'amen' from around the bar followed.

"Before he passed, I promised him I'd keep an eye on you both, and I've stayed true to my word. I've seen you fall, get up and fall and get up again. I've mostly seen you fall, but I still love you, you little shit. Under all this," he gestured to Warren from scalp to pinky toe. "There is a decent human being struggling to get out."

"Oh, come on, Hank. I'm not—"

"I'm not done, son. Despite your idiosyncrasies and habitual stupidity, I've always thought of you as a gentleman. Stupidity can always be outshined by the actions of a gentleman. You screwed up big time when you lost Ashley. She's a good girl, and she's good for you. I see the change Amber made on Greg, and I like it. If you want to continue your life bouncing from one failed relationship to the next, that's your call, but there is a level of chivalry you maintain where you still come out as the good guy instead of an asshole. If I ever hear of you talking to a woman that way again, your ass will get real cozy with the tip of my boot. Do I make myself clear?"

Warren leaned over the bar and looked at Hank's steel-toed pointed cowboy boots and gulped. "Crystal."

Warren looked over at Greg. "I can't believe you threw me under the bus."

"Oh, no you don't," interrupted Hank. "Don't project your own shortcomings on your brother. I'd have found out one way or another. You know I would. I always find out."

Warren slid off his stool, pulled out his wallet and threw his credit card on the bar. "I don't need this shit. I'm calling it a night."

Hank pushed the card back. "Your money's no good here. Go home and sleep this off. Things'll be better once the buzz has gone and your head is clear."

"I doubt it," said Warren as he grabbed his card. He turned and headed to the exit.

Hank held out his hand and coughed. "You forget something, sunshine?"

Warren stopped and looked back. "Huh?"

"Keys. You're not getting behind the wheel. I don't want your blood on my hands."

"Go fuck yourself, Hank. This ain't your business, sunshine."

"Because you're shit-faced, and for the sake of not kicking your ass from here to the library, I'm going to pretend you didn't say that."

"Whatever helps you sleep at night, buttercup. Kiss my ass, I'm done."

A stunned silence ripped around the room like a tsunami as Warren fished his keys out of his pocket and dangled them in front of his face. "You want these? Ain't gonna happen, sugar tits." He stumbled to the door and ripped it open with a bang. Snow blew in over his feet as he looked back. "Maybe everyone would be happier if I died, so you wouldn't have to look at this fuck-up every day."

"That's not what I'm saying, and you know it," Hank shouted after him.

Warren dismissed him with a wave of his hand and staggered outside, slamming the door.

Greg looked over at Hank. "I've got this."

"You want me to call a cab?" asked Hank.

"Nah, I'll get him home."

◆ ◆ ◆ ◆

Warren stepped out of Jacob's into the cold evening air and zig-zagged towards his car.

"At least I still have you," he said as he caressed the hood. "You'll never break my heart."

"You're not driving, Warren. Don't make a bad night worse."

Warren turned to see Greg standing behind him. "I don't need a fucking lecture from Hank, and I certainly don't need one from you."

"I'm not lecturing you. I'm saving your ass."

"I don't need you watching out for me either. I can take care of myself."

"Because you're doing such a fantastic job so far," argued Greg.

"I'm doing fine on my own."

"Yeah, you're sitting on top of the fucking world. You're a thirty-one-year-old who can't sort his life out because he's too busy trooping on towards the next fuck up."

"Fuck off, Greg. This is my life, and I'll live it how I want."

"I get you're hurting now, but you're being ridiculous. You're damn lucky Hank didn't kick your ass."

"I could have taken him."

"No, you couldn't. Come back to my place so you can sleep this off. You'll feel much better in the morning."

"No, I won't."

Greg held his hands to his head in frustration. "Dammit, Warren, what is your fucking problem?"

"I'm hurting."

"You're hurting? Because of Ashley?"

Warren nodded.

"For Christ's sake, Warren, you were going to dump her. You're fucking her best friend."

"I was fucking. Past tense."

"The semantics change nothing. You have a get out of jail free card where you don't have to be the bad guy, and instead, you're moping about how hurt you are because you were dumped first. Guys would kill to be in your shoes."

"Well, other guys can have it," pouted Warren.

"You know what, princess?" said Greg as his patience started to disappear. "Maybe if you'd treated her halfway decent, instead of being such a complete and utter dick, you wouldn't be hurting. You treated her like shit, and I can't believe she took this long to dump you. She only hung around because she didn't want things to get weird with Amber and me if you two broke it off."

"It's all about you, isn't it?"

Greg stabbed a finger towards his brother. "Fuck you, Warren. I love Amber. Don't fuck this up for me."

Warren pulled the door hard, and it slipped from Greg's grasp.

"Get out of the god-damned car, Warren."

Warren slammed the lock and raised a middle finger as the engine started and the car sputtered forward.

Greg clenched his teeth in frustration. Warren was going to get himself killed if he did nothing. He pulled out his phone and dialed. "Lee, it's Greg. Warren's doing something stupid again."

◆ ◆ ◆ ◆

Warren barely made it two blocks when he saw the flashing of red and blue behind him.

"Shit." He pulled over and stopped.

Instead of the customary two or three minutes where the cop ran the plates to build unnecessary anxiety, Lee immediately climbed out and headed towards Warren. "Get out of the car and place your hands on the hood," he ordered as he approached the window.

Warren sighed and followed his directions.

"Turn and face the hood."

Warren obliged and placed his hands out in front of him. Lee pulled out a pair of handcuffs and clamped them on Warren's wrists.

"What are you doing, man?"

"Saving you from yourself. You'll thank me in the morning."

"Not fucking likely," said Warren as Lee escorted him to his car. "You might as well shoot me and be done with it. My life fucking sucks."

"No can do," said Lee. "One, no bullets, and two, that's way too much paperwork. I keep telling you that."

CHAPTER 13

The Mortality Division huddled around the table in conference room 7G and waited for God to arrive. Raphael, God's right-hand man, nervously paced around the room and rubbed his chin. He hated these ad-hoc meetings, nothing good ever came from them.

Gabriel and Ezekiel sat with their heads together, trying to brainstorm while Ceraphim read through his notes. Amitiel, Ecanus, Valoel, Mary, and Roger completed the group and spoke quietly among themselves. Ceraphim lowered his notepad and started to speak when the door opened and God stormed in, obviously in a foul mood. Everyone began to rise out of their seats.

"Sit your asses down," said God as he waved them back into their seats

The group sat as God moved to the head of the table and stopped next to a large whiteboard and flip chart. He picked up a wooden stick sitting on the board and started tapping his hand. After a few nervous glances, he cleared his throat.

"Can anyone tell me what is wrong with this picture?" He spread his arms wide, waiting for someone to answer. A second passed by, and then ten. "Anyone?"

The room remained silent.

"Here's a clue. Look at my clothes."

Amitiel raised her hand.

"Finally," shouted God as he pointed to her.

"You're wearing white after Labor Day?"

God reached over to the flip chart and started ripping off the pages in frustration. He quickly composed himself and turned back to the group. "No, I'm not wearing white after Labor Day. Anyone else?"

Ceraphim raised his hand.

"Anyone who isn't inherently stupid?"

Ceraphim lowered his hand. God had garnered a strong dislike for him from the moment they met. Back then, Ceraphim, a fresh-off-the-boat intern on his first day, inadvertently pressed the wrong button on the elevator and trapped God with the Born Agains for thirty-five of the most harrowing minutes of his life, and he never forgave him.

"You're wearing vertical stripes, and they make you look fat?" said Roger.

God's cheeks flushed with rage. "Okay. The next one of you ass-clowns who makes fun of my clothing gets bathroom duty for three months. Now let's try this one more time. What do you notice about what I'm wearing? In particular, my pants?"

"You're wearing golf pants?" said Ecanus.

"Give this man a fucking cookie," said God. "Now, why am I wearing golf pants?"

"Because you're ready to go play golf?" deduced Ecanus.

"Bingo. So can any of you imbeciles tell me why I am standing here instead of getting ready to swing my number nine with the British Prime Minister?"

Gabriel raised his hand. "Sir, the British Prime Minister isn't dead."

"Not yet." God looked down at his watch.

The phone on the wall beeped, and Nancy's voice rang through. "*Sir, the Prime Minister is in the waiting room.*"

"He's just going to have to wait for me," said God. "I have an issue in here to deal with." He turned back to the group. "I have a handicap of one hundred and ninety-seven. ONE HUNDRED AND NINETY-FUCKING-SEVEN. I golf like an asshole. I need to practice, holy fuck do I need to practice, but instead, I'm stuck here with you morons. I was going to ask if any of you knew why we were here, but as you didn't even notice my pants, I feel it's probably a pretty fruitless exercise. I just had the misfortune of Death paying me a visit this morning. Can anyone explain why I had an unscheduled meeting with Death?"

The room remained silent.

"Raphael, what do you have to say? I haven't heard you speak up yet. I'm sure you have something of value to add to the discussion."

Raphael despised these meetings as the proverbial shit always rolled downhill into his lap. "I didn't know he visited you, sir."

"Well, he did, and he dropped quite the gem on me. Does anyone care to take a stab at what the Grim Reaper dumped on my desk this morning?"

Amitiel raised her hand.

"Yes, Amitiel?"

"He doesn't like it when you call him that."

God pointed a finger at her. "Fuck him and fuck you. Sit down and zip it. Anyone else?" He looked around the room. "No? Okay, well, let's try this then. Who did the lists today?"

Raphael shifted nervously. He hated ratting anyone out, but his staff left him little choice. "It—"

"I did, sir," said Gabriel.

"Oh, you did, huh?" God started tapping the stick on his palm again.

Gabriel swallowed and nodded.

"And do you know what happened with them?"

Gabriel shook his head.

"You don't know?"

"I did an export and mail merge as I always do. I assumed it was right."

"You assumed? Do you know what happens when you assume?"

"I make an ass out of you and me?" asked Gabriel.

"No, don't drag me into this mess. I'm not the ass here, you are. Asshole. When you assume, you're wrong. Never assume. Check. Double-check. Do whatever it takes to make sure something is right. The lists were wrong. There were names on there of people who weren't supposed to be reaped."

"Impossible," said Gabriel impulsively in his defense. He regretted the words the moment they passed his lips.

"Are you calling me a liar?"

"No, sir. Of course not. I'd never dream of doing that."

"I don't know what's worse. The fact you messed up the lists, or the fact you have no idea you did it."

"Raphael said you needed them in a hurry, and I don't know how to use the new software."

Raphael squirmed and made a mental note to reprimand Gabriel after the meeting ended.

God ignored the protest. "Do you know what happened when we sent The Grim Reaper a list of souls he wasn't supposed to reap?"

"He got upset you called him the Grim Reaper," said Amitiel.

God pointed his stick at her. "You, shut your pie hole. One more peep from you, and I swear to Christ—"

Raphael cleared his throat.

God composed himself and continued. "Death has threatened to skip a reaping if we don't sort this out."

A stunned silence swept the room.

"He wouldn't," said Ecanus, his eyes wide with shock.

"That's what he claims," said God.

"But, that goes against the most important rule in the universe," proclaimed Valoel, her eyes as wide as Ecanus's.

God lowered his voice. "Perhaps now you see the severity of this situation. Why is it you all begged me for empowerment so I don't have to micromanage you, yet an issue of this magnitude falls into my lap? Raphael, can you shed any light on this?"

"We have new database software implemented. I think there might be a bug in the system," said Raphael.

"When did we get a new database?" asked God.

"Two weeks ago."

"Why wasn't I informed of this?"

"You were," said Raphael.

God frowned. "Are you sure?"

"Yes, you signed the purchase order."

"So why wasn't I told about the bug."

"You were. I debriefed you last week about it."

"Was that the meeting where I was eating ice cream?"

"Yes."

"I probably wasn't paying attention," said God as his mind wandered back to his delicious dessert.

"Well, it wasn't an issue until now. I think the data import feature is corrupt. We also haven't been given sufficient training on it yet to figure a workaround."

"You haven't been trained yet? That is going to be your excuse?"

"Well, sir, your memo last month told us we needed to slash twenty percent from our budget this upcoming fiscal year. We didn't have the money to pay for training."

"Did you think to swing by my office and ask for more money? Pop your head, and in say, '*hey boss, we need training*'."

"I did, sir. Twice."

"And I wouldn't give it to you?"

"No, sir. In fact, your words were, and I do quote, '*Ooh, can I have more money? What am I, a fucking ATM? Get the fuck out of my office*'."

"I said that?"

"Yes, sir."

"It does sound like something I'd say. So, what are our options?"

"We were rather hoping you'd have some direction for us, sir. This whole situation is rather unprecedented."

"Unprecedented? The shit you say?"

"It isn't in the manual. No one has created a process for this as it's never happened."

God looked around the room. "Can anyone tell me what will happen if Death skips a reaping?" He looked around the room. "Anyone? Valoel, care to take a stab?"

"Nothing?" she said.

"Stupid. Anyone else?"

Ceraphim raised his hand.

"Oh, this should be good."

"The fabric of space and time would fracture?"

God stared at him.

Ceraphim shrugged. "What?"

"You quoted Doctor Who. Why don't you say it's a big ball of wibbly-wobbly timey stuff?"

Ceraphim slipped out an unintentional laugh.

"Is something funny, Ceraphim?" asked God.

"It's timey-wimey, sir."

"I'm well aware of what I said."

"You said timey stuff. The correct line is wibbly-wobbly timey-wim—"

He never finished the sentence. God waved his hand, and Ceraphim fell to his knees, choking and grasping his throat. Seconds later, the color drained from him, and he collapsed in a lifeless heap.

God lowered his hand as the group stared at Ceraphim's body. "I'm done with you lot."

Raphael sighed in frustration.

"Something on your mind, Raph?" God's fingers tensed up for a second round of choking.

"Sir, we're already short-staffed and under-trained. Killing my team members won't make this any easier."

"Do you want to be next?" He pointed the stick at him.

"No."

"Then shut your yap and let me finish. Don't make me Dark Vader anyone else."

No one in the room dared to correct him.

"Let's all assume, for argument's sake, money isn't an issue. What's it going to take to get you all trained on the new database?"

"We need to outsource someone to come in and train us," said Raphael.

"And that will cost?"

"About a hundred and fifty."

"All this over a hundred and fifty dollars?"

"Thousand."

"THOUSAND? A hundred and fifty thousand to learn a database?

Raphael shook his head. "It's not dollars, it's Kuwaiti dinar."

"And how much is that in a currency I understand?" asked God.

"About half a million dollars," said Raphael.

"We could make our own database for that."

"But, we'd still need training, and I thought you said money wasn't an issue."

"Of course it's an issue. It's always an issue. I guess we'll have to shift funds around. Have you cut a purchase order yet?"

"Right here, sir." Raphael pulled out a three-sheet carbon copy purchase order and a pen.

"Give me that." God snatched the pen and paper from Raphael. He wrote his signature, but no ink appeared. He scribbled across the paper in exaggerated sweeping lines. "Pen."

Raphael took the pen and paper. "Mary, could you get us another pen, please?" He flipped to the second page. Large carbon scribbled lines made most of the purchase order illegible. "And a new PO."

A minute later, Mary returned with a new pen and a fresh purchase order. She stepped over Ceraphim and handed them to God. He quickly skimmed over the order.

"McNeil and Associates. Why does that name sound familiar?" asked God.

"Mary's husband owns a software development and training company. They wrote the software," said Raphael.

"Well, isn't that convenient?" God scribbled his name and roughly handed it back to Raphael.

"How soon can he be here?"

"Next Wednesday. Isn't that right, Mary?"

"Yes, sir."

"Next Wednesday? That's—" God started counting on his fingers. "Five days."

"Seven, actually," corrected Raphael.

"You're not helping," said God. "So, what do we do in the meantime?"

"Maybe we wait and hope the new lists Death has are correct," said Ezekiel.

"Great plan, Zeke."

"Thanks," said Ezekiel with a grateful smile.

God stepped over and punched him on the arm. "No, you moron, it's a stupid plan. Does anyone have a better idea?"

A few hands thrust skyward.

"A plan which doesn't involve waiting of some sort."

The same hands were lowered.

"Anyone?" asked God.

Raphael opened his mouth to speak, then thought better of it. The rest of the room stayed quiet.

"Okay, everyone out, this meeting is adjourned. I have a golf game to get to. In the meantime, if any of you idiots can come up with an idea, one that doesn't involve waiting, then I'm all ears."

The group started to rise and headed to the exit. The hushed muttering followed them out.

"Not you, Raph," God called after him.

Raphael stopped and waited for the room to clear.

"Raph, I know you're holding out on me. Speak."

"I didn't want to say this in front of the team, but I have thoughts on what will happen if Death follows through on his threat."

"Al right, spill it."

"It's just a theory, and a radical one at that. But I believe they wouldn't pass on."

"What do you mean by 'wouldn't pass on?'" He fingered the quotes for emphasis.

"I mean they wouldn't go to Heaven or Hell."

"That isn't such a bad thing. Isn't that what Purgatory is for? A catch-all for everything else?"

"Technically, yes, but to be eligible for Purgatory, you need to have died and be processed via the correct measures. This is way outside the realms of Purgatory."

"Meaning?" Considering he created much of the universe, God could be a little slow on the uptake at times.

Raphael paused for a second. Obviously, he needed to explain it in layman's terms. "Purgatory is the waiting room for those who show up on Death's reaping least, but it hasn't been determined if they come up here or go down to Lucifer. Last-minute repenting is the most common reason as it causes confusion. If Death doesn't reap someone, they don't qualify for Purgatory."

"So, they'll stay dead and rot?"

"I believe it could be worse than that. It's a radical theory, though."

"What's worse than a stinky dead person?" asked God.

"I think they will come back to life."

"Are you talking about reincarnation?"

Raphael shook his head. "No."

"Good, because I didn't create reincarnation. I don't believe in it. Who'd want to come back as a slug? They're fucking gross."

"Didn't you create slugs?"

"Yeah, doesn't mean I don't think they're disgusting, and most likely you'll get stepped on at some point. How's that for a kick in the karma nut sack? You come back with a life span of less than a week." He paused. "I can name a few people I'd like to step on." He had drifted again.

Raphael coughed politely.

"Sorry. Continue," said God.

"I believe if Death skips a reaping, they'll either come back as one of the living dead or as a demon. I'm unsure. It may be a combination of both."

"The living dead?" asked God. Not quite sure what Raphael was trying to explain.

"Yes."

"You mean like a zombie?" asked God.

"Yes."

"Monsters from cheap horror movies?" God mimicked a zombie with his arms outstretched and groaned.

"Yes."

"Mythical creatures created by Hollywood and authors, that, well, don't actually exist?"

"Yes. Or demons."

God blinked.

"You're staring," said Raphael.

"Demons? That's quite a hypothesis, Raph."

"I know, but I've run through every possible scenario, and the outcome ends up the same. The victim will be invalid. I have no idea who or where, but wherever Death decides to make true on his word, all hell is going to break loose."

"We're going to need to keep a close eye on his movements for the next few days," said God.

Raphael nodded in agreement.

"Let's keep this demon zombie thing amongst ourselves until we have a grasp on what is going on," said God. "There's no sense in scaring the troops." He paused before leaving the room. "Oh, and Raph, can you resurrect Ceraphim before you leave? He's going to stain the carpet." God scrunched up his face in mild annoyance. Golf was still going to have to wait.

CHAPTER 14

Much like God, Death owned an office. However, his base of operations appeared far less celestial. He worked out of a quaint Victorian-era office in the town of Cedar Grove, West Virginia. The perfectly manicured front yard flourished with vibrant color and nose-tingling aroma. Two rows of miniature pine trees flanked the pathway leading to the front entrance, and a smattering of flower beds wrapped around the edges. To passersby, the building appeared to be a life insurance company, and the irony amused Death. He liked the small-town lifestyle, and it allowed him to work in peace. On the front door hung a small wooden sign which read '*No hawkers, philistines, or Jehovah's Witnesses*'. Nobody knocked or rang, and the office sat unnoticed.

He established a routine he followed without fail. Each morning, the overhead bell rang when he opened the heavy oak door. He hung up his robe and put his scythe in the umbrella stand. After the coffee brewed, he poured himself a cup of black, no sugar. While he avoided being grim, no one called him a morning person.

As he finished his fourth cup of coffee, Susan, his short-sighted, but ridiculously competent secretary, handed him a magical reaping list printed on enchanted paper. When he checked off the last name at the bottom of the page, it magically refreshed and continued the list from the top. Sure, using a smartphone or tablet would be easier, but he found it far more enjoyable to use physical paper lists. He loved the theatrics of crossing someone's name off. The modern version of clicking and deleting from a digital device presented far less of an impact and seemed so impersonal and cold. Plus, he never remembered to charge up his cell phone. It would be unacceptable for him to appear at a reaping with a dead iPad. No one liked to be kept waiting. Granted, he reaped souls, but he could do it without being clinical and heartless. Besides, he used a quill, and there were insufficient opportunities to use one in most careers.

Death loved how classy the ink from his feathered scribe looked. For eight hundred years, he used the same quill, and the print quality was as good as the day he acquired it. The feather came from a hawk that frequented his farm and killed the field mice running wild through the crops. One morning, it experienced a boost of bravado and killed Death's six-week-old puppy. That night, Death received his quill and enjoyed a tasty side of roasted hawk leg for dinner. It was also the last time he owned a pet.

Death worked well without modern technology helping him do his job. The older ways proved efficient long before the internet and cell phones, and he believed if something worked, leave it be. He always had a taste for the dramatic and picked the right profession to nurture that side of him.

Equipped with his two lists, his quill, and a pocket watch, Death wandered the Earth, locating his targets, tapping them on the shoulder, and sending them on their way. A tap on the left shoulder ascended them to Heaven, a tap on the right sent them to Hell. Decked out in black, he looked like a Gothic repo man with a cape and scythe, although, the scythe acted as more of a prop than a functioning weapon. Despite widely held belief, Death never used it for reaping. In the early days before the worldwide population boom, he owned a farm and spent half his time reaping souls and the other tending to his crops. His wheat raisin bread often won first prize in the Planer County Fair, and his blueberry muffins were to die for. When Death started reaping, he left a bread and muffin basket on the doorstep of the families he reaped. While a simple, heartfelt gesture, most preferred their loved one back over a fucking bran muffin.

Back before the population became so dense and healthy, infant mortality rates were so bad he could walk an entire street and have at least fifteen children die of the bubonic plague. He frequently completed ninety percent of his daily reapings before noon. On more than one occasion, he removed four or five souls from the same household and spent the remainder of the day cutting wheat stalks and grinding oats. In the centuries which followed, with the advent of new medications and better medical equipment, people had healthier children, and they, in turn, produced healthier children. Those children grew up to have their own, and the population expanded. Before long, Death spent more time traveling than harvesting, the job took longer to perform, and his other interests started to suffer. After one harvest passed by and Death's crops withered and died, he decided he needed to choose. A few weeks later, he sold his farm, gathered up his cloak and numerous Bread Master Trophies, and walked the Earth reaping souls full-time. Soon after, he stopped with the gift baskets too.

In the early days, he used to wait around to watch the victim's soul leave their body. He found it an extremely peaceful and cathartic moment, watching them become one with the universe. Regardless of the direction of their afterlife, the separation of body and soul was a breathtaking sight to behold, and few experiences in life came close. Nothing gave Death a greater sense of purpose, but as with all good things, it too eventually came to an end. As Death's lists grew into tens of thousands a day, reaping started to consume every waking minute. As fast as he could reap, the next name came up on his list. Fortunately, he loved his job, so the increase in workload bothered him little. One minute he visited New Orleans sending a billionaire oil baron to his maker behind the pearly gates, and the next, South America, sending a retired Brazilian teacher to the depths below.

Death shared Earth's reaping responsibilities as each religion used its own assigned bringer of death. In the early days, he reaped everyone regardless of faith, but as new religions formed and old religions changed to serve the current populace, it became too much, and the role was divided. Death stayed with Christianity and the various spin-offs, but even those kept his days full.

He acted unusually restless as he reached into his inbox and picked up the two reaping lists Susan left for him. He sipped his coffee as he flicked through the pages, unsure of what to look for. He could not tell if God had sorted his shit out or not. The list looked precisely the same as it did the day before, or any other day for that matter. All he could do was head on out and hope for the best. He was honest when he told God he intended to skip a reaping, but had no idea of the possible consequences, nor should he, for he always followed the process.

Susan noticed his odd behavior and slipped out a muffled cough to get his attention. "Is everything okay? You don't seem like your usual self."

Death stood from his desk and walked over to Susan. "How would you feel if one morning you came into the office and the mail wasn't sitting in the mailbox, Darren didn't stop by to deliver the water, and the nine o'clock news on NPR didn't air?"

Susan stayed silent for a moment, giving serious thought to her answer. "Why I'd probably snap and kill everyone in a file mile radius. This is my routine. Without it, I'm nothing. Why do you ask?"

"No reason."

She did not buy his dismissal. "What are you doing to my routine?"

"Nothing."

Susan frowned. "I've worked for you long enough to know when you're lying. Because you're not very good at it."

"Let's just say things may be getting a little tense around here," said Death.

"What do you mean?"

"Client issues."

"Which client? You only have two."

Death straightened a stack of papers on her desk. "How long have you worked for me?"

"Almost fifty years." She took the papers away and moved them to another pile out of his reach. She became extremely irritable when people started messing with her filing system.

"And have we ever had a problem with our lists?"

"Never. Is this about my anniversary? A day off would be nice."

He paused a second. "Susan, take the day off. Happy anniversary." With that, he pulled up his hood and disappeared.

◆ ◆ ◆ ◆

He reappeared in Des Moines, Iowa, and found himself in a crowded Walmart parking lot. Walmart heart attacks were a far more common cause of death than one might think. It most likely related to the out-of-shape people who stumbled out of the entrance. They crammed their faces with all kinds of genetically manufactured junk food and keeled over from a heart attack before they reached their crookedly parked cars.

Death pulled out his list and found his next customer. Julie Tanner, twenty-seven, originally from Edmonton, Kentucky, would meet an untimely demise not focused around a cheeseburger or Twinkies. Death read over the details of her death, and all signs pointed to it being messy. In these cases, he appreciated being invisible and avoiding the dry-cleaning bill.

He desperately wanted God to have fixed his issues, but the nagging feeling in the pit of his stomach told him he grasped onto a pipe dream.

He hated having his bluff called, and taking such drastic steps was far from his first choice, but rules were in place for a reason. God may be omnipotent, but even he found himself tethered to the laws of the universe.

As Death faced Julie, he prepared for the worst. On a typical day, her soul would be reaped, and he would be ten further down his list. Instead, he stood and stared at her as she loaded her groceries into the trunk.

Her shopping cart contents confused Death. She certainly did not look like the type of person who lived on cheap synthetic cupcakes and lab-manufactured potato chips. When she returned to the car, Death saw the intended recipient of the food. In the passenger seat sat her twin brother Dale, who pushed four hundred pounds. Death shook his head at her complete disregard for his health, but could not help but laugh at the irony of her dying first.

As she backed away from the window and headed to the driver's side, Death followed her around the car. In thirty seconds, Death expected an RV to enter the parking lot, and its poorly maintained brakes would fail, taking out Julie and her car door. As he reached out to touch her shoulder, he hesitated. It had nothing to do with sentiment. He simply wanted to believe Heaven had sorted its shit out and the reaping would work without a hitch. Her time needed to come to an end, because the fate of the universe depended on it.

On cue, the RV pulled into the parking lot.

Death looked down at his list and saw Dale listed right behind her. The reaping promised a twofer. They cropped up once or twice a day. Approximately twenty-six seconds after Julie died, Dale should suffer a widow-making heart attack, killing him instantly.

He tapped Julie on the left shoulder, and the RV turned her into goo. The oversized vehicle crashed into the open driver's side door head-on and slammed it closed on her, severing her head, and snapping her legs mid-shin. Her decimated torso fell into the car, spraying blood throughout the interior. Dale, covered in gore, grabbed at his chest in shock. He gasped for breath as pieces of his sister dripped down from his face.

Death moved around to the passenger side of the car and reached in to reap Dale.

Nothing.

Death gritted his teeth. "Are you serious?"

It made no sense. How could a guy his size with arteries the size of pins witness such a devastating scene and survive?

He tried one more time.

"Dammit, Gary," Death said to himself. "Okay, if this is how it's gonna be."

He looked at the list for the next reaping, closed his eyes, and disappeared.

♦ ♦ ♦ ♦

A moment later, he reappeared on the outskirts of Oceanview. The snow had finally stopped. However, the road was a dead-end, and he looked around in an effort to find his bearings. Death had visited all four corners of the planet, from shanty towns in India to multimillion-dollar estates of Beverly Hills and all styles of residences in between. But in all his years, he never visited a town so piss-poorly organized as Oceanview.

"Where am I?" He spun around, trying to get his bearings. A second later, he disappeared and reappeared at the end of Port Road. He looked across the street and saw the Paradise Bay condominium complex, neither in a bay, or remotely considered paradise. He glanced at his list. Harriet Jenkins, one of the elderly residents, would die of a heart attack. At least if God had bothered to fix his list.

Harriet was snoring loudly when Death appeared in the room. A respirator covered her mouth, aiding her erratic breathing. Her eyes suddenly opened, and she grasped at her chest. She pulled the respirator away from her face and tried to shout. No words came as she gasped her final labored breath.

Death leaned over her. "I am so sorry," he said. "This isn't personal."

As the last of her life slipped away, Death did nothing. He did not touch her left shoulder, and he did not touch her right. Harriet did not go up, and she did not go down. "Sorry, Oceanview, it looks like you drew the shit straw," he said.

Death looked up and saw a picture of Jesus above Harriet's bed. "Are you watching? If so, this is all on your dad." Death closed his eyes and promptly disappeared.

♦ ♦ ♦ ♦

Susan quietly ate her lunch and ingested the daily tabloids when the front door ripped open, and the ordinarily chipper bell screamed loudly. Susan put her sandwich down and wiped her mouth.

"Lunch is over, Susan. Take a memo," said Death as he stormed over to her desk. "Wait, didn't I send you home?"

Susan tossed her napkin in the trash and turned to her keyboard. "I'm just about to leave."

"You'll have to take a rain check," said Death.

"Why am I not surprised?" Susan muttered under her breath.

Death wasted no time dictating. "Dear Gary," he started. "I warned you, and you didn't listen. I'm a man of my word, and I am not responsible for what follows."

Susan quickly started typing as Death continued to speak. "Excuse me, but what is going on exactly?"

"A major breakdown in procedure."

"Shall I sign it from Steve or Death?"

"I don't give a damn how you sign it, Susan. Draw a big red skull and crossbones for all I care."

Susan stopped typing and glared at Death. "Just because you are having a bad day, do not take it out on me."

"Just write the damned letter. You can lecture me when it's blown over."

"Until what's blown over?"

"That's just it, I don't know." He took a step towards his office and stopped. "Susan, hold off on faxing it until tomorrow."

"Why?"

"I'm changing the rules."

Death turned and stepped into his office and closed the door behind him. "You want to play with the big boys, Gary? This is how it's done."

By mid-morning Thursday, Death still hesitated on sending the memo. He wanted each passing minute to feel like an hour to God. At ten minutes to four, he finally gave Susan the order to send it.

◆ ◆ ◆ ◆

Within thirty seconds of Susan pressing the Send button, Raphael grabbed the memo from the fax machine and sprinted down the hall to God's office.

Ecanus and Valoel were deep in conversation at the water cooler when Raphael plowed through them.

He looked back over his shoulder. "Sorry, guys, I'm trying to prevent a universal crisis."

"Drama queen," Ecanus mumbled. "Everything is a crisis with him."

As God's second-in-command, Raphael handled most of the serious business that needed attention. It often involved cleaning up behind his boss.

♦ ♦ ♦ ♦

God sat at his desk reading a newspaper, when he heard a soft knock at the door.

It slowly opened, and Nancy meekly stuck her head in the office. "Excuse me, sir?"

God ignored her. After a moment, she coughed to try to get his attention.

"What does the little white sign on the door say, Nancy?" he said from behind the paper.

"Do not disturb."

"And?"

Nancy ducked back behind the door and looked at the sign. A second later, she reappeared. "Nothing else."

God sighed and lowered the paper. "What do you want, Nancy?"

"Raphael is here to see you."

"I guess my lunch break is over then."

"It's only nine-thirty."

"Don't judge me, Nancy. You may as well send him in. My Pop-Tarts are stale now anyway."

"You just opened them."

"And they're stale. Organic food does that."

"Pop-Tarts aren't organic."

"They have strawberries in them, and the last time I checked, strawberries were organic. So, your logic is flawed."

"But —"

"Nancy? What's the number one rule around here?"

"Never forward memes of babies with teeth, as they freak you out?"

"No. The other one," said God.

Nancy shrugged. "I don't—"

"Never speak ill of Pop-Tarts."

"I'll just —" She points at the door.

Nancy disappeared behind the door, and Raphael entered the room.

"What is it, Raph?"

Raphael never uttered a word. The expression on his face said everything.

God dropped his newspaper. "He didn't?"

"He did. I got the fax."

"Where?" God paused. "Wait, he sent a fax?"

Raphael nodded.

"Who uses fax machines these days?"

"Death apparently. But we don't know where."

"Who?"

"We don't know that either. Or even when."

"Well, what do we know?"

"Nothing. We don't know who he skipped, where he skipped them, or when he skipped them. We don't even know how many he skipped."

"How many people died today?"

"Ballpark, about a hundred and fifty-four thousand."

"Shit. Can't we check the reports?"

"No, the database is still broken."

God groaned and slammed his fist against his desk. "Are we certain it happened today?"

"No."

"So, it could be three hundred thousand people on the list."

"Or more."

"So, what is your master plan?"

"I don't have one, Gary." Raphael was one of the few people in the universe allowed to call God by his real name, but only when others were out of earshot. "We don't know if he skipped one person on his list or everyone. We don't know if it's just today, or if he's on strike. We could wait it out and see." Raphael cringed. He knew it sounded like a bad idea.

"We wait?" confirmed God. "Wasn't that also your plan leading up to this point?"

Raphael nodded.

"And how's that working out for you?"

"I don't see us having many options. He skipped a reaping. We have no idea what, if indeed anything will happen. So, we turn the department on its ass trying to figure out a possible solution to a problem we may or may not have, or we wait it out and see what damage control we have to do."

God shrugged. Raphael had a point, as he typically did. "Could he be bluffing?"

"I suppose he could be. Doesn't seem like his M.O., though. I've never known him to talk unless he meant what he said. I'd take the threat seriously."

"Get him on the phone. We can settle this now."

"And say what? This could also be a power play to see how you react."

"You just said bluffing wasn't his M.O."

"It isn't, he may have skipped the first reaping yesterday, or he could skip one tomorrow. He isn't bluffing as far as the skip goes. He will skip one, I have no doubt. I just don't know when he'll do it. The best thing we can do is wait to see how this plays out."

God chewed on his lip as he mulled the situation over. "Get back out on the floor and keep your ear to the ground. If something out of the ordinary comes up, I want to be the first to know."

CHAPTER 15

Ding dong.

Silence.

Ding dong.

Greg's doorbell chirped at an hour far too early for his liking. It rang a third time. Then a fourth, and again, and again, until Greg's eyes snapped open.

"Hun," he said softly as he rolled over. He reached for Amber on her side of the bed but found nothing. After a moment of feeling the empty bed, he remembered she had spent the night with Ashley at her parent's house.

Ding dong.

"Who is it?" he shouted.

Ding dong.

He snapped upright and climbed out of bed.

Ding dong.

Greg stormed downstairs and headed to the front entrance. "Someone better be dead," he muttered as he opened the door. "What?"

"Have you accepted the word of God into—" The man in his Sunday best stopped talking.

Greg stood butt-naked in front of him.

Unsure where to put his eyes, the man thrust a magazine at Greg. "Watchtower? God always has room for a lost penis."

Greg raised an eyebrow.

"Lamb, lamb. I meant lamb. God always has room for a lost lamb."

Greg looked down at his wayward penis, looked back up at the man, and slammed the door shut. He walked into the kitchen to find his cell phone flashing, notifying him of three missed calls from Lee. He yawned and scratched his head as he tried to wake up and get the energy to go and get Warren.

◆ ◆ ◆ ◆

"Rise and shine, kiddo," said Lee cheerfully as he banged on the cell bars with his coffee mug. "You want to play nice, or do you need another night in here?"

Warren lay face-down on his cot.

Lee banged on the bars again. "Wake up, sunshine. You alive in there?"

Warren stirred from his sleep. He raised his hand in the air and gave a half-assed thumbs up. "Yup," he said, muffled by the pillow. He sat up and swung his legs over the side of the bed. As he stretched, his back cracked with a loud, satisfying pop.

"Coffee?" said Lee with a smile.

Warren yawned. "Yeah, that sounds great."

Lee returned a few moments later with a red coffee cup with 'Warren's Mug' stamped in white on the side. The ingrained coffee stains his jail version of frequent flyer miles.

Lee unlocked the cell and handed Warren his drink.

"Thanks, Lee."

"Don't mention it. Greg's on his way over to get you."

"Oh, man, this is early for him. Did he sound pissed? I'm pretty sure I owe him an apology."

"Nah, he's fine. You don't owe him an apology. I'd be more worried about Hank."

Warren turned pale. "Shit. What did I do?"

"You don't remember?" Warren shook his head.

"You told him to go fuck himself."

Warren shrugged. "That's not so bad. I've done it before."

"And then called him buttercup."

"Shit. That I haven't done."

"And then sugar tits," said Lee.

"Or that. Maybe I'll stay here an extra day or two."

"Negatory. Time to face the music, or at the very least an angry bartender."

"Can I apply for diplomatic immunity?"

"No, that's outside my jurisdiction."

"Well, I guess I know what I'm doing first this morning."

Lee escorted Warren through the hallway to the lobby. "Liz has bagels."

Warren stopped at her desk as she offered him his circular breakfast. "You're a lifesaver, Liz." He grinned as he swiped a cheese bagel from the plate and took a seat in the waiting room.

Lee walked back to his desk to file paperwork unrelated to Warren's incident. No charges were being pressed. He offered the lockup as more of a courtesy to a friend rather than laying down the arm of the law and making an example of him. Truth be told, Lee held few people in town for more than a single night. Oceanview experienced no crime, and most issues stemmed from people having one too many beers and trying to drive home. He considered it a community service to pull them off the streets.

The front door opened, and Greg entered. He nodded at Lee and Liz. "Morning," he chirped.

"Hey, Greg," said Liz.

"Has he behaved?"

"Perfect tenant," said Liz with a smile.

"God knows he's had enough practice," said Greg.

Lee dismissed the arrest. "It's just a sleepover. Nothing serious. His hangover, on the other hand."

Greg smiled and turned to Warren. "And you, little brother, did you sleep well?" he said, a little louder than necessary.

"Yeah."

"The usual bed?"

"Yep."

"Breakfast?"

Warren held up his mug of coffee and a bagel. "And coffee. Can you keep it down a bit, my head's pounding."

"Nope." said Greg as he turned to Lee. "What do I owe you for breakfast?"

"On the house. Just happy to see him go home in one piece." Lee smiled from behind the counter. "He's going to feel a little rough today. You might want to get him something for that headache."

"Well, let's not tie up any more of Lee's time. Thank the nice man, Warren."

"Thank you, Officer Adams."

Lee laughed. "Get out of here, you two, and stay safe. The roads are slick this morning."

Warren stood and followed Greg to the exit. He swiped a second bagel from Liz as he passed her desk.

"It's coming out of your rations next time," said Lee.

Warren flashed her a smile. "Bill it to my room."

◆ ◆ ◆ ◆

Warren walked a few steps behind Greg as they left the station. "Hey, wait up, man."

Greg stopped, and Warren quickly caught up to him. "What are you doing up so early?"

"Fucking Jehovah's Witness."

"Ugh, sorry, man."

Greg grinned. "Not as sorry as he was." He cast his mind back to flashing the poor man.

"Are we cool?" asked Warren.

"I don't know. Are we?"

"Yeah, I guess. I supposed you were the one who called Lee to come get me?"

Greg nodded. "Yep. You weren't listening to anyone last night. You didn't give me much of a choice. I wasn't letting you drive home in that condition."

Warren smiled, appreciative of the gesture. "Thanks for watching out for me, man. What happened to my car?"

"It's still at Jacob's. Lee had someone at his office take it back there for you."

"Who?"

"Why does it matter?" asked Greg. "It's safe. You're safe. That's all that counts."

"That car is my pride and joy," said Warren. "I don't want just anyone driving it. Why did you let them take it? Couldn't you have driven me back?"

"I didn't think you'd want to barf in it on the way home," said Greg. "I figured you'd rather spend the day nursing your hangover rather than scrubbing vomit out of your seats."

"Good point. Where's your car?"

"I left it at Amber's. Figured I'd be driving you home, and I didn't want you throwing up in my car either. I wasn't expecting you to be so shit-faced. I'm picking it up later."

"Wait, we're walking?"

"Four blocks won't kill you. You're crashing with me for a few days while Ashley moves out.

Warren nodded. "Thanks, Greg."

"Don't thank me yet. We still need to stop by Jacob's later, so you can apologize to Hank."

"He's going to kill me."

"Probably," said Greg grinning ear-to-ear.

CHAPTER 16

friday arrived with little fanfare. The sky did not rain blood, and the Four Horsemen did not appear. God paced his office like a caged hamster, and Death methodically progressed through his reaping lists, happily collecting souls as though nothing had happened. Surprisingly, every new name on God's list since Harriet processed correctly, and Death almost felt bad for his actions. Almost.

Far below the heavens, the residents of Oceanview were putting the finishing touches on an event the entire town cherished. The only thing about Oceanview which should not have been considered a joke was the annual Forefather's Day festival. However, the town's founding forefather, Jason Reynolds, had not died, and in fact, lived in a sprawling mansion at the end of Lindsey Hill.

While most places celebrated their long-dead founders with slightly exaggerated stories of heroism and daring, most of the residents of Oceanview could be called out as plain and simple bullshitters. Reynolds did not kill a sleuth of bears or fight a violent tribe of an indigenous race. He did not cross the country on foot, foraging for whatever food he could find, or live under a flour sack for the winter, barely clinging on to life. He did not fight velociraptors or stand up against an alien invasion. The real story contained far less romance. He pointed to a spot on a map, determined it was not on state land or located in Native American territory and jammed a thumbtack in it. The origins of Oceanview could not have been any more vanilla or unromantic.

To counter this, the town created a celebratory anthem of the worst type of contrived and self-indulgent tripe. The fact that it blatantly ripped off '*Oh Tannenbaum!*' was disregarded entirely.

Oh, little town of Oceanview
Our forefather has founded
A Phoenix rising from the ash
Where bears and lions pounded
With rivers deep and mountains high
He fought natives from either side
So on this day we give him thanks
For all that he's endur-ed
Jason Reynolds is the man
Who all our ailments cur-ed

This travesty harped on for five more verses, three bridges, and four choruses and highlighted everything Reynolds did not do when he founded the town. The only parts missing were a Velociraptor attack and a duel with an alien. However, the town's fiftieth anniversary was only fifteen or so years away, and all signs pointed to the changes happening then.

To celebrate the rich history of a town not even forty years old appeared weird to outsiders, but to Oceanview, it seemed as normal as the salmon and jalapeno scones Judy Deacon sold in her coffee shop.

Reynolds started Forefather's Day thirty-five years ago to celebrate his prized creation. Its origins, however, were far from tacky. The first year's events were little more than him driving down Port Road waving to the crowd from the back of his brand-new Cadillac convertible. It stroked his already massive ego, but it wasn't tacky. That naturally came later once the residents of Oceanview slapped their grubby little paws on it. And come it did. Over the years, the talons of bad taste grabbed hold tight, and the event quickly became populated by carnival booths, overpriced hotdogs, event memorabilia, and a ticker-tape parade. Reynolds still cruised Port Road waving to the crowd in his new Cadillac convertible, but the cheese factor spread like cancer.

The town was too young to have any impact on history, so having a Forefather's Day appeared to be nothing more than an excuse for the citizens to have a party and be drunk in public. Reynolds was still in his sixties, so he could not come to the stage and grace the crowd with tales of the great depression or his struggles to break out of poverty. He spent his life with a silver spoon jammed firmly up his ass, and the weekend-long annual butt-kissing event did nothing to circumvent it.

To someone outside Oceanview, Reynolds appeared to be a complete and utter dick. Although, to be fair, he was a complete and utter dick. He enjoyed being better than the town's citizens and telling them what to do, and he acted like royalty to them. Every once in a while, he came down from his ivory tower and mingled with the lower classes for photo ops and free cupcakes. Of course, his people leaked his arrival time to generate a buzz, so when he showed up, there were throngs of admirers waiting for him. Reynolds signed a few newspapers or photos, kissed a few babies, and then retreated to his palace. One would be forgiven for thinking the Queen of England lived at the end of Lindsey Hill.

In its early days, Forefather's Day started as the last Friday evening in September. A few years later, it changed to the first Friday of December and included the annual Christmas tree lighting ceremony. Soon after, it spread to Saturday, and for fifteen years, the entire weekend became dedicated to Forefather's Day and kissing Reynolds' ass. Each year they added something new, and the setup and organization took longer and longer.

Of course, the citizens set up a committee to help with the planning. They felt it essential to discuss the minutia ninety-nine percent of the town cared little about. The Tuesday before the festivities, they spent their meeting deciding where the glass raffle bowl should be placed when Mayor Beck did the prize drawings at the end of the evening. The discussion turned ugly, the committee member's true colors came out, and insults flowed freely. Mrs. Hamilton accused Mrs. Sibley of having ambition without scruples. Mrs. Sibley called Mrs. Flack the Queen of the Harpies, and Mrs. Flack told Mrs. Crowley her stomach had more rolls than a bakery. The issue was dropped at the same time as the bowl. As Mrs. Sibley picked up the pieces, she mumbled about anarchy without order.

Despite the glass bowl setback, the planning continued without any other significant hitches, and by Friday night, the carnival rides were set up, and the Fry Bread was soaked in liquid death. Mr. Hughes donned his clown costume and made balloon animals for the children and giant phalluses and breasts for the adults. Mayor Beck used his clout as Mayor to cut to the front of the line to be sure he purchased the first deep-fried Twinkie.

The citizens who owned a store or restaurant set up a booth at the downtown park, and prices were immediately doubled. The Oceanview baseball caps which were ten dollars Friday morning, increased to twenty dollars during the fair. And without fail, they sold out. Despite the fact on Monday morning, prices went back to their original cost. Town pride spread like an infection, and it caused the residents to spend money like morons.

The fair opened at five o'clock with the usual ribbon-cutting ceremony. The grey sky threatened to dump more snow on the already frozen town as Mayor Beck took the stage and stood next to the town's giant Christmas tree. Earlier in the afternoon, the town's landscaping crew pushed much of the snow off the park, and enormous piles circled the festivities. Beck loved to use his giant golden scissors, and every event in the town involved a ribbon-cutting ceremony. New park? Ribbon-cutting ceremony. New ice cream flavor on the menu at Freeze? Ribbon-cutting ceremony. Broken ribbon cutting scissors? Let's just say that was a dark day for Oceanview. Costing over $15,000, the new pair of gold-plated scissors caused quite a stir when Mayor Beck insisted on adding them to the budget at the expense of three stop signs around town. Mayor Beck said the scissors were a necessity for the town's reputation. He said any mayor worth their salt owned a pair, and no one could take the town seriously without them.

During the press conference, as Mayor Beck pleaded his case to a few reporters that a good pair of ribbon-cutting scissors were critical for photo ops and media events, a report came in of a car accident. Clara Wilson, one of the town's oldest citizens, died at the intersection of Jefferson and Miller, where one of the planned stop signs should have been installed. In her honor, Mayor Beck took to calling the scissors Clara; however, the gesture overshadowed the fact the town traded a life for a pair of scissors. It was merely one more item to an extensive list of insensitive actions the town accepted as perfectly normal.

After a few token lines about town pride and a brief paragraph distorting the facts about Clara sacrificing herself for the good of the town, Marshall, her widower, teared up at the mention of her name. As he wiped the tears on his sleeve, Mayor Beck sliced through the purple ribbon with Clara's namesake and officially opened the Forefather's Day Festival to a roar of approval from the crowd. He stepped over to the giant Christmas tree, picked up two extension cords, and enthusiastically thrust the two ends together. Barely a quarter of the lights on the tree spluttered to life and the rest remained dark. The few less than enthusiastic cheers were as half-assed as the tree.

Warren cheered when Mayor Beck mentioned Clara. Her car had been in the shop the day she died, and Warren loaned her his car as a good-faith gesture while he worked on changing her tires. She came in driving a Mercedes and left in a Ford Escort. Marshall felt so bad after the accident he let Warren keep the car as payment for destroying his. Shocked by the impromptu upgrade, Warren took exemplary care of the vehicle. On Sunday afternoons, he scrubbed and detailed the inside and gave the body a fresh coat of wax. Sure, the car was fifteen years old, but it meant everything to Warren. He considered himself part of the social elite, and to further cement his place in a new social class, he tried ordering caviar one evening to improve his palate. He ended up vomiting all over the table, and the restaurant owner threw him out. He compromised by wearing a tie out in public occasionally, but mainly stayed with safe food groups.

Reynolds walked onto the stage a little after seven. Casually late was as on time for him as he could be. The townsfolk dropped what they were doing to go and listen to his annual speech and state of the town address. With Reynolds being the wet-behind-the-ears-entrepreneurial-developer-douchebag-hipster who named the town, it was only natural he had a personality as equally douchey. Two armed security guards in dark glasses escorted him onto the stage and moved to the back as Reynolds approached the microphone.

"Good evening, peasants," he yelled at the audience,

Surprisingly, the crowd cheered at the demeaning label, and ripples of laughter rang loud.

"Another year has come and gone in our beautiful town, and as the holiday season rapidly falls upon us, we find ourselves happier and more prosperous than ever before. Our schools are testing well, our businesses are thriving, and crime is below point one percent."

Reynolds paused as excitement echoed through the crowd.

"Justin Pearsall, if you're in the audience this evening, I'd appreciate it if you didn't graffiti the wall beside the town hall. Your vandalism tendencies are messing up our perfect crime stats."

The crowd all turned to pinpoint Justin as his mother hit him on the back of the head. A court system seemed unnecessary when public shame and a quick motherly hand acted as a far more effective deterrent.

"And it's fuck *the* police, not *da* police. If you're going to vandalize, use proper English, and I'm sure Sheriff Adams doesn't appreciate the sentiment."

Justin received another smack from his mother for his poor writing skills.

"Despite this minor blip on our record, the town is in fine standing," Reynolds continued.

He paused to receive a loud round of applause.

"Thank you, thank you. While I am pleased to report the town is doing well, that isn't the most exciting part of my speech. As you are no doubt aware, our poor football team is still struggling, so next year, we will be breaking ground on the new state-of-the-art sports facility, which can hopefully generate a winning spark and see us to victory."

A loud cheer rang out.

"Of course, this means a small increase in sales tax to cover construction."

A few grumbles bounced around.

"But, the price of victory isn't cheap. How many of you want to see another trophy in the Town Hall? I know I certainly do."

Every hand in the crowd shot up in the air.

"Can you put a price on victory?" he raised his arms to the sky like a delinquent prophet.

Scattered '*no's*', and words of support floated back from the crowd as Reynolds lowered his arms.

"Then we need this facility." He stabbed a finger at the audience, emphasizing each word. "I already have my architectural firm drawing up the plans." He could sense the crowd's hesitation. "Fear not, good citizens. The burden won't be yours alone. There will be a tax increase on car rentals and hotel rooms to make sure out-of-town visitors pay their share."

The crowd cheered in approval, oblivious that ninety-five percent of car rentals over the past ten years were from town residents whose vehicles were in for repair. Reynolds wrapped up his speech and sent his sheep back to the festival to throw more money into the town's economy.

The crowd walked away feeling uplifted, even though he just swindled the whole damn lot of them again. While Reynolds was no politician, he certainly needed to be. He possessed the knack of telling people what they wanted to hear and made even the worst idea sound like something they could not live without. His charm bought the town numerous facilities and amenities no one needed. The art museum on the west side displayed little more than pictures from the elementary school students and a few slightly more talented local artists. Certainly nothing that warranted a two-million-dollar price tag. Yet Reynolds convinced them promoting the arts benefitted the town. The only thing his ridiculous ideas benefitted involved his own wallet. Reynolds Construction oversaw the architectural projects that happened in the town, and Reynolds continued to live comfortably on the town's dime.

By nine o'clock, the fair kicked into full swing. Prizes were being won, food scoffed down, and money spent in abundance. By all accounts, Forefather's Day XXXVI, or Forfeathers Day XXXIX, as the three-hundred-and-fifty misprinted shirts read, could be deemed a tremendous success. Most of the town came out for the event and the park overflowed with bodies.

Amber enjoyed the evening and appreciated that Greg was the more outgoing of the two brothers. Her arms were full of stuffed toys and trophies that Greg won at the various carnival games, and he proudly wore a princess crown Katie Yan awarded him when he helped her win the duck shoot. Amber always beamed when she saw him with children. She heard rumblings he planned to propose to her on Christmas Day, and she could hardly contain herself. Despite her parents wanting her to date out of town, she wanted nothing more than to be Mrs. Greg Hart.

Warren continued to reel from his breakup with Ashley and struggled to enjoy himself. Finally, Greg and Amber told him to go home after his repeated sighing and whining. His passive aggressive '*I should go. I'm just going to bring you guys down*' backfired when they agreed and told him to go away. After acquiring heartburn from the funnel cake, he decided to call it a night and headed back to Greg's house.

David squeezed his way through the crowd towards one of the many food vendors lining the central strip. His quest to find something vaguely healthy to eat failed miserably. The fair ranked poorly for someone on a diet. Anything that could be dunked in oil and deep-fried became a sacrifice to the batter gods. About the only thing on the menu not dipped in batter and fried until its contents reached three thousand percent of a person's daily allotted trans-fat intake was a diet coke, and even then, vendors served it with a scoop of ice cream. David sighed and stepped back out of the line.

"Blessed are the churro's," yelled a tipsy Reverend Ellis from behind him. He pointed to the churro vendor and flicked holy water in its general direction. He gestured to another nearby booth. "Blessed are the t-shirts and the baseball caps." He stumbled off towards the popcorn stand to continue his benediction crusade. "Blessed is the wasabi popcorn."

"He's been at this all night," said a voice from behind.

David turned as Cam stepped in line, carrying a bottle of water.

"Really?" he asked.

"Yeah, he's blessed half of Main Street. He just finished up at TK's gun store."

He pointed to her drink. "Seems you found the only healthy thing here."

She shook her head and swished the bottle. "Vodka."

"Straight?"

Cam nodded with a sly grin. "Damn right."

"Smart woman." He smiled and nodded over his shoulder. "I wouldn't bother with this line unless you have no use for your arteries."

"Oh, cheer up, you miserable old bastard. It's a fair, we're supposed to willingly shave years off our lives at these events. It's a rite of passage."

"Well, you'll have to forgive me if I don't leap in with both feet. I'd rather not slowly kill myself with poison."

"No, you'd rather use gin." Cam grimaced at her comment.

David blinked. "Ouch."

"I'm sorry," said Cam. "Cheap shot. I've just got something on my mind."

"What's wrong?" he said, automatically jumping into shrink mode.

"Ever since that chat with Donald, I've been feeling bad. He's bound and determined to get the hell out of here."

"Can you blame him?"

"I'm joining him."

"You're leaving too?" said David, a little surprised.

"No, I'm going to help him pack. What he said in Jacob's hit home."

"Which part?"

"The part about sitting here and rotting. I must have seen him a thousand times, and I barely so much as inquired about his day. I can't help feeling I'm part of the problem."

"Do you have feelings for him?"

"Oh, God, no, he reminds me of my dad."

"You still miss him, don't you?" asked David.

"Of course I do. That's a fucking stupid question." Cam caught herself again. "I'm sorry. I didn't mean that. It's the vodka."

David laughed. "Yes, you did. It's okay, it's a stupid question. Sometimes my mouth runs off before my brain kicks in."

Cam smiled.

"It's good news about you and Donald, though." He nodded over her shoulder. "You'd have broken Kit-Kat's heart."

Without turning, she knew he stood ten feet behind her. "He's been following me around all night. I keep dropping things on the floor to bend over in front of him. It embarrasses the shit out of him. Watch."

She dropped her water bottle and bent over to retrieve it. She deliberately arched her back for emphasis and held the pose a few seconds longer than necessary. Kit-Kat immediately turned his usual shade of red, spun on his heels, and walked in the opposite direction.

"It never gets old," said Cam as she straightened her back.

She finally made it to the front of the line, and the zitty kid behind the window suddenly perked up as he received a clear view of her cleavage.

"What can I get you?" he asked Cam with adoring puppy-dog eyes.

"Two beers, please," she said with a beaming smile.

"May I see your I.D., please, miss?"

"Oh, I like you," flirted Cam as she plucked her driver's license from her purse.

The cashier handed over two bottles. "On the house."

Cam smiled and blew the blushing kid a kiss. "Thanks, sweetie."

David shook his head in disbelief. "So, what are we toasting to?"

"Donald."

"Good idea," said David.

Cam smiled. "No, the other one's for Donald. I'm sorry, but you're on your own, buddy."

"I can't take this much rejection in one night," complained David jokingly.

"Toughen up, sunshine, the night's still young," she said as she playfully patted his back.

David laughed. "What is it with everyone growing a pair of balls around here lately?"

"Must be the end of the world," said Cam with a grin as she turned away.

David looked at the crowd having fun and remembered why he fell in love with Oceanview. Maybe seeing out life in the crazy little town was not such a curse after all.

He had inadvertently stepped back in line, and the zitty kid behind the window looked at David with what could barely be called disinterest. David's breasts were smaller than Cam's, so he did not deserve as much of the kid's attention. With an ear-to-ear grin, David ordered a bacon cheeseburger with fries, a deep-fried Twinkie, and a large root beer float. He did not need those extra years anyway.

CHAPTER 17

Donald was not screwing around when he said he wanted to get the hell out of dodge. He skipped Forefather's Day and spent the evening packing. While under no strict deadline other than what he set for himself, each second he waited kept him away from his new life.

The contents of his rather sad wardrobe were spread across his bed as he carefully picked through the carnage. He decided to keep a beige suit and white shirt, but the lime green wool cardigan ended up in the trash pile. Uncertain of what society considered fashionable, he sighed in relief when he heard a knock at the front door.

"It's open," he instinctively yelled from the bedroom, clueless as to who it could be.

The front door opened as he walked into the living room.

"Need a hand?" asked Cam with a smile. "I brought beer."

"Oh, hi," said Donald, a little surprised.

Cam closed the door behind her. "Expecting someone else?"

"No, I wasn't expecting anyone, actually. I never have unexpected guests."

"Do you always yell '*come in*' to strangers?" she said with a smile.

Donald laughed. "Sorry, packing distracted me. What are you doing here?"

"I came to help you pack."

"You want me gone that fast, huh?"

Cam's eyes widened. "Oh, I didn't mean it that way."

"I'm kidding," said Donald with a smile. "Your timing's perfect. I'm sorting out my clothes and could use a woman's eye."

"What can I do?"

"Make yourself comfortable and give me a thumbs up or down."

"I can manage that," she said with a smile and sat on the couch. She promptly gave him a thumbs down to the red and blue pin-striped jacket.

"Wow, you're not wasting any time, are you?"

"Hey, I can give a thumbs up if you want to look like a Vaudeville barbershop quartet singer. All you need is a curly mustache and a straw hat, and you're set."

"Okay, okay, I get it. No on the jacket."

"And the pants."

"What's wrong with my pants?"

"The seventies want them back. So they can give them back to the sixties."

He removed the coat and headed back into the bedroom. A few minutes later, he came out wearing a light brown corduroy jacket with paisley elbow pads. Cam stuck her fingers in her mouth and pretended to gag.

Donald furrowed his brow until he saw himself in the mirror. He disappeared back into the bedroom as Cam turned around and started looking at the heavy dark wood bookshelf behind the couch.

Her eyes widened as she scanned over the spines. Dickens, Shakespeare, Lee, Kerouac, Tolstoy, Hemingway. Not a single piece of fluff among them. Cam loved literature and held a deep-rooted appreciation for the classics.

"Your collection is amazing," she said.

"I take it you don't mean my wardrobe?" Donald replied from the bedroom.

Cam laughed. "Your library, it's incredible."

"Thank you." He stepped out of the room wearing a green and cream argyle vest and tan pants.

"Ooh, now that's a keeper." She said as her attention diverted back to the books. "I didn't know you were so well-read."

"Most people don't. No one bothered to ask me."

"I could say the same," Cam muttered.

"Yeah, it sucks, doesn't it? How long have you been into the classics?"

"All my life. My grandfather used to read To Kill A Mockingbird to me. While most other kids were getting Doctor Seuss and looking for Waldo, I got Harper Lee and Dickens. I know I'm not too smart in other parts of life, but I love to read."

"There are worse ways to spend your life." Donald disappeared back into the bedroom.

"Hey, did I tell you I earned an A in my Creative Writing class?"

Donald feigned ignorance. "That's wonderful," he shouted.

"It's the only A I ever got. Damn proud of it too. I wish I had more book smarts, though."

"Smarts aren't everything. You're very pretty. That counts for a lot. It isn't all about the brains."

The edges of Cam's mouth dropped. "That's what people say to idiots. It's the reverse of telling a smart ugly person that it's what's inside that counts," she said, her voice tinged with sadness.

Donald stepped back out of the bedroom. "I wasn't calling you an idiot. I happen to find you quite endearing."

"You're incredibly sweet, Donald, but let's be real. I'm the town whore."

"You think I have it any better? I'm the town's weird old man. If you'd shown me this life forty years ago, I'd have never believed it could be me. I had plans and ambitions." He gestured to the apartment around him. "Not this."

"I don't think you're weird."

"Yet you barely said a word to me before last week."

"I—" Cam stammered.

Donald headed back into the bedroom. "I'm sorry. I didn't mean that."

A few minutes later, he reappeared wearing a baby blue turtleneck and red golf pants. "I guess I never gave you a reason to talk to me."

"Definite no on the pants. Keep the sweater."

Donald turned to go back into the bedroom and stopped. "Why are you here?"

"You inspired me," said Cam.

He looked back at Cam, mildly amused. "Me? What did I do?"

"By leaving."

"I'm sorry, I don't follow."

"You've lived in Oceanview all your life, and you could have easily stayed here until you died." She paused a moment. "You're not dying, are you?"

Donald frowned. "Why does everyone keep asking me that?"

"It's okay if you are. I mean, no, it isn't okay, I mean—" Cam fumbled for the right words.

"I'm not dying."

"So, you really do just want to get out and see the world, before—" she stopped the thought before it came out.

"Before I die?"

"Yeah, sorry. That came out wrong again. I should stop talking."

Donald smiled. "It's okay. It's the exact reason I'm going."

"I wish I could leave."

"Why don't you?"

"Where would I go? I don't know anyone outside Oceanview."

"Neither do I. Why don't you come with me?" Donald blurted out. The words were spontaneous, and they shocked him with their bold nature.

"What?" said Cam as her eyes widened.

"Come with me."

"Donald, you're old enough to be my father."

He laughed. "Not as my girlfriend, as a traveling companion. To find yourself. Two lost souls looking for a new beginning to our happy ever after. Let's escape this place together. This town holds nothing for us anymore. Let's head east and don't look back."

"I don't know if I want to run away."

"I'm not running away. I'm going to find out who I am."

"That isn't what I meant, Donald."

"I know, I'm sorry. Everyone keeps telling me I'm running away. To be running away implies there is something I'm moving away from. There's nothing for me here. I'm not running away, I'm running towards. Same speed, different direction."

"I guess I never thought of it like that. I just didn't think I'd ever leave Oceanview. It'd be a huge leap for me."

Donald sat on the couch next to her. "It is for me too, but I need to find myself. To be surrounded by people who give a crap about me. I don't deserve to sit here in this town and rot. I could die in this apartment tonight, and no one would notice for a month. I deserve better. Hell, I'm sixty-three, and I still live in an apartment. I've never even owned a house. I've already been here for thirty-five years. Odds are I won't have another, and if I do, then God knows I want to spend it doing something for me. If I don't get out there and see what the world has to offer me, then what is the point to all this? My entire life would have been wasted. Thanks to my overbearing mother and a father who didn't give a shit, I am emotionally stunted. I'm scared of my own damn shadow, and I want to break free of this so I can be treated like everyone else. For one last moment, I want to feel alive and that all of this meant something."

Cam smiled. "I like the sound of that."

"Who knows, maybe you could fall in love?"

"Falling in love is not all it's cracked up to be," said Cam softly.

"It is when you truly find it. What you found wasn't love, I could see it in your eyes. You sit at the bar every night desperately looking for someone to truly love and validate you. You won't find it getting hit on by the same drunk guys all the time. You deserve better. If this town can't give you what you want, then you need to go out there and find it. Don't settle. Our happy endings live way beyond the boundaries of Oceanview."

Cam smiled. "Why couldn't you have been twenty-five years younger?"

Donald laughed. "You'd tire of me within a week. Besides, I'm not available."

"You're dating?"

"Heavens, no," he said with a sad smile.

Cam studied Donald's face. "But your heart belongs to someone else. Have you told her?"

Donald nodded. "She knew."

"She left?"

"It happened a long, long time ago."

She could see the discomfort in his eyes. "You don't have to talk about this."

"It's fine. It might do me some good. I've never really spoken about it." Donald exhaled a heavy breath. "Her name's Laura. We met in the last year of elementary school and were inseparable from then on. Two years after we graduated, I proposed to her."

He paused for a second, and Cam saw his eyes look off into the distance. She saw something new on his face, a look she previously missed, the face of a man holding back years of incredible pain and loss.

"What happened to her, Donald?"

Donald sat back on the couch. "You want the unabridged version or the Cliff Notes?"

"The one you're comfortable telling."

"I lived in Maine at the time. One night after work, a few days after I proposed, we planned to meet at a restaurant with our friends and family to break the news. We waited an hour, but she never showed."

"Cold feet?"

"That's the conclusion I'd come to. I thought she'd changed her mind and ran. It seemed to make sense." He let out a heavy sigh and paused. "People started running past the front of the restaurant, and someone screamed for an ambulance. We stood up to check on the commotion. One of our local police officers stopped me as I left and pulled me aside. He told me Laura had been hit by a drunk driver crossing the street two blocks away. The coward drove off and left her dead against a dumpster. The woman I loved and gave my entire heart to was killed by some drunken bastard who didn't even have the guts to hang around and deal with it.

"Oh, Donald, I'm so sorry. Did they catch him?"

"Yeah, about an hour later. Someone saw his license plate. By the time the cops got to his house, he'd hung himself."

"That's at least something, right?"

"No. I didn't even get to confront him. I wasn't happy he died. I hated that he wasn't alive. I had nothing to direct my anger towards. I didn't see him on trial. I didn't get to see him punished for what he did."

"But he died. Isn't that the ultimate punishment?"

"It didn't matter to me. I wanted him to hang on my terms. His death came of his own choosing. He took the easy way out, and he didn't get to pay for what he'd done to me. I wanted to talk to him, to shout at him, to punch him. To show him what he'd taken from me, and I couldn't. He denied me that."

"Don't you think he'll be judged in the afterlife?"

"I don't believe in all that bullshit anymore. If there's a god, he wouldn't have taken her from me. I got sick and tired of all the pity *'she's in a better place now'* or *'it's all God's plan'*. Fuck that and fuck him. I did nothing wrong, and he saw fit to punish me for who knows what."

"I guess it's the last thing you want to be hearing. Some people don't know what to say."

"Then don't. Telling me she's in a better place does nothing to make me feel better. We were already in good a place. She carried my child too. We'd planned to tell everyone at dinner. I didn't just lose my fiancée, I lost my family. I lost the man I was supposed to be. It's impossible to pick up the pieces after that."

"I am so sorry."

"Don't be. It isn't your fault." Donald smiled sadly. "You're actually the first person I've told this to in its entirety."

"All the sessions with David, and you never told him?"

"What's the point in talking about it? All the therapy in the world won't bring her back. You know what they say about time healing all wounds?"

"Yeah."

"It's bullshit, it's all bullshit. It never gets better. I never got over Laura, and I never will. Sure, as the years went by, I thought of her less, but the times when I do, it hurts. It hurts as bad as the day she died. Time doesn't heal shit. It's lip service when there's nothing else to say. Shortly afterward, my mom fell sick, and I ended up getting stuck helping out. We ended up here, and you know the rest of the sad story. That's my sorry life in barely a minute."

"And you never dated again?"

"No."

"But you're a good-looking guy, surely someone chased you?"

Donald smiled. "I'm not saying women weren't interested in me. I wasn't interested. How could I be? I didn't get any closure. It's not like a divorce or a separation where you have one or both of you falling out of love. The day she died, I was unequivocally in love with her. You don't stop loving someone, and you don't fall out of love with them over time. You can't. The feeling never goes away. I loved her then, and I love her now. I could never date again as they'd never have all of me."

Cam sat in silence, processing what she heard. She no longer saw the strange old man who sat behind her in the bar for so many years. "So, you weren't watching my ass, were you?" She instantly cringed. "I'm sorry. That sounded horrible."

Donald smiled again. "It's okay. It isn't to say you don't have a nice ass, but my mind is always on another."

"I guess I feel a little better. I was worried I was losing my touch."

Donald laughed, and the mood started to lighten up. "I tell you what, I leave tomorrow night. If you want to come with me, I will leave some room in the car. I'll stop by at eight to get you. I won't come up, I'll just honk twice. That way, if you don't want to come, there is no weird face-to-face interaction, and I head out on my own. Deal?"

"The only gives me a day."

"Some of the best decisions are done in the spur of the moment."

Cam smiled. "Fair enough. Deal. Oh, and Donald, keep the blue suit. It matches your eyes."

Donald stood up from the couch and headed back to the bedroom. "Lose the scarlet letter."

"The what?"

"The scarlet letter. Third row, fourteenth from the left."

Cam turned to the bookshelf. She scanned to the third row and counted fourteen in, and pulled out '*The Scarlet Letter*'. As she glanced over the back synopsis, she looked down at her shirt, and her jaw dropped. "Oh, fuck me. How long have you known? Does everyone laugh at me?"

"It's okay. To be honest, I don't believe most of the town even noticed the connection, but it certainly draws attention to your chest." Donald reached into a pile of clothes on the bed and pulled out an old, faded Star Wars T-shirt with a picture of Han Solo in all his 1970's glory emblazoned on the front of it. "Catch," he said as he threw it out of the bedroom.

"What's this?"

"Wardrobe change. It's a little geeky, but at least it will be an improvement."

She stood up and took off her shirt.

Donald caught her reflection in the bedroom mirror and smiled sadly. "I miss you, Laura," he muttered under his breath.

"Did you say something?" Cam shouted from the living room.

"I said it suits you."

"I'm more of a Luke Skywalker kind of girl," she said with a smile. "But this will do."

"I'd have thought you'd be drawn to the scoundrels."

"What can I say? I happen to like nice men. I have enough scoundrels in my life."

Donald smiled at the movie reference. "I'm a nice guy," Donald whispered softly.

"Yes, you are." Cam walked up from behind and planted a quick kiss on his cheek.

Donald flushed red with embarrassment.

"You know you're the first guy who has had me in his bedroom without putting the moves on me."

"Should I apologize?"

"Not at all. I actually like it." She smiled as she sat on the edge of the bed and smoothed out a crease from the comforter. "This is new territory for me. You make me feel safe. I wish more guys took the time to get to know me. I wish I'd taken the time to get to know you."

Donald opened his mouth to answer.

"You don't have to say anything. It's my own fault. But, you're right. I do need a change."

"So, you'll come?"

"What about all my stuff? I can't leave it all here."

"Do what I'm doing. I'm bringing the essentials and have arranged for the rest to be picked up when I find a place to settle in. The apartment owner owes me a favor."

"I could ask David to help me." She paused, genuinely considering the proposal. "Is there enough room in your car?"

"Plenty."

"I wouldn't need to bring a lot of stuff, just a bag or two."

"So, is that a yes?"

"It's a definitely maybe. Let me think about it. It's a lot for me to process. Tomorrow?"

"At eight."

"It doesn't give me a lot of time." She flashed him a smile and hopped off the bed. "I have a lot of thinking to do."

Cam left the bedroom and let herself out.

As the door slammed, Donald fell back on the bed and held his hands to his face, unsure if his ridiculous proposition had been the right thing to do. He barely knew her. As he closed his eyes, images of Laura bounced around his head. Since talking to Cam, he felt a great load lifted. As though the crushing weight on his chest lessened. Part of him wondered if he had done it sooner, maybe the pain would have subsided faster. He pushed the question aside. For a moment, the heartache that ravaged his core for forty years finally started to subside.

♦ ♦ ♦ ♦

Cam's mind also raced with a million thoughts as she descended the stairs and headed to her car. She was shocked she was contemplating leaving, as she barely knew the man. She had resigned herself to seeing out the rest of her life in Oceanview. Now suddenly, she found a new option on the table that she had never seriously considered before. While a creature of routine, the opportunity of leaving excited her. Over the years, the thought casually crossed her mind, but never extended past more than idle daydreaming. Her head told her packing up and running was something twenty-year-old kids do, not a woman in her mid-thirties. But, she felt a knot in her stomach telling her to run like hell and never look back. She always followed her head. Perhaps now she finally needed to trust her gut.

♦ ♦ ♦ ♦

By Saturday evening, the Forefather's Day celebrations in Oceanview had slowed to a crawl. Twenty-four hours remained of the event, but most of the residents were drunk, broke, in a food coma, or various combinations of the three. Festivities were planned for the closing ceremony on Sunday, but it looked doubtful if anyone remained coherent enough to attend. It was not the first time, as every year, the same thing happened without fail. Maybe one day, the organizers would get smart enough to figure out that minor detail. In a few short hours, attendees reduced the downtown park to a pile of empty cups and junk food wrappers, and a few of the more inebriated citizens were collapsed under the various trees scattered throughout the park. The threatened snowfall finally arrived a little after four o'clock, and many attendees gave up and vacated the park in favor of their warm homes.

Earlier in the day, Hank won the hotdog eating contest. Well, win was a bit of an overstatement. He fell to last place until he announced that anyone who beat him would have their tab cut off at the bar and full payment due immediately. Suddenly the pack slowed down, and Hank deep throated his way to victory. The quickest way to his competitor's hearts always came down to alcohol.

Cam skipped most of the Saturday evening festivities and instead spent the time pacing her apartment. She wanted to stay for the Hobbit toss, but as Mayor Beck took the stage to introduce the event, it quickly became evident the town did not, in fact, have a little person in its ranks, and he left the stage amid loud boos and jeers. Someone in the audience suggested a mayor toss, and Beck's security detail whisked him away before the idea came to fruition. As Cam left, she saw Kit-Kat being pulled on stage as the substitute sacrificial Hobbit.

By the time she pulled out of the parking lot, her mind raced with thoughts. She failed to notice her speed increasing until she noticed blue and red lights flashing in her rear-view mirror. She glanced down and saw she was thirty over the limit. A two-hundred-dollar speeding ticket was a fine she could ill afford. While Lee generally never arrested anyone for minor DUIs, he was less lenient on felony speeding on a residential street.

"Shit," she muttered to herself as she pulled over and reached into her glove box. She rummaged through the junk inside when Lee walked up to her window and tapped gently on the glass. A flurry of papers fell onto the floor.

"Shit," she said again as she sat up and lowered the window.

"Evening, Cam," said Lee with a smile, his breath visible in the brisk air.

Cam turned her attention back to the pile of papers on the floor. "Oh, hey, Lee."

"Where are you heading in such a hurry?"

"Was I speeding?"

"Do I need to answer that?" He pulled out his pen and ticket book

She finally found her insurance and registration and offered them to Lee.

"Cam, I don't need these. I've pulled you over so many times I have your policy number and license memorized."

"Yeah, I guess you do," she said as she placed them on the passenger seat.

"Do you want to take a stab at how many lights you ran?"

Cam cringed. "Shit. I'm sorry, Lee. I didn't realize. I—"

"You didn't. I wanted to see if you're paying attention." He looked at her intently for a moment. "Where are you?"

"Huh?"

"You're obviously somewhere else. Where is that head of yours?"

"I'm leaving town." She had not said the words out loud before, and they surprised her.

"Shut the fuck up. Are you drunk again?"

"No, I'm not drunk. When have I ever drank and drove? I'm going home and packing up my shit and getting the hell out of here."

"You're serious."

"Yeah."

"Are you going alone?"

"I'm going with Donald."

Lee was taken aback. "Donald? Isn't he a bit old for you?"

"Not in that way, you smart-ass."

"Hey, it isn't wise to upset the man with the pen. I may not be able to shoot you, but I sure as hell can write you a ton of tickets. Do you have any idea many I could give you right now?"

Cam opened her mouth to answer but thought better of it.

Lee closed the notepad. "How can I ticket you if you're leaving?"

"I can't believe I'm even talking about it."

"Seems to be something in the air lately. First Donald, now you. David's talking about it, and last night at Jacob's, Greg said when he and Amber get married, they're moving out of state."

"They are? Warren's going to be pissed."

"Yeah, he is." Lee laughed at the thought.

"Times are changing, Lee."

"I think the world's coming to an end." He smiled. "Try not to forget us."

"Impossible" said Cam with a grin.

Lee banged on the roof of her car. "Go home and pack, Cam Harris." Cam pulled away and Lee headed back to his cruiser.

His radio crackled with a static burst. "Lee, we're getting reports of a disturbance at Paradise Bay. Can you check it out?"

Lee thumbed the switch on his radio. "Send Joe over. I'm on the other end of town. I'm going to check the park for drunks. I don't want anyone dying of hypothermia tonight."

◆ ◆ ◆ ◆

The streets were quiet for a Saturday evening, and Cam made it home in ten minutes. It took her another ten to get out of the car and go indoors. She could not believe she was about to pack up and run. Donald could call it what he wanted, but she would be running if she left. As she walked inside, she looked up at the clock in the kitchen. She still had a couple more hours to mull it over before Donald arrived. Cam headed upstairs and drew a bath.

◆ ◆ ◆ ◆

On the other side of town, Donald finished packing and looked around his bedroom. Everything of value to him was stuffed in a pile of four boxes. He picked up a picture of Laura and sat down on the bed. "I'm not in love," he said to the photograph. "I promise. She's kind, she's safe. For the past forty years, my heart has never wandered. I've never allowed it to." He sighed softly. "Everyone kept telling me you'd want me to be happy. I know they're right, but it doesn't make it any easier. Sometimes I think if it'd been me hit by the car, what would I have wanted for you? I don't think I'd want you to date, but I wouldn't have wanted you to live life alone and unhappy. I supposed I should practice what I preach, huh?"

He flipped over and read the inscription on the back. *'I can't promise you an eternity, but I will love you for one. Always, Laura'*. As he placed the picture down on a pile of papers on the bed, a postcard of Niagara Falls caught his eye. Another handwritten note adorned the back. *'Two hundred and forty-seven days and counting'*. A countdown to their honeymoon. He wiped away a tear and put the picture in his suitcase. He zipped up the bag and carried it to the living room.

As evening fell, Donald closed the door of his apartment for the last time and walked down to his car. He looked back up at the living room window, his mind a torrent of emotions.

◆ ◆ ◆ ◆

He pulled up in front of Cam's apartment a few minutes before eight o'clock. Light snow had started to fall again, and the streets were quiet. Donald sat patiently in his car and stared at her front door. While he desperately wanted to get the hell out of town, he craved for Cam to come with him. He struggled with his offer and began to regret inviting her. It felt like the right thing to do at the time, but having dwelled on it for a few hours, he thought it was nothing more than a spur-of-the-moment knee-jerk reaction.

As the seconds ticked by and eight o'clock approached, his head swam with thoughts. He had no interest in her romantically, but taking the giant step alone terrified him. Having a friendly face by his side might make the trip less daunting, but then again, was it not the main reason for leaving to begin with? To get away from the familiar, to head east and find himself. How could he do it with a piece of his past in tow?

Donald let out a long sigh. "I'm sorry, Cam."

He put the car into drive and pulled away.

Seconds later, the apartment door opened, and Cam stepped out carrying two suitcases. "Don't leave," she screamed after him as she watched his taillights disappear with her dreams riding shotgun. "Come back," she pleaded as tears cascaded down her cheeks. Cam let out a heavy, defeated moan of anguish between heavy, racking sobs, watching her last chance at happiness vanish. She closed her eyes and fell to the ground. "Don't leave," she said again, her voice barely audible.

CHAPTER 18

The start of the apocalypse should have had far more impact than it did. It did not resemble what is typically seen in horror movies. The sky did not turn blood red, and dark-winged demons with eyes like black holes did not swoop down from the heavens. No rotten arms were thrust out of the ground, and decayed bodies did not pull themselves out of their graves as people took to the streets screaming. There were no explosions or car crashes. The power grid stayed on, and there were no riots at the grocery store as people trampled each other to get the last bottle of water. No, it was far less dramatic. You could probably go as far as calling it completely fucking boring. In fact, the first person to return from the dead went unnoticed for three days.

After Death skipped Harriet Jenkins, she stayed locked in her home until help arrived. She turned ninety-six days before and had perched on death's door for years. Unfortunately, when she finally arrived, Death did not lead the way, so instead of moving on to the next world, she lay still for a few minutes, emitted a deep throaty growl, rolled over, and fell out of bed. Twenty minutes later, she climbed back on her feet. Her eyes as black as the darkest cavern, and her veins, a violent, angry red. Mrs. Alvarez, her home nurse, would not arrive until Saturday, and so the first living creature Harriet saw was her cat, Mr. Giggles.

Which she promptly ate.

Its bony frame offered little sustenance, but it held her over for a short time. For three days, she waited, staring at the front door with Mr. Giggles congealing on her chin. Shortly after three o'clock on Saturday afternoon,

Mrs. Alvarez knocked quietly on the door. Harriet possessed a weak heart, and she tried to avoid any unnecessary shock by ringing the doorbell and barging in like a hurricane. She started tapping, gradually increasing the noise until Harriet heard her and opened the door.

The knocking increased in volume, but Harriet didn't answer.

"Hello," she asked in broken English as she fumbled for her key.

She knocked once more before letting herself inside.

The apartment was dark as she reached for the light switch. The lights snapped on brightly, and it took her eyes a moment to adjust. As the room came into focus, she saw Harriet standing in the middle of the floor. Mrs. Alvarez's eyes still processed the light and squinted as she crossed over to her.

She saw the bloodstain on the front of her nightdress, and before she could check on Harriet, the old woman came at her. The struggle only lasted a few seconds, but to Mrs. Alvarez, it felt like time slowed to a crawl. Harriet bared her teeth and moved straight for her neck, biting off a chunk of flesh. Mrs. Alvarez screamed and grabbed at her throat as a fountain of blood spurted from the wound. She tried to form words, but nothing came except a bloody gurgle. A second later, Harriet attacked again and tore into her forearm. Mrs. Alvarez toppled backward under the weight and crashed into a marble coffee table. Blackness mercifully followed. A few minutes later, her eyes snapped open. Black, lifeless eyes.

And then there were two.

The Paradise Bay apartment complex comprised sixteen apartments. Eight on the top floor and eight on the bottom, split into two groups of four facing each other. Mrs. Sally Jepson from 2B opened her front door after hearing a loud bang outside. She peeked out into the hallway to see Harriet stumbling from her apartment across the hall. A streak of dark red blood dripped her chin and onto her chest, Mrs. Alvarez a step behind.

"Harriet, are you okay?" Sally said, her face awash with concern as Harriet moved towards her. "I'm calling Doctor Palmuth. You're hurt." She turned to step back into her apartment and picked up her cell phone.

It was her last move. She bled to death thirty seconds later.

As the group grew, they became louder, and more residents came out to investigate. While the three of them made quick work of the condo residents, it would be a few more hours before the situation became dire.

Rick Kenlan, the manager of the complex, woke shortly before ten to frantic banging on his front door. He stumbled out into the brisk night to check on the noise. The outbreak may have stayed contained to the area had he not decided to climb into his car, clutching the bloody wound on his neck, and head to the hospital. He made it three miles before he slumped over the steering wheel and slammed his car into a tree.

The homeowner across the street rushed out to help. Rick's black eyes flicked open, and he bit down on the man's arm. At that moment, the small, contained infection became an outbreak.

♦ ♦ ♦ ♦

A little after midnight, Cam stumbled out of Jacob's, a broken and depressed woman. After three hours of crying into her beer about her fading looks and barren womb, Hank threw her out for scaring off customers. Donald was gone, and her last chance at happiness disappeared with him. As his taillights faded, she immediately drove to Jacob's to seek solace in either the bottom of a glass or the arms of the first man who spoke to her. The glass won.

A plow had pushed a pile of snow from the street and onto her car, blocking the driver's side door.

"That's fucking great," she muttered to herself as she crossed around to the passenger side and fumbled for her keys.

She opened the passenger door and climbed over the center console onto the driver's seat. As she leaned back in her seat, she saw her reflection in the rear-view mirror. She no longer recognized the woman staring back. Her eyes were red from hours of tears, and mascara danced chaotically across her cheeks. How could it have come to this? She had dreams and goals and wanted to be someone of value instead of a two-bit bar tramp who lifted her skirt at the drop of a complimentary word. For five minutes, she stared at herself, trying to figure out when she became lost and how the fuck she could get her life back on track.

Too buzzed to drive, she rested her head on the steering wheel and closed her eyes. An hour became two, but sleep never arrived. She sat mourning the past, hating the present, and dreading the future.

A loud bang snapped her eyes open as a body scrambled over the hood of her car and slammed hard against the windshield. "Hey!" screamed Cam. Do you fucking mind? I'm having an epiphany, you asshole."

Her train of thought derailed, she tried to make out what the man was screaming at her. His black eyes bored into her soul as he clawed at the glass. Cam thought he must be one of those druggies from the big city. She heard they did all kinds of weird substances which did unnatural things to the body. She only tried pot a few times, never any of the hard drugs. Aside from the copious amounts of unprotected dick, she was careful of what she put in her body.

"Get off my car, you fucking crack-head," she yelled as the man struck again.

A trail of blood oozed down his chin as Cam leaned into the windshield for a closer look. He bared his teeth and banged harder on the glass, making her jump back in surprise. Cam flipped on her windshield wipers in hopes of knocking him away, but only succeeded in pissing him off further. The next impact left a large crack in its wake. Tired of his bullshit, she threw the car into reverse and hit the gas pedal. The man lost his grip and tumbled onto the snowy street.

Cam pulled forward and took off down Port Road. She grabbed her phone from the seat next to her and dialed the police station. The phone rang five, fifteen, twenty times, but no one answered. "Shit," muttered Cam. They never ignored a call, someone always monitored the front desk.

She stopped at the light at Seventh Avenue and turned left towards the station. Despite no one answering the phone, it still seemed like the best place to go. As she made her way through town, she saw other people moving erratically. One stood hunched over, eating something on the sidewalk she could not identify.

Cam gazed up into the sky. A full moon shined brightly over the town. "Well, that explains it," she said to herself. "Fucking moon."

Minutes later, she pulled up outside the station. Usually, there were at least one or two cars parked out front, but the lot was vacant. She climbed out and headed towards the entrance to find the door locked and the lights off. The police station never closed.

"Where is everybody?" She leaned against the glass and peeked into the lobby. "Hello?" Unsure of her next move, she stepped back from the door.

A loud siren blared behind her, making her jump. She turned to see a police cruiser stopping in front of the station, and the driver's door swinging open.

"Finally," said Cam as she walked over.

Lee climbed out of the car and stopped behind the door, his gun drawn.

"Stop right there." He raised his weapon towards her chest.

"Very funny, Lee," said Cam as she walked towards him.

"I said stop."

Cam squinted at him in confusion. "This isn't funny anymore."

"I said fucking stop," ordered Lee.

She stopped walking.

"Put your hands in the air."

Cam slowly obliged. "Lee? What's going on?"

"Have you been bitten?" he asked, his tone deathly serious.

"Huh?" she said, clueless as to what he meant.

"Has one of those things bitten you?"

"You mean the crazy meth head who owes me a new windshield?"

"They're not on crack, Cam. Just answer the goddamn question. Are you bit?"

He kept his gun trained on her.

Cam rolled her eyes as she stepped towards him. The town had gone all kinds of crazy. "Lee, we both know you're carrying blan—"

Bang.

He fired a warning shot above her head. Lee appeared to have his bullets back.

"JESUS FUCKING CHRIST," Cam clutched at her ringing ears. "WHAT THE FUCK?"

"I said, are you fucking bit?" Lee yelled back at her.

"No, goddammit, I'm not bitten," she screamed as she stamped her foot. "What the fuck is going on?"

Lee lowered his gun and came around from behind the car door. "Wait here."

She turned as Lee walked past her.

He kept his pistol drawn. "I SAID, WAIT HERE." He picked up speed and ran towards the station door. He unlocked it and disappeared inside. A minute later, he returned with a large black bag and a rifle slung over his shoulder. He left the door open behind him.

"Christ, Lee, are you going to war?"

He walked around to the trunk and threw the bag inside. "Get in, Cam. It isn't safe out here."

"No shit. The fucking cops are shooting at me."

"Get in the damned car," he said as he slammed the trunk shut. "I'm not asking."

"My car's right there," she said as she pointed to her beat-up Hyundai parked twenty feet away.

"Don't argue with me. I'm keeping you safe."

"Yeah, by fucking shooting at me," Cam muttered under her breath.

She reluctantly complied and opened the passenger door as Lee climbed in the other side. He put his pistol down on the center console.

"What's going on?" she said as Lee flipped on the siren and pulled away. She was still shaken from the gunshot.

"I don't know. We were called out to a disturbance at Paradise Bay a few hours ago, and I sent Joe out to investigate. Thirty minutes later, I get a frantic call that one of the old women bit him."

"Bacon, it's what's for dinner." Cam smiled.

"Not the time, Cam." Lee inhaled sharply. "He's dead."

"Get the fuck out of here."

"He's dead."

"Joe? Joe's dead?" Cam felt sick to her stomach. Joe ranked as ex-husband number three and one of her favorite failed marriages.

Lee nodded. Cam noticed his hands were shaking, and his skin was as white as the snow on the ground. It was a miracle his shot missed her. Maybe it had been unintentional.

"Lee, what's going on? A mad man jumps on my car, drooling God knows what on my windshield, and now you're saying Joe's dead?"

"When I got there, I saw him sprawled on the lawn out front, and two of the old ladies were leaning over him. I thought they were giving him CPR. There was blood on the grass, and it looked like he'd been shot. I told them to back away, but they ignored me. They kept moving over him."

"Who?"

"Mrs. Jenkins and Mrs. Foster."

"Aren't they, like, eighty?"

"Yeah. I figured they were deaf. I shouted for them to back away, and they ignored me. I pulled out my weapon, and as I got closer, I heard these weird tearing sounds. It was like nothing I'd heard before. When they refused to move, I fired a warning shot, and they stopped moving long enough to look up. Mrs. Jenkins went back to leaning over him, but Mrs. Foster stood up and headed towards me. I told her to stop, but she didn't listen. She kept coming at me. There was blood all over her. So much fucking blood."

"Joe's blood?"

Lee nodded.

"She shot him?"

"He hadn't been shot. I don't even know how to say this. She'd been eating something."

"Something? Like what?"

"Something living. She had all kinds of weird shit hanging off her chin. Then I saw Mrs. Jenkins pull back from Joe with a mouthful of his flesh."

Cam gasped.

"As Mrs. Foster came closer, I fired another warning shot, but she kept coming. Her face was covered in blood. I shot her in the leg. She stumbled for a second, and she kept moving towards me. I hit her in the stomach and her chest, and she kept coming."

"Adrenalin?"

"No. No one could keep moving after that, even with adrenalin. I aimed for her heart. Cam, I could see right through her chest. I left a big fucking hole where her heart should be, and she kept moving. She lets out this scream like nothing I have ever heard before. I aimed for the head. It's the only thing that put her down."

"Drugs?"

"Have you seen a drug where someone moves without a heart? Use your damn head."

"You don't have to be an asshole."

Lee brushed her off. "I don't know what the fuck to do. The academy doesn't teach you how to deal with cannibals."

"So, where's Joe now?"

"I have no clue. I ran."

"You ran?" Cam was appalled.

"What else could I do? Before I left, I saw him get back up. Half of his stomach fell out, but I'll be damned if he didn't climb to his feet as if nothing happened."

"I thought you said he's dead."

'There is no way he could be alive," said Lee. "It's impossible."

"We should go get him."

"We can't. It's like this all over town. I saw a dozen people being attacked driving here."

"What is it?" asked Cam.

"I don't know, some kind of virus maybe. I keep seeing their eyes. I've never seen eyes so devoid of light, of humanity. It's like nothing of this Earth."

Cam thought back to the man on her hood and his dark soulless gaze. "The man who attacked me looked like that. I tried calling the station, but no one answered," she said as she gazed out of the window. She saw another scuffle on the side of the road as they drove by.

"I sent them home. Until I figure out what this is, I don't want to put them at risk. I don't know what's going on, but it looks like death has taken a fucking vacation."

Lee's phone on the dashboard started ringing. He glanced at the display. "It's Nikki. I need to take this." He held a finger to his lips to silence Cam as he picked up the phone.

"Hi, sweetheart." He paused to hear her response. Cam watched him turn a paler shade of white. "Are you hurt?" He waited for an answer. "Good. Stay in the bedroom and lock the door. I'm on my way." He hung up the call and turned to Cam.

She opened her mouth, but Lee spoke first.

"Someone showed up at the house and attacked her. I need to go home."

Cam nodded. "Fine. I'll wait in the car."

Lee shook his head. "You know you can't come. Nikki will kill me if she sees me with you. I have to drop you off. I'm sorry."

Cam's eyes widened. "WHAT?"

"I'm sorry, Cam." He pulled the car over to the curb and stopped.

"Fucking really?" Cam was incredulous as rage washed over her.

"I don't have a choice."

"The fuck you don't. You just told me people are being eaten all over town, and you're booting me to the curb? Is your bitch of a wife that fucking petty?"

"Don't make this harder than it needs to be."

"Harder? Because dumping me on the street isn't hard enough? You told me to come with you. I'm nowhere even near my fucking car now. Can you at least take me back?"

"I can't. I have to go. She needs me."

"First you tell me it isn't safe to be out here, hold a gun to me, and insist I come with you. Now you're telling me to get out and fend for myself? What the fuck is wrong with you?"

Lee fell silent. Even though he and Cam dated, nothing had happened between them since. For reasons only known to Nikki, she held a grudge. She never liked Cam and made no efforts to change the situation. Now her unfounded hatred was going to get Cam killed.

"I'm sorry, Cam."

"Not as sorry as I am."

"This isn't easy for me. I—"

"Fuck you, Lee."

He reached out to touch her arm in empathy.

"Don't you fucking touch me, you fucking asshole" she said as she slapped his hand away.

"Once she's safe, I'll come back for you," said Lee.

"Don't do me any favors. I can take care of myself."

She opened the door and climbed out. "I hope she's getting fucked as hard as you've just fucked me," she yelled as she slammed the door. "You fucking coward."

Lee turned the car around and took off, sirens blaring. He tried to gloss over the reason someone could be at their house at such a late hour, but Cam most likely guessed correctly with her crude assessment.

As the siren faded, Cam looked around to get her bearings. Fortunately, everything appeared quiet. She saw the Circle K with the broken 'I' and realized Lee had dropped her on the corner of Fourth and Miller. He had only driven nine blocks before unceremoniously dumping her on the sidewalk. Cam looked at her shoes and determined running in six-inch heels may not be the smartest option. She would break an ankle before she made it a block. She bent over and slid them off her feet.

"Fucking—" she shouted as she threw the first shoe at a large propane tank next to the gas station. The shoe flew wide. "Prick," she yelled as she lobbed the second one. It found its mark and bounced off the tank with a loud clang.

She paused for breath and smiled, for she had unearthed a bright side to her predicament. Despite being without shoes, Cam was better equipped to survive than five minutes ago. She had stolen Lee's pistol.

CHAPTER 19

Eleanor Barrett was a little bit of a bitch, and she hated technology. Depending on the time of day, her hatred of technology overshadowed her disdain for people, and she toned the bitchiness down slightly. The rest of the time, she reached a seventeen on the ten-point bitch-o-meter.

She nagged her poor husband Paul every waking moment, and on occasion, he even heard her complaining about him in her sleep. He suffered hearing damage in Vietnam when a gun fired inches from his head. The severity of his deafness weighed heavily on how much nagging occurred at that particular moment.

Sunday morning was a technology hatred day. She hated microwaves, and she hated dishwashers. She cooked her meals on a wood-burning stove and washed the dishes by hand. She despised how lazy technology made people, and she felt all the world needed to get back in order was God and a dose of good old-fashioned elbow grease. That is not to say the twenty-first century dragged her in kicking and screaming. There were a few exceptions, most notably the television. She could not live without it. Truth be told, she would trade Paul before parting with her Sony. Her entire world revolved around doing chores and watching her 'soapies', and often, she enjoyed both simultaneously. The advent of the DVR allowed her to record multiple shows and watch them at her convenience. When people called her out, she simply said she could only watch one show at a time, and the DVR did not make her lazy. It made watching her soapies easier, and she would vehemently argue with anyone with the gall to highlight her blatant hypocrisy.

Eleanor woke at the early whispers of dawn, and while she typically stirred at a respectable hour on Sunday, it was premature even for her. While most of the town was recovering from the Forefather's Day festivities or dying, she started her housework.

"Do you need anything from the store?" Paul yelled from the hallway.

She hated it when he shouted, so she ignored him and continued watching the TV by the sink.

Paul stuck his head in the kitchen. "I said do you need anything from the store?"

"I heard you the first time, dear," she said with an exaggerated smile.

"Then why didn't you answer me?"

"Because I'm not a dog, dear. Inside voices for inside people. If you want to shout, go get a dog and sleep in the kennel."

Paul rolled his eyes. "I'll take that as a no, then?"

"Just my usual spices and a scratcher."

Paul mumbled under his breath. He hated spending his pension on lottery tickets. He felt it was a waste of money as they never won anything more than a dollar or two. After a few months of scratching them off on the way home, he started handing Eleanor the old tickets and telling her they were losers. If she handed it back to him, he pretended to throw it in the trash. If she took it upon herself to dispose of it, he fished the old ticket out of the garbage when the television distracted her and slide it into his pocket.

Paul grabbed his glasses from the kitchen table and kissed Eleanor on the cheek. "Back in fifteen."

"Take your time, dear. Breakfast will be ready when you get back. Unless you're late and I fed it to the cat."

The cat in question was a fat little shit named Dew Drop. Eleanor treated the damn thing better than she did her own husband. She fed it at every opportunity, and it waddled around the house in a constant food coma, licking its lips and drooling. Its mewing became more of an agonized wail, and its stumpy little legs threatened to give out any moment. Each morning, Eleanor let it out in the front yard to wander around and get fresh air. Within ten steps, it keeled over and wheezed until she came outside and carried its twitching body back into the house.

Eleanor heard the door slam and turned her attention back to the dishes in the sink, and a stubborn piece of chicken skin fused to a baking sheet. Paul never used silver foil when he cooked and always left a huge mess to clean up the morning after. It ranked as one in a rather long list of things he did that irritated her. While she hated cleaning up the mess, she enjoyed taking a night off from cooking every once in a while. Although Paul's cooking certainly did not justify the cleanup, with her soapies on the television, she soon lost track of time. She was deeply distracted by an unrealistic relationship between a world-famous plastic surgeon and a part-time waitress when she heard a loud bang on the front door. She jumped, and the glass in her hand crashed to the floor, smashing into a hundred tiny pieces.

"For goodness sake, Paul, do you have to slam the door? I broke one of the good glasses."

Paul did not answer.

"Paul?" She carefully stepped over the broken glass and headed to the door. Another bang echoed as she passed through the living room.

"Hold on. I'm coming."

Paul most likely forgot his wallet and keys again and would be on the receiving end of a verbal dressing down due to his lack of organization. As Eleanor approached the door, she saw the familiar silhouette of Tony, her straw-hatted landscaper, through the frosted glass. He was three hours early. If he expected a tip, banging on her door acted like a sure-fire way to go home empty-handed.

She wrenched the door open ready to give him a good tongue lashing. "Now you listen here, young—"

Tony looked at her. Only it was no longer Tony. Well, it looked like Tony, but the man who usually cared for her lawn looked different. Blood covered his overalls, and he held something furry and bloody to his mouth.

"Tony, are you okay?" Then she noticed the collar and tag of the thing he chewed on. "DEW DROP?" She screamed.

Tony looked up at her with a dark demonic stare and snarled, baring his bloody teeth. He dropped what remained of Dew Drop and started towards Eleanor.

Fast for a woman of her age, she pushed him away and slammed the door in his face. She turned the lock and stepped back as she straightened her apron. "Damn hippies," she muttered.

The door shook under the overture of a heavy bang, and she screamed again. Despite the fancy window, it consisted of the typical entry-level piece of shit plywood that barely kept out roaches, let alone one hundred and eighty pounds of pissed-off, undead landscaper. Another few blows, and Tony would break through. The next impact sent splinters flying.

Eleanor ran over to the mahogany wet bar and started looking for a weapon. She looked for anything she could use to bludgeon Tony's skull. On the fourth impact, he pushed his torso through the door.

She reached up and grabbed a bottle from the wine rack.

As Tony charged in through the splintered door, she spun it in her hands to see the label. "Wait, this is the '58 Bollinger. I can't—"

She never finished the sentence. Tony reached her in an instant and tore out her throat before she hit the floor. The Bollinger fared no better.

A few minutes later, a bloodied Eleanor climbed back on her feet and stumbled outside, just in time to greet Paul, who had returned home to pick up his wallet and keys.

Greg was in a deep sleep when he heard Warren's voice crawl its way into his subconscious.

"Greg?" Warren asked again.

As Greg's eyes slowly came into focus, he saw his brother standing at the window, looking down into the street.

"Did you hear me? Something weird is going on outside," said Warren.

"What the hell are you doing in my room, man?" asked Greg as he pulled the covers up.

"Your room has a better view of the street," said Warren.

"That doesn't explain what you're doing in here."

"Come and take a look."

"Wasn't my door locked?" asked Greg.

Warren shrugged. "Yeah. What's your point?"

"I'm glad my privacy means so much to you."

"Are you going to come and see?"

"I'm not exactly dressed to be walking around the room, if you get my meaning."

"Oh, for Christ's sake." Warren looked around the floor and spied a pair of jeans. He picked them up and threw them at Greg. "Hurry, there's something really weird going on."

"Weird? Like weird, how?"

"Just come and look," Warren pleaded.

"Dude, I'm tired," protested Greg. "Can't this wait?"

"There's a thing in the street."

"A thing? What thing?"

"A zombie thing."

"What? For fuck's sake, Warren, it's—" Greg fumbled for his cell phone on the nightstand. "It's 6:27 on Sunday morning. I have a raging hangover and an even bigger boner. I did not want to wake up to your ugly mug telling me there is a fucking zombie outside."

"Get over here, man."

Greg yanked the jeans under the comforter and fumbled around for a few seconds while he pulled them up.

"Fucking zombies. How much did you drink last night?" He climbed out of bed and walked over to the window, yawning. "You sure there wasn't some happy powder in your cigare—"

On the sidewalk below, their neighbor Eleanor kneeled over what looked like her husband Paul, or rather what remained of him. Eleanor's face dripped with blood as she ripped out his intestines and shoved them in her mouth.

Greg promptly shut the curtains. "The fuck?"

"I told you I saw something weird."

"Weird? Weird would be a javelina pissing on the trash can. Maybe a lost deer. That's not weird. That's fucked up."

He opened the curtains slightly to take a second look, certain his eyes were deceiving him. Eleanor continued to chow down on her Paul buffet.

"I thought she was giving him head," said Warren.

"In their front yard?"

"Yeah."

"She's sixty."

"I've seen weirder." Warren peeked between the curtains. "What should we do?"

"Did you try calling the cops?"

"Yeah, no answer. I left a message."

"We should go and help," suggested Greg. "She's just an old lady. We can take her."

"I'm not going go out there."

"Why?"

Warren shrugged. "It's cold, and my jacket is in the car."

"No, it isn't. It's in the dining room."

"It doesn't matter. He's a little past help now anyway."

"Well, we can't leave him out there, can we?" Greg opened the curtains and saw movement across the street. "Look."

On the other side of the road, the front door of Ed and Kathy Fisher's house swung open, and Kathy ran out into the front yard screaming and clutching her neck. Mr. Fisher stumbled out after her, still in his postal worker's uniform. She saw Eleanor across the street and frantically ran over to her, waving her arms.

"Eleanor, call 9-1-1. Help me," she screamed. "Ed's gone crazy."

She reached Eleanor and skidded to a halt when she saw she was in no better condition than her husband. Kathy looked back at Ed and again to Eleanor. It would be her last move as Ed knocked her to the floor and started tearing into her.

Greg held his hand to his mouth and closed the curtains again.

Warren tried to register what he saw. "What do we do?"

"Check the news?" suggested Greg.

"Good idea."

"The remote's on the dresser." Greg headed to the closet to find a shirt.

Warren snatched up the remote, and the T.V. flickered to life. He flipped through the channels expecting to find something, anything, about the events unfolding on the front lawn. All he saw were a few overzealous morning news hosts and a handful of infomercials. "Oh, for fuck's sake. The zombie apocalypse is playing out in our yard, and this damn town isn't even important enough for a thirty-second segment."

Greg stepped out of the closet with a fresh shirt. "So, what do we do?"

"Well, I don't know about you, but I can't even begin to function without coffee," said Warren as he cycled through the stations a third time.

"We just watched our neighbor get torn to pieces, and all you can think about is coffee?"

"I'm a bitch without caffeine. Do you want me on my A-game, or do you want me cranky?"

Before Greg could respond, a loud crash of breaking glass echoed from downstairs. The brothers looked at each other nervously.

"That came from the kitchen," said Greg.

"You think it's whatever's outside?"

Greg shrugged. "Why are you asking me? I don't know."

"You should go and take a look," suggested Warren.

"Thank you for volunteering me to be the meat stick, oh chivalrous one."

Greg carefully crept out of the bedroom to the top of the stairs. Outside the bedroom door was a small loft that looked down into the kitchen and dining room. Another crash of glass echoed. "I hope he hasn't fucked with my Christmas tree," whispered Greg. "Amber spent hours decorating it."

He placed a foot onto the first step and could see the broken back-patio door and a lone figure standing in the kitchen.

"It's Mr. Kent," said Greg as he quietly started moving down the stairs. Mr. Kent faced away from Greg, but the town's attorney was easily recognizable by his mess of shaggy black hair and ill-fitting suit.

"What are you doing?" whispered Warren.

"I'm going to see if he's okay."

"He could be one of those things."

"Or he could be hiding from them," said Greg.

"Or he could be one of those things."

Greg smiled and continued creeping forward. "Let's go see."

"Greg. What the hell, man?"

"Where's your sense of adventure?"

Greg reached the bottom of the stairs, Warren still a few feet behind. "Mr. Kent, are you okay?" asked Greg.

He slowly turned around. It was the same story as before. It was Mr. Kent but was not Mr. Kent, and he possessed the usual criteria for a flesh-eating demon. Black eyes, bloody mouth, an appetite for human sushi, and he chewed intently on a severed arm.

"Oh shit," said Greg.

"Is that what I think it is?"

Greg nodded.

"He's eating an arm, Greg. Why the fuck is Mr. Kent in our kitchen eating an arm?"

Greg shrugged.

"Whose arm is it?" asked Warren.

"How would I fucking know? Why don't you ask him?"

"Mr. Kent," Warren shouted. "Where did you get the arm?"

Greg turned and punched Warren on the arm. "I was kidding, you idiot."

Mr. Kent looked up and faced the brothers, no longer interested in the appendage. He staggered towards the stairs with his arms outstretched and let the half-eaten limb fall to the floor.

"Oh, fuck," said Warren as he backed up the stairs.

"Distract him," yelled Greg as he leaped over the banister. Mr. Kent turned to follow him.

"What?" Warren could not recall a time he needed to act as a distraction to a cannibal before and was unsure of the correct protocol.

"Distract him. I'm going behind," said Greg.

Warren let out a frustrated sigh. He started banging on the wall. "Mr. Kent. Yeah, you. Over this way, you goofy looking fuck."

The plan worked as Mr. Kent turned around and moved towards Warren. "Greg. Whatever you're doing, do it faster," he pleaded.

Greg disappeared down the hallway as Mr. Kent reached the bottom of the staircase and bared his teeth.

"GREG!" Warren panicked and started backing up towards the bedroom.

Greg reappeared behind Mr. Kent, his arm raised high.

Warren's eyes widened as he saw what Greg held in his hand. "No."

The coffee pot crashed down on Mr. Kent's head, shattering the glass. Mr. Kent's skull followed in a similar manner. Blood trickled out of the wound, and he wavered slightly before collapsing to the floor.

"Boom," exclaimed Greg cheerfully as Mr. Kent hit the ground. "Bitch goes down." He grinned until he saw the scowl on Warren's face. "What?"

"Everything in the damn kitchen, and you grabbed the fucking coffee pot?"

"Sorry, man. It's the first thing I saw."

"If we die because of my lack of coffee, I'm blaming you, dude."

"Christ, Warren, we'll hit Starbucks in a few."

Warren was taken aback at the suggestion. "You want to leave?"

"You think it's any safer in here?" countered Greg. "The back door is fucked, you need coffee, and I'm out of deodorant. All in all, it's building to a shitty conclusion."

"Where's your car?" asked Warren.

"It's at Amber's. She dropped me off last night. Yours?"

Warren shrugged. "Still at Jacob's. I never picked it up."

"How did you get home last night?"

"Bob dropped me off."

"Holy shit. You let Bob drive you home?" asked Greg. "You must have been hammered."

"Yeah, thankfully, I blocked out those thirty minutes of my life."

In addition to being a less-than-stellar mechanic, Bob was also legally blind. Yet somehow, he slipped between the cracks and still maintained a valid driver's license. People gave him a wide berth when they saw him on the streets, and it became common practice to allow him a thirty-minute head start when leaving Jacob's.

"I want to see how big this thing is," said Greg. "There's nothing on the news, so it can't be too bad."

"When has the news ever been right?" asked Warren.

"Good point."

"You're calm considering what we just saw," said Warren, wringing his hands nervously.

"I don't think there is any need for us to panic yet. We don't know how bad it is. Maybe it's only on our street."

◆ ◆ ◆ ◆

David deeply regretted partaking in his fairground food binge. His sensitive stomach kept him in the bathroom for most of the previous ten hours, unable to settle on sitting on the toilet or shoving his head in the bowl. Aside from the constant flow of gin he poured down his throat, he stuck to a healthy diet and mostly ate organic foods, so all the alien preservatives and deep-fried batter hit him hard.

A little before 6:00 a.m. Sunday morning, his head once again hovered over the toilet bowl when he heard his alarm clock chirping in the bedroom. Convinced his desire to barfing had dissipated, he grabbed a towel and wiped his face. He stepped into the bedroom and hit the off button as he flopped down on the bed. A long run of throwing-up played havoc on his throat, but his stomach had finally settled down to a manageable level. His cell phone buzzed on the nightstand to remind him of the day's appointments. His first patient was due in four hours, so he could still find time to sleep, at least for a little while. He found it hard to feign interest at the best of times. To do so with barely ninety minutes of sleep seemed impossible, so he lay back down on the bed and closed his eyes. Some days he regretted opening his office on Sundays.

Barely twenty minutes passed when the doorbell rang. Within thirty seconds, it had screeched fifteen more times. Floating in the early stages of a deep sleep, David took a moment to get his bearings. Meanwhile, the doorbell continued to scream frantically.

"For fuck's sake," he cursed under his breath. "I'm coming." He hated it when patients showed up at his house unannounced. Even though each one of them signed an agreement explicitly promising to schedule an appointment, without fail, at least once a month, someone showed up at his front door on the verge of suicide due to one issue or another. They were well aware if they mentioned the S-word, they left David no choice but to let them in. He swung his legs out of bed and stormed off down the hallway as the doorbell continued to ring.

"Doctor Hewett. Please, for the love of God, let me in," a voice shouted as the doorbell chimed again.

"I'M COMING. AND STOP RINGING MY FUCKING DOORBELL."

He recognized Nick's voice. Nick frequently arrived early for his appointments, but David did not remember him being on his schedule for the day.

"Please, it's an emergency. You have to let me in," the voice pleaded.

"It always is," David thought to himself as he walked down the stairs. Nick needed to come back during normal business hours, as David would be useless in his current condition.

"I'm going to die if you leave me out here."

And there it was. Nick planned to off himself on David's doorstep. He had successfully reached a new low just as David reached his breaking point. A loud thump echoed against the door and confirmed his suspicions.

He grabbed the handle and ripped it open. "Listen, you little shit. I—"

It took a second for his brain to register what his eyes were seeing. Nick's death had not been a suicide. He lay sprawled out on the floor and Kathy Fisher, or at least who David thought looked like Kathy Fisher, gorged on Nick's lower intestines.

"Sorry," said David weakly as he closed the door.

A few seconds later, another loud bang rang out, and he jumped back.

"What the fuck?" he yelled again.

He slowly opened the door. Kathy looked up at him with a snarl, pieces of Nick stuck to her chin. She slowly rose to her feet and moved towards the door. Before he could slam it, her full weight crashed against it, and both tumbled into the entryway. David landed hard on his back, knocking the air from his lungs. Kathy twisted as she fell. She hit the tile, and her forearm snapped with a sickening crunch. David caught his breath and climbed to his feet. He backed away as she started to stir. Kathy rolled onto her stomach and pushed herself upright. The broken ulna pushed against the skin, and a sliver of bone pierced through, ripping the flesh open.

David held up his hands. "Oh, Christ. Kathy, you're hurt. We need to get you to a hospital."

She climbed to her feet and moved towards David. He could now see her eyes, the usual blue replaced with the now-standard demon black.

Yet, she could still see David and continued moving closer to him. David backed further away, trying to put distance between them.

"Kathy, you need help." He held up his hands and took another step back.

She bared her teeth and growled.

David turned and picked up a vase off the table by the kitchen door. "I'm warning you. Back off, or I will use force."

She emitted an ear-piercing yell and charged. This time David was the faster of the two and swung the vase. It connected with the side of her head and shattered against her skull. Blood sprayed the wall, and she collapsed.

David ran to the kitchen and grabbed his phone from the counter. He dialed 9-1-1 and promptly received a chorus of repeated beeps.

He hung up and dialed again. The busy line beeped its response as he dropped the call and looked down at Kathy. His mind ran a mile a minute. There was a dead body on his front doorstep and one in his hallway. It looked bad from every angle. Was Arizona a stand your ground state? Could he claim self-defense against a woman barely five feet tall? He watched enough crime shows on TV to know to make sure any dead bodies on his property should be dragged inside to help support the self-defense claim.

He opened the front door to retrieve Nick, only to find him already standing. Nick turned as the door opened, his guts in a bloody pile at his feet. He stepped on the intestinal rope as he moved towards David and lurched forward. He fell into the door frame and split his forehead open. David promptly slammed the door shut before Nick could come inside.

He picked up his cell phone again but hesitated before dialing. Who could he call? A friend? He visualized the conversation. '*Oh, hey, it's David. I'm doing good. I have two dead bodies in my house and a lot of blood on my hands, both figuratively and literally, you?*'.

David's mind raced as he put the phone back down on the counter, clueless as to what to do next. He looked around to see if anything jumped out as a solution. Then it hit him. He walked into the dining room, grabbed a glass and a bottle of St. George's Terroir from the bar. He needed gin. Lots and lots of gin.

CHAPTER 20

Cam's parting words echoed as Lee pulled up in front of his house. There were no other cars outside, so whoever came over to see Nikki either walked over or she picked them up herself. Any time Lee harbored any suspicions about Nikki and her students, he dismissed them as a byproduct of an overactive mind of a police officer. His job required him to look for evidence of a crime, and with the right theories and circumstantial evidence, anyone could seem like a criminal. He obviously still loved her as he drove halfway across town with his siren blaring breaking countless traffic laws. He saw more disturbances in the four-mile drive, but he kept his foot all the way to the floor. All that mattered was he made it home.

He switched off the siren a block away and quietly pulled up in front of the house. He had no idea if he was being stealthy to avoid disturbing other creatures in the area or if he simply wanted to catch Nikki red-handed. He climbed out and looked at the house. It sat in darkness except for a single light coming from the master bedroom window. The significance was not lost on him. However, he could see no movement inside and tried to focus on the issue at hand. He reached down to the console to grab his pistol, but his hand grasped air.

"Goddammit, Cam," he cursed as he realized his gun had a new owner now.

His heart thumped in his throat. Lee was no stranger to stressful situations, but none were ever on his front doorstep before. He pulled the keys out of the ignition, grabbed the shotgun from between the seats, and took off across the yard. He stopped at the front door and leaned against it, listening for any kind of movement. Hearing nothing, he turned the handle and pushed. The door didn't move. Lee quietly slid the house key into the lock and pushed the door open. The house seemed silent. He flipped on his flashlight and swept it across the room. Seeing nothing out of place, he headed towards the staircase. Each step creaked under his weight as he slowly ascended. At the top, he turned left to the master bedroom and tried the handle. Locked.

"Nikki?" he whispered against the door. He felt his cell phone buzzing in his pocket and fished it out. "Nikki?"

"*I'm in the bathroom,*" her voice said through the phone.

"Are you okay?"

"*No. Someone came to the house and attacked me. I'm scared.*"

"I'm here now. Can you unlock the door?"

"*No, he's in the bedroom. I'm trapped.*"

He? Bedroom? Lee could feel pangs of anger clawing through his body. Nikki's story screamed bullshit. If the attack had been random, the front door would not have been locked. As much as he wanted to write off his suspicions as hyperactive police paranoia, the evidence was damning.

"Who is it?"

Nikki stayed quiet.

"Who is it, Nik?"

"*Kyle.*"

Lee recognized the name as a student of hers. The typical clichéd blonde, blue-eyed, tall, and muscular captain of the high school football team. Nikki tutored him a few times in the past, and like a fool, Lee believed her that it was purely vocational.

"Is he hurt?" asked Lee.

"*He has a nasty cut on his arm.*"

"I'm going to come in, but I need you to help me. When I hang up the phone, I want you to start banging on the door to get his attention."

"*Okay, please don't hurt him. He's just a kid.*"

"I'm hanging up now." Lee dropped the call, and instantly, he heard Nikki banging and yelling. He waited a few seconds and kicked the door open.

On the far side of the room, Kyle pounded against the bathroom door, wearing nothing but a sneer.

"Hey, shithead," said Lee.

Black-eyed Kyle turned to face him. Lee could see pink lipstick marks covering his neck, torso, and penis. He screamed and came at Lee. Lee raised the butt of his shotgun and swung it at Kyle's face. The boy hit the floor instantly.

"You can come out now," Lee said, barely able to hide the anger boiling in his stomach.

The bathroom door slowly opened, and Nikki timidly stepped out wearing a towel and a shade of smudged lipstick suspiciously similar to that on Kyle's cock.

Lee opened his mouth to speak but thought better of it. There was nothing left to say. He turned away to leave, having seen enough.

"Lee, I'm sorry. He came over and said he'd been attacked on the street. I didn't know what to do."

Lee stopped and sighed. "How about you run this story by me one more time, but this time you rethink the part where you confuse me with a clueless fuckwit?"

"Honey, I don't think you're a—"

"Shut your fucking mouth. You want to tell me why he doesn't have any fucking clothes on, Nik? Or why your lipstick is the same color as his dick?" Lee continued before Nikki could respond. "Forget it. I don't even want to fucking know."

"This isn't the time to be talking about his. He attacked me, Lee. I'm the victim here."

"No, it's the perfect time to be discussing this. I've turned a blind eye to you since day one. I see the looks you get when we're out. I see the pity looks I get. Everyone knows but me."

"Lee, I'm sorry."

"So am I. I left a good person on the side of the road to come home and get you, and I quite possibly got her killed. Her blood is on your hands now, Nik."

"Who?"

"It's not important." He paused. "Fuck it, you know what, it is. I gave Cam a ride."

"That fucking bitch." Nikki transitioned from victim to predator in an instant as Lee hit his breaking point.

"No, you don't. You don't get to do this. When you called me, I unceremoniously dumped her ass out like a good little puppy dog and came trotting home to you. You see what's going on in this room? These creatures? It's all over the town. It's fucking everywhere. The dead are coming back to life."

Nikki ignored the Armageddon comment and remained focused on

Cam. "The bitch got what she deserved. What, were you getting a bit of road-head before coming home?"

Lee stabbed a finger at her. "Fuck you, Nik. Don't you dare try and push this on me. Unlike some people in this room, I can keep my dick in pants."

"But you were just happening to be giving an ex-girlfriend a ride." She emphasized ride with condescending finger quotes.

"I found her at the station when I arrived. I gave her a ride and then shoved her out to fend for herself when you called me to come running."

"Always trying to get into your pants until the bitter end."

"She isn't the one banging a high school student under her husband's nose. I've been suspicious for a while, but like a fool, I decided to assume it was the result of a cop's imagination. All day, I deal with liars and cheats, and I didn't want to accept my wife was no different."

"It isn't like that."

"No, what is it like then?"

Nikki opened her mouth to answer.

"How long has this been going on?"

Before she could answer, a loud bang echoed from the closet, and the doors flew open. Two more naked and bloody teenage boys with bright pink dicks charged out at Lee. He dispatched both with rapid blows to the head.

"Fuck," he said. "How many more are in here?"

Nikki's eyes quickly darted to the bed. Lee stepped around to the other side, and sure enough, he saw a fourth lying on the floor in a puddle of blood with an equally suspicious colored penis.

"What the fuck, Nik?" said Lee.

She wrung her hands nervously. "Some of the boys came over for a study group."

Lee snorted in disgust. He had arrested felons who told better lies than his wife.

"Kyle complained about a scratch he got from a homeless guy on the way here."

Lee held up his hands. "I don't want to hear it. I'm done." He stopped and clenched his teeth. "I have one question. Is it even mine?"

Nikki looked down at her stomach. She placed her hands on the first-trimester child and shook her head ever so slightly.

Lee turned away in disgust. "Fucking figures."

He turned to leave as Kyle and the other two boy creatures started to stir.

"Where are you going?" Nikki's voice dripped with fear and panic. "You can't go."

"They're all yours."

"What? You can't leave me here. I'll die if you go."

"Yeah, I'm hearing that a lot tonight. I'm going to see if I can go and fix my first fuck up."

Kyle climbed to his feet as Lee headed to the door, Nikki a step behind him. Lee stopped before leaving and turned. He put his hand on Nikki's chest and pushed her back into the room.

"What about the baby?" she pleaded as she fell backward.

"It's not my baby."

"Lee!" she screamed as he slammed the door shut. "Don't do this to me, Lee!"

Nikki banged hard on the other side as Lee jammed his nightstick underneath the door handle and against the frame. The door shook as she frantically pulled the handle.

"Lee," she yelled again. "HELP ME!"

He reached the bottom of the stairs when he heard a piercing scream. His eyes welled up as the front door closed behind him, and he headed toward his cruiser. As he reached the driver's door, he saw the 'To Protect and Serve' slogan emblazoned on the side and with a scream of anger, he kicked the door, leaving a large dent in the panel. He climbed in and put his head in his hands.

"Fuck. Fuck. Fuck. FUCK." Each curse emphasized with a bang on the steering wheel.

He reached into his pocket and pulled out his phone. He thumbed through the contacts and dialed Chris. No one answered, especially no one called Chris, but Cam's prerecorded voice quickly spoke. "Hi, you've reached Cam. You know what to do." Beep.

"Cam, it's me. I'm so fucking sorry. I'm coming for you. If you get this, call me, and let me know you're okay."

Lee hung up the phone. He changed her contact name to Chris after Nikki's jealous streak came to the surface. He hated going behind her back, but he was honest when he said he never cheated. Cam only came to mind when Nikki started one of her tirades. She thought about Cam far more than he did. Most of the town was on his phone's contact list, but it meant little to Nikki. She convinced herself he was cheating, and he could do little to change her mind.

At Seventh Avenue, he turned right and floored it.

♦ ♦ ♦ ♦

The zombie outbreak spread across Oceanview like the proverbial wildfire. As the sun peeked over the horizon, many of the townsfolk set about their daily routine, oblivious to the events unraveling around them.

Judy Deacon noticed a few of the creatures stumbling around as she set out her plastic chairs on the sidewalk out front of her coffee shop. She assumed it was residual drunks from the Forefather's Day event, and while she certainly disapproved of such debauchery, she avoided passing judgment. She knew God would sort the heathens out in time.

As she brought the second from last chair outside, she wondered what could have distracted David. He should be the one putting the chairs out. If he thought he deserved free coffee, he was gravely mistaken. She placed the chair on the sidewalk, and as she turned to head back inside for the last one, she saw the paperboy coming down the street towards her.

"Good morning, Sam," she said as she stepped back inside. A closer inspection of her paperboy would have revealed something quite wrong with him. Of course, there were the usual fucked up eyes, but his top lip was gone and exposed his teeth in a maniacal grin. By the time Judy came back outside, it was too late.

She backed out of the front door, struggling with the chair. "Be a dear and grab this for me," she said in the same sickly niceness she used to sucker David every morning.

Sam launched at her before she could drop the chair. They both fell forward as he latched onto her neck. The chair slid forward, and they both toppled over into the entryway of the shop. Judy tried to push the boy away from her to no avail.

"Sam, what is wrong with you? Get off me."

She clawed at the ground to get away and dragged her nails over the concrete. Her right hand caught the door frame, snapping the middle fingernail back. She cried out in pain, and in the second of distraction, Sam leaped onto her back. He bit down on her neck and ripped off a large chunk of bloody flesh. With her remaining strength, Judy rolled and pushed Sam to the ground. She slowly climbed to her feet and almost made it to her store when a second creature rounded the corner and joined in the assault. Minutes later, Judy joined their ranks.

The story repeated for Carl, the church groundskeeper, also for

Morgan, the garbage man, and pretty much anyone else up before dawn. By the time the rest of the town awoke, the outbreak was in full swing. Pastitsio Boulevard collapsed into chaos, and an accident involving two cars at the intersection of Moreland Avenue and Fifteenth Street blocked the only way out of town. One by one, the line of cars started to grow as people fled to the intersection to make a break for it. Horns honked, and people cursed, yet no one displayed the common sense to get out and push the disabled vehicles out of the way. As the impatient drivers sat honking, the undead pulled them out kicking and screaming and devoured them in the street like a manic roadside buffet.

CHAPTER 21

"Is it clear?" Warren tried to peek over Greg's shoulder as he looked out of the front door.

Greg pushed him back. "If you get off me, I'll look." He poked his head outside. "All clear. Well, except for Mr. and Mrs. Barrett wandering around."

"What do you mean Mr. *and* Mrs. Barrett? I thought Mr. Barrett was dead."

"Take a look for yourself."

Greg swung the door open. Sure enough, both Mr. and Mrs. Barrett were standing on their front lawn and looking the worse for wear.

"Oh, shit," Warren said, a little louder than he anticipated.

Greg smacked him on the head. "Quiet, you dumb-ass. They'll hear us."

He carefully pushed the door closed as Mrs. Barrett started heading in their direction.

"What do we do?" Warren whispered.

"We should make a run for it. There's a few, but we can outrun them."

"The fuck we can. I ain't going out there."

"Where are your balls, man?" asked Greg.

"They took a leave of absence when Mr. Barrett got the shit torn out of him on our doorstep. I'll be damned if I'm letting his wife park her fat fucking face around my arm."

Greg turned to face him. "This place isn't safe."

"The hell it isn't. It'll do until we can figure out a plan."

"One of those things could break in here at any minute." Greg closed the door. "Grab the La-Z-Boy. We'll use it as a barricade while we come up with a plan."

Warren dragged the brown recliner to the front door and wedged it under the handle. "There, that should hold them."

In response, a loud bang rang out from the other side of the door, and the La-Z-Boy slowly tipped over on its side. Greg turned to Warren and held his hands up, his mouth wide open in dismay.

Warren shrugged. "What?"

"You can't even jam a door shut? You're going to get me killed the second we step outside, aren't you?"

"Probably," said Warren with a grin.

"That's not funny," said Greg as the door splintered under another heavy thud. "That's our cue."

"We're leaving now?"

Greg nodded. "Head out back. If the alleyway is clear, we'll hop the fence." He took off into the kitchen. "Grab your jacket. It's cold out."

"What if we run into one of those things? We need to defend ourselves."

Greg stopped at the dining room table and tipped over one of the accompanying chairs. He kicked at the chair and a leg snapped. Moments later, he removed a second. "Here," he said, offering Warren a leg. "Better now?"

"Now I'm somewhere between peachy and fucking keen. How the fuck do you think I'm doing? The only fucking thing fucking standing in between me and getting my fucking throat ripped out is a fucking chair leg. I'm fucking spiffy."

Greg continued to the back door. Warren hesitated a moment, and another bang against the door spurred him into action.

"Wait for me," he shouted after his brother.

Greg peeked over the top of the back fence as Warren stepped outside.

"That way's clear," said Greg as he pointed to the right side of the alley that stretched along the back of eight neighboring houses.

"What's to the left?"

"About a dozen or so of those things, but even bloodier."

"Right it is then." Warren climbed over the fence and dropped down on the other side.

The brothers started walking away from the pack of creatures.

Warren glanced back at the bloodied group. "What do you think this is?"

"No idea," said Greg.

"It's probably Russian."

"Why the hell do you think it's Russian?"

"Isn't everything?"

"Not since the eighties."

"Could be those GMO's I've read about."

"You've read about GMO's?"

"Yes, Greg, I do read sometimes."

"Okay, Einstein, what does GMO stand for?"

"Gigantic mutated object."

"You are a fucking idiot."

Warren shrugged. "Al Quesa?"

Greg sighed in defeat. "Quesa?"

"I still think they're zombies."

"Don't be ridiculous. Zombies aren't real, Warren. They're biologically impossible. Everyone knows dead tissue can't reanimate."

"The dead have come back to life, and they're eating people. It's your classic zombie."

"Look at their eyes, Warren. Zombies in the movies don't have black eyes like that. I'd say they are demons."

"Wait, so zombies aren't real, but demons are? How does that work?"

"You read the Bible, you know what demons are. Let's face it, neither one of us knows what this is. We can stand here spouting fucktarded theories, or we can keep moving and get somewhere safe."

"Fine, we keep moving." Warren stopped walking. "Wait, did you call me fucktarded?"

Greg grinned as he continued to walk. "If the fucktarded shoe fits."

The brothers jogged another hundred feet when a group of zombie-demon creatures appeared at the other end of the alley blocking their exit.

"Shit," Greg muttered. "Quick, over the fence."

Before Warren could respond, Greg cleared the wall and landed on the other side. As Warren dropped down beside him, Greg held a finger up to his lips, prompting him to be quiet.

The groaning became louder as the creatures moved down the alley toward them. The noise attracted the other group, and within minutes, over a dozen were milling around behind the fence, trying to find where their lunch had disappeared to.

"What do we do?" whispered Warren. "We couldn't have gone more than four houses."

"No!" said Greg. "That puts us at—"

"Boys," a shrill elderly female voice rang out.

Greg's head fell limp. "Mrs. Andrews' house."

"Great fucking plan, Einstein," said Warren.

"Oh, boys?" she called out again.

Warren stood up and mounted the fence. "Fuck it. I'm taking my chances with the zombie things."

Greg grabbed him by the back of his shirt and pulled him back down off the wall. "Oh, no you don't. You're not leaving me alone with her."

"Then come with me. We can't stay here."

The glass patio door slid open, and Mrs. Andrews stepped out. "Boys, over here."

"Shh, they'll hear you," Greg half-whispered, half-yelled.

"Boys?" she shouted again.

The groaning behind the fence increased in volume, and Greg cringed.

"Come around to the front. I'll open the door."

Warren looked at Greg, gauging his reaction.

"We don't have much choice now. Our escape route is blocked. It beats sitting out here in the open," said Greg.

"The fuck it does."

"Well, until you can come up with a better one, this is our plan."

"I could shit a better plan than this."

"Well, relax that sphincter and get cracking, genius. I don't want to be here any longer than you do."

Greg and Warren realized their mistake in taking shelter with Mrs. Andrews when she told them to take their shoes off before stepping into the house.

"Uh, uh," she said as she blocked the doorway with her arm. "Shoes off first. Don't forget your manners, boys."

Greg's jaw dropped as he looked at Warren.

Mrs. Andrews sensed their disapproval. "I just cleaned my carpets. The end of the world is no reason to track mud across them."

"But, our shoes aren't—" He never finished the sentence. A loud groan across the street rushed their decision.

Thankfully, the creature focused its attention elsewhere.

"Good morning, Esther," shouted Mrs. Andrews to the creature.

Undead Esther turned and started to cross the road. The boys frantically untied their shoes and kicked them off.

"Uh, uh. In a straight line, please," ordered Mrs. Andrews.

Greg groaned and bent down to straighten the shoes.

"Can we come in now?" The level of urgency in his voice increased.

"Can we come in now, what?" asked Mrs. Andrews.

"Huh?" said Greg, his eyes darting back to the creature shuffling across the street.

"Can we come in now, what?" she repeated .

Greg rolled his eyes. "Can we come in now, please?"

"Of course," she said and opened the door fully.

Undead Esther stumbled into the yard as Greg and Warren piled into the house.

"Please, take a seat," said Mrs. Andrews, gesturing to the living room.

Warren started to sit down on a recliner.

"No, not that one." Mrs. Andrews held her hands up in a panic. "That's Harry's chair, bless his soul."

Warren stopped mid-sit, his butt dangerously close to tarnishing the seat. "I'm sorry for your loss. Did the zombie-demons get him?"

"Zombie-demons?"

"The creatures outside, we're calling them zombie-demons."

"He is calling them zombie-demons," added Greg. "I think it's ridiculous. They're just demons."

"No, of course they didn't get him," said Mrs. Andrews while completely ignoring Greg.

Greg tried to look concerned. "When did he die?" he asked, not really caring at all.

"He didn't."

"Okay," said Greg, slightly confused.

"He left me fifteen years ago for a twenty-something floozy he met at the office."

"Oh, well, I'm still sorry," said Greg, unsure which words of comfort to offer.

"Don't be. I hope the cheating bastard burns in a pit of fire and that Lucifer doesn't swallow."

Greg threw Warren an uncomfortable *'get me the fuck out of here'* look.

"So, what are you boys doing up so early?"

"Trying to survive," said Warren.

"Yes, the traffic can be awful this time of day."

"I didn't mean the traffic."

"I know, dear."

Warren frowned in confusion. "You do realize we were just attacked and almost eaten alive out there, right?"

"Oh, don't be such a negative Nellie, Master Warren. Esther wouldn't hurt a fly. I see no need to be blowing this out of proportion. The lord doesn't look well upon people who exaggerate in his presence."

"Yeah, well, the lord really threw us in the shit," said Greg.

"Master Greg, you will keep a civil tongue in your head while you are in my house, do you understand me?"

Greg nodded. If he opened his mouth again, he would likely say something he would regret.

"Maybe I should put the kettle on, and we can sit down with a nice cup of tea and wait for this to blow over. Master Greg, would you like a cup?"

"No thanks, I'll pass."

"Master Warren?"

Warren raised his eyebrows in confusion. "No, I don't want a fucking cup of tea. The whole world's gone to shit, and you want to break out the good fucking china?"

Mrs. Andrews' hand moved a lot faster than it should for a woman of her age as she slapped Warren across the face. Warren rubbed his throbbing jaw as she stepped away.

"Master Warren, just because the end of the world is here, it does not excuse you from being a gentleman, and you do not qualify for the good china."

Warren turned to Greg. "She hit me," he whined to his brother.

"Quit your bitching," Greg muttered. Two seconds later, he found himself rubbing his own jaw.

"That goes for you too, Master Greg."

"What did you do that for? Bitch isn't a bad w—"

Mrs. Andrews slapped him again. "Are we done?"

Greg nodded as he held his stinging jaw.

"Okay then, I'll be in the kitchen getting us tea." She turned and left the room, leaving the brothers alone.

"Do you like scones?" she said from the serving window separating the two rooms.

Neither answered.

"I'll bring some out anyway."

"Do you like scones?" mimicked Greg.

Warren laughed at his brother's impression of the old lady.

Greg stood up from his chair. "I don't know about you, but I'd rather take my chances out there than be locked up with his crazy bitch. I want somewhere where I can keep my shoes on."

"And curse," added Warren.

"Fucking right."

By the time Mrs. Andrews returned from the kitchen with her tray, the brothers were gone.

"Fucking idiots," she muttered under her breath.

Instead of jumping the back fence, Greg and Warren decided to hop over the neighbor's adjoining wall and cut through their yard. The moaning in the alleyway increased while they were inside, and Greg wanted to put as much distance between them as possible.

The first two yards were quiet. In the Mitchell's backyard, their waterfall ran into the pool and masked their clumsiness as they tried to climb over the fence.

The fourth yard presented a different story.

Greg landed softly on the grass, and before he could stand, he heard a deep rumbling growl. "Shit! Bain."

Greg scrambled back up the wall as Bain, a one-hundred and twenty-pound pit bull, came around the corner. It bared its teeth and sprinted at Greg, barking and foaming at the mouth. Warren reached the top as Greg launched himself back over and slammed into him. They crashed down on the other side and landed hard on the concrete pool deck.

"I think I broke my spleen," groaned Warren as he lay on the ground clutching his chest. The dog continued to bark and claw at the other side of the wall.

Greg rolled onto his back. "Do you even know where your spleen is?"

"Yeah, it's where I'm hurting now."

Greg struggled to find sufficient breath in his lungs to argue.

After a few moments of wheezing and catching his breath, Warren finally spoke. "So, what do we do now?"

Greg slowly stood up. "There's flesh-eating fuck-knows-what that side. We've got Satan's hound this side, and a crazy old bitch over there," he said as he pointed to each direction for emphasis. "I'm all out of ideas."

"We need to get to a car and get out of here," said Warren. "Mine is closer."

"That is the smartest thing you've said all day," said Greg. "Car keys?"

Warren patted down his pockets. "Shit."

Greg fished out his own keys. "Okay, so we go get my car then. It's an extra two miles. Are you up for the exercise?"

"No," replied Warren.

"Good. I want to pick up Amber anyway."

"Do you think she'll come with us?"

"I hope so."

"What about Ashley?" asked Warren.

Greg forgot about the two of them separating. "Is it going to be a problem?"

"I don't know. She did dump me, in case you forgot. I hardly think fighting my way across town to save her is on the top of my to-do list."

"You really expect to fight your way across town? You can't even make your way through a crowd at the mall without hyperventilating."

"My survival instincts are going to kick in. In times of fear and danger, people are capable of superhuman feats."

"Is this before or after your coffee?"

"Probably after. We should also get guns," Warren added.

"Have you ever even fired a gun before?"

"No, but I'm a quick learner."

"A quick learner picks up tennis or golf, not how to shoot things."

"You point the end with the hole in it at the thing you want to kill. Simple."

"Warren, you can't even use a wrench without dropping it. Guns are a bad idea."

"How do you propose we defend ourselves? We left our chair legs at Mrs. Andrews' house."

"We'll find some garden tools or sports equipment or something. I'll get you a large stick."

"I can't fight these things off with a pointy stick. I want a gun."

"I said nothing about the stick being pointy."

"Now you're being an asshole."

Greg grinned. He enjoyed getting under his brother's skin.

"I won't shoot myself."

"I'm not worried about you shooting yourself. I'm worried about you shooting me. I see me climbing over a fence and you shooting me in the ass because I'm moving too slow."

Warren laughed. "Yeah, I probably would do that."

"That isn't helping your case."

"Yeah, I know, but we do need to protect ourselves, though. These things are killing people."

"I'll think about hitting TK's Guns after we get Amber."

Loud groans from the other side of the fence spurred them into action.

"Time to go," said Greg. "After we get onto the street, stay close to me. We're better off hitting the back streets as much as possible."

"What if there's more of those things?"

"Then we start jumping fences again. On three."

CHAPTER 22

Nancy sighed as her phone rang for the seventh time in less than fifteen minutes. She let out another sigh as she picked it up, knowing full well the question God wanted answering.

"*I heard that,*" said God through the handset.

"I'm sorry, what?"

"*You sighed.*"

"I didn't s—"

"*Has he called yet?*" asked God yet again.

"No, sir, he has not."

"*Call me when he does.*"

"I know. Call you when Death calls. You've said that already. Many, many times." Nancy hung up the phone and turned back to her computer

Immediately, the phone rang again. "*And stop sighing,*" said God

She hung up the phone one more time and turned back to the email she struggled to finish. Her shoulders slumped as the phone rang once more.

"*Has he called yet?*"

"Yes, he just called. He's on hold. I'll transfer him over."

"*Really?*"

"No, he hasn't called. And you calling me every thirty seconds is not going to speed this up.

"*Nancy?*"

"Yes?"

"*Don't be sassy.*"

Nancy sighed again. Death needed to hurry up and confirm whether he skipped a reaping. She understood the fate of the Universe was at stake and Death's action could have devastating consequences, but her patience had worn thin.

◆ ◆ ◆ ◆

"Send me a priest, Foz," said Kit-Kat into his headset. "I'm dying here." He was nine hours deep into a mission on World of Warcraft, and fatigue had taken its toll.

His five cyber teammates were also tired and snippy.

"That's a negative, LM," a male voice replied over the speaker. "I'm a little tied up right now." Fozzie acted as the group's resident healer and struggled with more urgent matters on his hands. "Ask Willis. I'm low on hit points. Another hit and I'm dead."

"Willis is a fucking druid," said Kit-Kat. "He can't do shit. His lame-ass needs to respec."

Laughter bounced around the chat room.

"Fuck you, guys," protested Willis.

"Fozzie, I have about twenty points left until you'll be needing a new tank," said Kit-Kat into his headset.

"Christ," Krigo, a third male voice, added. "Desimia is still freaking AFK."

"Didn't I tell you she'd do this mid-instance? That damned kid of hers probably needs feeding again," griped Fozzie.

"That damned kid is six weeks old," said Kit-Kat in the absent Desimia's defense. "Give the girl a break, Foz. You knew this could happen when you logged on,"

"Well, she shouldn't have come. She's going to fuck everything up."

"It's just a game, Foz," added Kit-Kat. "Always a person behind the keyboard."

Fozzie muttered under his breath about the abundance of amateurs.

Krigo started to get irritated at the lack of order. "Can someone heal him? If LM dies, we may as well pack this shit in and go to bed."

"Well, if Wing Nut hadn't Leeroy Jenkinsed the damn dungeon, we wouldn't be in this cluster fuck," said Kit-Kat.

Kit-Kat's headset erupted with bursts of agreement as they called Wing Nut every derogatory name under the sun. He smiled as he picked up a can of Mountain Dew from a large cluster on his desk and shook it to check for contents. After three attempts, he found a half-full one and downed the rest.

"Guys," Kit-Kat said as his character fought off another winged demon on his computer screen. "I really need help here." His patience finally diminished, and the Mountain Dew ceased working.

Fozzie finally made it over and healed Kit-Kat's character, saving the group from immediate death.

"Thanks, Foz."

"Sorry guys," said a female voice. "The little one got hungry."

"Welcome back, Des," said Kit-Kat.

"Did I miss anything?"

"Foz almost fucked the instance, and Willis is still a lame-ass druid."

"Fuck you," said Foz. "It was Wing Nut."

"Willis needs to respec," added Desimia to laughter from the group.

Minutes later, the cyber squad cleaned the room of digital demons, and they paused for breath. Kit-Kat had been awake since escaping the dwarf toss at the Forefather's event. His video game clan started playing a particularly challenging instance in the game that lasted well into the early hours of Sunday morning. What he lacked in social skills, he more than compensated with his talent in online roleplaying games. As the owner of one of the strongest characters on his server, his name was known across the kingdom. Well, rather his Lady's Man 69 pseudonym was.

"Okay, we cut that a little too close," Kit-Kat said into his microphone. "Wing Nut, the next time you get the urge to be a fucking idiot and charge into a room, do us all a favor and fucking log off. From now on, until you've earned your name back, I'm calling you Fuck Nut."

The rest of the group laughed as Kit-Kat stood up and stretched, clueless to the events unraveling mere feet from his front door and that his entire world would change in less than a minute.

"Guys, can we camp here for a few hours? I'm wiped. I need sleep."

A loud bang echoed from his front door, muffled their response.

"Let me in," a female voice screamed out.

"Hold on, someone is outside," he said into his headset as he walked over and looked through the peephole. The cute college co-ed from the apartment below stood outside the door. "Guys, I've gotta go. The hot chick who moved in downstairs just showed up."

"You really are delirious, man," said Fozzie. "Go to bed."

"Funny, douche," said Kit-Kat as he took off his headset and threw it down on the couch.

The knocking came again.

"I'm coming," he shouted. Kit-Kat opened the door, and the young woman threw herself at him.

"Thank you so much," she panted heavily as she pushed the door closed behind her. "I'm so scared."

Kit-Kat seemed more than a little confused. He never considered himself a hit with the ladies, and this sudden attention sent up a dozen red flags. No woman had ever literally thrown herself at him. Let alone someone as hot as the gorgeous brunette dream queen with the perkiest boobs he ever laid eyes on currently wrapped around his neck.

He wriggled out of the stranglehold and put a little distance between them. "What's going on? What do you want?"

"There's this—" she panted, still trying to catch her breath. "This strange man banging at the kitchen window."

"What did he want?" asked Kit-Kat.

"He didn't say. He looked messed up."

"Messed up how?"

"He had blood all over his cloths. I went outside to check on him, and he bit me." She rolled up her sleeve to reveal a bloodied bite mark on her forearm

"Holy shit," muttered Kit-Kat. The wound looked bad. The edges of the bite were angry and red, and the veins surrounding it were swollen. "We need to get that cleaned up. I have peroxide in the bathroom."

She followed him down the hall and waited as he disappeared into the bathroom.

A moment later, he appeared with peroxide, bandages, and a towel. "Let's go in the kitchen, and we'll sort you out."

They walked back to the kitchen and stopped at the sink. Kit-Kat turned on the water, and she carefully rinsed the blood off.

"Do you live here alone?" she asked.

"Yeah."

"I love your decorations," she said as she nodded towards the various mounted animals on the living room wall.

"It's a hobby, well, a job, really," said Kit-Kat as he turned off the faucet and patted the skin dry around the wound. The bite looked mostly superficial but still needed attention. "You should probably go see a doctor. People's mouths aren't the cleanest of places." He grabbed the bottle of peroxide. "This might sting a bit."

She flinched as he poured the liquid on the wound. The peroxide bubbled aggressively as it contacted the infected skin. "I'm Rachel, by the way."

Keith nodded politely. "Keith, but everyone calls me Kit-Kat."

"Pleased to meet you, Kit-Kat. Sorry it isn't under better circumstances. I've been meaning to stop by and introduce myself."

"It's already infected," Kit-Kat said as he reached for the bandage. He noticed sweat beading on her forehead. "Did you try calling the police?"

"I just got a busy signal."

"Let me try. Maybe a line freed up," said Kit-Kat as he finished wrapping her arm and picked up his phone. He dialed 9-1-1 and instantly heard a busy tone.

"Still busy?"

Kit-Kat nodded as he hung up the phone. He walked over to the back window in his living room and parted the curtains. On the grass below, a man in ripped jeans and a white T-shirt stumbled around with what looked like wet dirt covering his face and shirt.

"Is that him?"

Rachel stepped over to the window and looked down at the group. "No."

"No?" Kit-Kat expected a different answer. "There's someone else?"

The words barely passed his lips when a second bloodied man stepped into view. "Is that him?"

Rachel shook her head.

"What did he look like?"

"Brown khakis and a blue shirt. It looked like Mort from the front office."

"I'm going down there."

She grabbed him by the arm. "Be careful."

Kit-Kat paused and smiled at her. "I'll be fine." Were he a character in a video game, his bravery level would have just increased two points.

Kit-Kat descended two flights of stairs and headed to the parking lot below. He walked around the back of the building and saw three men standing around Rachel's window. The man with the blue shirt stood among them.

"Hey, guys. What's going on? You're kinda freaking out my friend. Could you—" He let the sentence hang.

The man in the blue shirt turned around, holding a severed leg.

"What the fuck?" Kit-Kat said to himself.

Then he saw the body on the snowy ground behind the man. From the gray overalls, Kit-Kat assumed it to be Pat, the apartment complex's landscaper. There were no other identifiable features. His intestines were spread across the grass, and most of his face was missing. Kit-Kat held his hand up to his mouth and quietly took a step back, remarkably calm considering the carnage before him. He reached the corner when his cell phone rang. The other two creatures slowly turned to face Kit-Kat and instantly came at him. Kit-Kat spun and sprinted back to the stairs. He raced up the steps and slammed his apartment door behind them.

"We need the police, bad," said Kit-Kat as he leaned back against the door, slightly out of breath. A loud bang echoed from behind, and he jumped away from the door. "Rachel?"

He looked around the living room, but she was gone. A clatter came from the kitchen, and he cautiously stepped forward to investigate.

Rachel stood with her back towards him, her shoulders slumped.

"We need the police," he said again. "Your friends down there are in bad shape. They fucking killed our landscaper. I'd guess they're on meth or something. Really fucked up shit." He paused as he caught himself. "Sorry for cursing."

The woman remained silent.

"Hey, are you okay?"

Kit-Kat took a step as she slowly turned around. Her eyes were black, and her jaw hung low. She uttered a deep guttural growl and moved towards him, picking up speed with each step.

"Shit," he muttered as he stepped backward.

Kit-Kat headed towards the bathroom and slammed the door in zombie-Rachel's face, but she stopped it before the latch could take. She pushed the door open and overpowered Kit-Kat. He stumbled backward and landed in the bathtub, pulling the shower curtain and rod down on top of him. In a flurry of arms and legs, he scrambled to free himself as she charged in. Kit-Kat frantically kicked at her chest as she tried to grab hold of him, the shower curtain the only barrier stopping her from biting down on his face.

One of his lashing feet caught her under the jaw, and she stumbled back. The move allowed Kit-Kat to untangle himself and stand up. He slid the remainder of the curtain off the rod and held the metal pole in front of him.

"Stay back," he ordered.

Rachel stood up and advanced on Kit-Kat again as he pushed the pole against her chest to try to keep her out of reach.

She pressed her stomach against the pole, and Kit-Kat stepped back. He abruptly stopped as the rear end of the pole hit the shower wall.

Rachel continued to push against the pole.

Suddenly, she started slowly moving forward again. Kit-Kat looked down and saw a circle of blood spreading across her abdomen as she impaled herself on the curtain rod.

"Fuck me," said Kit-Kat as he put all his weight behind the pole, and she moved another foot closer to him. With one last burst of energy, he pushed her out of the bathroom.

The added effort pushed the pole completely through her torso and punctured her back as she lost balance and fell. Kit-Kat stepped over her lashing arms and headed for the front door.

"Fuck," he yelled again as he ran outside and slammed the door. He stopped at the top of the stairs. The entrance to his neighbor's apartment was open, and the creatures previously banging on his door were inside, tearing the tenants apart. As Kit-Kat leaped down the stairs, a piercing scream came from behind. He paused, tempted to run back. Instead, he pulled his keys from his pocket and ran towards his car. The alarm chirped as he ripped the door open and jumped inside.

"Fuck," he screamed again as he started the engine and his bravery points receded back to lower than their previous level.

CHAPTER 23

Greg and Warren arrived at Amber's parent's house with little trouble. They mostly kept to back alleys and side streets and only encountered two creatures and were easily able to avoid them. The desire or need to kill them on sight had not yet materialized.

The McKenzie's lived in the more upscale area of town and faced a large park surrounded by a red brick wall. The closed gates kept the monsters out, and the brothers crossed the snow-covered grass with ease. They stopped at the wall, and Greg peeked over to look for the car. "It's still there."

"Well, that's a good start. Is it clear?" asked Warren.

"Looks like it."

The brothers climbed over the wall and dropped down onto the flowers on the other side.

Warren followed Greg over to the car. "Why did you park at her parent's house anyway?"

"I didn't. She borrowed the car. She's keeping Ashley company. Don't worry, their parents are out of town."

"Good. I was beginning to think you started liking hanging out with her folks."

"Hell no. I'm just happy they aren't home. It should make this a lot easier."

While the parents liked Greg slightly more than Warren, that could not be considered high praise.

Warren stopped at the car, but Greg kept walking. "Where are you going?"

"To get Amber. I won't leave without her." Greg stopped at the door and rang the doorbell and waited. He rang it again as Warren trotted over to him.

"No one home?" asked Warren.

"Doesn't look like it. Maybe they left."

A small window to the side of the door slowly opened, and a shotgun barrel slid out.

"Get off my porch, or I'll shoot you," said a deep male voice from inside the house.

In a panic, Greg raised his hands. "Whoa, whoa, whoa. Mr. McKenzie, don't shoot. It's Greg and Warren."

"I know."

"We're not one of those things."

"I know."

"We haven't been bitten."

"I know."

Warren looked at Greg, slightly confused. "Wait. Did he—"

"Yep," said Greg.

"And he's still going to—"

"Yep."

The shotgun cocked back with a loud *cha-chic*.

"RUN," screamed Greg.

The wooden pillar where Greg's head had been moments before exploded in a shower of splinters.

The shotgun cocked a second time.

Warren looked relieved. "He missed."

"No, he didn't," yelled Greg. "I fucking ducked."

Greg grabbed Warren by the arm and dragged him off the yard. Another shot rang out, and the ornate garden urn by their feet turned to dust.

The brothers kept running until they were behind Greg's car and out of the line of sight.

A third and fourth boom shattered the silent street as the brothers caught their breath.

"What in the ever-loving fuck? gasped Greg between heavy breaths. "My girlfriend's dad just tried to kill me. Who does that?"

"That's going to put a damper on the wedding plans," Warren said with a grin.

"They weren't supposed to be home." Greg reached up for the handle and quietly opened the car door. "Get in the back."

"Where are we going?"

"Out of range."

Both quietly climbed into the car. Greg put the key in the ignition and started the engine.

The car pulled away, but no other shots followed. Greg looked up at the rear-view mirror to see if Mr. McKenzie pursued them. The street appeared empty, and Greg finally exhaled, confident they were out of danger.

"You're bleeding," said Warren.

"Huh?"

"Your neck. Looks like he nicked you."

Greg put his hand up to his neck and felt around. Sure enough, his fingers came away with blood on them. "I didn't even feel it."

"Sorry about Amber, bro," said Warren.

"Thanks."

"At least her dad didn't kill us."

Greg laughed. "Yeah, I suppose there is that. Though it wasn't through lack of trying."

"So, what do we do now?"

"We need to find somewhere with weapons and food and ride this thing out."

"Jacobs?" suggested Warren.

"I said a good plan."

"Why? What's wrong with Jacob's?"

"Well, for one, it's probably closed," said Greg.

"Yeah, but I could use a drink. Hair of the dog and all that shit. I know how to use a tap. I've watched Hank do it a thousand times."

"Didn't you want coffee?"

"Oh yeah. Starbucks?"

"For the coffee or to hole up?" asked Greg.

"Either?"

"I'm not hiding out in Starbucks."

"Walmart?"

"The closest Walmart is forty-five miles away."

"How about an abandoned farmhouse or castle?"

"Well, if you know where there is a castle, I'm in."

Warren thought about it for a moment.

"Do you have any ideas you haven't seen in a movie? Are you even taking this seriously?" asked Greg.

"Okay, so what is your plan, Mr. I-know-how-to-survive-the-god-damn-zombie-demon-apocalypse-because-I-went-to-a-hoidy-toidy-university-and-I-know-every-fucking-thing?"

"Are you done?"

"Yep."

"A, I never learned about the zombie apocalypse in university. I went to community college, and it wasn't on the curriculum."

Warren rolled his eyes.

"B, we don't know that this is actually the zombie apocalypse."

"Zombie-demon apocalypse, Greg."

"We don't even know what this is, and three, we still need a plan."

Warren opened his mouth to speak.

"One which doesn't involve calling me a stuck-up twat."

Warren closed his mouth.

Suddenly, the engine sputtered and died as the car coasted to a stop.

"What the—" Greg looked at the flashing gaslight. The tank was empty.

"No gas?" said Warren.

Greg shook his head. "Nope."

"Good going, dipshit. The end of the world rolls around, and you can't even remember to put gas in the car. Are you sure it's going to be me who gets us killed?"

"I filled her up two days ago."

"You sure about that?"

"Of course I'm—" he stopped mid-sentence and sniffed. He pushed the door open and leaned under the car to see a large puddle of gas trailing off behind them.

"Fuck," he said.

"What's wrong?" asked Warren.

"Charlton-fucking-Heston must have hit the gas tank."

The brothers climbed out of the car to survey the damage.

"Shouldn't it have exploded?" asked Warren.

Greg shrugged. "No idea. But now we need a new plan."

"Jacob's?" Warren suggested again.

"Stop with the Jacob's thing. It's a bad idea."

"It's close, has snacks and there's a Glock in Hank's office. You said we need guns and food. Jacob's has guns and food."

"Pork rinds and peanuts aren't food. And for the last time, I'm not comfortable with you having a gun."

"Well, it has one thing we don't," said Warren.

"What?"

"My car."

Greg sighed. "You don't have your keys, remember?"

"Yeah, I do," said Warren as he pulled them out of his pocket.

"You said you didn't have them."

"I didn't feel like driving."

Greg stared at his brother, unsure if he wanted to walk away or punch him in the face.

Warren nodded to the road behind Greg. "We should get moving. We're drawing attention."

Greg turned to see a group of zombie-demons shuffling in their direction. "Time to go."

They climbed back over the wall and took off across the park towards Jacob's.

◆ ◆ ◆ ◆

David set down his half-empty glass on the kitchen counter and looked at the carnage in his living room. The body count had doubled in less than an hour, and four bloodied bodies were piled in the middle of the floor.

Shortly after dragging Nick into the house, he heard more commotion outside the door. Through the peephole, David saw Edna and Scott Wallace from two houses down standing on his porch. He opened the door, and they charged in, blood and sinew covering their faces. David quickly dispatched the two assailants and added them to the pile. He desperately needed a cop.

He picked up his phone from the kitchen counter and called 9-1-1 for the seventh time. Finally, he reached the station's voicemail.

"Hi, it's David Hewett," he said after the beep. "I may have a bit of a situation. I have a dead body in my house. Actually, I have four dead bodies in my house. All piled up on my living room floor. I didn't kill them. Well, actually, I did, but I'm pretty sure they were already dead. I haven't been drinking. Well, I have, but this isn't because of that. I—" he paused. "Just send someone over. I can explain this better in person."

"Well, I'd lock me up if I heard that," he said to himself as he hung up the phone. David picked up his glass and looked at the pile of bodies for the hundredth time. He felt reality slowly slipping away. There were no violent bones in his body. He never so much as run over a duck, let alone kill someone. The fact he had killed four someone's seemed impossible, but there he stood, staring at a tangled mass of arms and legs. He let the thought hang as distant sirens announced the police were already on their way. David swallowed nervously. They were not wasting any time. He took a deep breath and opened the front door. It made no sense for them to kick it in. He wanted to make this as peaceful as possible. Well, as peaceful as he could, considering he had massacred four people in his living room.

David stepped outside with his hands raised and stared at the flashing red and blue lights at the end of the street. He sucked in a deep breath and took a few steps away from the house. The siren became louder as he laid face first on the snow-covered grass, his arms spread to show he was unarmed. The cold ground took his breath away as his heart pounded in the back of his throat. In a few short moments, he would be kneeled on, cuffed, rolled over, read his Miranda rights, and unceremoniously stuffed in the back of a police car.

His breath grew heavy as the siren's volume increased. What would his neighbors say? Mild-mannered shrink one minute, killer the next. Was he a serial killer or a mass murderer? He was unsure of what constituted serial and what was mass. He killed them one after another, so technically, that was a serial killing, but the large pile of bodies in the living room screamed mass murder. Which one gave the death penalty? '*Oh shit*', he thought to himself. '*I'm going to get the fucking chair*'. His eyes started to tear. He saw his name plastered all over the media and his mom finding out her son had been fried for being a murderer on Fox News. David hated Fox News.

He took another deep breath and surrendered himself to the inevitable. The siren grew louder and louder as the blood pumped in his ears.

"Oh God, oh God, oh God," he said as he screwed his eyes up tight. The cop car reached the end of his yard.

David waited for the imminent '*freeze mother fucker, don't fucking move, or I'll blow your fucking brains out*', but it never came.

The cruiser flashed by, and the siren faded away.

David opened his eyes. "What the hell?" he said as he lifted his head. Slowly, he pushed himself up to his knees. Wherever the cop headed, he seemed to be in a hurry, but he did not want to stop for David. What could be more important than a man who just killed four of his neighbors? More imperative than apprehending the Oceanview Butcher? He realized how ridiculous he looked and glanced around to see if anyone saw him, but the street remained quiet. His block housed just two active busybodies, and one resided at the bottom of the pile in his living room. After taking a few seconds to compose himself, David stood up and brushed the snow off his clothes. He let out a long, heavy breath and headed back inside.

♦ ♦ ♦ ♦

Lee's eyes stayed focused on the road as he barreled past David's house. His mind could only think about getting back to Cam. He prayed he could undo his mistake and reach her before she came to any harm. Cam was nine blocks from her car. Hopefully, she made it back and found safety. He struggled to keep his mind on the destination as Nikki's screams echoed loudly in his mind. A few desperate civilians tried to flag him down, but he ignored their pleas and kept driving.

At Hatcher and Fourth, he drove past a particularly nasty scene as a man feasted on a woman in the display window of TLC Flowers. Blood sprayed across the window as he ripped into her jugular. Lee let off the accelerator slightly, his instinct to help kicking in, but he quickly regained speed. The woman could not be saved, and every minute he stopped to help someone was another minute he left Cam alone.

Lee finally spotted the Circle K with the broken 'I' and pulled into the parking lot. He grabbed his shotgun and climbed out.

"Cam," he shouted. "It's Lee. Where are you? I'm really sorry." He realized how ridiculous the words sounded. He may as well have said, '*I'm sorry for choosing my whoring wife over you and kicking you to the curb when the town has been overrun by flesh-eating monsters*'. Somehow, he doubted Hallmark made a card for such an occasion.

The gas station seemed quiet as Lee looked across the courtyard, desperate to see any signs of escape or struggle. As he headed back to his car, he saw something sparkle by the propane tank and stepped over for a closer look. One of Cam's shoes lay on the ground. Lee heard a low moan and moved around the side of the tank. A woman with long blonde hair sat with her back against the metal, looking away from Lee. A large pool of blood collected on the concrete next to her, and his pistol lay at her feet.

"Cam?" he said as he squatted down in front of her. "Oh, Christ. I'm so sorry."

Lee reached in and moved the hair from her face to find the other shoe buried heel first into her left eye. Blood covered the front of her shirt. She growled and slowly looked up at him. The face did not belong to Cam.

"Thank God." Lee stepped back as the woman climbed to her feet. He raised his shotgun. "I'm giving you one warning to back down, or I will drop you."

She growled and lunged. Lee fired, and her stomach exploded. The force sent her backward, and she hit the ground hard. He picked up his pistol and slid it into his holster. His stomach knotted as he headed back to his car. One, possibly two women died on his watch. As he reached his car, he heard a growl and a wet slap. He turned and saw the woman standing up, her intestines in a pool at her feet. Lee aimed at her head and fired. She did not get up a second time.

CHAPTER 24

Judging by the trail of chaos left in his wake as he hightailed it out of town, going down with the ship was a term unfamiliar to Mayor Beck.

When Oceanview started to crumble, he had been shacked up at the Off-Ramp Motel with his secretary, Eve. Naturally, the town planners allowed the motel to be built ten miles from the nearest off-ramp. It was located in the seedier area of town, surrounded by a strip club and half a dozen run-down warehouses. Eve wished Beck splurged a little more, but he explained the cheaper motels were necessary to hide their affair, as no one expected a mayor to be holed up in a discount daily-rate shithole.

The room acted as his home away from home with Eve for eight toe-curling months. They tried to be discreet, but he was terrible at keeping his mouth shut. Everyone in town hall knew about their fling, but they were also smart enough to keep quiet if they wanted to stay employed. Even his wife Melody knew better than to question him. Unless she was okay with the Lexus and seven-bedroom house vanishing. If she were to be completely honest, he repulsed her, and the less she needed to touch him, the better. To say she felt grateful for his bit on the side was a stretch, but she enjoyed someone else being pawed.

Suite 9b, with its bedroom, kitchenette, and living room all rolled into one, was far from the level of comfort to which he was accustomed, but all he cared about lay underneath the sheets. He had no intentions of leaving Melody. While a dead fish in bed, she looked stunning for her age and a good trophy wife to be seen on his arm at social and press events. Eve understood where she ranked and suffered no false pretenses that the situation may change.

Things started going downhill for Eve when Beck recently told her he no longer wanted to wear a condom as the experience felt better without it. Although a blonde, she taught herself to be smarter than that. The last thing she wanted was to get pregnant by the man, and kids with anyone were at the bottom on her to-do list. Even if life ever did change, she could not bring a love child into the world. She took birth control, but still wanted to avoid the risk. He already stiffed her on agreed payments, so stalking the guy for child support did not sound appealing. She found it hard enough to look Melody in the eyes when they met at the office. Getting pregnant seemed awful all around.

She had tired of the deal. When she first started seeing Beck, he spoiled her with gifts, made payments on her car and mortgage, and generally made life more comfortable for her. After a few months, the rewards stopped. Then he skipped a payment or two. If Beck stopped lavishing her with gifts, then why stick around? She felt no attraction to him. Hell, she faked every orgasm since they first met. She laid on her back, moaned and thrust her hips a couple of times a week, and it was over. A good payday while it lasted, now she lay spread-eagle on the bed so he could have his way with her for free. Eve never felt like a whore when he paid her, but without the rewards, she was just a cute twenty-something getting pounded by a fat old guy for nothing. She found herself in a bind. If she ended the relationship, her job may be in jeopardy, a job she could ill afford to lose. So, where she once screwed for comfort, she now screwed for survival, but even that motivation neared its end of shelf life. The time had finally arrived to break the arrangement off, consequences be damned.

Beck had been fucking her like a rabid bunny for over an hour and showed no signs of stopping. Eve lay on her back in the usual position, but her mind wandered elsewhere. Anything to make the time go faster.

After her first pseudo-orgasm, she tapped Beck on the shoulder. "Billy, we need to talk."

"I'm almost done," he rasped in her ear.

Almost done. Beck made it sound like cleaning the garage. Eve sighed and squeaked an obligatory moan of faux ecstasy. Beads of sweat fell from his brow onto her chest, doing little to help with her repulsion of the man.

Suddenly, a loud bang echoed at the door, and Beck lost his momentum. He continued thrusting into Eve for a few more seconds before another thud rang out.

"Who the hell is it?" he screamed into Eve's face, spraying her with spit. "You're fucking up my rhythm."

No one answered, but the door shook again.

"Quit banging on the fucking door. I'm coming. Actually, I'm not cumming. That's the problem," he mumbled to himself.

Beck climbed off Eve and grabbed a sheet from the floor. He wrapped it around his portly waist as he walked to the door.

Eve sighed, relieved to be free from the crushing weight on her chest. A sigh far more real than the ones she used in the throes of passion.

"Who is it, Billy?" Eve pulled the comforter over her naked chest as she watched Beck lean into the peephole, convinced Melody had discovered their secret love nest.

"I can't see." He jumped back as another loud bang crashed against the door. "But I can tell you they are pissing me off." He stepped over to the kitchen table and grabbed Clara out of his bag. Beck took his damn golden scissors everywhere.

"Is that necessary?" asked Eve as she sat up in concern. He held his forefinger up to his lips to silence her. Frustrated at the disrespect, she flopped back down on the bed as her mind wandered again.

Beck grabbed the door handle, ready to give the visitor a verbal dressing down. "Somebody better be dying," he said as he twisted the knob.

As the door started to open, the uninvited guest smashed into it again. The door flew open into Beck's face, and both he and the intruder fell to the floor in a tangle of limbs and sheets.

Eve screamed as the man looked up at her. Blood dripped down his chin, and Clara protruded from his stomach. He snarled as more blood drizzled onto Beck's naked body. Beck shifted his weight, dumped the creature to the floor, and pulled out the scissors. The man snapped upright and scrambled onto the bed, no longer interested in Beck. Eve yanked the comforter over her head as she continued to exercise her lungs.

Faster than most believed possible of a man of his size, Beck leaped to his feet and pulled the sheet up around him. "I'm sorry, Eve, I can't— I just don't— I— I'm sorry."

Eve screamed out in pain as the man bit into her left forearm and jerked his head away, tearing skin and tissue from the bone. Beck ignored her screams as he swiped his keys off the table and fled.

"Bill, you fucking—" Eve screeched.

It was the last thing Beck heard as he dashed out of the door. Eve met her bloody end moments later. After thirty seconds of silence, she reanimated and shambled out into the world as naked as the day she was born.

Beck waddled his fat ass down the stairs as fast as possible. One hand struggled to keep the sheet up while the other grasped his scissors and keys. Halfway down the stairs, he stepped on the edge of the fabric, and it swiftly unraveled itself, leaving him butt-naked. He left the sheet behind as he continued to the bottom of the stairs and ran over to his SUV parked a dozen spaces away. Beck fumbled with the remote to unlock the doors, and the alarm politely chirped.

A woman peered out of the window of room 7a, her jaw slack as she stared at the large naked man trying to get into his vehicle. "Good morning, Mayor," she shouted through the glass, unaware of the chaos unfolding upstairs. "Is everything okay?"

Beck did not bother to respond. He pulled the door open and hauled his naked ass into the driver's seat and started the engine.

As he put the truck into gear, he glanced out of the windshield, and for the first time, saw the carnage spreading across Oceanview. Large plumes of smoke drifted in the distance. A woman sprinted past the front entrance screaming and disappeared behind a row of bushes lining the street. Moments later, two bloody black-eyed men shuffled after her. A few spaces down, Beck noticed a car with the driver's door open. A person leaned over the front seat, gorging on the hapless driver.

"What the fuck?" said Beck, as he slammed the door shut.

As the vehicle pulled away, movement in his rear-view mirror caught his attention. Eve, naked and covered in blood, stumbled out of the room onto the balcony and headed towards the stairs. Beck pushed the accelerator to the floor and peeled out of the parking lot.

He felt the impact of the motorcycle before he saw it.

The bike plowed into the passenger side of his vehicle, sending the rider flying over the hood. Beck hit the brakes, and the SUV skidded to a halt. Frantic, he looked out of his window and reached for the door handle. The rider rolled to a stop at the end of a twenty-foot-long bloody skid mark. Beck paused, but the body remained still. He pulled his hand away from the door, threw the truck back into gear, and finished his turn.

The motorcycle was the first of two details he missed as he tore out into the street. Death stood by the motel's front sign as Beck decimated the motorcyclist and floored it.

Death had stopped by over a dozen times in as many hours to see how the skipped reaping affected the population of Oceanview. He was not there to reap Bill or Eve, or even the bloody skid mark on the tarmac as none were on either of his lists. He simply wanted to see how the situation was unfolding. None of the bodies he encountered were on his lists. There was no way they could be. Every one of their deaths was a direct result of a skipped reaping. The process was broken. All established rules were off the table, and the longer the system stayed broken, the higher the body count became. Death expected God and his team to be scrambling to fix the mess, so he wanted to enjoy it while it lasted.

Death smiled as he watched the chaos unfurling around him. He wished Lucifer could see it. He reached down and grabbed his pocket watch from inside his robe. As much as he wanted to sit back and watch the body count rise in Oceanview, he needed to get back to work. He returned the watch and promptly disappeared.

◆ ◆ ◆ ◆

Beck floored the accelerator as he barreled down Miller Avenue. The closer he traveled to the town center, the worse the scenes of carnage became.

At Eighteenth Street, he saw a woman being pursued by a gang of bloodied townsfolk. She made it another ten feet before they pulled her to the ground and tore her to pieces.

At Fifteenth Street, he saw a man sprawled on the sidewalk with a group of children tearing at his abdomen.

As Beck reached Thirteenth Street, he started to block the images out of his head.

At Twelfth Street, a body lay face down in the street. It still moved, but Beck could not tell if it was human or one of the maniacs. It was, in fact, human, but Beck kept the accelerator down, and his giant wheels crushed the man's head like a melon. All regard to traffic laws and others around him went out of the window. Beck had no direction. He simply wanted to get as far away from the motel as he could.

At the Eighth Street light, he narrowly missed a truck pulling into the intersection, and on Seventh Street, he grazed the side of a car that had stalled at the traffic light in front of him.

By the time he reached the stop-signless intersection at Jefferson and Miller, his luck had run out.

Beck fumbled in the glove box for his backup phone and swerved dangerously between lanes. He never saw the beat-up Ford Escort pull out in front of him. Beck sat up as he plowed into the side of the car. The impact killed the driver on contact, and the mayor fared no better. In his haste to leave, he neglected to put on his seat belt, and the ramifications were immediate. He launched out of his seat and through the windshield.

There were two things Beck did not know before his face and the tarmac became one. He had no idea, Mr. Wilson, the husband of Clara's namesake, drove the other car, and in less than five years, Beck killed both Mr. and Mrs. Wilson. The second was all three of them died at the same stop-signless intersection. The irony was wasted. Still, at least his scissors were unscathed.

♦ ♦ ♦ ♦

Cam waited until she heard Lee climb back in his car and pull away before she moved. He might have found her if he had bothered to perform a more thorough search of the area and looked over the wall behind the propane tank. She crouched behind a bush and bit down hard on her lip as she trembled. She heard him yell, but let her emotional side take over and threw all logic to the wind. She knew staying with Lee seemed the smartest choice, but she fumed over the way he abandoned her. While she most certainly needed his help, she refused to accept it. Her stubbornness did little to alleviate a possible untimely demise, but she would figure it out on her own.

She already struggled to subdue the woman on the other side of the wall, and had more creatures joined, she would have been overpowered. Lee barely pulled away the first time when the woman stumbled around the corner and came at her. Cam aimed the pistol and fired, but nothing happened. Gun operation was foreign to her, and she overlooked turning off the safety.

In the ensuing panic, the woman reached her and knocked the weapon from her hands. Cam lost her balance and fell to the ground. The woman landed on Cam's legs and clawed at her face, snapping her teeth as she moved. Frantic, Cam reached around for something, anything to use as a weapon. She grabbed one of her shoes and swung at the woman's head. The heel made impact with her eye, and Cam felt a sickening pop as the mushy organ gave way and the shoe slid deep into the socket. The heel stopped an inch short of damaging the brain, but penetrated enough to shift her weight so Cam could throw her off and escape over the wall. She stayed hidden in the bushes, shoeless and unsure of her next move.

When she heard Lee leave for the second time, she stood up and peeked over the wall. The woman he shot lay in a bloody mess on the ground. Cam climbed back over and did her best to avoid looking at the remains as she removed the woman's left sneaker. She held it against her foot to compare sizes. It was three sizes too big, but preferable to running around barefoot. She carefully removed the other sneaker and put them on her own feet. She already started to feel a little better. While she did not know how to fire a gun, she did know how to run. As she laced up the shoes, she saw a movement out of the corner of her eye.

The woman, or rather what remained of her, climbed back on her feet.

"Fuck me," Cam whispered to herself as the woman turned to face her. Her shoulders carried no head, her chest no heart, and most of her intestines were on the sidewalk. Cam tried to process what she saw. How could she kill something that could function without a heart or brain? As winning the Nobel Peace Prize was not on Cam's to-do list anytime soon, so she saw no point in hanging around to figure it out. She ran past the mangled woman and left the parking lot.

CHAPTER 25

The few citizens of Oceanview fortunate to have successfully dispatched one of the blood-thirsty demons by destroying the brain, either intentionally or purely by accident, thought they were getting the upper hand, albeit a bloody one. They were oh, so wrong. While destroying the brain stopped more traditional zombies dead in their tracks, it didn't work on demons. Celebrations turned back to terror as within an hour, and in some cases, mere minutes, the creatures were getting back up and picking up where their bloody rampage left off. Across town, the dead which came back to life and subsequently died, were once again coming back to life. It took less than an hour for the town of Oceanview to realize it was completely and utterly fucked.

◆ ◆ ◆ ◆

With the police paying little interest in David's living room massacre, he retreated into his house to rethink his next move. Staying inside with a pile of bodies felt unappealing, but little else came to mind, and his gin buzz had worn off. He expected to spend the night in a cell, so to be home gave him a sense of appreciation not felt since he first received the keys.

David closed the door and leaned back against it. He rubbed his face and sighed heavily. His heart raced a hundred miles an hour, and he could feel it beating its way out of his chest. Nothing made sense anymore. The dead were coming back to life, and the police cared little that he killed them.

"Get it together, Dave," he said to himself as he pushed off the door and headed to the kitchen.

His half-full glass of gin sat on the counter where he left it. He picked it up and took a sip. The long-melted ice watered down the taste of juniper berries, but it helped his nerves. As he put the glass down, he noticed his hands were shaking, unsure if he had dodged a bullet or if something far more serious was going on. Although he could not fathom anything more dangerous than a man with four dead bodies in his living room. This was not exactly the norm for Oceanview. The most drama the town saw was minor fender benders in the grocery store parking lot, or a drunken Jacob's patron singing too loudly in the early hours of the morning. Clara's fatal car accident easily ranked as the worst incident in the town since he moved there. He stepped over to the sink and parted the curtains. Nothing in the street seemed out of place. If anything, it appeared quieter than usual.

David grabbed the remote from the counter and flipped on the television. The channels displayed the usual fluff, and the few that broadcast locally either showed reruns of Jerry Springer and Maury, or car title loan commercials. There were no reports of anything strange in his sleepy little town. It came as no surprise as little in Oceanview ever made the news. The closest it ever came to fame occurred when Air Force One flew Jimmy Carter over the town in 1977 while heading to Phoenix.

The remaining channels were the typical bunch of national tripe. Different reruns of Jerry Springer or Maury and news stories about people being ripped off by car title loans. He turned it off and tossed the remote back on the counter. David considered himself a practical man and figured there must be a logical explanation, but for the life of him could not figure it out.

Most of the morning passed as a blur. His phone buzzed on the counter and notified him of three missed appointments.

"Shit." He picked it up and looked at the calendar.

It would cost him dearly. He rarely missed appointments, but the few times he did, the patients never let him forget. It went down the same way each time. *'You ruined my weekend because I wasn't able to talk about my mommy issues'* or his favorite, *'I contemplated suicide because you weren't there to talk me out of it'*. He closed the calendar notifications and navigated to his voicemail. There were no messages. There were no *'this is a life-threatening emergency'* calls, nothing.

He found it impossible to believe none of his patients called to complain, especially Peter, his first appointment of the day. Peter frequently started leaving voicemails if David did not open the door precisely one minute before the start of his appointment. His OCD allowed for nothing less.

David started to get concerned. He opened his contact list and searched for Peter's phone number. Peter's phone never rang more than twice. On the sixth ring, he figured something was wrong and canceled the call before leaving a message. He looked back at the dining room window and saw two more bloodied people standing at his back door. He had no intentions of making the death tally six, so he grabbed his keys and his jacket and headed to the garage.

He opened the door and reached for the remote switch on the wall. The garage door slowly started to rise, and he could see three pairs of feet standing on the other side. He jumped in his SUV and started the engine.

When the door finished opening, the rest of the creatures on the other side were revealed. As with the pile in his living room, they were covered in blood and ready for their next meal. He hit the accelerator and plowed through them. All three fell under the front of the vehicle. He bounced in his seat as the truck drove over the bodies, and he inadvertently added numbers five through seven to his kill list. Unbeknownst to David, he ascended to Oceanview's number one zombie-demon killer at that point in time. Although he only held the record for seven minutes as the pile of bodies in his living room started to stir and reduced his total to three.

David pulled into the street and floored it. He picked up his phone and called Cam, uncertain she would even answer.

"*David?*" panted an out-of-breath voice on the other end.

"Cam?" he said, surprised she picked up.

"*What the hell is going on?*"

"I don't know. You've seen this too?"

"*Hell yeah, I have. I've been dropped balls-deep in the middle of it.*" Cam always did cut to the chase.

"Where are you?"

"*I just got back to the police station. Fucking Lee dumped me in the middle of nowhere and took off.*"

"Nikki?"

"*That obvious, huh?*"

"Educated guess. Do you need me to come and get you?"

"*Nah, I'm nearly at my car. It's fucked out here. I'm trying to figure out my next move.*"

"Yeah, I'm doing the same."

"*What are they, David?*"

"I'm not sure. They look like us. But—" He trailed off, unsure how to finish the sentence.

"*But they sure as hell ain't us.*" Cam finished it for him. "*Have you seen what these things can do?*"

"Yeah. I got a little too close." David turned onto Miller and saw the sign for Interstate 17. "I'm thinking about heading to Phoenix. I have friends down there. You're welcome to join me if I do. We can hang there until this blows over."

"*Do you think it's going on down there?*"

David paused. The possibility never crossed his mind. "Then I guess we're totally fucked."

◆ ◆ ◆ ◆

Bar-owner Hank had unsuccessfully tried to watch '*The Golden Girls*' for the better part of two hours and finally lost his patience. He asked for little out of life, but he insisted on watching his shows in peace. He turned his phone off, and those close to him avoided ringing his doorbell during television time.

Hank's interruptions were not related to unwanted guests showing up unannounced and everything to do with the television. Every thirty seconds, the picture disappeared, and turned to static. Five seconds later, the image returned to give another short sampling of the show before the static interfered again. He had seen the rerun of the episode over a dozen times, but it did not make the disruption any less irritating.

He stole his cable television from his neighbor, and his bootleg line ran undetected beneath the gravel driveway between the two houses. Anytime his neighbor's tacky hipster electric car pulled up or he walked to the mailbox, the image temporarily cut out. The disruptions were brief and only occurred a few times a day, thus a small price to pay for free television.

Although the sun perched high in the sky, Hank always kept the curtains drawn and the lights on. An aggressively private person, he hated the idea of strangers peeking in at him. He climbed out of his recliner and hobbled over to the window. He parted the curtains to get a better view of the driveway, and sure enough, he spied Marty French, his pompous British neighbor standing on the cable, rocking back and forth.

Hank tapped on the window to draw the man's attention, but Marty stood still and paid him no mind. Frustrated, he pulled the curtains closed and headed to the front door. Not bothering to put on pants or a shirt, he stepped outside in his tighty-whities and ketchup-stained under-shirt. Hardly a presentation of class or social decorum. Marty continued to face the street with his back to him, so Hank coughed to try and get his attention.

"Hey, Marty—" he said as he trudged through the snow. His voice trailed off as he realized he could not ask his neighbor to stop standing on his stolen cable. A different approach to the disruption was required. "Are you okay, son? I saw you standing out here while taking out the trash," he lied.

The fallacy was irrelevant. The Marty who turned around cared little about trash or stolen cable. It also did not resemble the same Marty that Hank had lived next door to for over five years. This Marty possessed black glossy eyes and a more gaunt than usual look to his face, as well as a large streak of blood down his shirt.

"Are you okay? You look pretty messed up." Blood had never been an issue for Hank. He had been around enough bar fights in his day and stepped forward to help the younger man.

Marty made eye contact. Without pausing, he bared his teeth and came at Hank. Hank turned and sprinted back to his house.

Hank slammed the door closed and turned the deadbolts. He waited with bated breath for a loud bang, but none came. While he could move fast when it counted, he found himself out of breath much faster than in his youth. He crossed over to the window and slowly parted the curtains again but saw no sign of Marty. Hank assumed him to be a victim of a rough night of partying. God knows Jacob's played host to plenty of customers having one too many at the bar. Even though he cut off those he deemed to be over the limit, he could not control it when others supplied the drinks behind his back.

He turned to close the curtains when a hand smashed through the glass and grabbed him by the shirt. Marty pulled hard on Hank's clothing. It usually took a lot more to bring Hank down, but the combination of being mid-step and Marty's weight were enough to shift his balance, and gravity did the rest. Hank fell sideways. His head slammed into the top of the window and smashed the pane. Marty continued to pull, and Hank toppled onto the broken glass. A long shard pierced deep into his stomach, and he collapsed on the frame. Blood sprayed from his mouth as he tried to yell for help. He could not even manage a scream as Marty bit down into his arm and tore a chunk of flesh away.

As Marty turned his attention to Hank's neck, the blood loss from the stomach wound became too much for Hank, and he mercifully blacked out.

When the regulars at Jacob's found out their beloved bartender died, they were going to be pissed.

CHAPTER 26

The trip to Jacob's had been considerably more exciting than the one Greg and Warren took to Amber's parents. After abandoning Greg's car, the brothers headed back towards the park, and the first creature crossed their path within a couple of minutes. Rather, the first seventeen. They climbed back over the wall and cut across the snow-covered grass. At the far end of the park, they saw the flashing lights of a stationary ambulance over the top of the wall.

"I guess 9-1-1 is working after all," said Warren.

"Let's go see what they know," said Greg. "Maybe the authorities already have a solution."

They took off across the quiet park. A few minutes later, they reached the opposite wall and climbed over. Greg looked around for the paramedics.

"Where are—" started Warren as he dropped to the ground next to Greg.

"Shh." Greg silenced him and put a finger to his lips. He pointed to the far side of the ambulance and signaled for Warren to wait as he slowly stepped around the back of the vehicle. He peered around the rear door, and his eyes widened. Sprawled on the floor were the remains of two paramedics, recognizable only by their bright yellow jackets. Greg estimated over a dozen monsters were tearing into the bodies.

"Did you find them?" Warren shouted from behind.

As one, the group looked up in Greg's direction.

Warren stepped forward as Greg tore around from the back of the vehicle in a dead sprint.

"Run, you fucking idiot." Greg waved at his brother to start moving.

"What?"

Greg grabbed Warren by the collar as he bolted past. Warren looked behind as one, two, five, and then all fourteen of the creatures came around the ambulance.

Greg continued running until they rounded the corner and put the ambulance behind them. He crossed the street and headed towards an alley, Warren a few seconds behind him. They disappeared into the alleyway and ducked down behind a large dumpster. Warren leaned against the green metal bin, trying to catch his breath.

"Out of shape, little brother?" asked Greg.

"Shit, I haven't run like that since my teens," said Warren between heavy breaths. "What the fuck was that?"

"The same shit we saw earlier, just more of them. These things really are fucking eating people." Greg carefully peeked around the wall.

Warren leaned around him, craning his neck to see. "Did they follow us?"

Greg shook his head. "No. Which means either they can't run, or they lost interest."

"Well, that's something at least."

"No, wait, here they come," said Warren.

The creatures slowly walked around the corner, but headed in their direction, nonetheless.

Greg nodded and appraised the situation. "Okay, so they can't run, which gives us the advantage."

"Where to now?"

"We stick to the plan and head to Jacob's." Greg looked back at Warren. "Look out!"

Warren spun around. A blood-covered monster stumbled towards him, gnashing its teeth.

"Mr. Pilano." Warren yelped as Sal Pilano, the undead pizza store owner, lunged at him. Warren grabbed Sal under the chin and pushed his head back. "Dammit, Greg, help me."

Greg froze. He carried no weapons or any means to subdue the creature. "I don't know what to do. We don't have our sticks."

"Open the dumpster," Warren shouted back to Greg as an idea started to form.

"What?"

"Open the damn dumpster," ordered Warren.

Greg lifted one of the large black lids as Warren pushed Sal over to the open bin.

"Close it and pin his head."

Greg pulled the lid down and leaned forward to put more of his weight on it.

"Keep it closed."

Sal's arms thrashed around as Greg pushed down harder.

"Whatever you're doing, man, do it faster." Greg pleaded as he tried his best to keep the dumpster closed.

Warren climbed up onto the trash can. "When I say let go, move back. On three. One. Two—"

As he reached three, Greg moved back, and Warren jumped hard on the lid. Mr. Pilano fell limp as his neck broke with a sickening crunch. Warren crouched down and jumped again. And again. And again. Until the headless body slid to the floor in a blood-soaked heap.

Greg held up his hands as Warren prepared to jump for the seventh time. "Warren, I'm pretty sure you killed him."

"What?" He looked down at the headless torso. "Oh, right." He stepped down from the dumpster.

Greg stared at the bloody mess on the ground. "Where the hell did that come from?"

"Somewhere down the alley."

"No, I don't mean the flesh-eater. I mean what you just did."

"The only way to kill a zombie is to remove the head. It seemed like the right thing to do."

Greg shook his head. "It's not a zombie, Warren. Those rules don't apply."

"Are you sure about that?" asked Warren as he nudged the body with his left foot. Mr. Pilano was definitely dead. "It seemed to work. Although this still highlights one thing, Greg."

"What?"

"We need weapons and fast. We won't have a dumpster around whenever we get into a jam."

Greg sighed. Warren was point. "Fine, we'll get them after we get your car."

"Aren't you forgetting something?" asked Warren.

"What's that?"

"Coffee?"

"Oh, right. Jacob's, Starbucks, TK's."

Warren grinned. "I love this plan."

Greg started off running down the alley. Thirty seconds later, the group from the ambulance shuffled into the alleyway behind them. Twice the size it had been moments before and included one headless pizza parlor owner.

◆ ◆ ◆ ◆

The remainder of the journey passed by uneventfully, and they arrived at Jacob's to find the parking lot empty except for Warren's car.

"That's weird," Greg said as he glanced around.

Warren knew precisely what Greg was referring to. "Where's Hank's car?"

"It hasn't left the parking lot during the day in twenty years."

"This really is bad, isn't it?" said Warren.

Greg slowly nodded.

"So, what do you think we should call them?" Warren said as he fished the keys out of his pocket and unlocked the car.

"Call who?" said Greg as he climbed in the passenger side.

"The zombie-demon things."

"I don't care. Why does it matter?"

"Well, we need a name for them. So, when it comes up in conversation, we're ready." Warren started the car and pulled away.

"Is this what bothers you?"

"Greg, barely fifteen minutes ago, one of those things came up behind me, and you shouted, '*look out*' and left it at that. I didn't know if you meant one of those things coming at me, or Mrs. Andrews or that little shit who keeps stealing my newspaper."

"Do you honestly believe I'd shout at you if I saw Scott?"

"He's due for an ass kicking. Those are my papers."

Greg rolled his eyes.

"What if it'd been a mugger?" asked Warren.

"Have you ever been mugged? Do you even know what a mugger looks like?"

"They usually dress in black."

"Okay, so the next time I see someone in black behind you, I'll be sure to shout mugger."

"I'm far less concerned about muggers than those things. I'm okay calling them zombie-demons," said Warren, his mind made up.

"Well, I'm not. It sounds ridiculous. How about calling them people?"

"People?"

"Yeah."

"They're not people, Greg. They're dead."

"Okay, dead people," suggested Greg.

Warren shook his head.

"The living dead people?"

"No," said Warren.

"The walking dead?"

"No."

"Chompers?"

"That makes them sound like old people's dentures."

"The unliving? The people who were once living and now are not?" offered Greg as his final half-assed suggested.

"Can you take this seriously?"

"What do you want me to say, Warren? The dead are coming back to life, and they're eating people, and all you care about is what we call them."

"Labels are important. Now more than ever."

Greg threw his hands up in resignation. "Fine, we'll call the damn things zombie-demons, but if a better name comes up, we're using it."

"Now who's caught up on labels?"

By the time the argument wrapped up, they had arrived at the Starbucks drive-through.

"Hey, no line," said Warren, genuinely surprised to see the drive-through empty.

"What did you expect?" Greg answered as he stared out of the window.

"There are usually five or six cars in front of me. It's why I'm always late for work."

"And yet it doesn't cross your mind to leave earlier?" asked Greg.

"Nope."

Greg turned his lip at his brother. "Do you honestly think they'll be open today?"

"Of course, they're always open on Sunday."

"That's not what I meant."

Warren leaned into the intercom. "Okay, I'm ready," he shouted.

Silence.

Greg shook his head as Warren tapped the horn.

Silence.

"Believe me, no one has bothered to come to work today," said Greg.

"Kevin hasn't taken a sick day in eleven years. He's always here."

"Today may be considered extenuating circumstances."

A muffled noise came from the intercom.

"See? A consummate professional," Warren said with a smile. "Perfect attendance. It'll be a cold day in Hell when Kevin doesn't come to work."

Warren turned back to the intercom. "Morning Kev, I'll have a grande non-fat vanilla latte and a raspberry scone." He turned to Greg. "Need anything?"

"Yeah, I need you to take this shit seriously."

Another grunt came from the speaker.

"That's everything." Warren pulled the car forward to the open drive-thru window. He saw movement inside and looked over at Greg. "Nothing to worry about. Get some coffee in me, and I'll be right as—"

He saw Greg's eyes widen, and before Greg could shout out a warning, Kevin reached through the drive-thru window and grabbed Warren by the shirt. He pulled Warren towards him, his teeth snapping, eager to take a bite out of Warren's face.

"The fuck?" Warren grabbed the steering wheel. "Safe word," he gasped.

"What?"

Warren kicked out with his feet, trying to break free of Kevin's grasp. He struggled to speak. "You were... supposed... to say... the... fucking... safe-word."

"What safe word?"

"Zombie—" said Warren as he fought for breath, "—demon." He gasped again. "You... were, you were supposed... to say—" He sucked in another breath. "—fucking zombie-demon."

"It's a stupid name," said Greg.

"Are you— going— to— help me?"

Greg leaned over, grabbed Warren's arm, and pulled. Kevin fell forward out of the drive-through window and into the car.

"That's not fucking helping," said Warren as he stomped on the floor, trying to reach the accelerator. "I can't reach the pedal."

Kevin's teeth inched closer to his face.

Warren frantically stabbed at the window button, and the passenger side window slowly descended. "Shit."

He tried again, and the driver's side window started to move. The glass caught Kevin under the chin and beneath his right armpit. His grip relaxed, but Warren kept his finger on the button.

"What are you doing?" asked Greg.

"Cutting his head off," said Warren as he gasped for breath.

"The motor isn't strong enough. You'll strip the gears."

"I know how to kill a zombie, Greg."

The glass pushed harder into undead Kevin's chin, and the motor started to grind as the gears skipped. It was enough for Kevin to release his grip and pin him in the window.

Warren rubbed his throat. He pushed down on the accelerator, and the car moved forward. "Time to get rid of our passenger."

Kevin's legs were still in the drive-through as the car started to move forward. His torso moved with the vehicle, but the lack of space between the car and the wall twisted Kevin in a grotesque manner. His back snapped with a loud crack as his limp body fell out of the drive-through window. The creature formally known as Kevin, continued to snap and bite the air around Warren as he left a bloodied skid mark along the wall.

Greg watched Kevin's body drag across the wall. "That's fucking gross."

The window started to crack under the weight.

"Shit." Warren should have listened to his brother.

The car left the drive-through and re-entered the parking lot. Warren lowered the window, and the rest of Kevin fell to the tarmac.

"You broke my window, you coffee-pouring fuck-dumpling," Warren protested weakly.

"That damned thing nearly chewed half your face off, and you're worried about a window?"

"It's an import. These things are fucking expensive." Warren rubbed his throat. "I still need coffee."

Greg shook his head. "Change of plan. We need guns next. Coffee will have to wait."

Warren sighed. "This day is really starting to suck."

Cam dumped the contents of her purse on the hood of her car and frantically sorted through the pile of makeup, feminine hygiene products, and receipts. Her keys were gone. She had misplaced them plenty of times before, but she never needed to search for them with the concurrent threat of being attacked by monsters. Tears welled up in her eyes as she stepped to her right and collapsed on the car roof. She buried her head in her arms and silently cursed the universe and any deity who happened to be listening.

Her loud sobs masked the shuffling of the demon moving up behind her, and it grabbed her arm before she noticed. Cam spun and fell backward onto the hood. The creature lost its grip as she flailed her arms, but it regained its grasp and quickly overpowered her. Cam barely mustered the strength to fight back as its teeth came closer. As her energy faded, it moved in for the kill. Cam closed her eyes tight and waited for the inevitable bite.

The next few moments were a blur as teeth gnashed an inch away from her face. A car horn blared beside her. She took a deep breath and pushed the creature as hard as she could. It stumbled back into the road, and the horn-honking car plowed into it, sending it crashing onto the hood. The tires skidded on the snow as the demon flew forward, becoming a long bloody streak on the frozen tarmac. The car backed up and stopped in front of Cam as the passenger window descended.

"Get in," a familiar voice commanded.

Cam looked up at the open window, and she gasped in shock when she saw the driver. "Donald, you came back."

Donald pushed the door open. "Come on. The streets aren't safe."

"That's an understatement." Cam gathered her purse contents and climbed inside.

The car pulled forward as Donald swerved around the broken body writhing in the street. "Are you okay? Did he bite you?" He tried to focus on driving but kept glancing across at Cam.

"I have no idea," she answered truthfully. Adrenaline churned through her body, but she was unsure if the man's teeth made contact in the chaos.

"Check. It's important."

She looked over her arms and touched her neck, but she was unharmed. "I'm okay," she said, sounding a little surprised.

"You were lucky."

"Thanks to you. If you hadn't come along, I'd—"

"Don't dwell on it," said Donald. "The important thing is I made it."

"I thought you left me."

"I did," confessed Donald. "I made it about fifty miles out of town, but I stopped at Point Pass and sat staring down in the north valley. I couldn't bring myself to leave. Something told me to come back for you."

"I came down as you left. I wanted to go with you."

"I'm so sorry."

"Why did you go?" asked Cam.

"I felt I was betraying Laura. I—"

Cam touched his arm tenderly, any feelings of anger gone. "You're here now. That's the main thing."

Donald smiled. "Shit really hit the fan, didn't it?"

"One minute I'm crying in my beer, the next I'm running away from psychos, and the cops are shooting at me."

"Lee?" asked Donald.

"Yeah."

"He got his bullets back?"

Cam nodded. "Oh yeah."

"Why did he shoot at you?"

"He thought I turned into one of those things. I don't even know what those things are."

Donald shook his head. "I don't know what's going on, but the dead aren't staying dead."

"End of days?" Cam was only half-joking.

"Then someone's god is pissed off with us," he said as he turned on First Avenue.

Cam noticed the change of direction. "Do you have a plan? Because I'm shit out of ideas. I've lost my car keys, and I'm wearing one of those things' shoes that are too damn big."

"We should go to my place. I have shoes of Laura's that should fit you."

"My place is closer," said Cam.

"Yeah, but Pastitsio is a disaster. Two huge wrecks have the east end completely blocked. Unless we want to chance it on foot."

"Hell no, I've done enough running for one day."

"We can use the back streets to my place. Shouldn't take us long."

Cam nodded in agreement as she pulled a stick of gum from her purse. "Hell of a day," she said as she stared out of the passenger window at the chaos unfolding around them. Her attention certainly was not focused on the bloodied bandage wrapped around Donald's left arm.

CHAPTER 27

Greg stared intently at his phone as Warren drove them across town. Amber was not answering his calls or text messages. When daylight abruptly disappeared, he finally looked up. "Where are we?"

"Car wash," said Warren.

"Are you fucking kidding me?"

"Have you seen the side of the car? It's going to be a bitch to scrub Kevin off if it dries."

"If it dries? Warren, half the town is trying to eat us, and you want to get your damned car detailed? Have you lost your fucking mind?"

"I'm not getting it detailed, just a quick wash and wax. This car is all I have, man. It'll take two minutes."

Greg shook his head in disbelief. "You really need to sort out your priorities." He resumed texting on his phone. After a few moments, he realized the car remained stationary and looked up at Warren.

"Do you have any quarters? I'm out."

"Oh, for fuck's sake." Greg shoved his hand in his pocket and pulled out a handful of change.

Warren grabbed the coins and lowered his window. The glass moved down in a slow, jerky manner. "Man, Kevin totally fucked my window," he mumbled under his breath as he fed the coins in the slot and raised his window. "Fucking coffee-brewing, zombie-demon, asshole. I should file a complaint with corporate."

"I'm sure you can do it on their website. Click the link that says, stupid fucking fucktards who have their priorities all fucked up."

Warren ignored his brother as the brushes moved back and forth across the paint and washed Kevin from the car. "I'm hungry. Can we get food?"

"If we get guns, we can fight our way to food. Do it the other way around, and I don't rate our chances fighting through a crowd of zombie-demons with a box of Strawberry Pop-Tarts."

Warren grinned.

"What's so funny?"

"You called them zombies-demons"

Greg missed the error. "You know what I mean."

"I still need coffee."

"Let's hold up at the shop," suggested Greg. "I picked up coffee and snacks Friday. If we move the vehicles around, we can block off the entry points. Shouldn't be hard for us to defend."

Warren shrugged. "Sure, it beats sitting out here."

The brushes finished their cycle, and the overhead dryer started up and blew the drops of water from the paint. As the dryers powered down, Warren floored it and pulled out of the carwash.

And promptly smashed into a zombie-demon stumbling across the exit.

Warren's jaw dropped. "Are you fucking kidding me?" He stopped the car and threw it in reverse.

"What are you doing?"

"Rewash."

"Goddammit, leave it, dude. We have far more important things to worry about."

"Like what?"

"That." Greg pointed towards a large group of creatures staggering across the parking lot towards them.

Warren grumbled under his breath, put the car into gear, and pulled out of the parking lot, watching the horde disappear in his rear-view mirror.

Although the streets were littered with monsters and chaos, the trip to the gun store passed by without issue. Greg directed his brother to stick to the back roads and alleyways, and they zigzagged across town. The undead they encountered were easily avoidable, and as they pulled into the parking lot beside TK's gun store, a loud explosion rumbled in the distance.

Warren turned in the direction of the noise. "What was that?"

Greg dismissed the distraction. "I dunno. Gas station maybe? Go check the front. I'm going to check the side and back." He disappeared around the back of the building, and a quick glance at the wall showed all the windows were barred. He stepped over to the closest window and pulled on the thick iron struts. They held fast, and the door offered the same resistance.

Warren walked around the corner. "Sealed up tighter than Mother Teresa's vagina."

"Eww, thanks for that visual."

"Anytime," said Warren. "How's it looking?"

"Same," said Greg. "The back door is locked. We're not getting in from street level."

Warren pointed across the parking lot. "We're already getting attention."

Greg followed the direction of Warren's finger. A large group of creatures were headed in their direction. "The roof," he said as he took off around the rear of the building. "There may be an entrance up there. The ladder's around back."

The caged roof ladder mounted on the rear wall stopped twelve feet short of the ground.

Greg looked up at the ladder. "Find something to climb on."

Warren ran over to the other side of the building. A moment later, he stuck his head around the wall. "Dumpster," he shouted.

"Will you keep your voice down?"

"Help me move it," Warren ordered loudly.

Greg rolled his eyes and ran over to help. The brothers put their backs up against the large metal bin and pushed it over to the ladder. Warren quickly climbed on top and reached up for the bottom rung.

"I still can't quite reach it. Jump up and give me a boost."

Greg hopped up next to him and cupped his hands together. Warren stepped on Greg's hands and wrapped his fingertips around the bottom rung of the ladder, and kicked off from his brother, clipping him under the chin with his swinging foot.

"What the fuck, man?" complained Greg as he rubbed his jaw. "Watch what you're doing."

The ladder hesitated for a second and suddenly dropped six feet in a second. The jolt shook Warren off, and he landed flat on his back.

Greg burst out laughing. "Karma's a bitch, bro."

Warren reached up his hand. "Are you gonna help me up or stand there being an ass-hat?"

Greg reached down and pulled him up. They quickly climbed onto the roof and looked around for a point of entry. The square hatch in the middle of the roof was locked from the inside, and their search presented no other way into the building.

"No entry?" asked Warren.

"Of course there's no fucking entry. Why would there be? That would make things too fucking easy for us, wouldn't it? Oh no, this whole fucking deal has to be a complete and utter cluster fuck. May as well climb our asses back down and go home."

"Greg, we ain't going anywhere."

"What do you mean?"

Warren pointed down behind the building. "Looks like our welcome wagon arrived, and they brought a few friends."

Greg stepped over to the edge of the roof. The dozen demons from the parking lot had arrived, as well as twenty or so more friends. "Where the hell did they come from?"

Warren shrugged. "What do we do?"

"Keep your voice down," whispered Greg. "It isn't going to take them long to figure out where we are."

"Do you think they can climb ladders?"

"Let's not give them a chance to find out. We need to stay quiet until they leave."

In response, a muffled cell phone started to ring.

"Shut it off," Greg whispered to Warren. "Shut the damned thing off."

"It isn't mine," said Warren as he pulled his phone out of his pocket. The device sat silent despite the continued ringing. "See? It's dead. I forgot to charge it last night."

"Shit," Greg muttered as he patted down his pockets, looking for his own phone. Coming up empty, he walked to the edge of the roof and looked down at the car. His phone lit up on the passenger seat through the open window.

The ringing stopped, and the brothers let out a collective sigh.

The phone rang eleven more times before the caller finally called it quits. Greg and Warren watched helplessly as the waiting hoard flocked towards the vehicle.

"Well, that makes a change," said Warren.

"What do you mean?"

"Usually it's me who fucks things. About time you stepped up."

"That's not funny."

"Yeah, it is. I wonder who called, as they just fucked us well and good. Could your phone be any louder?"

"I hope it wasn't Amber."

"Maybe she killed Ashley as she turned into one of those things and tried to eat her," said Warren cheerfully.

"You really know how to make a bad situation worse, don't you?"

"Hey, it's just a thought. All I'm saying is I'd be okay if it happened."

"She dumped you, man—"

"Yeah, thanks for reminding me," said Warren.

"If you'll let me finish. She dumped you, that's it. Nothing else. She doesn't deserve to die. Dumping the almighty Warren Hart is not a crime punishable by death, despite what you may think. Give the poor girl a break."

"She broke my heart, man."

"You were cheating on her. You are not the victim here."

"Do you have a plan to get us down from here?" asked Warren changing the topic.

"Well, we ain't getting down until they disperse. There's a bunch of tarps over there. May as well get comfortable. We might be here a while."

"Wait, what?"

"We're sleeping up here until someone rescues us," said Greg.

Warren turned his nose up at the idea. "Dude, it's fucking freezing. Are you shitting me?"

"Do you want to go downstairs and hang with our cannibal friends?"

"No."

"Well then, until another scenario crops up, we're sleeping up here. Help me get the tarps unfolded. We'll make a tent and blankets."

"I am going to die of hydrothermia in this weather," said Warren as he exhaled, billowing hot air from his mouth for emphasis.

"Hypo," corrected Greg.

"No, not in the slightest."

Sometimes Greg wondered if Warren spoke a foreign language. "Call someone to help us then if you don't want to wait up here."

"I told you my phone is dead. We could use yours if you had it with you."

"At least I charged mine."

"Whatever. You get to be big spoon then," said Warren with a grin.

CHAPTER 28

"Come in," said God in response to the gentle tapping coming from his office door.

The door slowly opened, and Raphael poked his head inside. "You wanted to see me?"

"Raph, come in and close the door," said God. "We need to talk."

Raphael pushed the door shut.

God stood and stepped around his desk. "Walk with me."

He crossed to a large pair of doors across from his desk and pushed them open. They stepped out onto a balcony and into the vast blackness of space and gazed at the Earth swimming below, in all its green and blue glory.

God leaned on the ornate golden railing and looked at the planet below. "It looks so peaceful from up here. It's like the ugly girl you see sitting across the bar. Good from far, but far from good. It's when you get up close the vision falls apart. The whole lot of them are a pain in my ass. Wars, famine, rape, poverty, murder, reality TV. There are times when I wish it didn't have my stamp on it."

"I'm sure you love them as you do all of your creations," Raphael countered.

"I never said I didn't. I just wish they'd sort their shit out. So much wasted potential. I swear I spend more time putting their crap in order than I do with any of my other creations. They're like the fifty-seven-year-old son who doesn't move out of your house because he sucks at life. Half of them don't even believe in me anymore."

"It's a work in progress. All the best pieces of art are."

"See, that's why I keep you around, Raph. You can always see the sunny side of a shit sandwich."

Raphael nodded his appreciation. "This isn't why you called me here, is it?"

God shook his head. "People are starting to talk. I don't like it when people start talking."

"I'm not going to lie. Rumors are starting to circulate about Death."

"Are we any closer to sorting this situation out?"

"We're very close," said Raphael.

"You promised me you'd do whatever it takes to get this taken care of. It's been what, two, three days, and we're no closer to getting this taken care of."

"I assure you, I have my best men working on it."

"Where? I don't see any activity outside the normal office worker type stuff. Who exactly do you have working on this?"

"You said you trusted me."

God sighed. "And I do, Raph. I just need this to go away. The Council is starting to ask questions I don't have answers to. If they come here to audit us, it's going to be a bad day for everyone."

"The Council of Deities is getting involved?" asked Raphael.

"Yeah, they sent an email asking for an update."

"How do they know?"

"They know everything. Now do you see why I'm freaking out? The Council never gets involved in my affairs. Ever."

Raphael sighed and pondered his options. "I think it's time I showed you the Invocation Room."

God turned to face Raphael. "Invocation Room? What the hell is that?"

"It's where we're fixing this. If you'll follow me."

Raphael stepped back into the office, and God followed him to the door and into the hallway. They stopped at the elevators in the reception area, and Raphael pushed the *down* button.

The elevator pinged, and the doors opened. Raphael entered and swiped his ID badge through a card reader. A previously invisible row of numbers appeared below the bottom row. He pressed the button labeled -5.

God raised an eyebrow. "A secret floor?"

"Floors. Plural."

"And I don't know about this because?" asked God.

"Plausible denial."

"Of course. Why would the executive director and exulted ruler be aware of a hidden floor in his own damn building?"

"It's a contingency plan. It seemed like a good idea, even more so now that the Council is involved. I'll explain everything in a few moments."

The elevator stopped, and the doors opened.

"This way, please." Raphael gestured for God to walk ahead.

God stepped out into a vast room filled with thousands upon thousands of large monitor banks and pieces of computer and surveillance equipment.

"Welcome to Invocation," said Raphael.

An employee sat at each terminal wearing a headset and staring at screens displaying either streamed video of varying quality or static snow. God looked around in bewilderment. There were at least ten thousand people in the room. It looked like the help desk from Hell, except no one spoke.

It took God a few moments to find the right words. "What. The. Fuck?"

Raphael wrung his hands nervously.

"What is this, Raph? Where did all these people come from?"

"We added it to the new hire initiation program. Recent acquisitions coming into Heaven spend a day here as part of their training."

"Well, that explains why I never noticed."

"We felt this was the easiest way to integrate without a big production."

"You don't consider this a big production?" asked God.

"In the grand scheme of things? No. Our options, however, are rather limited."

"Why isn't anyone talking?"

"They're monitoring. They don't interact."

Monitoring what?"

"Prayers."

"Whose?"

"Everyone."

"EVERYONE?" echoed God in shock and surprise.

"Yes. It's amazing, isn't it?" Raphael beamed with pride.

"No. How long have you been doing this?"

"The past few days."

"Oh, shit." God shifted uncomfortably as he cast his mind back to the masturbation session in his private bathroom earlier in the day while watching porn on his phone. "Even up here?".

Raphael smiled. "It's okay, it's just Earth. Nowhere else"

God patted Raphael on the back. "Good man. However, I'd rather not start this precedent. Besides, isn't it a waste of resources and manpower?"

"We have a process for such emergencies. We never expected it to be on a scale this big."

God looked around the room, clearly flustered at the sight. "We never act on prayers. Never have, never will."

"Humans don't know that."

God moved towards one of the monitor banks. "What am I seeing here?"

"Mobile devices and camera feeds," said Raphael.

"Pretend I'm five. Explain it to me in simple terms."

"We're capturing audio and, in some cases, video from anything that has a microphone or camera. Cell phones, tablets, laptops, ATMs, traffic lights, security cameras, Alexa, Facebook, Google. Everything. We figured we may hear something that could give us a lead on Death's skipped reaping."

God stayed silent.

"I know what you're thinking," said Raphael.

"You do?"

"Yes, this is morally wrong."

"No, that isn't what I'm thinking."

"Sir?" Raphael was confused.

"I'm thinking you ripped this entire thing off from The Dark Knight."

Raphael expected a different response and a berating of unknown intensity. Of course, God was absolutely right. "You saw The Dark Knight?

"Of course I did, I love Batman, and I'm one of Heath Ledger's biggest fans. I thought Jack Nicholson nailed the Joker, but damn, Heath was born to play the role. I made sure the Academy took note during Oscar season. It made me really happy when I saw his name on my list. We always grab a coffee on the second Thursday of the month. He does this great Batman, Brokeback Mountain monologue that has me in stitches." God drifted again.

Raphael cleared his throat to get the conversation back on track.

"Right, sorry," said God. "So why do some of the monitors have static?"

"Audio only."

"I see."

"So you approve?" asked Raphael.

"My approval is irrelevant. Do what must be done, but let's not start this answering prayers bullshit. I'd rather we didn't start that precedent." He pointed to one of the employee's headsets. "May I?"

"Of course," said Raphael.

The young female operator stood up and offered God her headset as she grinned like a maniac.

God smiled at her reaction. "Is everything okay?"

"You're him," she said, barely able to contain her excitement.

"Him?"

"You're God. I'm a huge fan of yours."

God smiled his thanks, but his groupie continued her fangirl freak-out.

"I had your poster on my wall as a kid. Well, not you, your son. I love him so much. He is so dreamy." She stopped a moment as her brain raced a million miles an hour. "Wait, is he here?"

God smiled graciously. "No, sorry, wrong religion. He's Jewish. He didn't qualify. He's out sleeping with seventy virgins or something."

"Isn't that Islam," asked the fangirl.

"I have no idea," said God. "Kids these days, eh? I can't keep up with their shenanigans."

The girl's gaze fell at the disappointing news.

God put the headphones on and listened for a few moments. "So, what do you normally hear?" he asked as he looked up at Raphael.

"The usual bullshit. Please let me win the lottery. Please don't let my wife catch me cheating. Please don't let it be herpes."

"Can we filter out all the petty mundane crap? Who do they think I am, Publisher's Clearing House? I won't help some dopey shit in Tulsa win the lottery because he is too lazy to get a job."

"No, we have to listen to everything."

God felt overwhelmed. The feed erupted with requests and orders. *Make me rich. Get me a promotion. Smite my neighbor. Let Chloe, Sarah, and, or Jenna sleep with me tonight. Don't let her be pregnant, else I'll have to stay with her. Let me be pregnant, and he'll have to stay with me*.

He took off the headset. "Is this what people pray for?"

Raphael nodded. "Ninety-nine percent of the time, it is."

"Do they think I'm a genie?"

"Sure seems that way."

"They don't need a god. They need Ed McMahon. So how do you

know what you're looking for?"

"We put a list of keywords and phrases together. Figured we may find something along the lines of '*Oh God, don't eat me*' or '*it's a fucking zombie or demon*'. Seemed like a good place to start."

"And no leads?"

"Well, we heard quite a few women talking about being eaten, but they were taken way out of context."

God spluttered a moment. Talking about sex made him terribly uncomfortable. Even his son needed to have a surrogate mother. He scrambled to change the subject. "How long has this been going on?"

"A while, but never on this scale."

"For fuck's sake, Raph, and you were going to tell me when?"

"We felt plausible denial seemed like the best option."

"What if they aren't Christian?"

Raphael swallowed nervously at the question he hoped to avoid. "We're listening to everyone."

"No? Everyone?"

Raphael nodded. "Muslims, Jewish, Hindus, Pastafarians, everyone."

"Jesus Christ, Raph. If the Council finds out we're encroaching on other religions, they will shut this place down without blinking." He paused and handed the headset back to the young woman.

"Well, keep at it."

"So you still approve?" Raphael asked again, wary of God's upbeat tone.

"Approve is a powerful word. Let's say I accept doing what needs to be done until this has passed. Hopefully, something comes up soon. If word gets out that we're actually listening to prayers, they'll never let up."

CHAPTER 29

Warren was in the middle of a mind-blowing sex dream when he felt his feet being kicked. One minute he was sandwiched between two unknown women, and the next, he found himself staring up at Greg and the bright morning sun.

"Wake up, princess. We're losing daylight."

"Man, you even cock block me in my sleep," Warren complained as he rubbed his eyes and sat upright. "Fuck me, it's cold."

"Tough shit, Tinkerbell. You need to get up and help me."

"I dreamed I was banging Ashley and Amber," he lied.

"Dick."

Warren grinned as he pushed the tarp off himself and stood up and stretched. "I don't suppose this end of the world bullshit sorted itself out overnight, did it?"

"As a matter of fact, it did. I woke up this morning, and every last one of those things was gone."

"Really?"

"No. The parking lot is full of them."

Warren walked over to the rear edge of the roof and glanced down at the creatures. The crowd had grown since he fell asleep. "That sucks. What's the time?"

"About nine."

"I thought you said we're losing daylight."

"The speed it takes you to do anything, we are."

Warren ignored the jab. "I'm surprised the sun is out."

"Why wouldn't the sun be out?"

"I expected the apocalypse to be more overcast. At least the power is still on." He nodded towards the digital price sign at the gas station across the street.

"Why would the power be off?"

"You know, in disaster films, it's always the first thing to go. I figured we'd be in darkness by now."

"This isn't the movies, Warren. The power grid is a little more stable than that."

Warren raised his eyes in anticipation.

Greg frowned. "What are you doing?"

"You said the power grid is more stable than that. In movies, that is the exact point it shuts down."

"God, you're an idiot." Greg swatted a hand in the air as he brushed off his brother's stupidity.

"So, what's our plan then?"

"We need to draw them away from the back of the building. Your car looks mostly intact. If we can get to it, we should be okay."

"What do you mean mostly?" Warren stepped back over to the edge. This time he focused his attention on his car. "She's fine. What are you talking about."

It was Greg's turn to grin.

"Dick." Warren looked back at the group. "Looks like they moved the dumpster."

"Yeah, I noticed. The drop shouldn't be too bad."

"How do we get them to go around the front?"

"That's the ten-million-dollar question, isn't it?"

"It's ten million now?"

"Inflation." Greg looked around the rooftop at their limited options. Aside from the tarps, they saw a bucket and roofing tar. Even MacGyver might struggle coming up with a halfway decent plan. He walked to the front of the roof to discover the parking lot empty. "I have an idea."

Five minutes later, three tarps were tied together in a crude rope.

Warren looked at the contraption suspiciously. "Will this hold me?"

"Pull on it, and we'll find out." He offered Warren the other end of the tarp.

Warren grabbed hold and pulled. The first knot immediately unraveled, and Warren fell to the ground, landing hard on his tailbone.

"Asshole. How are we going to climb down if the knots won't hold?"

"We're not," said Greg as he re-tied the knot.

"What?" Warren rubbed his ass as he stood back up.

"They're going to be a distraction. I figure we can drape them over the side and catch their attention. We then walk around the roof and lead them to the front so we can use the ladder."

"So the goal isn't to climb down the tarp then?"

"Hell no," said Greg. "The knots wouldn't hold."

"I fucking hate you."

Greg smiled as he threw his side of the tarp over the edge of the roof. "Come and hold this. I'll go to the front and make some noise."

Greg handed Warren the tarp and crossed over to the front of the roof.

Warren looked over the side and started to wave the plastic sheet. "Hey, meatbags, come and get it."

Greg took off his right sneaker and placed it on the edge of the roof. He reached over and started banging on the acrylic store sign. For thirty seconds, he slammed against the plastic. Thirty seconds turned into a minute which turned into five. None of the creatures took the bait and rounded the corner.

"Warren, what's going on?" he shouted over his shoulder.

"We might have a problem," Warren suddenly said, standing a lot closer than Greg expected.

Greg jumped and dropped his shoe to the parking lot below. "What's wrong?" he said with an exasperated and defeated sigh.

"There's a chance I may have inadvertently dropped the tarp."

"So all the demons are still back there?"

"Yeah. You dropped your shoe."

"I know I dropped my fucking shoe," Greg said as he stood back up on his feet. "Congratulations, dipshit. You screwed our only chance of getting off this damn roof."

"It was an accident."

"Your life is one giant accident. If you're not fucking something up, you're not breathing."

"You don't have to be a dick," said Warren.

"And you don't have to be such so fucking useless."

"It's easy for you, Greg. You were always dad's favorite."

"What the hell does that have to do with anything?"

"Everything."

Greg stabbed a finger at his brother. "Not now, Warren. I don't want to get into this again."

"Why? You never want to talk about him."

"This is neither the time nor the place."

"Then when is, Greg? God knows if we're even going to survive this."

"I don't plan on dying unless your sorry ass gets me killed, and I certainly don't want to spend this time arguing with you."

"Are you two finished?" a voice called from the street below.

Greg looked down at the street to see David standing by his car.

"One of you dropped a shoe," said David as he held it up in the air.

"Oh, fuck me. Anyone but him." Warren complained.

"What are you doing on the roof?" asked David.

"We wanted to get inside so we can get guns, but we got stuck," said Greg.

"I'll help get you down. Even Warren."

"I don't need your fucking help."

"What seems to be the issue aside from the obvious?"

"Why don't you go on around back and find out for —" said Warren.

"Don't," interrupted Greg. "There's a swarm of them back there. We can't use the rear ladder, and the inside hatch is locked," said Greg. "Can you create a distraction and get them to clear out?"

"Or I could go in the store and open the hatch from the inside."

"Don't bother. The front door is locked."

"Are you sure about that?"

"Yeah, Warren tried it." Greg turned to Warren. "Right?"

"It's locked. He's trying to make me look bad."

David stepped away for twenty seconds. He reappeared, carrying a pistol and shotgun. "No, I'm pretty sure it's open."

Greg turned to Warren, seconds away from losing every last bit of his shit. "Did you try the door?"

"I pulled it. It's closed."

"Did you push it?" asked Greg. "Doors open both ways."

"Maybe."

"Then we're stuck on this roof freezing our tits off because you couldn't be bothered to push a fucking door handle?"

Warren shrugged. "Technically, we're stuck because I dropped the tarp."

David pointed to the door. "If you're finished, I'll go inside and get the hatch open."

David disappeared back inside the store, and a minute later, the hatch popped open.

"This way, gents," he said as he offered Greg his sneaker.

Greg slid on his shoe and pushed Warren out of the way as he stepped down the ladder. He dropped into the store and wasted no time heading for the front door.

Warren landed on the floor behind Greg. "Where are you going?"

"To call Amber."

"Don't you want a gun first? Those things are still out there."

Greg stopped. Occasionally his brother did have a valid point. "Fine," he said and headed back inside.

"I feel like a kid in a freaking candy store," Warren said as he spun around and looked at the various gun racks and display cases.

"No, you don't," said Greg as he picked up a pistol from a display case.

"How do you know how I feel?"

"Because in a candy store, you'd know what all this stuff is. This is more like you being a kid in a Japanese candy store. Everything looks awesome, but you don't know which shit has wasabi in it. One minute it's fruity gummy goodness. The next, your eyes are watering, your tongue is on fire, and you're flapping around like a demented pigeon because your esophagus is melting."

"Do you have to ruin everything for me?" asked Warren. "This is a big moment."

"All I'm saying is you don't know half of what this shit is, and you're likely to shoot yourself, assuming, of course, you can even get the damn gun loaded."

"I know what I'm doing."

"Have you even been to a gun store before?" asked Greg.

"Yes," said Warren.

"Okay, which one?"

"Walmart."

"That doesn't count."

"Of course it counts."

"If your shopping cart contains Twinkies, cheap aftershave, and ammunition, it isn't a gun store."

"It doesn't mean I can't be excited."

"Just go and find bullets. I'll grab the guns."

"Can I pick a gun?" asked Warren, barely able to contain his excitement.

"Fine."

Warren walked over to a large display behind the counter and grabbed a shotgun. Five minutes later, the trio gathered a cart full of guns, ammunition, and camping supplies.

Greg quickly loaded his pistol. "Okay, we have weapons. I'm going out to the car to get my phone."

Warren stared at Greg as his brother deftly loaded the weapon. "How did you learn to load a gun?"

"Dad taught me."

"When?"

"A long time ago."

"What?" protested Warren. "He never showed me."

"I said, not now." Greg cautiously pushed the door open and stepped outside. He moved to the edge of the wall and peered around the corner. The demons had moved away from Warren's car, but he could still hear moaning and growling. Seconds later, he reached the car and jumped inside. He slid the key into the ignition and closed the windows. His cell phone flashed, announcing twenty-three missed calls and ninety-eight text messages. As he feared, all were from Amber. He grabbed the phone off the seat and headed back to the store, dialing Amber as he ran. It rang once.

"Honey, I'm sorry. Are you—"

"*Where the fuck are you, Greg? I called you all fucking night.*" Amber never swore.

"I'm sorry, I couldn't get to my phone. Those creatures cornered us, and we couldn't get out."

"*Why didn't you come to get me? I need you.*"

"I did yesterday. You were the first place we went to." Greg stepped back inside the store and closed the door.

"*Why didn't you knock?*"

"I did. Your dad shot at us."

"*That was you?*"

"Of course it was me. You think I wouldn't come for you?"

"*He told me looters tried to break in.*"

"That prick. You were the first person I came for. He shot at me and trashed my car, so we escaped on foot. Kind of upsetting if I were to be completely honest."

"*Greg, he's been bitten.*"

Greg stayed silent, unsure of how to respond. Saying good, felt like the right response. The old man got what he deserved, but he could not say that to Amber. "I'm sorry," was all he could muster.

"*Someone came into the yard and attacked him when he went outside.*"

"Did he hurt you?"

"*Dad?*"

"Yeah."

"*No, we put him to bed last night, and he had a fever. When we woke this morning, he started smashing up the house. We're locked in my parent's room. Come get us, please,*" she begged.

"I've got guns. I'm on my way."

"*Guns? Why do you need guns?*"

"It's bad out here. This shit is happening everywhere, love."

"*You're not going to shoot my dad.*"

"If he has turned, I won't have a choice."

"*YOU ARE NOT GOING TO SHOOT MY DAD,*" she screamed.

Greg moved the phone away from his ear. "Sit tight. I'm on my way." He hung up the phone and dropped it in his pocket.

Warren looked genuinely concerned. "What's wrong?"

"Walter's been bitten."

"Good, he's a douchebag. And Ashley?"

"She's safe."

Warren looked genuinely disappointed.

"Warren, just don't," Greg put up a hand, dismissing his brother.

"Hey, a man can dream."

Greg pushed past him.

"Where are you going?" asked Warren.

"To get Amber, and I'm taking your car. Take the supplies and go back to the shop and barricade yourselves inside."

"What?" said Warren incredulously. "How do I get there?"

"With David."

"No fucking way."

"Listen, I don't care what pissy little squabble you two have," said Greg gesturing to Warren and David. "Get over it, or you're going to get us killed."

"But he said he's an atheist, I can't ride with a heathe—" Warren started.

Greg held up a dismissive finger. "I said, I don't care. Take a look around you. We're knee-deep in shit. If we can't get past our petty differences, we won't survive."

"But—"

"Grow the fuck up, Warren. This isn't up for debate." Greg turned to the front door as the breaking of glass echoed through the store.

A bloodied arm thrust through the bars and broken glass on the sidewall across from them. The shards of glass sliced through its skin, leaving bloodied streaks on the frame.

"Okay, we move now," said Greg.

David ran up to the door and cracked it open. "We're still clear out front."

Warren pushed the cart outside and turned back to his brother.

"Don't die out there." It was the closest he could get to affection

Greg nodded. "You too." He turned and ran towards the car.

Three demons were banging on the passenger side window as he approached the vehicle. He raised the gun and fired three times. All three took shots to the head and hit the ground. He was glad Warren missed the feat. He did not feel like explaining why their father also taught him to shoot.

CHAPTER 30

"**D**o they fit better?" asked Donald loudly from the living room.

Cam sat on his bed and wiggled her toes in the new sneakers. "Loose, but better than what I had," she shouted back.

"There should be socks in the dresser. Top right drawer." He coughed loudly.

"Are you okay?" asked Cam as she walked over to the dresser and pulled out a pair of white sports socks.

"Yeah, it's just the cold air. These old lungs aren't a fan of winter."

"It's a good thing you came along when you did. God knows what could have happened," said Cam entering the living room.

Donald sat on the couch staring at the floor as Cam flopped down next to him.

"That's twice you've had me in your bedroom this week. A girl could be forgiven for thinking you have other intentions," Cam said with a smile.

Donald stayed silent.

"Donald?"

He groaned softly and looked up at Cam.

"Oh, come on, I'm joking."

Donald smiled weakly. "We should figure out a plan," he said, changing the subject.

"Why can't we stay here?" She noticed sweat beading on his forehead. "What's wrong?"

It's nothing. It's just a little warm in here. I'm fine."

"Want me to turn the heating off?"

Donald shook his head as she put the back of her hand to his brow.

"You're burning up. You're getting sick," said Cam.

"No, really. I'm fine."

"We can't be running around town if you're coming down with something."

Donald shook his head again. "We must keep moving. Those things are dangerous."

"We can stay here a while. I'll jam something in front of the door. Nothing's coming in. I can go and find supplies."

Cam stood up and crossed over to the thermostat. The heat was off and had been since Donald left town. It registered fifty-three degrees, nowhere near warm enough for him to be breaking a sweat. She looked back at Donald. "We should get you in bed. It looks like you're getting the flu. Great timing, dude." She looked back at Donald and saw the bloodied bandage on his arm. "Donald?"

He remained silent as he stared into nothingness.

"Donald?" Her tone became more serious.

He looked up at her with distant and glazed eyes. "Huh?"

"Show me your arm."

Donald drifted back to the present and looked down at his arm. "It's nothing."

She walked back over to him. "Show me."

"It's just a scratch. I'm fine."

Cam stared until Donald resigned and pulled up his sleeve. A bloody bandage wrapped his left forearm. He pulled it back and flinched as the gauze snagged on a bloodied bite mark. Cam helped move the cloth away from the wound. The skin and veins surrounding it were dark and angry.

Cam's mouth fell open, but no words came.

"I'm so sorry," said Donald.

"What happened?" Cam did not know what to say or do.

"When I came back, I saw a car stalled in the middle of the road. I thought there'd been an accident, so I got out to help. I found a woman in the driver's seat, and she looked in bad shape. I reached in to help her, and she bit me."

"I don't understand. Why did she do that?"

"It's what those things do."

"They bite?"

Donald nodded. "Apparently." He smiled faintly. "I'm sorry, bad time for a joke."

"I don't understand," she said again.

"We've moved a step down the food chain. You haven't seen it?"

"No. I've only seen that you can't kill the damn things."

"Oh, it gets worse," said Donald.

"I don't see how."

"The bites turn people."

Cam frowned. "Turn them into what?"

"Into one of those creatures."

"That's not possible."

"It is. I saw it happen with my own eyes."

Cam's heart dropped. "Lee asked me if I'd been bitten when we were at the station. I didn't understand."

Donald nodded. "He was right to be worried."

"What can I do? How can we stop the infection?"

"There's nothing you can do. You should go. You're not safe here."

"Maybe we can remove the infected area?"

"You are not cutting off my arm. Besides, that time has passed. You need to leave. You know what these creatures do to people. I don't want to hurt you."

"I won't leave you. You deserve better than that."

"Cam, it isn't safe here. If you won't leave for your sake, then leave for mine. If I turned and attacked you, I'd never—"

Cam stayed quiet as tears welled up in her eyes.

Donald reached out and softly held her hand. "Please don't cry."

"You stupid old man. You wouldn't have been bitten if you hadn't come back for me."

"And you'd be dead if I didn't."

"You can't do this to me. You can't. I didn't ask you to trade your life for mine."

Donald shook his head. "Cam, it's okay. We all die sometime. There's nothing you could have done."

"Why did you have to try to be the hero?"

"Isn't the hero always supposed to survive?"

Cam smiled sadly. "Why didn't you tell me sooner?"

"What's the point? I've seen what's coming. Look on the bright side. I get to be with Laura now."

"I didn't think you believed in all that?"

"Let's just say I'm going to repent like hell in the hopes of being reunited."

"What are you talking about, Donald? You have nothing to repent for. You're a good man, and you've led a good life."

"Now I'm faced with all this, my views have changed. All I want is Laura. So if there's a chance, no matter how remote that I could get to spend eternity with her, I'll pray to whatever god I need to make sure it happens."

Cam leaned over and hugged him. "Thank you."

"For what?"

"For showing me true love does exist. I want someone to have the same love in their heart for me as you do for Laura. I deserve that."

Donald's brow glistened as the fever slowly took over his body. "Don't get all mushy on me, princess." He cracked a weak smile.

Cam found no humor in the Star Wars joke. She opened her mouth to speak.

"You should go now," he interrupted. "It isn't safe here. I could turn at any moment. I'm already on borrowed time."

"I'm not going to leave you."

Donald stood and looked at Cam. "Please go. I'm begging you." Cam shook her head as Donald sighed and turned.

"Where are you going?"

"To the bedroom. If you must stay to the end, lock me in there. You'll at least have a chance to get out."

Once again, Cam found herself without words. She sucked at goodbye at the best of times, but she had never said it to someone about to die. Nothing felt like the right words to say.

Donald sensed her fumbling for words as he sat on the bed. "You don't have to say anything. You've done enough."

"I don't want you to go through this alone."

"I won't be." He pulled a picture of Laura from his shirt pocket.

Cam focused on the picture and smiled. "She's beautiful. Tell her I said hello. She's a lucky woman."

"I didn't think you believed in all that either?" he said as he lay back on the bed and rested his head on a pillow.

"I don't, but if a little faith helps, I'll do my part and put in a good word."

"Thank you." Donald smiled weakly and closed his eyes. "Cam? One last thing."

"Anything."

"Inside my jacket, there's an envelope. It's for you. Please take it before you leave. It's on the couch."

"But—"

"Promise me you'll take it."

"But you're—"

"Promise me."

"I promise." She leaned in and kissed him gently on the forehead.

"You should go," he said softly and closed his eyes.

"Goodbye, Donald. I'm glad I got to know you." Cam stepped back, expecting a response, but he stayed quiet. "Donald?"

Silence.

"Donald?"

He stirred slightly. "Don't leave."

"I'm not going anywhere."

"Laura?" muttered Donald. "Is that you? I love you, Laura."

No other words came.

"Donald?" Cam stared at his body. She had never seen someone turn before and was uncertain how long it took or, indeed what happened during the transformation. Cam looked around the room and spotted a pen and notepad on the nightstand. She quietly stepped over and picked them up, never taking her eyes off Donald. Before leaving his bedroom for the last time, she stopped at the foot of the bed and looked back at him.

His eyes were open. Black, piercing eyes.

"Oh, Donald, no. No. I'm so sorry." Cam gasped and took a step backward as he looked up at her.

The man who was once Donald was gone.

Heavy sobs took over as she took another step towards the door, clutching the notepad to her chest.

Donald groaned and rolled off the bed. He slowly climbed to his feet and bared his teeth as Cam backed out of the room and closed the door behind her. She knew the humane gesture would be to kill him instead of letting him turn, but she could not summon the strength.

She found the jacket on the back of the couch and pulled out a white envelope from the inner pocket. Inside she found a check for three hundred and seventy-five thousand, four hundred and sixty-three dollars written out to Cam Harris. She held her hand to her mouth in shock and half expected someone to jump out behind her like a demented game show host.

Donald slammed against the door and violently jerked her back to reality. She wiped her tears on her sleeve and sniffed, wondering if she would live long enough to cash it.

Donald hit the door again. Cam glanced around the apartment, looking for his car keys. Another loud bang and the bedroom door splintered. She gave up her hunt and left, pulling the door closed behind her.

Her phone vibrated in her pocket, and she quickly answered.

"*Cam, it's David. Where are you?*"

"Donald's dead."

"*Oh, god, what happened?*"

"Someone bit him," said Cam.

"*Are you hurt?*"

"No, just shaken. It's the bites, David. The bites turn you."

"*I know. I've seen it. Are you somewhere safe?*"

"No. I'm leaving his place now. I don't know where to go."

"*We're at the Hart's garage. Can you get over here, or do you need me to come get you?*"

"I couldn't get Donald's keys. I'm stuck here."

"*Sit tight, I'm on my way.*"

She hung up the phone and turned back to the door. She rested the notepad against it started to write '*A good man is dead inside*'. Cam ripped off the top sheet of paper and spat out her gum into her hand. She stuck it to the back of the page and pinned the note to the door.

Greg's car screeched to a halt in front of Amber's parents' house. Five houses away, a fire burned, and dark smoke filled the street. The wind lashed the flames across the yard as a pine tree on the edge of the driveway smoldered. Half a dozen creatures shuffled in the direction of the fire, and it took the attention away from Greg as he climbed out and quickly scanned the area behind him.

The ride over had not been without incident, and Warren would be unhappy about the dent on the hood. Greg needed to choose between a demon and a parked car, and the demon lost. He stayed on the phone with Amber the entire drive, and the fifteen-minute trip felt like time had frozen.

He grabbed the gun from the passenger seat and closed the car door. The snow-covered grass crunched loudly as he crossed the front yard.

"Okay, I'm here," he said into his Bluetooth earpiece.

"*What's burning?*"

"The Gerhart house."

"*We heard an explosion about half an hour ago. Is it bad?*"

"Yeah."

"*Oh, God. I hope they weren't home.*"

"It's heading this way. The whole street will go up if the wind changes."

"*Mom won't leave the house.*"

"She may not have a choice. The fire is going to decide for her,'" said Greg as he reached the front door.

Amber ignored the comment. "*Are you out front or back?*"

"Front door, but it's locked."

"*Come around back. You'll have to hop over the gate. It's padlocked,*" said Amber. "*The back door is open.*"

"Is Ratchet locked up?"

"*He's in the backyard.*"

"Fuck," Greg muttered to himself. If matters could not get any worse, he now needed to go face-to-face with her parent's eighty-pound shithead dog who attacked anything not family, and even a few who were.

He quickly crossed the lawn and headed to the gate on the side of the house. He jumped up, swung his legs over, and dropped into the backyard. The R.V. gate on the rear fence opened into the alleyway, but the yard looked empty and Ratchet long gone. Greg sighed in relief at one less creature in the house that wanted to kill him.

"I'm at the back door," said Greg as he approached the sliding glass doors.

"*Be careful,*" said Amber quietly. "*Ratchet?*"

"No idea. The back gate is open. It looks like he bolted. Where's your dad?"

"*I think he's upstairs, Greg, promise me you won't hurt him.*"

Greg stayed quiet.

"*Greg?*"

"I'm here."

"*Promise me you won't shoot him. He's not dangerous, he's just sick.*"

"Amber I—"

"*Promise me.*"

Greg sighed. "I promise."

"*Can you leave the gun in the car?*"

"Not fucking likely," he said under his breath.

"*What?*"

"I said I'm coming in. Greg cursed under his breath again. He did not want to go in unarmed. He knew what the creatures could do, and it did not fill him with comforting feelings. The situation suddenly became a lot more complicated.

He looked through the patio doors. The living room appeared empty. "Where are you?"

"*Upstairs in my parent's room.*"

Greg slowly slid the door open and entered the house. In the corner of the room, the McKenzie's Christmas tree flashed randomly, casting an eerie glow on the walls. He could see the stairs at the end of the hallway, and he quietly crossed the carpet.

He almost cleared the room when he stepped on one of Ratchet's toys. It emitted a loud, punctuated squeak. Greg stopped and slowly lifted his foot. The toy let out another long, exaggerated squeal as it refilled with air. Greg held his breath, trying to hear movement, confident the rubber terrorist was going to get him killed. The seconds clicked by loudly as his heart threatened to jump up into his throat, but the house remained quiet.

He walked up to the hallway and peeked around but did not see Walter. "*He's by the bedroom door. I can hear him,*" whispered Amber from the phone. "*You need to distract him.*"

"Well, of course I need to fucking distract him."

"*Don't take that tone with me. This isn't any easier for us.*"

"Goddammit, Amber. Your father is likely going to attack me the second I set foot upstairs. What do you want me to do?"

"*Get him away from the door.*"

Greg sighed again. "How?"

"*There's a magazine on the couch.*"

"I'm not going to hit your dad with a rolled-up magazine."

"*It's Vogue. It's pretty thick.*"

"He's not a dog, Amber."

Greg stepped back into the living room and looked for something to defend himself with. How could he fend off two hundred pounds of flesh-eating future father-in-law without hurting him? He felt like Goldilocks as his eyes darted around the room, trying to locate a weapon.

A poker. Too pointy.

A cushion. Too comfy.

A broom. Well, it was far from just right, but it would have to suffice.

He tucked his pistol into the front of his jeans and picked up the broom. The house was quiet as he tried to focus his hearing on any unusual sounds. As he reached the staircase, he cautiously looked up, hoping to see signs of Walter.

"We're at the end of the hallway," Amber whispered in Greg's earpiece. Greg slowly climbed the stairs, carefully shifting his weight to avoid making any unnecessary noise. If Walter heard him, he stayed quiet. Finally, Greg reached the top step. Walter stood ten feet away with his back to him. Greg raised the broom, and as his foot touched down, the floorboard cried out with a long, pained creak.

Walter remained still as Greg stepped into the hall. He moved forward, unsure of how to subdue him. Suddenly, Walter turned and advanced. Greg barely had time to react as he spun and shifted his weight. Walter stumbled and fell over Greg's legs, smashing into a glass table by the wall. The top shattered with a loud crash.

"*Greg?*" asked Amber, her voice heavy with concern.

"We broke the table."

"*You or dad?*"

"Your dad."

"*Dammit it, Greg. I told you to be careful with him.*"

"Would you have preferred it be me?" asked Greg as he moved towards the door.

"*That's not what I'm saying.*"

"Your dad is out here, and he is trying to kill me. I am not going to be able to handle this with peaceful negotiations."

Greg stepped towards the bedroom door as Walter grabbed his legs and Greg fell to the floor hard. He yelped out in pain as he rolled onto his back and held the broom across his chest. Walter scrambled to his feet and launched himself at Greg.

"Christ." Greg pushed the broom handle under Walter's chin and tried to get some distance from Walter's gnashing teeth.

"*What's wrong?*" Amber's voice said from the earpiece.

"I fell on my gun."

"*I thought I told you to leave it outside?*"

"Can we talk about this later?" Greg struggled to hold the broom, trying to keep distance between Walter's teeth and his face. Walter put all his weight onto the wood, and Greg started losing the struggle. The handle cracked loudly and left only a few seconds before it snapped in half. With a surge of strength, Greg pushed up hard, and Walter fell backward.

Greg quickly stood up and pulled the gun from the front of his pants, intending to tuck it in the back waistband.

As Greg moved towards the door, Walter grabbed his ankle, and his balance shifted. Greg reached out to keep from falling, and his hand hit the floor. The gun fired, and a loud scream came from behind the bedroom door.

"I didn't shoot him, I promise!" shouted Greg, expecting Amber to be pissed at the accidental discharge.

Greg kicked the creature in the chest, and the thing formally known as Walter reeled under the blow. He stumbled back and disappeared from view with a series of loud thumps.

Greg climbed back on his feet and stepped over to the top of the stairs. Walter lay still at the bottom, his body a mangled mess. His right leg and left arm were snapped backward, and his head contorted in a grotesquely unnatural position.

"Shit," Greg muttered.

Walter's eyes snapped open, and he started thrashing around.

"Oh, thank God."

Greg turned to head back to the bedroom and paused. He turned back to Walter's twitching body. "Before I forget, do I have your permission to ask your daughter's hand in marriage?"

Walter growled and gnashed in response.

"I'll take that as a yes," said Greg.

A second demon appeared behind Walter and launched herself up the stairs, her black eyes focused on Greg.

"Who the fuck are you?" said Greg as he stepped back.

She moved a lot faster than Walter and cleared the steps in seconds, barely giving Greg time to pull his gun. The bullet hit her between the eyes, and she too, fell down the stairs. Greg sighed in relief and finally headed to the bedroom door.

"Amber, it's me. Let me in," he said as he knocked. "I didn't kill your dad, I promise."

The door lock clicked, and Amber pulled the door open. Her eyes were red from crying. Greg followed her into the room. Ashley sat on the floor at the foot of the bed with their mother's head in her lap as she gently stroked her hair. Greg understood Mrs. McKenzie's paralysis. Her husband of thirty-two years had mutated into a flesh-eating monster and tried to kill her future son-in-law. She had every right to be in shock.

"Is everyone okay?"

Amber looked devastated. "What did you do?"

"I had no choice, he attacked me. Then some other woman came out

233

of nowhere." Greg suddenly noticed blood on Amber's shirt. "What happened? Are you bit?"

Amber continued crying as she shook her head.

"Amber, what happened?"

"You," said Ashley.

Greg pointed to his chest. "Me? What did I do?"

"What did you do?" Ashley hissed in anger. "You shot our mom."

Greg stared at her lap. Sure enough, a bullet hole centered Mrs. McKenzie's forehead. "Christ, what happened?"

"What happened? You fucking shot her," said Ashley said between clenched teeth. "That's what fucking happened."

"No, I didn't."

"Yes, you did. With the gun Amber told you to leave in the car."

"How?" asked Greg.

"Through the fucking door. Right where you aimed it."

Greg looked behind him to see a bullet hole two feet from the bottom of the door.

His eyes widened in shock. "Oh, God, I am so sorry. It was an accident. I never meant to sh—"

"Liar," shouted Ashley, cutting him off. "You never liked her."

"That's not true. I liked your mom."

"Then why did you kill her?" asked Ashley.

"I would never intentionally shoot her."

"You're worse than your brother," she added.

Oh, come on. That's uncalled for."

"At least he didn't kill our mother."

"Ash, I didn't do it on purpose."

"Right. This was the perfect opportunity for you to make it look like an accident."

"It was an accident."

Ashley snorted her disapproval.

"You'd closed the fucking door. How the hell could I have known?"

"I don't know. You just did. Our parents were right to want us to stay away from you."

Greg turned to Amber with a pleading look in his eyes. "Amber, you must believe me. I liked your mom. I never wanted to shoot her. You know me better than that."

"You shot her, Greg, even after I repeatedly told you to leave the gun outside," said Amber. "If you'd listened to what I told you, she'd still be alive."

"And I'd be dead if I didn't. Your dad was trying to kill me."

"I suppose you shot him too?" accused Ashley.

"No, he fell down the stairs after he attacked me. He's a little banged up, but he's fine."

"And the second gunshot?"

"Someone else came in the house," said Greg.

"No, they didn't," accused Ashley.

"She's lying at the bottom of the stairs. Want to go see?"

"Did you kill her?" asked Ashley.

"No, Ash, I gave her a harsh talking to and told her to reflect on her ways. Of course I fucking killed her."

"I don't care for your attitude," Amber interjected. "You need to leave."

"Amber, you're not thinking straight. I didn't do it on purpose. Your dad came at me, and we fell. It wasn't my fault."

"If you'd left the damn gun in the car like I said, my mom would be alive."

"And, as I said already, I'd be dead. That's twice in two days your dad has tried to kill me."

"Greg, you killed my mom," said Amber as she sniffed back a tear. "How rational would you like me to be?"

"I'm sorry I killed your mom. I didn't do this on purpose. If I came in unarmed, I'd be dead now."

"Better you than her," said Ashley.

Greg turned back to Amber. "We need to go. It isn't safe here."

"We can't leave, Greg."

"If the zombie-demons don't get in, the fire at the Gerhart's house will. You're out of options."

"Zombie-demons? I don't understand," said Amber.

"It's what we're calling them. The dead aren't staying dead anymore."

A loud crash of glass came from the living room to emphasize his urgency.

Greg pointed downstairs. "That's the patio door. We need to go now."

Amber looked at Ashley. "Greg, we can't leave her."

"She's gone, Amber. We have to go."

"Greg?" Amber pleaded.

"Listen to me. Those things are coming this way. If they head for the stairs, we're screwed. We need to leave."

"She's awake," said Ashley as Mrs. McKenzie opened her eyes. "Mom's awake."

Greg looked at her soulless black eyes. Mrs. McKenzie was no longer home.

"Ashley, stand up right now," shouted Greg urgently.

"We need to get her to a hospital."

"Ashley, please, listen to—"

"ASHLEY, GET UP RIGHT NOW," Amber screamed as she noticed the eyes.

Ashley jumped up quickly as Mrs. McKenzie climbed to her feet. She turned to her daughter and snarled.

Greg pointed to the door. "Everyone out, now," he shouted.

As Amber and Ashley ran for the door, Mrs. McKenzie moved on Greg. He pushed her chest, and she fell backward. The few seconds of distraction gave him enough time to scramble for the door and slam it shut. Amber and Ashley were already halfway down the stairs.

Ashley stopped after a few steps. "What did you do to our dad?"

"He's not dead." Greg pointed. "See, he's still moving. I told you I didn't shoot him."

"No, you saved that for our mother."

"And it was an accident," said Greg.

"So you said."

"And there is the woman I shot." Greg led them past Walter and the dead woman and headed for the front door. Seven of the creatures were already in the living room, and Greg could see more in the backyard. They ran outside moments before the horde swarmed the house.

CHAPTER 31

Jason Reynolds, the founder of Oceanview, sat in his office enjoying a rare couple of hours of downtime. His feet were propped up on his desk as he sipped a glass of wine. Muted porn played on his computer screen, but his attention focused elsewhere instead of the three women ravaging each other. He stared into the fireplace on the opposite wall. The curtains were closed, and the room was silent but for the crackling of the flames. He seldom watched local television or went online to read the goings-on in his town, so he was clueless about the atrocities occurring outside.

His eyelids were getting heavy when a gentle knock sounded at the door. Reynolds stayed quiet and chose to ignore it. A second knock followed.

"Sir?" The voice belonged to Vernon, his butler for the past sixty years.

"Come in," said Reynolds eventually as he rubbed his eyes.

Vernon entered, carrying a silver tray. "Dinner?"

Reynolds took his feet off the desk and sat up as Vernon placed the tray in front of him. His focus never left the fireplace. "Thanks, Vernon."

Vernon lifted the lid of the serving tray, and the pleasant aroma of braised rack of lamb filled the room. A favorite meal of Reynolds', he would generally be champing at the bit to dive into the beast. Instead, he continued to stare at the fire.

"Is everything okay, sir?" Vernon always nailed Reynolds' mood when something looked out of sorts.

"Yes. I don't know. Possibly?"

"Possibly?"

"Are you getting tired of all this?" asked Reynolds.

"This, sir? Sorry, I don't understand."

"Ruling this town."

Vernon frowned. "Sir?" Something was definitely wrong. The Reynolds he had known most of his boss's life would never have thought such a question, let alone say it out loud for someone else to hear.

"These pedantic ass-kissers need to grow a collective backbone. I'm starting to find this whole existence rather hollow and dull."

"Did something change, sir?"

"No, Vernon. That's just it. Nothing has changed."

"So, what brought this on?"

"The Forefather's Day events this year kind of cemented it for me."

"But you love Forefather's Day."

"I used to. This year bored me. It's the same people doing the same thing year in and year out. It's like this town is the land that time forgot. What's the point in ruling a giant pile of mediocre?"

"And you're deciding this now after almost forty years?"

"I know, right? I'm getting too old for this shit."

"I must say I'm surprised. Don't tell me the famous Jason Reynolds is finally growing a heart?"

"I wouldn't go that far," said Reynolds with a laugh.

"I thought you wanted a town full of people kissing your ass?"

"Me too. I thought a town full of people bowing to my every whim would be wonderful, but I must admit it's grown stale. There isn't a single one among them who'd stand up to me. I called them peasants, for God's sake, and they still cheered. I suggest a new stadium, and we build it. I want a new art museum? Done. There's no challenge anymore. It's like stepping on ants, and fucking retarded ones at that. If I have to kiss another baby, I going to puke. I wish I had a cold sore so I could give them all face herpes."

"I don't know what to say, sir. How about something stronger, whiskey perhaps? Maybe this will pass?"

Reynolds lifted his wine glass and looked at the contents. "You're probably right."

As Vernon turned to leave, there came another knock at the door.

Reynolds nodded, and Vernon let the visitor in.

"What is it, Randy?" said Reynolds as his head landscaper walked into the room, clutching at his cap.

"Sir, something is going on at the front gate. A bunch of the townsfolk have gathered outside."

"What do they want?" asked Reynolds.

"They said they want to come in."

"Are they crazy? I don't offer tours of my mansion."

"No, this is something different."

"Are they Christmas carolers? I fucking hate Christmas carolers. They stand on my front porch and warble some out-of-tune drivel about their savior and then expect a tip. And they don't go away until I pay them to. It's quite the racket they've got going on. It's fucking extortion. Tell them to fuck off. I have their tip right here." He grabbed his crotch for emphasis.

"They aren't carolers, sir."

Reynolds minimized the porn on his desktop and clicked on a camera icon. A video application opened, showing a bank of video screens. He clicked on the Camera Two link, and a live feed from the roof was displayed on the screen.

Reynolds moved the camera and zoomed in on the group. Sure enough, a group of twenty-five or so Oceanview residents stood at the gate.

"What do we have here?" he said as a grin spread across his face

Vernon leaned into the monitor. "Can you switch to camera five?"

"What do you see?" asked Reynolds as he switched cameras.

"Can you zoom in a bit?"

Reynolds zoomed the camera in on the crowd. "What am I looking for?"

"There," said Vernon as he pointed to the screen.

Reynolds leaned in closer to the screen. "Am I seeing this right?"

Vernon nodded as it became apparent a few of the group carried guns.

"Why are there armed citizens at my front door?"

Vernon shrugged. "I have no idea, sir."

Reynolds watched the monitor for a few more seconds with a look of amusement.

◆ ◆ ◆ ◆

Outside at the gate, Kit-Kat and several other residents were desperately trying to find shelter. The zombie-demon ranks were growing by the hour, and places of refuge were getting fewer and more precious. Reynolds' mansion sat behind a large stone wall, twelve feet high and two feet thick. It formed the perfect stronghold, if the miserly bastard would let them inside.

After fleeing his apartment, Kit-Kat ran into the small group and felt safety in numbers seemed wiser. Despite being a level one-hundred and twenty Tank in World of Warcraft, he could hardly be considered combat-ready, and his hours spent in-game did little to prepare him for violence in the real world. As the group moved across town, a few more joined up with them. Then a couple were eaten, then a few more joined, and then a few more were eaten.

As the numbers ebbed and flowed, the pulsating group slowly made its way to Reynolds's mansion. By the time they reached the front gate, they were twenty-five strong, and the longer Reynolds kept them standing outside with their collective asses hanging out, the more irate they became.

They jumped and waved at the camera above the gate, hoping to grab Reynolds' attention.

♦ ♦ ♦ ♦

Inside, Reynolds could see the crowd pushing into the gate. Lips were moving, but no sound came.

"I wonder when one of them will be smart enough to figure out the intercom."

Twenty seconds later, a static-infused voice chimed through the speaker. "*Hello?*"

"There's a clever Muppet." Reynolds tapped the intercom button. "What do you want?"

A quick static burst rang out as Kit-Kat's voice piped through. "*Yeah, Mr. Reynolds. It's some of...*" static "*...from town. We...*" static "*...wondering if we...*" static "*...in and take shelter...*" static "*...you?*"

"Take shelter?" Reynolds looked genuinely bemused. "From what?"

"*The whole town...*" static "*...gone to shit.*"

Reynolds flipped off the intercom and looked up at Vernon. "Didn't I tell you to get that fixed?"

"He's due out next week."

"What does he mean, gone to shit? Do either of you know what he is talking about?"

Vernon and Randy both shook their heads.

He keyed the intercom again. "Please repeat."

"*The town...*" static "*...gone to shit.*"

"Yes, I heard that part. Are we having a homeless issue at the bus stop again? You know it's a police issue, right? Do you need their number?"

Kit-Kat may have called him a pompous, self-righteous prick, but more static distorted his voice. "*The dead...*" static "*...come back to life and are tearing the...*" static "*...apart. We need somewhere safe...*" static "*...hide out.*"

"Did he say what I think he said?"

Vernon and Randy nodded again.

"Fucking druggies." He flipped on the intercom. "I'm sorry, there isn't any room, but I believe the rehab is taking new patients."

The intercom crackled as Kit-Kat's voice piped through again. "*Rehab? What are...*" static "*...implying?*"

"That you're on drugs, I thought I made that clear. You'll have to go somewhere else."

"*Somewhere else? There...*" static "*...nowhere else.*"

"Not my problem, pee-on."

"*Pee-on? I'll give you fucking pee-on, you stuck...*" static "*...piece of shit. We put you in...*" static "*...damn mansion. The least you can do...*" static "*...let us take shelter.*"

"I don't have room."

"*What? You...*" static "*...fifteen bedrooms.*"

Reynolds was tired of the games. "I won't say this again. Get off my fucking property, or I will be forced to defend my domain."

"*Or what, you'll shoot us? Not...*" static "*...we shoot you.*"

Reynolds's eyes widened as he leaped up from his chair. "Vernon, you know what this means? The fucking peasants are revolting. Quick, go grab my gun."

"Excuse me, sir?"

"Get my gun. I'll show them how I deal with trespassers."

"Technically, they aren't trespassing, sir. They are standing in the street, which is town property."

"A town I built."

"It won't make any difference. They aren't trespassing."

Reynolds reached under his table and pressed a button.

♦ ♦ ♦ ♦

The front gates slowly swung open.

Despite their desperation, the group hesitated before stepping through the gates.

"See, I told you he could be reasonable," Kit-Kat said with a grin and stepped over the perimeter threshold. "Let's get off the streets and get this gate closed."

♦ ♦ ♦ ♦

Reynolds smiled as he opened his office window. "And now they are trespassing." He raised his rifle.

♦ ♦ ♦ ♦

Kit-Kat looked down as a red dot appeared on his chest. "Give me a break."

A gunshot rang out, and Kit-Kat flinched. He stared at a gaping hole where his heart previously occupied. He dropped to the snowy ground as his life slipped away.

The group screamed as the intercom chirped and Reynolds' voice piped through. "*Anyone else want to come in?*"

♦ ♦ ♦ ♦

Reynolds looked back at Vernon as he put his rifle down. "That is how you deal with trespassers," he said with a grin and sat returned to his chair. "Shut the window, Vernon. It's getting cold in here."

"I'm relatively certain that was murder, sir," said Vernon as he pulled the window shut.

"Don't be ridiculous. I feared for my life, and they were trespassing with guns. Who is a jury more likely to believe?"

Vernon frowned in frustration as he opted to stay quiet. It was a fight he would not win.

Reynolds reached under his desk and pushed the gate button. He watched it close on his monitor as the crowd quickly dispersed. He looked rather pleased with himself. Vernon had witnessed Reynolds commit a lot of underhanded deeds over the years, but murder was a first. Suddenly, Reynolds was not the only one in the room having doubts about their place.

"Vernon, is the limo ready?" asked Reynolds.

"Of course, sir. Where are we going?"

"I want to go into town and see what all the fuss is about."

"Are you sure that's wise?"

"Why?"

"The dead coming back to life?"

"Oh, Vernon, they weren't serious. They wanted to come in and steal my shit. I thought you'd know better than that. The town is full of potential thieving degenerates. Give them an inch, and they'll wipe me out. I know how this ends." He paused. "Meet me outside in fifteen."

Ten minutes later, Vernon stood holding the car door open as Reynolds stepped outside into the cold air. He walked briskly to the limo but paused before getting in. He cocked his head and listened. "What is that noise?"

"I don't know. It started just before you came outside,' said Vernon. "I can't tell what it is."

"It sounds like farm equipment," said Reynolds. "Is Andre cutting grass?"

"No, sir. All the equipment is locked up. The lawn is under a foot of snow."

Reynolds looked around, trying to pinpoint the location. He turned to the front entrance as a large yellow backhoe smashed through the heavy metal gate, pushing its twisted form aside. The citizens jogged behind it as the anti-peasant barrier crashed open.

Reynolds stared at the group. "Where the fuck did they get a backhoe? Those assholes fucked up my gate. What is wrong with these people? I swear, you kill one peasant, and the entire fucking town goes ape-shit."

"Sir, we should go back inside and call the police. This is out of our hands now. There are too many of them. More blood is going to be spilled if we stay outside."

"Vernon, you underestimate—" And then he saw something.

The angry mob cleared the gate, but Reynolds ignored them. The movement behind them stole his attention.

At first, one, then ten, then fifty, and within fifteen seconds, at least two hundred demons shuffled through the open gate and towards the mansion. Reynolds lost track of the citizens. He no longer cared.

"The fuck? Are they—"

"Dead, sir?"

Reynolds nodded.

Loud groaning echoed across the lawn as the army of the dead continued to pour through the gate.

"May I suggest a change of plan, sir?" asked Vernon.

Reynolds nodded.

"It's time we moved you to the panic room."

Reynolds nodded.

"Sir?"

Reynolds nodded for the fourth time, frozen in place.

Vernon grabbed his arm. "Jason, it's time to go," he said, using his name for the first time since Reynolds had been a child.

Reynolds looked at him with panicked eyes, his cocksure attitude gone. Vernon no longer saw the arrogant ruler of Oceanview, but the young child he met all those years ago.

"Come on, let's get you inside."

Reynolds and Vernon ran back into the house. Vernon hit an alarm inside the front lobby, and the remaining staff on duty headed to the panic room in the basement. The plan would have worked if Reynolds bothered to check everyone for bites before they entered. Andre, one of the newer gardeners on the property, turned about thirty minutes after Reynolds sealed the doors and locked himself and his entire staff inside with him.

To Reynolds's credit, he disposed of five assailants before they finally overpowered him and tore him to pieces. He also unwittingly created a truthful verse that could be added to the Forefather's anthem. Unfortunately, no one stayed alive long enough to share the news with the rest of the town.

He tore five creatures limb from limb
Until they bit then devoured him
Oh, little town of Oceanview
Is overrun with zombies.

CHAPTER 32

Warren sat in the front office of his garage with Mr. Yan when a loud knock came from the side door. Warren stood up and quickly headed out back as the knock rang again. A heavy desk blocked the door, but he hesitated before moving it.

"Who is it?"

"A zombie-demon," the muffled voice on the other side answered.

"Huh?"

"It's me, you idiot. Let me in."

Warren put his weight against the desk and pushed it aside with a loud groan. He unlocked the door and pulled it open as Amber and Ashley stepped in, their arms around each other for comfort. Greg followed close behind and hurriedly closed the door.

"Not funny, dude," said Warren. "I thought you were one of them."

"Do they knock?" asked Greg.

"They might."

"Or introduce themselves?"

"Seemed like the right question to ask in light of what's happening."

"You know those things can't speak, right?" He nodded to the desk. "Need help?"

"Sure."

The brothers pushed the heavy table back in front of the door.

Greg noticed Mr. Yan sitting in the front office. "Who else is here?" he asked.

"A couple of people. I found survivors on the way back."

Amber escorted Ashley to the mechanic bay as Warren nodded at the girls. Greg stopped next to him.

"Where did you get to, man? You've been gone three hours," asked Warren.

"I killed Jackie," said Greg.

"What?"

"I killed Jackie. It was an accident."

"She turned?"

Greg shook his head. "Not when I shot her, she hadn't."

"The fuck?"

"Walter went ape-shit and tore up the place. He jumped me, there was a struggle, I fell, and the gun went off."

"Was she helping you?" asked Warren.

"No, they were in the bedroom. The bullet went through the door and hit her in the head."

"YOU SHOT HER THROUGH THE DOOR?" Warren said a little too loudly.

"Will you shut up. The girls aren't exactly taking this well," said Greg in a hushed tone.

"Can you blame them? You shot their mom."

"You're not helping," said Warren.

Warren shrugged. "I'm just saying."

"Did David make it back with you?" asked Greg.

"Yeah, but he left to get Cam."

"Cam?"

Warren nodded. "Donald got bit and turned into a zombie-demon. David went to pick her up."

Greg nodded, but his mind dwelled on Jackie. He felt immense guilt about killing his future mother-in-law and wondered how he would explain her death to his future kids.

"Did you hear what I said?"

"Yeah," said Greg. "David left to get Cam."

"No, I mean about the bites. They bite you, you die. You come back as a zombie-demon."

Greg looked at Warren, snapping out of his haze. "That explains Walter then."

"What happened?"

"They said a man in their garden attacked him and bit him on the hand defending himself." He started pacing as the pieces of the puzzle began to fall into place.

"How fast did he turn?" asked Warren.

"Amber said about two hours based on the noises they heard." Greg nodded towards Mr. Yan in the office. "When did he show up?"

"We saw him out front when we got here. They jumped him trying to leave town."

"Where's Min and Katie?"

Warren shook his head. "They didn't make it."

"Fuck. Are you serious?"

"He tried to pack his car to get out of town and got attacked. They ripped Katie right out of the seat in front of him."

Greg looked visibly ill. Katie Yan gave him a pink princess crown to wear at the Forefather's Day festivities a few days prior. It felt like a lifetime ago. "She's just a kid." The gravity of the situation finally kicked in, and it made him sick to his stomach. "Is he bit?"

"No, but he ain't saying much."

"I can't say I blame him. It's getting really bad out there, Warren."

"There's one more thing."

Greg continued to pace the floor, his mind racing.

"Greg. You might want to sit for this."

Greg stopped and looked at Warren. "I can't take any more bad news today."

"We picked up someone else on the way back."

"Good. Strength in numbers," said Greg.

"Not necessarily. Open the blinds."

Greg stepped over to the window and parted the blinds to the workshop to see Mrs. Andrews seated in the mechanic bay. He watched as she ran a finger over the edge of a workbench to check for dirt. She shook her head in disgust.

"What the fuck, Warren?"

"Dude, I saw her running down the street when we drove by. What would you have done?"

"Left her. I did not plan on spending the zombie apocalypse with her miserable ass."

"So you've accepted it then?" asked Warren.

"Do I have much of a choice? She's here now."

"Not Mrs. Andrews," said Warren. "I meant that this is the zombie apocalypse."

"You mean zombie-demon?' asked Greg. "I guess."

Warren smiled. "I'm glad the name is finally sticking. What are we going to do?"

"Maybe we can trick her into leaving," said Greg.

"Not her. I mean here. What is our next move?"

"We need to take stock of our weapons and do a supply run for more food and water. Maybe get some blankets."

"You want to stay here?"

"Why not? You blocked up the front window easily enough. The backyard is fenced in, and we have electricity and running water. We can protect ourselves."

Warren's cell phone started to vibrate in his pocket. He pulled it out and checked the caller I.D. "It's Bob."

"Answer it."

"Hey Bob, what's up?" Warren said cheerfully to their aging mechanic. He listened for a moment. "What are you doing in the Circle K freezer?" A pause. "Trapped?" Another pause. "We're on our way, Bob," said Warren as he hung up the phone. "Well, that sucked."

"Is he bitten?"

Warren shook his head. "I wish we knew someone called Barbara."

"Why the hell do we need to know someone called Barbara?"

"Because I wanted to shout into the phone, '*We're coming to get you, Barbara*', you know, like in zombie movies. 'We're on our way, Bob' kinda sucked."

"Are you serious?"

Warren nodded.

"For fuck's sake." Greg ducked behind his desk and reappeared with a phone book.

"We still have a phone book?" asked Warren.

"It's propping up a leg." He flipped it open and started scanning through the names. After a few seconds, he stopped, pulled out his cell phone, and dialed.

"Here." He handed the phone to Warren.

"*Hello, this is Barbara*," an elderly woman on the other end answered

Warren's face beamed. "We're coming to get you, Barbara," he said triumphantly.

"*Who is this?*" she said meekly.

"It doesn't matter. Just know we're coming to get you, Barbara."

The voice became distant. "*It sounds like the young man from the dial-a-ride. I think he is coming to take me to the senior center. Maybe you could speak with him?*"

The phone clattered as Barbara passed it to her son.

"*This is Bob.*"

"Fuck off, Bob." Warren's shoulders slumped as he cut off the call and promptly hung up the phone.

Greg raised an eyebrow.

"Never mind," Warren whined. "I—"

Loud, frantic banging from the side door cut him off mid-sentence.

"Let us in," a voice screamed from behind the door.

Warren looked at Greg. "Who is it?"

Greg shrugged. "I don't know. Help me with the desk."

"Hurry," the voice yelled.

Greg and Warren pushed the table aside, and Greg unlocked the door. The door pushed open, and Cam and Lee staggered in, carrying David between them.

"What happened? Are you okay?" Warren's genuine concern surprised both David and himself equally.

"Lee shot me," said David through clenched teeth.

"It was an accident," mumbled Lee.

"There's a lot of that going around," said Ashley as she walked over to check on the noise.

Lee helped move David to a table and set him down carefully. "What does she mean?" he asked.

"He shot their mom," said Warren, matter-of-factly. "Long story."

"Seriously?" said David as he carefully laid back, obviously in a considerable amount of pain. "That was rude."

"We need to get you taken care of," said Lee.

Warren grinned at Lee. "You got your bullets back?"

"That isn't funny, Warren," said Lee.

"Yeah, it is."

"No, it really isn't," said David as he grimaced again.

"How do we know you weren't bitten?" asked Warren.

"Because I have a bullet hole in me, Warren," David said with a pained look on his face. "Amazed you're still alive. Figured you'd be one of the first to go."

"Because I'm a few pounds overweight?"

"Because you're an idiot," said David.

"I'd rather be an idiot than a heathen," argued Warren.

"I can always stop being a heathen, but you'd still be an idiot."

"What are you going on about?" asked Greg

"David here feels here is better than everyone else and doesn't believe in God."

"So?"

"So? Greg, I don't trust a man who doesn't believe in the Lord."

"I don't believe, and you trust me."

"But at least you go to church."

"But I don't enjoy it," said Greg.

"But at least you go," he said again.

David rolled his eyes. "Idiot."

"Do you want a piece of me?" Warren challenged belligerently as he turned to face David.

"Okay, calm down, sweetheart," said Lee, getting between the two men. "You can compare cock sizes later. Right now, we need to get David fixed up." Lee turned to Greg. "What medical supplies do you have?"

"Nothing major. Band-Aids and Neosporin." He pointed to a medicine cabinet on the wall.

"Christ, Greg," said Lee. "You work in a garage. What if you seriously hurt yourself?"

"I'd put ice on it, and we'd use the urgent care. It's like four blocks away."

"We could treat him liked an injured horse and, you know—" Warren put two fingers together to make a gun and pretended to fire it. "Pow."

Lee shook his head in disbelief. "Not helping, Warren. The bleeding has stopped, but I need something to clean the wound and bandage him up. I can use what you have, but we'll have to hit the pharmacy later. Do you have weapons?"

"Yeah," said Greg. "Warren, go grab what we found."

Lee looked around the workshop. "Is this place secured?"

Greg nodded. "Yeah. The back lot has a nine-foot chain link fence. The bay doors are closed and locked. We parked a couple of cars in front of the front office door. The side door is barricaded from the inside. Nothing is getting in."

"Good. So, what do we know about these things?" asked Lee.

"It looks like the dead are coming back to life," said Amber.

"You mean like zombies?" asked Cam.

"See," said Warren as his face lit up. "We're actually calling them zombie-demons because of the black eyes."

"And our friends are dumping us on the curb to fend for ourselves," Cam continued. She quoted 'friends' with her fingers for emphasis.

Lee cringed. "Cam, I'm sorry."

"Save it," she said. "Not interested."

An awkward air of silence washed over everyone at the unexpected confrontation.

Lee finally spoke. "Seems we're all in agreement on them being dead. It also looks like a shot to the head takes them down."

"Not true," said Greg. "Mrs. McKenzie was shot in the head, and she came back."

"Are you sure it was a headshot?"

"Oh, he's sure," said Ashley. "Right between the fucking eyes. He made certain of it."

"But she hadn't been bitten," added Greg. "And she still came back."

"Yeah, she had," said Amber from behind.

Greg turned around. "You never told me that."

"Dad bit her on the arm while we were trying to get into the bedroom," said Cam. "We'd bandaged her up before you came over."

Greg opened his mouth to reply, but Lee interrupted. "So we know it isn't airborne then. It's definitely the bites. I shot one in the head, and she died. I saw her on the ground."

"No, you didn't," said Cam.

"You haven't seen me shooting one yet."

"I did. At the Circle K."

"But you weren't there."

"I was hiding behind the wall. If you'd bothered to look over it. You know, right after your bitch of a wife made you dump me in the middle of the fucking apocalypse. The woman you shot in the head got back up a few minutes after you left. Headshots don't work."

"She had no head. I blew it clean off her shoulders," said Lee.

"And she got back up."

"I smashed Edna Wallace in the head with a vase," said David. "No way she should have gotten up after that."

"You hit a little old lady in the head with a vase?" said Warren as he returned, carrying a large box of weapons. "What is wrong with you?"

"It was self-defense," said David. "She came at me."

"You're a real hero."

Greg stepped in to defend David. "Get off your high horse, Warren. We've all killed someone. You decapitated Mr. Pilano."

"Aw, not Sal. I liked his pizza," moaned Cam. "I swear to Christ, if Hank is dead, I'm giving up right now. No pizza and beer, I might as well be dead."

Lee faced the group. "So, how do we kill what we can't kill?"

"What if we took their legs out," Warren offered as he dropped the box on the workbench next to Lee. "It won't kill them, but it'll slow them down."

"That's actually not a bad idea," said Lee. "Do you happen to have a machete in that box of yours?"

"Don't know, let's look." He picked up the box and dumped the contents out. Guns and boxes of ammunition spilled across the surface.

Lee's eyes widened at Warren's carelessness.

"What?" Warren picked up on Lee's disapproval.

"You haven't been around guns very much, have you?" asked Lee.

"No, why?"

"Just a hunch."

Warren shrugged as he continued to rummage through the weapons. "I don't see a machete in here."

Lee started to sort through the pile and picked out a couple of the guns and put them on the workbench. He gave the boxes of ammunition a quick once over and shook his head. "Who grabbed these?"

"Greg, David, and me."

"Where?" asked Lee.

"TK's. What's wrong with them?"

"Most of this is useless. Hardly any of the bullets match up to the damn guns." Lee turned to David. "I figured you would know better."

"Me? Do I look like an NRA member to you?"

"I thought with you having a doctorate you'd know how a gun works," accused Lee.

"I guess I skipped the '*match a bullet to the gun*' part of my thesis. Besides, I didn't grab guns. I grabbed sleeping bags and camping equipment. Warren grabbed the ammo."

Warren picked up a pistol.

"What are you doing?" asked Lee.

"Loading the gun. What does it look like?"

"You're putting the bullets in the barrel."

"Yeah."

"They don't go in the barrel."

"Of course they do. How do you think they come out when you pull the trigger?"

Lee shook his head. "You're confusing it with a Nerf Gun. Maybe you shouldn't have a weapon." He reached out and snatched the pistol away from Warren.

"Toss me a clip then," said Warren as he picked up a shotgun and pointed to a box on the table. "I'll show you how it's done."

"It's a magazine."

"Same thing."

"No, a magazine holds shells under spring pressure in preparation for feeding into the gun's chamber. A cartridge clip doesn't have a spring, and it doesn't feed shells directly into the chamber. It holds cartridges in the correct order for charging a firearm's magazine. The clips feed magazines, and the magazines feed the firearm." He held up a clip. "Clip." He put it down and picked up a magazine. "Magazine. It's not rocket science."

"Whatever, dude, I just need some bullets," said Warren.

"You're holding a shotgun, for Christ's sake."

Warren looked down at the gun. "Can I have some bullets for my shotgun, please?"

"Shotguns use shells."

Lee picked up a box of ammunition from the table and pulled out a magazine. He loaded it into the gun and pointed it at Warren's chest.

Warren's arms automatically shot skyward in surrender as the McKenzie sisters screamed.

"What the fuck, Lee," Greg yelled. "What are you doing?"

Lee pulled the trigger.

Bang.

Warren instinctively flinched and grabbed his chest. Nothing. No pain, no blood, and certainly no death.

"WHAT THE FUCK, MAN?" he screamed. "I nearly shit myself. You almost fucking killed me."

"Not with blanks," said Lee. "Half of the bullets you grabbed are fucking blanks. They're worthless."

"How were we supposed to know? I have no idea about guns. I've never even held a gun. How am I supposed to know what fucking bullets to get," said Warren, still trying to compose himself. Part of him thankful to be alive, and the other half wanting to kill Lee.

Lee held up a box. "Because it fucking says blanks on the fucking side."

Warren shrugged, unable to argue the point. "Oh."

David shook his head. "Figures. This is like sending a vegetarian to get burgers."

"What's that supposed to mean?" asked Warren.

"What do you think it means? It means you're the wrong fucking man for the wrong fucking job. It means you are a fucking idiot, and to be quite frank, the last person I'd want to be around who's holding a gun. I'll take my chances with the demons if our brilliant plan is to arm you."

Warren pointed to the door. "Okay, quack, you and me, outside right now."

"Outside?"

"Yep. What are you, chicken?" challenged Warren.

"Are you kidding?" said David.

"What's wrong with going outside? Have the wuss fairies foreclosed on your nutsack?"

"The place is crawling with flesh-eating fuck knows what."

"They're called zombie-demons, David. What, all your fancy, big city edjacashion didn't teach you about zombie-demons, boy?"

David started to move. "That's it."

"Enough," yelled Greg. "If you two don't knock it off, I'm throwing you both outside."

"You wouldn't dare," said Warren.

"Keep pushing, and you'll find out."

Warren thought about it for a second and took a step back. "Fine, I've got better things to do with my time."

Greg turned to Lee. "What exactly do we have to work with then?"

"Not much. Four pistols with about eighty bullets, including mine. Seven pistols with incorrect ammunition. Four rifles with seventy-six bullets and two shotguns with no shells."

"Five pistols." Greg pulled his gun from his pants and put it on the workbench. "With ammo." He handed Lee two boxes of correct ammunition and turned to Warren. "I told you to get ammo for the shotgun."

"You told me to get bullets, so that's what I grabbed," said Warren.

"Shotguns don't use bullets," said Greg. "They use fucking shells. Everybody knows that."

"How would I know? I'm a pacifist," said Warren.

"You're a moron," said Greg.

"I didn't see you grabbing shells," countered Warren.

"No, I grabbed bullets for the damn pistol. I assumed you could handle the simple task of grabbing a box with a label on it."

Lee started to lose his patience with the brothers. "Are you two done?"

No," said Warren.

"Yes," said Greg.

"Warren, I'll ask again, are you done?"

"Over a hundred bullets isn't bad," said Warren, ignoring Lee's question.

"Depends on how long we're stuck here. If those things get determined to come in, we don't have enough to stop them," said Lee.

"Plus, we need to save nine bullets," said Warren.

Greg frowned. "What for?"

"Well, I don't know about all of you, but if those things get in and we can't get out." He put two fingers to his temple and pulled the imaginary trigger.

"He has a point," Amber agreed.

Greg had no interest in killing himself. His family suffered enough premature death with their dad's suicide without him and Warren taking the easy way out. "Nobody is shooting anyone. Should we go out for more ammo?"

"Not now. It's getting dark out," said Lee.

"Isn't that the best time to go? They won't be able to see us," asked Warren.

Lee shook his head. "And we won't be able to see them. It's too risky, we can go in the morning. We'll grab medical supplies too. How is the food situation looking?"

"It isn't," said Ashley. "Just vending machine snacks. But it's at least full."

"Dibs on the Skittles," said Warren.

Ashley already had her eye on the same candy. "Why?"

"Because they have fruit juice in them, and I don't want to catch scurvy."

David laughed.

"Something funny, David?"

"Yeah, a few things."

"Such as?" asked Warren.

"Scurvy?"

"It's cold outside. If I have vitamin C in me, I won't catch scurvy."

"Scurvy isn't something you catch in the winter. It's a severe vitamin C deficiency that particularly affected poorly nourished sailors in the eighteenth century. Scurvy hasn't been an issue in the civilized world in two hundred years, and even if it was, a bag of Skittles isn't going to cut it."

"There has been a recent outbreak," said Warren.

"Oh, really. Where did you read that?"

"Online. Just because you have some hoidy-toidy doctorate, it doesn't make you smarter than me."

"Actually, it does. It's why I have the capital D and little r in front of my name."

"Yeah, well, I don't see you offering us a better solution," said Warren.

"Good plans take time. They aren't something you come up with on the spot."

"Which is hoidy-toidy speak for I ain't got a fucking clue."

"I don't hear your grand plan, Warren."

Greg needed to deflate the situation before someone ended up shot with real bullets. "Okay, Warren. Time to put your Google M.D. to bed. David, rest up. We'll get you clean bandages and painkillers tomorrow. We'll figure this out in the morning."

"You can count me out then," said Warren.

"Now what?"

"Tomorrow's run. If it's for David, I'm staying here. I won't risk my life for a man who doesn't believe in God," said Warren firmly.

"So much for loving your fellow man," said David.

"It only works when your fellow man isn't a heathen."

"So, God's unconditional love does, in fact, have conditions then?"

Greg had tired of the fighting. "Fine, I'll go on my own. You can stay here."

"What?" said Warren.

"I'll go on my own. I won't force you to do something you don't want to do."

Warren gritted his teeth. His brother needed a wingman and deep down he knew it needed to be him. "Fine. I'll go with you. I don't want your death on my conscience."

CHAPTER 33

"**I** do not want a cup of tea, Gary. I don't drink tea, I don't even like tea," said Death, as God placed a steaming teapot in front of him.

God looked shocked. "Who doesn't drink tea? Everyone in the universe drinks tea."

"Well, I don't."

"Oh, so you're a coffee person?"

"I'm a '*why did you call me to your office to talk about beverages, when I have far more pressing things to do*' type person."

"Whiskey? I have whiskey."

"Gary, my patience is wearing dangerously thin. What do you want? I'm a very busy man."

God leaned back in his chair. "You know what I want. I was hoping you'd call me."

"Why would I call you? I don't like you."

"I want this reaping thing fixed."

Death stared at God for a moment and a smirk spread across his face. "You still haven't figured it out yet, have you?"

God shook his head in the negative. "We've been trying."

"It's been what, five days?"

"And now the Council are getting involved. They have demanded we meet to resolve this."

Death raised an eyebrow. "The Council of Deities ordered this meeting?"

"Yes, and they have directed you to help."

Death did not believe him. "Show me."

"Show you what?"

"Their directive."

"They emailed me."

"Then show me the email," ordered Death.

"They called me."

"Uh, huh. There is no directive, is there, Gary?"

"Oh, come on, Steve. You must help me contain this. If this gets out of the town and spreads, the entire planet is fucked, and I will lose my seat on the Council. It took me six thousand years to earn it. Do you have any idea how many special brownies I baked to get in?"

"This isn't rocket science," said Death. "Run a database query."

"The programmers are still working on the database. Queries won't be available for another week."

Death laughed. "Your IT team is dreadful."

"This isn't funny," griped God. "The Council is asking questions I can't answer. This is your mess."

"My mess? Are you blaming this on me?"

"Well, if you hadn't let that man in London fall by the wayside, we wouldn't have a problem."

Death smiled at God's pathetic attempt to coerce information from him. "I see what you're doing, Gary. Don't bait me. I won't tell you who I skipped, so don't bother asking. If you'd sorted it out when I asked you to and got me the right list, we wouldn't be here. This is all on you."

"Did you have to make them flesh-eaters? This situation wasn't bad enough, so you went and made them a bunch of fucking flesh-eaters."

"I didn't know they'd be cannibals. That's just an added bonus. We both know this whole thing is unprecedented. I didn't know what would happen. I'm as shocked as you, but I'm much happier with the outcome."

"Are you intentionally trying to make things harder for me? We have a list of invalids growing by the hour."

"Invalids?"

"It's what we are calling everyone who dies during this mess. They are invalid. None of them are supposed to have died yet. Your little stunt has snowballed, and half the universe is watching."

"I'm well aware of the attention it has garnered. Why do you think I did it in the first place?"

"What is it going to take to put an end to this?" asked God.

"You sorting your act out. I'm still getting incorrect names on my lists."

"What about you robe?"

"What about it?"

"I know some of the best tailors in the universe. Your robe must be awfully uncomfortable. Synthetic fibers have come a long way in recent years. I can get you a nice new one."

Death shook his head. "There's nothing wrong with my robe."

Gary reached into his drawer and pulled out an envelope. He slowly removed a crisp one-hundred-dollar bill and placed it gently on the desk.

"No," said Death.

God added four hundred to the pile.

"No."

One, five, and ten thousand were thrown at him as Death rose from his chair. "We're done here."

"Pounds? Rubles? Francs? Yen? Doubloons? Throw me a bone, Steve. Which currency do you prefer?"

"I'm not for sale."

"Everyone's for sale."

"Well, I'm not,"

God grew desperate. "Please, I need you to fix this."

The office door swung open, and Nancy poked her head inside. "Sir?" she said softly.

"What is it, Nancy?" said God, clearly irritated.

"Raphael is here to see you."

"Can it wait? I'm a little busy here."

"He said it's important."

"Really? Is he smiling?" asked God, his hopes rising.

"Ear to ear."

God smiled himself. "Well, in that case, send him in. He must have good news for me this time."

Nancy's head retreated from the door.

A second later, Raphael entered the room, grinning from ear to ear. "We've found her."

"You have?"

Raphael nodded.

God looked at Death. "Well, it looks like we won't be needing your help after all," he said as he grabbed the pile of money off the desk.

God stepped around his desk and headed to the door. Death started to follow him, curious to know what they had found.

"No, it's okay, Steve. We'll take it from here. You can see yourself out."

259

God followed Raphael as he walked briskly to the elevator. Raphael pressed the down button and stepped back, barely able to contain his excitement.

"You're pretty sure of yourself. This isn't a wild goose chase, is it?"

"I'm two hundred percent sure."

The elevator pinged, and the doors opened. Raphael swiped his ID badge at the number bank, and the hidden numbers appeared. He pressed -5, and the elevator started to drop.

A few moments later, the doors opened, and they stepped out into the Invocation Room.

A young man leaped up from his terminal. "We got her," he shouted triumphantly.

God looked at Raphael as they walked over to him. "Repeat," ordered God.

"I said we got her."

"The correct verbiage is 'we have found her'," said God.

"Whatever, dude," he said as he offered his headset, unaware of to whom he was speaking.

God furrowed his brow at the brush off as Raphael reached out for the headset and held it up to his ear.

"Replay in broadcast."

The young man punched a few buttons on his keyboard and a static-ridden female voice broadcast from the terminal. "Oh, my God, it's coming this way."

Raphael turned to God and smiled. God shrugged, clearly not impressed, or convinced.

Incoherent. Static. "... *it's fucking dead.*" Static. "*...you bit her, you crazy fuck.*" Static. "*.. run.*" Static. "*...it's a fucking zombie, Josh..*" Screams. "*... get it off me. Oh, God, help me, please. Oh, God, oh, God, oh, God.*" Gurgles. Growling. Silence.

"Aren't zombies supposed to say brains?" asked God.

"Only in the movies. It turns out real zombies are quite different."

"Where is it?" asked God.

The young man typed again. "Oceanview, dude."

"Oceanview, where?"

"Sorry, dude. Oceanview, Arizona, dude." He jotted down the location on a piece of paper and handed it to God.

God raised an eyebrow. "There's an Oceanview in Arizona?"

"Apparently," said Raphael.

"That doesn't make any sense."

Raphael gestured to the elevator. "Shall we?"

God started back towards the elevator. "How can a town in the middle of Arizona have a view of the ocean?"

The young man looked at Raphael expectantly.

"Sir?" Raphael called to God.

God stopped and turned around. "What is it, Raph? We're losing daylight."

Raphael nodded over to the young man. "Shouldn't we reward him?"

"Yes, yes, of course." He turned to the young man. "You got yourself a raise, dude," he said as he stepped into the elevator.

"Thanks, dude," the young man said with a grin. Then as the elevator doors started to close, he shouted after them. "Wait, you don't pay us."

God smiled as the elevator doors started to close, and he slowly raised his middle finger.

"Dick," the young man mumbled under his breath.

As the elevator doors closed, God turned to Raphael. "So, what next?"

"We cross-reference Oceanview with our reports. It shouldn't be hard to find at all."

"What about the database?" asked God.

Raphael shook his head. "We don't need it. We can use the printouts."

"Then what?"

"We send someone down there to check things out and find our rogue corpse. I've already called the team together."

"Good idea. I was about to suggest that," lied God.

The team quickly assembled and was talking excitedly when God and Raphael entered. The chatter stopped as they walked to the front of the room.

"As no one around here can keep their mouth shut, you've probably heard we have located the person Death skipped," said God.

More hushed talking hissed around the room.

God raised his hands to silence the room. "Enough. While we do know Death skipped Harriet Jenkins of Oceanview, Arizona—"

Ezekiel's hand shot skyward.

"Yes?" said God pointing at him.

"There's an Oceanview in Arizona? That doesn't make any sense."

"I know, right?" said God. "I thought the same thing. How can a state which doesn't border any of the two major North American oceans have a view of them?"

"Maybe it's on the top of a mountain?" offered Ezekiel.

"Possibly," said God. "It would be a tall mountain, though."

"You're wandering, sir," Raphael whispered in his ear.

"Right. So, anywho, we know Mrs. Jenkins is the person at the center of all this trouble. What we don't know is what we are supposed to do about it."

Ceraphim raised his hand.

God rolled his eyes. "Not now, Ceraphim."

"But I have an idea."

"Of course you do."

"This is a good one."

"I don't care."

Ceraphim put his hand down.

"Does anyone else have an idea?" God looked around the room. "Anyone?"

No hands were raised. A few moments later, Ceraphim slowly lifted his hand again.

"Anyone but Ceraphim?" He glanced around the room once more time. "Anyone? Please?" He sighed in defeat. "Ceraphim?"

"I believe it's the patient zero scenario."

"The what?" asked God.

"It's the concept that every disease and outbreak has a single starting point. If we can successfully bring Mrs. Jenkins into Heaven within the parameters of the process, then everything else should rectify itself. If there is no source of the outbreak, then the outbreak never existed. If she is dead, then everyone she infected will reset."

God turned to face Raphael. "Is this true?"

"Actually, sir, it is."

God turned back to Ceraphim. "You're assuming she is still alive."

"She can't be dead."

"Of course she'll be dead. She's a damn zombie."

"No, I mean, she can't have been killed since becoming one of the undead. If she's dead, we're done," said Ceraphim.

God shook his head. "That can't be the endgame."

"This is our only chance. Without patient zero, we can't stop this," said Ceraphim.

"What are the chances of her being alive?"

"She's old, which means she is predictable. Old people are nothing if not predictable. I'm sure there is some shred of humanity left in her to keep her sticking to her old ways. Besides, she's got a bad hip. She could barely make it downstairs. It's doubtful she could get very far before hitting the ground."

"I've read the reports," said Raphael. "This town is a bunch of pacifist hippies. Even the sheriff shoots blanks. I doubt a single shot has been fired. We find her, we have Death reap her, and we pretend this never happened."

"Simple as that, huh?" said God.

"Yep."

"I like it. So how do we send Mrs. Jenkins and everyone else on if they are already dead?"

"Resurrection, sir," said Ceraphim.

"Go on," ordered God.

"If we can resurrect Mrs. Jenkins, we can then get her back on Death's reaping list. The system resets everything that has happened since, and the problem fixes itself."

God looked at Raphael. "Raph?"

Raphael rolled the theory around in his head. "As much as I hate to say it, he's correct. The bigger question is, will Death play ball?"

"He'll have to. We're fixing the database, and Harriet is a legitimate customer." God clapped his hands together. "Okay, so who wants to go to Oceanview?"

◆ ◆ ◆ ◆

Greg stood on a desk and stared out of the front window at the parking lot.

"Let me see," asked Warren as he waited for his turn.

"It's pretty bad," said Greg as he hopped down so his brother could climb up and take his place. "A bunch more joined them overnight."

Warren leaned against the glass. From over the top of the dumpster parked in front of the window, he could see hundreds of zombie-demons shuffling aimlessly around the parking lot.

"You weren't shitting. Where did this lot come from?"

"No clue. You see one bloody dead person, you've seen them all."

"Could they have followed us here?"

"I hope not. I've fucked things up with Amber enough. I don't want to be responsible for leading an army of the dead to our doorstep."

"What's your plan?"

Greg nodded at the side door. "The plan is to get your car. I'm going to head out back and go around the front to distract them."

"What should I do?" asked Warren.

"When they're all following me, you go out the front and get the car. I'll do a loop around the back and come out on the other side by the fence. Pick me up, and we'll drive to the clinic."

"Why do you get to be the distraction?"

"I've seen you run," said Greg. "You'll be out of breath before you reach the end of the building. Think you can run to the car?"

"Of course I can. Besides, they can't run. I'll be fine."

"It will be if you don't fuck it up," said Greg.

"Is it all clear out back?" asked Warren.

Greg nodded. "Yeah, I already checked. The alleyway's clear. Are you ready?"

"Wait, we're doing this now?"

"No, I'm having pizza delivered. Let's do it afterward."

"Okay." Warren paused a second. "There's no pizza, is there?"

"No, Warren, there is no pizza."

"Did I hear someone say pizza?" Cam walked into the office behind them.

"I wish," said Warren. "It's part of Greg's shit plan."

"Does it involve getting pizza?" asked Cam.

"No," said Warren. "It involves us running out into the apocalypse and probably dying."

"Do you have a better idea?" asked Greg.

"No," said Warren.

"Then it's the best plan we have and by default, makes it a good plan. Are you ready?"

"No."

Greg moved over to the back door as Warren headed to the front window of the store. Greg reached down to push the desk blocking his exit, when a soft voice spoke from behind.

"Where are you going?"

Greg turned around to see Amber, her face painted with concern.

"The clinic. We need medical supplies for David and food for the rest of us."

"Please come back to me," said Amber. "I've lost so much. I can't lose you too."

"I thought you hated me."

"I don't hate you, Greg. I lost both of my parents in less than an hour. My mind is a mess. I know it was an accident, but it doesn't make it hurt any less."

Greg grabbed her hands and kissed them. "I'm so sorry. If I could take it back, I would. I never meant—"

"I know."

Greg leaned in and kissed Amber. "I won't be gone long, I promise."

"When did you become so brave?"

"When the woman I love got caught up in the apocalypse."

Amber smiled as Warren started to push the desk away from the door.

"Close up behind us, we'll come back this way," said Greg as he opened the door and disappeared outside.

◆ ◆ ◆ ◆

The alley was quiet. Greg headed to the right and jogged to the end of the wall. Cautiously, he peered around the corner, but could only see part of the parking lot. Over a dozen creatures were milling around. The plan would fail if he could only draw a few of them away. He needed to get closer so more would see him.

He sided up against the wall and slowly moved around the front of the building. The sun reflected on the opposite wall, and shadows were his ally. Greg stepped out into the open. The rest of the parking lot overflowed with the dead. He opened his mouth to yell.

"Is it working?" said a voice from behind.

Greg spun around to see Warren. "What the hell, man? You're supposed to be inside."

"I figured you could use help out here, and we run to the car together."

"Goddammit, Warren, you are the bane of my existence."

Warren grinned. "Just keeping you on your toes, bro." He nodded behind Greg. "Looks like they saw us."

Greg looked back, and as one, the group turned and headed their way. "Time to go," he said as he started running back the way he came.

Warren gave a quick look at the shuffling horde as Greg disappeared around the corner. His eyes widened in terror, and he started running.

"Greg," yelled Warren.

"What?"

"We've got a big problem, man."

"What's that?" Greg shouted over his shoulder.

"A really big problem. These fuckers can run."

"The fuck you say?" shouted Greg.

"Look behind you."

Greg turned his head to see a mob of three hundred creatures tearing around the corner.

"Jesus fucking Christ, when did they start running?"

"I told you this is a shitty plan, Greg. If I die out here, I swear to fucking God I'm coming back and eating you first."

"I'll be sure to give you indigestion then."

"Why not? You're already a pain in my ass."

The brothers reached the end of the building and headed towards the parking lot.

♦ ♦ ♦ ♦

Amber stood on the desk and looked out of the front window as Greg and Warren sprinted towards Warren's car.

Cam stepped up behind her. "What's going on?"

"They're running."

"Who?"

"The boys. There's something behind them." Amber gasped. "Holy shit, we've got a problem."

"What's wrong?"

"Well, it looks like the zombie-demons can run now."

"Are you serious?" asked Cam. "When the hell did they start running?"

"Apparently now." Amber watched as Greg and Warren sprinted towards Warren's car. She let out a heavy sigh. "They made it."

"Well, this complicates things," said David as he shuffled into the room, clutching his wound.

Cam shook her head. "Should we go and help them."

"And do what?" said David. "We'll only get ourselves killed."

"My future fiancé is out there," growled Amber. "He's getting supplies for your ass. You may want to be a little more appreciative."

David lowered his eyes. "I'm sorry, I didn't mean anything by it."

Amber sighed. "I know. I just want them back and for this nightmare to end."

♦ ♦ ♦ ♦

The brothers reached Warren's car and stopped. Greg looked around as Warren patted his pockets.

"Greg?" asked Warren.

"What?"

"I need to tell you something."

"It can wait. Open the damn doors."

"I've left my keys inside."

"What?"

"I. Left. My. Keys. Inside," he repeated, pausing for emphasis after each word.

"I fucking heard you," Greg stepped back and swung his gun at the passenger side window, smashing it into a hundred pieces.

Warren held up his hands. "What the fuck?"

"Problem solved, now get in," said Greg as he reached in and unlocked the doors.

"I meant the shop. I left my keys in the shop. You owe me a window, you dick."

"I don't fucking believe you," shouted Greg. "The whole plan was to fucking drive."

Warren pointed to the large dent in the hood Greg acquired on the way to pick up Amber. "What the hell happened to my car?"

A loud groaning came from behind them. The brothers turned to see the horde pouring around the corner.

"Run," yelled Greg.

"Where?" Warren screamed as he took off after his brother.

"Anywhere."

Warren hated the change of orders. "This is a shitty plan," he yelled.

"It wasn't until you fucked it up."

Greg and Warren broke into a sprint and left the parking lot.

Warren pointed to a plume of smoke a few blocks away. "Something's burning."

"Looks close to the clinic," said Greg. "Shit." He picked up speed and headed toward Cactus Road.

CHAPTER 34

"**F**uck no," protested Ceraphim. "There is no way in hell you are sending me down there."

Raphael looked at God. It was time for the exulted one to turn on the salesman charm.

God turned to face Ceraphim. "Ceraphim, did you or did you not ask, nay, beg me for more responsibility?"

"Well, yes, but this isn't what I meant. You can't send me to Earth. They're barbarians."

"They were created in my image," said God.

"Well then, you fucked up."

"Excuse me?"

"I'm complimenting you."

"Ceraphim, you belong to the highest order of the ninefold celestial hierarchy," God said as he put his arm around Ceraphim's shoulder. "You are the beacon of light, ardor, and purity. You carry a ceaseless and eternal revolution about Divine Principles. You are a champion for their heat and keenness. You are tireless in your elevative and energetic assimilation of those below. You kindle them and fire them to their own heat and wholly purify them by a burning and all-consuming flame. And by your unmatched, unquenchable, changeless, radiant, and enlightening power, only you can dispel and destroy the shadows of eternal darkness."

The speech inspired Ceraphim no matter how little sense it made. God could sell ice to an Eskimo if the situation required it. Raphael raised an eyebrow in God's direction. God noticed but refused to acknowledge it.

It was a conversation best saved for later.

"I don't—" started Ceraphim.

"So, Ceraphim, I ask you again, will you be the unifying force to bridge Heaven and Earth? Will you be the angel who brings an end to this tragedy that has befallen us?"

Sold.

"I will!" Ceraphim said proudly.

"Okay, then, I'll need you at the transit bay in fifteen minutes."

Ceraphim left the meeting room as Raphael closed the door behind him.

"Where did you get that monologue? Your unmatched, unquenchable, changeless, radiant, and enlightening power?"

"Wikipedia."

◆ ◆ ◆ ◆

Ceraphim arrived at the transit bay and looked around in awe as Raphael directed technicians working on the giant teleporter in the center of the room. It consisted of two giant metal rings rotating around a semi-sphere.

"I have good news and bad news," Raphael said as Ceraphim crossed over to him. "The good news is the chamber is ready to go."

"And the bad?"

"We cannot transport non-organic matter. Clothes won't transport, just carbon-based life forms. You'll have to go naked."

"What?" Ceraphim missed that clause in the manual. He sighed as he started to take off his pants.

One of the technicians walked over with a chart. "Maximum cyclic charge is imminent. Terminal velocity reached in three minutes." He looked at Ceraphim. "What is he doing?"

Raphael shrugged.

"What are you doing?" the technician asked Ceraphim.

"Getting ready," said Ceraphim.

"Why are you taking off your pants?"

Ceraphim stopped with his pants around his ankles. "Raphael said—"

The realization hit him like a train. "I fucking hate you guys," he said as he pulled up his pants to roars of laughter.

"Are you ready?" asked Raphael with a grin.

"Considering I'm about to save the universe, you could be a bit nicer to me."

"Probably."

Ceraphim waited for an apology, but the only offering to come from Raphael was an earpiece.

"Put this on," said Raphael as he turned to another technician. "Audio test."

Ceraphim clipped the electrical device to his ear. "Test, one-two."

The technician gave a thumbs up and echoed the test. Ceraphim nodded when the audio piped through.

Raphael gestured to the transporter. "If you'll step this way."

Ceraphim followed him over to the machine. He climbed up a short ladder and stepped into the center of the lower semi-sphere.

"Pay attention, Ceraphim. This part is important. When the transfer starts, you will feel a jolt as you fall. Whatever you do, don't move your arms from your sides."

"Why?"

"Just don't. It affects the slipstream."

The rings started spinning around Ceraphim as a mechanical whirring increased in volume.

"How many people have used this?" shouted Ceraphim over the roar of the machine.

"You're the first," lied Raphael.

"What the f—"

A loud crack of electricity bounced around the room, and a bright ball of light swallowed Ceraphim and he disappeared.

"I'm heading to Invocation. Go live and forward the feed," Raphael ordered the technician.

The tech pressed a few buttons, and his monitor shared Ceraphim's video feed and audio.

Ceraphim appeared outside Port Road and landed hard face down on the street with a muffled yelp. The receiver in his left ear crackled as it found its channel. Broken laughter buzzed through.

"*Happy landings?*" Raphael fell into a fit of hysterics.

"I thought—" he groaned in pain. "I thought you... said to... leave my arms by my side?" He coughed, trying to get his breath back.

"*Sorry, did I say at your sides? I meant to say put them up in front of your face.*"

More laughter confirmed Ceraphim's hazing on his first teleportation.

"Fucking assholes," he wheezed. He slowly stood up and rested his hands on his knees.

"*Do you see anything?*" Raphael tried to compose himself enough to get back to business.

Ceraphim remained silent.

"*Ceraphim, can you stand up straight? All we see is concrete.*"

Ceraphim continued to draw pained breaths as he coughed and grabbed his chest. "Give me... a... minute. Still... can't... breathe."

The laughter piping over his earpiece finally stopped.

"Looks like a war..." Another breath. "... zone down here."

The street was decimated. Glass from broken display windows littered the sidewalk, and a half-dozen cars blocked the road. Bodies were strewn everywhere as a few creatures feasted nearby.

♦ ♦ ♦ ♦

A handful of blocks away, Greg skidded to a halt in front of the clinic. "Goddammit." He reached out and grabbed Warren by his jacket as he ran by. "Wait."

Warren stopped and joined Greg in staring at the burning building. The fire had destroyed anything inside worth salvaging. However, the raging fire and loss of supplies were the least of their concerns. The five hundred demons standing in front of the flames, mesmerized by the orange glow, however, were. Periodically, one strayed too close and stepped away with smoldering clothing.

"Now what?" asked Warren.

"We hit the Walgreens on Eighth."

They started running towards Port Road, and as they turned onto the street, they saw a lone creature standing in the middle of the road, hunched over.

"There's one," said Greg.

Warren raised his pistol and fired, hitting the creature in the back of the head. It slammed to the floor in a pool of blood.

"Nice shot!" yelled Greg as the brothers high-fived each other.

"Told you I'd be a natural."

♦ ♦ ♦ ♦

In the Invocation Room, loud static rang through the computer, and the video turned black.

Raphael frowned. "What happened to his feed?"

"I'm not sure. We lost contact," said the technician.

"Well, get him back."

"I'm trying, sir. There is no feed. It's gone."

"Can you get me an alternate visual?"

"Sorry, sir,' said the technician. "I can't find anything in the area. It's a total blackout."

"That's impossible," said Raphael. "There has got to be a camera somewhere around there. An ATM, traffic camera, cell phone, something. Keep looking."

"Negative, sir. The closest live feed we have is two blocks away."

"Someone get me a fucking feed," he yelled. Thirty seconds passed, and Raphael could feel his blood pressure soaring.

"We have a feed, sir," shouted another radio operator from his cubicle six spaces down.

Raphael sighed in relief and ran over to the operator. "Where is it?" he asked.

"One just came live in the area. Looks like a cell phone."

The operator pressed a button, and Warren's face filled the camera, grinning ear to ear. He turned his cell phone around to focus on the body he had shot.

Raphael watched helplessly as the two brothers crossed over to a body lying face down in the snow. A streak of dark red blood pooled around the head, a stunning and violent contrast to the white street.

"*Well, I don't think he will be getting back up again,*" Warren said through the phone.

"*Could you tell who he was?*" asked Greg off camera.

"*No idea.*"

"*He was dead, wasn't he?*"

"*Looked like it. You saw how he got up. He sure looked dead to me.*" The camera turned once again to face Warren.

"*What are you doing?*" asked Greg.

"*Taking a selfie for Facebook.*"

"*What?*"

"*My first headshot. I want to capture the moment.*"

Greg's off-camera voice filtered through the phone. "*Who's going to see it? You don't have any friends on your page outside Oceanview. Most of them are dead or in hiding. Besides, I'm pretty sure posting pictures of dead bodies is a violation of*

Facebook's terms of service."

"Remove the stick, Greg."

♦ ♦ ♦ ♦

Raphael reviewed the video feed in silence as Warren's head stopped in front of the body. Warren smiled as he snapped the picture.

"Is that—" the radio operator started.

"Shh." Raphael silenced him.

As the camera closed in, it became painfully clear they were looking at Ceraphim.

The room fell silent.

"They killed him," the operator finally said.

Raphael held his hands to his mouth in stunned silence.

"He died down there," said the operator.

Raphael nodded.

"This is really bad."

More nodding.

"The manual says if you die on Earth, you can't get resurrected."

"I KNOW WHAT THE FUCKING MANUAL SAYS," screamed Raphael as he grabbed his head. His grip on reality slipped away by the second.

"This has never happened before," said the operator.

"Shut up," yelled Raphael at the technician. "Shut the fuck up. Fuck. Why does this happen on my watch?"

"What are you going to do?"

"I don't fucking know," said Raphael. "We haven't lost an angel in over three thousand years. This is going to look terrible on my review."

"You have to tell God," the operator chimed in again.

"I can't. He'll freak out."

"He's going to want an update."

Raphael reached his wit's end. God was going to be pissed.

♦ ♦ ♦ ♦

Greg and Warren were far less stressed about the universal catastrophe they set in motion and were clueless about the issues they had just caused. After Warren's grim digital portrait, they left the scene of the incident and resumed running.

273

Warren took a deep breath as he followed his brother. "Let's hope Walgreens hasn't burned to the ground too."

"You're not funny," said Greg.

"I wasn't joking. I've had my years' worth of exercise today. I'm done running."

"It's just a few blocks. You can make it."

◆ ◆ ◆ ◆

Ten minutes later, they arrived at Walgreens to find the door smashed and glass scattered across the sidewalk.

"Shit, it's already been hit," said Greg, surveying the damage. "Keep your guard up. It isn't only the zombie-demons who can kill us. I expect survivors to be a bit jumpy and shoot first."

"And fuck the questions."

"Exactly." Greg raised his pistol and stepped through the broken door. The glass crunched loudly beneath his feet and echoed in the otherwise quiet store. He strained to listen for other signs of movement. Reasonably sure the store was empty, he silently signaled Warren to follow as they swept across the aisles, scanning each row as they passed by.

"The place looks clean," said Greg quietly as they reached the end of the store.

A few of the shelves were picked over, but mostly alcohol and cigarettes were missing. The typical staples of looting.

"What do you need me to do?" asked Warren.

"Go find peroxide and bandages. They should be in aisle four. I'll get painkillers and see if I can get behind the counter for something stronger. Grab any food you see."

Warren nodded and headed to the right side of the store. Greg looked up at the signs hanging from the ceiling to see the painkillers were one aisle over. He silently headed towards them and scanned the shelves for supplies. He found the Tylenol halfway down and shoved a couple of bottles into his pockets. It felt weird to steal. He never so much as stiffed a waiter on a tip, let alone walk through a store, shoving items into his pockets without paying.

He moved to the end of the aisle to check on the pharmacy. The metal security door was down, but he pulled on it to be certain it wasn't locked. The loud clang echoed his suspicions.

Warren came up behind him, pushing a shopping cart. "Here, I shoplifted these," he said, offering Greg a cigar.

"We're not shoplifting," said Greg.

"Okay, look what I looted."

"And we're not looters either."

"What's the difference?"

"We're only taking essentials. We're foraging for supplies. Shoplifters and looters take booze, Nike's, and DVD players."

"Why don't they take Blu-ray players?"

"What?"

"Why take inferior equipment if it's free? It doesn't make sense."

"It isn't free, and it doesn't matter what level of technology they take. The fact is they are taking non-essentials and are therefore, looting."

"Cigars aren't essentials, are they?"

"No."

"I guess I'm looting then. I'm okay trying new things."

Greg looked over the contents of the cart. Warren did well despite the looting. It was full of food, bandages, Neosporin, peroxide, and water. "Well done."

Warren smiled at the compliment. "Any luck with the pharmacy?"

"Locked tight. I grabbed some regular painkillers, though. Better than nothing."

They both heard the crunching of glass at the same time and instinctively ducked. Greg signaled for Warren to go to the back of the store while he headed to the front and surrounded who or what walked in. Before Greg reached the end of the aisle, a single gunshot rang out, and he froze.

"Warren?" he half-whispered.

Nothing.

He stopped at the end of the shelf and looked around. "Warren," he said louder, adrenalin sending his heart into overdrive.

Nothing.

"WARREN?" he screamed. Unconcerned with giving his position away. He raised his gun and prepared to step around the corner.

"What?" his brother said from behind. "Why are you shouting?"

Greg turned and slugged him on the arm. "You asshole, I thought you'd been shot."

"No, why?"

"I shouted, and you didn't answer."

"I figured I'd surprise you."

Greg shook his head in disbelief.

"I did bag me another headshot," said Warren cheerfully.

"Get the cart, and you can show me on the way out. We've probably brought attention to us."

Warren ran back to the pharmacy counter for the supplies as Greg waited, trying to calm his nerves. He found it difficult adjusting to living so close to imminent death. A few seconds later, Warren reappeared with the cart.

Greg looked at the contents and noticed a stack of movies he did not see before.

Warren sensed his disapproval. "What? You can't have a Blu-ray player without movies."

"You took a Blu-ray player?"

"Yeah, it's at the bottom of the cart."

"Can we just get out of here?" asked Greg, unwilling to fight with his brother.

They headed to the exit, and Greg threw more food in the cart as they passed a snack display. At the checkout, another creature stumbled through the door. Then ten more piled in after it.

"Shit, we're trapped," said Warren. His mind raced with ways to get out of the store.

Without pausing, Greg ran to the door and turned at the makeup aisle. "Follow me, you zombie-demon fucks," he yelled.

"Goddammit, Greg. What are you doing?" Warren shouted after him.

"Diversion. Get out of here."

"I'm not leaving you."

"Yes, you are. I'll be right behind you. Go."

Greg led the group further back into the store, clearing the entrance for Warren to make his getaway.

Warren hesitated before moving.

"Go," ordered Greg again.

Warren pushed the cart out of the door. A few more gathered on the street and were heading his way. He looked back at the store, but there was no sign of Greg. "Fuck," he yelled as he took off, trying to avoid dumping the shopping cart on the uneven and snow-covered sidewalk.

He made it a block before he stole a glance back over his shoulder. As he took his eyes off the sidewalk, the cart hit a pothole and flipped. Warren fell over it, landing hard on the cold concrete. His hands and elbows scraped across the ground, leaving bloody abrasions on his skin.

He winced as he pushed himself upright. "Dammit," he mumbled to himself.

A loud moan sounded from behind, and he turned as a creature lunged at him.

"Shit." He held his hands to his face and waited for the inevitable bite.

Bang.

The demon's head jerked back violently as a plume of blood burst out of the back of its skull. It toppled over onto the sidewalk.

"Need help?" said Greg as he offered Warren a hand.

Warren was visibly shaken. "I thought I was done for." He grabbed Greg's hand and pulled himself up off the ground.

"You're welcome," said Greg as he picked up the shopping cart and started putting the scattered supplies back in the basket. He looked back at the store. "Can you carry this?"

"Yeah, why?"

"Look behind you."

Warren turned. At least a hundred bloodthirsty monsters were tearing down the road after them.

"Run," yelled Greg.

The brothers picked up the cart and took off.

CHAPTER 35

God unsuccessfully tried to hit a golf ball into a tipped-over coffee cup for the eighty-second time when he heard a timid knock at the door.

"Enter," he yelled.

The door opened, and Nancy poked her head around.

"Nancy, has my coffee cup shrunk?"

She looked at the cup. "I don't believe so, sir."

"Are you sure?"

She squinted her eyes and gave the oversized cup a second review. "Yes. In fact, it looks like you're using a bigger mug than usual."

"Something isn't right. Normally I get at least one ball in. Maybe the moon is off."

"The moon?"

"Yeah, you know how it affects oceans. Maybe the gravitational pull is screwing with my game."

"I couldn't say. I'm unfamiliar with such things. Raphael is here to see you."

God smiled. "He must have more good news for me."

Nancy squirmed. "I don't know about that, sir."

"He must have good news. I explicitly told him not to return unless he brought good news."

"I wouldn't be so sure, sir. He has a very serious look on his face."

"He always has that look on his face."

"It's the look you don't like."

God sighed. "You mean this look?" His face became a grumpy, stern scowl.

"That's the one."

"Ugh," griped God. "Fine, send him in."

Nancy disappeared behind the door, and Raphael stepped past her.

God turned his attention back to his coffee cup. "Hello, Raph. Nancy says you have that look on your face I don't like." He prepared to take another swing when he saw the look on Raphael's face. "Oh, you do."

"I have some bad news, sir. It's about—"

"Up bup, bup, bup," said God, rudely interrupting him. "I've had way too much bad news this week. Between Death, Oceanview, and my coffee cup shrinking, I'm emotionally spent. I swear to Christ I'm one 'I'm sorry, sir' away from becoming a cutter."

"But, Gary—"

"How about you say it in a way that doesn't make it sound like bad news."

"Excuse me?"

"Tell me the bad news in a way that makes it sound like good news."

"Okay." Raphael paused as his mind raced to spin the news in a positive manner. "You know how much Ceraphim grates on your nerves?"

"I'm listening."

"Well, he's been relocated to a different department."

"Well, that isn't so bad," said God cheerfully. He turned his attention back to his golf ball and his mysteriously shrinking coffee cup. He swung his club, and once again, his ball went wide.

Raphael sighed with relief. "If there's nothing else then, I'll be going," he said as he turned and headed briskly to the door. He almost made it out.

"Which department?"

Raphael stopped and exhaled as he tried to come up with an answer.

God leaned on his club. "Which department did you transfer Ceraphim to?"

"I—"

With each second that ticked by, the chances of God asking the right question increased.

And then he asked it. "What happened to Ceraphim, Raph?"

"He's dead."

"He's WHAT?"

"Dead."

"I'm sorry. Did you say the angel we sent to Earth has died?"

279

Raphael nodded.

"That isn't good news at all. That's about as far from good news as you can get. On the scale of good news, one being the worst, this is a minus seventy."

"I'm sorry."

"How? He can't be dead. It's impossible. An angel hasn't died in over two thousand years."

"Three thousand."

"Well, that's even worse. What happened?"

"The humans killed him."

God walked back to his desk and collapsed onto his chair. "How the hell did they do it?"

"One of them shot him in the head."

"They did what?"

"They shot him."

"How?"

"With a pistol."

God stared at Raphael. "A pistol? No fucking shit. Not how, *how?* Humans aren't supposed to be able to kill angels. They are immortal. It's one of the perks."

"A freak shot. One in a million chance."

"I take it he didn't find patient zero then?"

Raphael shook his head. "He wasn't there thirty seconds."

"They killed someone who'd only been there for thirty seconds? What is wrong with these people?" God didn't wait for an answer. "Send Ezekiel. We need to finish the mission."

"We already did."

"And did he find patient zero?"

"No, they killed him too."

"The same people?"

"No, someone else. Another one in a million shot."

"Ecanus?"

Raphael shook his head again. "One in a million."

"Either they are incredibly lucky, or a million doesn't hold the same weight it used to."

"They must be using holy weapons."

"Holy weapons? Where the hell could these morons get holy weapons from?"

"Hard to say. The only way is a priest blessing them."

"What kind of lunatic does that?" asked God.

Raphael shrugged. "This town isn't normal."

"Why do they keep killing my angels, Raph?"

"Well, you did start the apocalypse. They are understandably a little jumpy."

"Technically, Death started it. Who do we send next? Valoel?"

"She won't go."

"Amitiel?"

"No one else wants to go. Morale is a little low at the moment."

"So, what are our options?"

"There is another way, but you won't like it."

"What did I say about telling me bad news?"

Raphael sighed as he played the news out in his head so he could soften the blow. "You know how you have always wanted the opportunity to go to Earth and visit your most treasured creation?"

God immediately read between the lines. "No, no, no. Nope. Fuck no. Don't even bother finishing the sentence. I'm not doing it."

"But—"

"I'm not fucking doing it, Raph. You have lost your fucking mind."

"I'm afraid there's no—"

God placed his fingers in his ears. "La, la, la, la. I'm not listening to Raphael while he's having a retard moment. La, la, la, la."

Raphael stared at God until he removed his fingers. "There is no other option."

"There is always another option."

"Yes, and we used it. This is it."

"Please don't make me go down there," pleaded God.

"I'm sorry, you have to. I wish there was another way."

"You've always told me it would be extremely bad if I went there."

"I know, but we don't have a choice. You're the only one who can fix this now. You're the best of what we have left."

"They shit bricks when my son's face appears on a cornflake. How the hell are they going to react if I show up?"

"You'll be treated like royalty," said Raphael.

"Did they treat Ceraphim like royalty? How about Ezekiel or Ecanus? Shit, they crucified my son, and he was a nice guy."

"That was different."

"How?"

"They weren't gods."

"How will they know I am?"

"They will just know. There is a symbiotic connection between a deity and their followers."

"And the atheists?"

"We're unsure. We don't know what will happen. Technically, they should be able to see you, but it's a bit of a gray area."

God shrugged. "Can't please everyone, I guess. Regardless, it's still a terrible idea."

"So, you'll do it?" asked Raphael.

"Do I have a choice?"

"There's always a choice."

"Then, no, I'm not going."

"Except this time."

"Of course, there is always a catch. You really enjoy shitting in my Cheerios, don't you?"

"Not at all," said Raphael.

"I think you do. So, what now?"

"Meet me in the transit bay in ten minutes. We'll be ready for you."

◆ ◆ ◆ ◆

Ten minutes later, God stood at the teleporter, ready to go.

"The transporter can only accept organic material," said a technician to God as he stood facing the machine.

"Excuse me?"

"It means no clothing. Only organic matter can go through." The technician tried to stifle a laugh.

"I know what it means, you idiot. I'm stunned you would try this on me."

The technician gulped. "Try what, sir?"

"The no pants prank."

The tech's eyes widened. "Oh, you know about it?"

"Of course I know," said God. "Who do you think invented it?"

He raised his hand to choke the technician. Raphael walked up behind him and coughed to announce his arrival.

"Sir, we're ready for you."

God lowered his hand, and the technician sighed in relief. "Raph, what if they're not happy to see me?"

"Relax. I'd expect nothing less than a red-carpet welcome, sir. You're their Lord and Savior. They will be elated to see you."

"I like the sound of that," said God. It indeed sounded pleasant.

"There's one more thing," added Raphael.

God raised an eyebrow. "More fine print?"

"You can't change anything."

"What do you mean?"

"I mean you can't directly affect the situation. The only person you can interact with is patient zero."

"Why?"

"It will create an alternate timeline."

"You mean like Back to the Future Two?" asked God.

"Exactly. But without the DeLorean or happy ending."

"Hoverboard?"

"Still hasn't been invented yet."

"Man, they are slacking. Can I pick up a Gray's Sporting Almanac?"

"No. Promise me you won't change things."

"I—"

"Promise me."

God sighed. "I promise." His disappointment was painted across his face.

"This is all brand new to us, so you can't interact with them. You've never gone down there before. Their tiny little minds may not be able to handle it."

"Aren't these the same people who have been clamoring for a look at me since the beginning of time?"

"Well, yes, but the events of the past few days are unprecedented. The truth is, no one knows what will happen if you interact. There are no rules for this. We're working on hearsay and hunches."

"I thought you said they'd be elated? How can they be elated if I can't interact with them?"

"It's hypothetical elation."

"Great. This should be a fun day then," God said as he stepped forward into the lower sphere.

CHAPTER 36

"Let me in," yelled a panicked voice from behind the side door as Amber and Cam pushed the heavy table aside.

"Hold on," shouted Amber.

The visitor started banging hard on the door. "Hurry the hell up."

Amber unlocked the door, and Warren stepped in breathing heavily and pushing the shopping cart ahead of him. He quickly closed the door behind him as Lee walked over to the cart to check on the supplies.

Amber looked behind Warren nervously. "Where's Greg?" she said, expecting to see her boyfriend.

Warren stopped and turned to look at Amber.

"Warren, where is Greg?" her face suddenly deathly serious.

"I'm so sorry, Amber."

The color drained out of Amber's face. "What?"

Warren reached out for her hands and held them in sympathy. "He didn't make it."

Amber let out a pained cry and fell to her knees. Ashley rushed to her side and threw her arm around her sister's shoulders.

Ashley looked up at Warren. "What happened?"

"The town is overrun with zombie-demons, and we got jumped coming back. A horde of them was waiting for us. I barely made it here." Warren grimaced at the delivery of the news, his face shadowed by sadness. "He told me to get the supplies here, no matter what. I tried to help him. God knows I tried. He told me to run. His last words were, *'tell Amber I love her'*. Or it may have been *'argh, get them off me'*. He was pulled to the ground screaming after that."

Amber wailed at the news as tears poured down her cheeks. Ashley pulled her in tighter, desperately trying to comfort her grieving sibling.

"I'm so sorry." He turned to walk away, but stopped and looked back at Amber. "Oh, I'm just fucking with you."

Amber looked up at him. "What?"

"He's out front moving vehicles so we can leave."

"WHAT?" she said, her voice rising in pitch.

"I said—"

The door opened, and Greg walked in.

"See?" said Warren with a broad grin.

Greg noticed everyone staring at him and frowned in confusion. "What's going on?"

"You're alive," Amber said as she climbed to her feet. She ran over to Greg and wrapped her arms tightly around him. Seconds later, she broke off the hug. "I'm going to kill your brother." Amber tore into a dead sprint at Warren.

Greg grabbed her and pulled her back. "What the hell is going on?"

"Your asshole brother told her you were dead," said Ashley.

Greg turned to Warren with one eyebrow raised.

"Seemed funny at the time," said Warren.

Greg let go of Amber's arm. "He's all yours."

Amber flew at Warren in a flurry of fists and fury. "You fucking asshole," she yelled as she beat on his chest.

Warren held up his hands. "I said sorry."

"I'll sorry you, you little shit." Amber had no intentions of letting up on him.

Greg let her beat on Warren for another thirty seconds before he cleared his throat. "I hate to break this party up, but we need to go. It's not safe here anymore."

"I thought you said this place was protected?" asked Cam.

"One or two of them may have followed us back."

"One or two?" said Lee.

"He means all of them," said Warren.

"Greg?" Amber looked nervous.

"Those things are everywhere," said Greg. "We didn't have a chance. We need to go."

"He means zombie-demons," clarified Warren.

"Of course he means the fucking demons," snorted Ashley.

"Zombie-demons," corrected Warren.

"Shut up," said Ashley. "The bigger question is, why did you lead them back here?"

"We didn't," said Greg. "They were coming here regardless. We need to go."

Lee disagreed with running without a plan. "What do you suggest? We can't take separate cars. If we get split up, we're screwed."

"We take the bus," suggested Greg.

"Bus?"

"Yeah. The school bus in the shop. Warren finished it the day before all hell broke loose."

Lee felt more comfortable with the idea of a larger vehicle, but he still wanted a general idea direction they were heading. "And go where? It's safe to say our town is fucked."

"Phoenix?" offered Greg.

"What if what's going on here is everywhere?" Cam echoed what others in the group were thinking.

Greg paused. That possibility eluded him. "Then we're screwed."

A loud crash came from the front office.

"That's our cue. Everyone into the workshop. I'll get the bus started."

Warren and Cam helped David to his feet as the rest of the group left the back room.

Amber turned to Mr. Yan who was sitting comatose in his chair, staring at the floor. "Mr. Yan, it's time to go."

"Leave me," he said softly. "I'm not leaving."

"They will be here at any moment," said Amber. "We have to go."

"I do not fear death," said Mr. Yan. "I embrace it. I have nothing to go to."

Amber pulled on his arm, but he stayed still. "You can't stay," she pleaded.

"You must go now," he said, looking up at her.

Amber gave Mr. Yan one last look and ran into the workshop to join the rest of the group.

"This is a pretty bad plan, Lee," David said through clenched teeth as Warren carried him to the bus.

"I know it is, but we're short on options." Lee pointed at the workbench. "Cam, Ashley, and Amber grab a gun."

The three women stopped at the table, and each picked a pistol. Lee gathered the remaining weapon as Greg loaded the supplies into the bus.

"Can you drive this thing?" asked Lee as he stepped onto the bus.

"Yeah, no problem," said Greg confidently as he sat in the driver's seat.

"Are you sure it's going to start?" asked David.

Greg frowned. "Yeah, why?"

"Didn't you say Warren worked on it?"

"I heard that," said Warren as he climbed into the bus.

Ashley quickly loaded the pistol and removed the safety to Warren's chagrin.

"How come everyone knows about guns but me?" whined Warren.

Greg fired up the engine, and it spluttered to life, much to his and David's surprise.

"See," said Warren. "Nothing to worry about."

"Hold on tight. We're getting the fuck out of here," said Greg as he pulled his keys out of his pocket and pressed a button on the remote.

Nothing happened.

He pressed it again.

Nothing.

Warren looked at the door and back at Greg. "What are you doing, man? Time to go."

Greg stabbed at the remote. "The fucking door won't open."

"You're kidding?" said Warren.

"No, the batteries are dead. You never picked up the replacements."

Warren cringed. "Oops, my bad. Now what?"

"We'd have to open it manually," said Greg.

"I've got it," said Lee.

"No, it's suicide," said Greg. "I can ram it."

"How thick is the door?" asked Lee.

"I don't know."

"Exactly, it's too risky. Let me do it, I'll be fine."

Lee stepped out of the bus and ran to the door. He grabbed a heavy chain hanging from the ceiling and pulled. Slowly the door started to rise. As it inched higher, he could see feet standing on the other side. "Shit."

Rapidly the feet became knees. Lee moved back to give as much distance between him and the door as he could, but the chain's length limited his movement. A hand grabbed at his ankle, its owner already halfway under the door.

"I don't have a clean shot," Warren yelled from the bus door.

A gunshot rang out, and the body went limp. Lee turned to see Ashley standing by the back of the bus. "I do," she shouted as she fired again and dropped a second. "Hurry."

Lee pulled the chain faster as another creature crawled under the door towards him.

"Let me."

Lee turned around to see Mr. Yan behind him.

He reached for the chain. "Go, I've got this." He wasn't asking.

Lee nodded and moved towards the bus as another demon climbed to her feet.

Warren stepped down out of the door and raised his gun, but he held off on firing.

"Shoot her, man," said Greg.

"I can't."

"Why?"

"It's Mrs. Halworth."

"So?"

"Dude, I can't shoot Mrs. Halworth. She taught me in second grade, for fuck's sake. She's like my grandmother. I can't shoot my grandmother."

"Fucking shoot her man. Put her down."

Warren lowered his gun. "I can't."

"Didn't she give you detention the time when Bulldozer ate your homework?" said Greg, casting his mind back to an incident where the family dog actually did indeed eat Warren's homework.

"Yeah."

"Didn't you also have to do summer school because of it?"

Warren's eyes widened. "That bitch." He raised his gun and fired. Mrs. Halworth dropped to the ground, a bullet hole between her eyes. "Time to go, Lee," shouted Warren.

Lee cleared the last few feet and jumped on the bus.

"Is everyone on?" yelled Greg.

"Mr. Yan's staying," said Lee.

"What? That's suicide," said Greg.

"He's made his choice," said Lee. "We need to go. Ashley, close her up."

"On it," shouted Ashley as pulled the rear shut behind her. "Let's go."

The garage door reached the top, and Mr. Yan dropped the chain as the first wave of demons spilled into the garage and pulled him to the floor. He looked up at Ashley, his eyes pleading for mercy. "Please?"

Ashley nodded, aimed at Mr. Yan, and fired off one more shot. The bullet found its target and spared Mr. Yan the agony of being eaten alive.

Warren pulled the door closed behind Lee.

The bus lurched forward and plowed into the crowd as they poured into the shop. The engine sputtered as it struggled against the wall of bodies.

"Come on," said Greg through gritted teeth. He pumped the gas, and the bus finally broke free of the crowd and careened into the parking lot. As he pulled away from his family's business, Greg looked into the rear-view mirror one last time and smiled sadly. He pulled out of the lot and turned onto Port Road. At the first light, he looked behind him at the group. "Shit."

"What's wrong?" asked Amber.

"I hate to say this, but where is Mrs. Andrews?"

Back at the garage, the bathroom door opened, and Mrs. Andrews walked out, drying her hands on her dress. "This bathroom is disgusting. Did either of you bother to get towels? My hands are soaked. Don't get me started on the stains. Disgraceful. You two are by far the most—"

She looked up at the lobby full of monsters. "Oh, fuck."

CHAPTER 37

For thousands of years, approximately thirty percent of humanity waited for its Lord and Savior to show his face on Earth. His real face in the flesh, instead of on cereal, dirty laundry, or slices of toast as so many believers claimed to have seen his son. Humanity champed at the bit for what seemed like an eternity to meet him, and then suddenly, there he stood on the outskirts of Oceanview in all his glowing white godliness. A choir of angels did not herald his appearance. No trumpets played, and the Pope neglected to lay down a red carpet. He simply appeared out of nowhere to zero fanfare. Anticlimactic felt like an understatement.

God looked around to get his bearings. He arrived at the east end of town and the opposite side he needed to be. A few flakes of snow landed softly on his shoes, a peaceful contrast to the chaos that consumed the rest of Oceanview.

"Raph, are you sure I'm in the right place?" he said into his earpiece.

"*Yes, why?*" Raphael's voice filtered through.

"It's a bit of a shit-hole."

"*Well, an army of demons tore through it. What did you expect?*"

"I don't handle dirty too well. There's a lot of smoke and debris. Are you seeing this?"

"*Yeah. The camera feed looks good.*"

God heard paper rustling through his earpiece. "What are you doing?"

"*Checking the map.*"

"Since when does Google rustle?"

"*I'm not using Google. The town doesn't register. The Google van got lost when it tried to get the imagery. Can you turn around so I can get your bearings?"*

God looked around as Raphael opened the map.

"Okay, it looks like you are on Port Road. There should be some small stores and a post office behind you."

"Yeah, I see them."

"Okay, well then you're about three blocks away from Mrs. Jenkins. You're going to have to walk the rest of the way."

"So, I have to exercise too? And why did you let me come here wearing white?"

"What do you mean? It's your favorite suit."

"There's a foot of snow on the ground. I look like a giant floating head."

A low groaning came from behind, and he spun around as a bloodied demon stumbled towards him.

"They're definitely demons, Raph."

"How can you tell?"

"Their eyes. As black as the shitty cupcakes Valoel brings in on muffin Mondays. I've told her god knows how many times that cupcakes aren't muffins. But does she listen? Oh no, I'm just God, I only created the fucking universe, and I don't know what a fucking muffin is."

"You're wandering again."

"This doesn't enrage you? What kind of moron can't tell the difference between a muffin and a cupcake?"

"I'll take it up with her tomorrow. Can we please get back to the task at hand?"

"Sorry, these things infuriate me." God sighed and tried to regain his focus. "Endus Lificus," he said triumphantly as he pointed a finger at the abomination stumbling towards him.

Raphael's voice crackled over the headset. *"What are you doing?"*

"I don't know. I'm new to all this. I don't know how Earth magic works."

"Humans can't do magic."

"What do you mean they can't do magic?"

"They can't."

"Not even a simple spell?"

"Nope."

"A Patronus? Surely they can do that."

"That's Harry Potter, sir."

"So there is no magical presence here at all?"

"A few people can bend spoons with their minds."

"Fucking spoons? Are you serious?"

"*Yes.*"

"But I created them in my image. How can they not do magic? I am outstanding, shouldn't they, by proxy, be outstanding too?"

"*I'm sorry, they just can't.*"

"Fucking Muggles. I must have used the wrong clay when I created these idiots. On the bright side, this damn creature isn't attacking me."

Kaboom!

God jumped as a loud gunshot rang out, and the demon's head exploded. It fell to the ground in a bloody heap. "What the hell?" yelled God.

"Get out of the street, dipshit," a female voice shouted from behind him.

God turned around to locate the source. "Excuse me? That was rude."

"I said get out of the goddamn street, asshole. You're drawing attention. Don't make me say it again." The voice came from the post office and belonged to Mrs. O'Grady, the postmistress.

"Why?"

"You're going to bring those monsters over here."

"The demons?" God said as he stepped over to the door.

"Yeah, those things. Now go away and find somewhere else to hide."

"I just arrived."

Kaboom!

A second shot rang out, and a puff of tarmac and snow exploded at his feet.

"WHAT THE HELL ARE YOU DOING?" screamed God.

"I'll be doing the asking. Why didn't it bite you?"

"I have no idea." God looked away from the body and back to the post office. The barrel of a shotgun poked through a crack in the door.

"They bite everyone. You seriously need to consider being open with me, shit-nugget, and I suggest you start right now. You can begin by putting your hands where I can see them."

God raised his hands. "I am being open."

"Are you with the gubbermint?"

"Excuse me?"

"Are you with the gubbermint? You're dressed mighty fine for someone entering a war zone."

"No, lady. I'm not with the government." He emphasized the correct pronunciation of the word.

"Don't lie to me. You're one of those Area 51 federal agents, aren't you? This is all your mess, and they sent you here to clean things up real quiet like."

"Well, part of it is right," admitted God. He declined to tell her which part though.

"I know how you gubbermint types clean things up. Our town will be wiped off the Google, and every last one of us will be slaughtered."

"Actually, your town isn't on Google."

"So you've already put your evil plan into action. I figured this day would come. You won't take us alive."

God sighed. "I'm going to go over here," he said, pointing north.

"Don't you walk away from me," shouted Mrs. O'Grady.

"Make up your mind. One minute you want me gone. The next I'm not allowed to leave. How am I supposed to play your silly little human game when I don't even know the rules?"

"What's that supposed to mean?"

"It means the rules keep changing."

"No, I mean the silly little human comment."

The door opened further, and Mrs. O'Grady stepped outside.

She lived her life as a woman of faith. Sure, there were times when she might have been less than generous with the collection plate, and times when she told her husband to shut the fuck up, but she mostly treated him well. She made sure the fridge overflowed with beer, and he received a blowjob on Saturdays. Had she known she was about to face her Lord and Savior, her choice of words may have been a little more refined.

"Fuck me in my Irish ass, you're—" she yelped as she made eye contact with God and spontaneously combusted.

God turned away from the fireball. Within seconds it disappeared, leaving little more than a pile of ash and a bare patch of charred sidewalk. The snow beneath instantly evaporated.

"Holy shit." God held his hand up to his mouth as he stared at the dusty remains of Mrs. O'Grady.

"*What the fuck was that?*" said Raph from the earpiece.

"The hell if I know," God stammered. "She was fine one second and a pile of ash the next."

"*We saw.*"

"YOU SON OF A BITCH! What the hell did you do to my wife?" yelled an extremely pissed off Mr. O'Grady, as he charged from the post office, raising his shotgun.

God turned to look at him. Seconds later, Mr. O'Grady joined his wife's pile of ashes, and turned a fluke into a coincidence. Ten seconds later, their eldest son, Liam, made it a trend.

Raphael's voice piped through the headset. "*What happened?*"

"I don't exactly know. There is a chance they may have spontaneously combusted."

"*What?*"

"They caught fire."

"*I know what spontaneously combusts means, sir. Did you touch them?*"

"Of course I didn't. Humans are gross. Raph, is there anything you may be holding back from me? I'm zero for three here."

"*Give me a second. Let me refer to the manual.*"

Another gunshot rang out.

God looked around to locate the shooter. "Hurry up, Raph. Another one of these assholes is shooting at me."

"*I'm looking, I'm looking. In the meantime, I suggest you get off the street, they probably think you are one of the undead.*"

"Great. I'm here to save their sorry asses, and they want me dead." He headed to an alley across the street.

Raphael jumped back on the intercom. "*Okay, it says here, 'and he said, thou canst not see my face, for there shall no man see me, and live'.*"

"Thou canst? That's not even a proper word. Are you sure you're reading this right?"

"*It's right here in Exodus 33:20.*"

"Oh, for fuck's sake. Are you kidding me? Wait, is that from the original manuscript, or the King Charles translation, which left out some of the bits they didn't agree with?"

"*Both, sir.*"

"And you decided to leave this nugget out because?"

"*I forgot.*"

"You forgot? You sent me on a mission to interact with humans without the ability to interact with humans?"

"*I'm sorry.*"

"Well, can I at least look at them if they can't see me?"

"*Yes.*"

"But, if they can't look at me, how am I supposed to finish my mission?"

"*You need sunglasses.*"

"Sunglasses?"

"*Yeah, the UV filter will protect them from you.*"

"Where am I supposed to find sunglasses?"

"The post office should have them."

"And I pay for them how, exactly? You didn't send me down here with a per diem."

"Just take them."

"So I take it the fourth commandment means nothing to you?"

"Remember the Sabbath?"

"No, the one about stealing."

"Well, technically, you've already broken the sixth one, so the rules are moot at this point."

"Bear false witness?"

"No, the murder one."

"Let's forget that then. Theft it is."

God stepped back out into the street and headed over to the post office. The front door was open from the ash family's quick exit. He stepped over the pile of O'Grady's and headed to the counter. Sure enough, he found a display of sunglasses.

"I don't do rhinestones," he said into his mic as he looked through the slim pickings.

"They'll have to do for now."

"I'm not wearing sparkly glasses, Raph. I'll look like a flamboyant seventy's pop star." God walked behind the counter and spied a cheap pair of dark aviator glasses beneath the register. He put them on as he left the post office and headed west to the Paradise Bay apartments to find Mrs. Jenkins. "This is unbelievable," he said as he walked through the wreckage that filled Port Road.

"What do you mean, sir?"

"Well, aren't these people supposed to worship me?"

"Many of them do."

"So far, I've been yelled at, shot at, and called a shit-nugget. I'm not exactly feeling the love yet."

"It may take them a while to warm up to you. It isn't every day someone gets to meet their Lord and Savior. They probably have deity anxiety, and you did recently kill three of them."

"Hey, that wasn't my fault. You withheld critical information vital to the success of this mission." God looked around as he walked down the snow-dusted street. "I expected a warmer welcome."

"Did you forget what they did to your son? They aren't exactly a friendly bunch to strangers. Give them time, they'll come around." Raphael paused. *"There's one*

more thing."

"Of course there is."

"It's about the three people you killed."

"I didn't kill them on purpose."

"It doesn't matter. They weren't supposed to die as they weren't in the database."

"Won't they disappear when we resurrect Mrs. Jenkins?"

"I don't know. The rules say everyone who dies must be reaped. It says nothing about deaths from God. That's a separate parallel."

"So how is it can we take care of Mrs. Jenkins?"

"Because she is in the database."

God stopped walking. "Can you fix the database?"

"Still working on it, sir."

"No, I know it's broken. Not fix, *fix.*"

"I don't follow."

"Obviously. Can you add the people who have died to the database?"

"You mean cheat the system for personal gain?"

God sighed. Raphael finally understood it. "Yes. I mean cheat the system."

"I can't do that. It's in direct violation of process 31709a."

"Which is?"

"You cannot cheat the system for personal gain."

"Of course, that'd make things too easy. What happens if we violate process 31709a?"

"We don't know, sir. It would be—"

"Let me guess, unprecedented? I get it. What exactly do you know, Raph? What information do you have I can actually use, because right now you're kind of worthless."

"I'm just telling you how it is. I didn't write the rules. We have no plan for this."

"Stop with the no precedent bullshit. Let's start a new precedent."

"We'd need a process in place first."

"Remind me to fire your ass when I get back to the office."

Bang.

A puff of dirt kicked up over God's shoes as another shot rang out.

God stepped out into the street. "Once more, motherfucker," he shouted

Bang.

He looked around for the shooter and spied someone on a roof across the street.

"Hey, asshole," he shouted as he stepped out into the street and lowered his sunglasses.

A flame leaped up from the roof, and the shooter disappeared.

"Anyone else wanna take a shot? Anyone?" shouted God. "Come on, I'm ready."

"*Sir, you're not making this any easier,*" declared Raphael. "*Killing them won't help.*"

"No, but it makes me feel better."

"*You're making things worse.*"

"Raph?"

"*Yes, sir?*"

"Fuck off."

CHAPTER 38

Greg stopped the bus at the traffic light at Miller and Seventeenth and cursed under his breath. The intersection contained a mass of smoking, twisted metal resulting from a cement truck plowing into a line of cars. A downed streetlight sparked with electricity, and dozens of creatures picked through the wreckage, eating the drivers who were too slow, too injured, or too stupid to leave their cars.

"Drive through them, man," said Warren from a few rows back.

Greg ignored him.

"We can't get through, can we?" said Amber softly.

Greg shook his head. "Not without damaging the bus, we can't. It's too risky."

"Just plow through," said Warren as he moved up to the front of the bus.

"Christ, use your head, man," said Greg. "The wreckage is twenty cars deep. We'll never make it."

"Greg, whatever you're doing, do it faster," said David. "We've got company."

Greg looked into the side mirror. A large group of zombie-demons was advancing on the bus. "I'm out of ideas," he said softly.

"Greg, do something," yelled Ashley.

"I'm out of fucking ideas," he yelled back. "I don't know what to do."

"What about the church?" suggested David.

"What about it?" said Warren curtly. "Nothing there for godless heathens."

"It's a stone building. The windows are high, and the main door is solid oak. We could hole up there."

"Not a bad idea," agreed Greg. "Does anyone have a better plan?"

No one answered.

"Okay then, we hit the church," said Greg.

"Hey, Greg," said Warren from behind.

Greg turned around. "What?"

"Can I drive?"

"What?"

"The bus. Can I drive it?"

"Why?"

"Never tried it before. I may not get another chance."

"No, you just want to ram shit with it."

"You have my word. We'll get to the church unscathed." Warren tapped the four points of a cross on his chest.

"Fine." Greg stood up and climbed out of the seat.

Warren quickly replaced him. "Okay, kiddies. Hold onto your tits."

He threw the gear into reverse and backed up, crushing the demon unlucky enough to be closest beneath the wheels. The bus rocked as the violent swarm slammed into the side of the vehicle. Warren finished the turn and pulled forward. He looked up at the rearview mirror as the blood-thirsty group started to vanish.

Despite only having to walk three blocks, God found himself lost six times. A trip that should have taken less than five minutes in a normal town took over forty-five minutes as the streets became dead ends and did unexpected U-turns. Winded and agitated, God finally found the Paradise Bay apartment complex.

"Okay, I'm here," he said, a little out of breath. "I fucking hate this town. Whoever designed it should be smited. Remind me to do that when I get back to the office."

"*Do you see her?*" responded Raphael through God's earpiece.

A large group of demons shuffled around on the street without direction.

"What does she look like?" asked God.

"*She's old, most likely gray.*"

"Old and gray, huh? The shit you say, Sherlock? Can you be a little bit more specific?"

"*She's white.*"

That removed the elderly African American lady.

"Anything else?"

"*What distinguishing features do you see?*"

"They're all covered in blood, pastels, and bad sweaters, Raph. They all look the same except the one in a nightie with a breathing mask around her neck standing in the street."

"*That's her. She has trouble breathing and uses a respirator while she sleeps. According to the reports, she died in her sleep. That has to be her.*"

God smiled and started to walk over to the bloodied woman. "Hello, Harriet, this is quite the mess you have caused us."

She slowly turned around and stared at him with black lifeless eyes.

God reached out to touch her on the shoulder. What happened next came so fast that he was unable to register what transpired. Before he could resurrect her, the school bus barreled around the corner and plowed into Harriet. She disappeared in an explosion of blood and gore.

"No," yelled God as he held up his hands.

The bus kept moving as God's jaw fell open.

His earpiece erupted with Raphael's similar shock. "*What the fuck was that?*"

God paused. "What's our backup plan, Raph?"

"*This was the backup plan.*"

"Well, we need another one. Patient zero is no longer an option."

"*What do you mean she is no longer an option? I thought you said you'd found her?*"

"A bus ran her over."

"*What?*"

"A bus ran her over. She's a skid mark. Shit, she isn't even a skid mark. She just vaporized."

"*How did she vaporize? That doesn't make sense.*"

"She's a flesh-eating demon, Raph. None of this makes sense."

"*That's it,*" Raphael said into the earpiece. "*That was our last chance. Game over, man.*"

God rubbed his chin pensively. "Raph, calm down. There has to be another way."

"*How are we supposed to resurrect a body for reaping when there is no body? We've played all our cards. There is nothing in the universe that can fix this mess.*"

"Raph?"

"Patient zero is dead. That's the endgame. We're finished." Raphael continued his freak out.

God's eyes widened as an idea formed in his head. "RAPH."

Raphael snapped out of his moment and tried to compose himself. *"Sir?"*

"What did you say?"

"I said it's game over."

"Before that."

"I said we've played all our cards."

"Raph, you're a fucking genius."

The bus sputtered into the church parking lot with the engine smoking and knocking. Blood and miscellaneous body parts covered the front. It had seen far better days.

"Everyone out," ordered Warren.

He waited until the rest of the group had exited the bus before standing.

Cam ran over to the heavy wooden door and slammed the brass knocker. "Help," she yelled. "Someone, please let us in."

Each passing second felt like an hour. Demons were already starting to appear at the end of the parking lot and were getting closer.

"Help," shouted Cam again.

Lee raised his gun and dropped the nearest one that ventured too close to the group. Ashley sided up next to him and took down a second.

Amber banged on the door. "Reverend Ellis, please let us in."

Ashley shot a third as a deadbolt clicked on the door, and it swung open. Reverend Ellis beckoned the group inside. "Quick, come in."

"Greg, help me with the cart," yelled Warren as he ran to the back of the bus and opened the door from the inside.

Greg ran around to the rear of the bus as the door opened. Warren reached up and grabbed the end of the cart as Greg pushed it out and jumped down onto the concrete.

"Greg, behind you," shouted Lee.

Greg spun around. A creature lunged towards him, its arms outstretched. Greg ducked under its reach and pushed it into the bus door. It lost its balance and fell to the ground. Ashley put a bullet between its eyes before it could sit back up.

"A woman with a gun is hot," said Warren with a grin.

"Shut it, or you'll be next," Ashley replied.

"You saved a bullet for me? You do love me."

"Whatever helps you sleep at night."

"Move," Greg ordered as he slammed the rear door closed and bolted it shut.

Warren lifted the front of the cart, and they ran to the church door. Lee pulled it shut behind them.

"Is everyone okay?" asked Reverend Ellis as the group gathered inside the entryway.

Lee nodded. "Yeah."

David raised his hand. "I've been shot."

"I've been bitten," said Warren clutching his left arm. As one, the group turned to him.

"What?" said Greg. "No."

"Sorry, bro. Happened outside by the bus."

"Dammit, Warren," said Greg as he held his hands to his head in shock.

Warren slowly pulled up his sleeve. Greg clenched his teeth, preparing for the bloody bite mark.

Nothing.

"Psych," Warren said with a grin.

"You're a fucking prick," said Greg.

The rest of the group mumbled their agreements.

"The good Lord does not look well upon those making light of such a serious situation," said Reverend Ellis.

"Oh, come on," said Warren. "Where's your sense of humor?"

Every last bit of Greg's shit disappeared. "My sense of humor? Our friends are dying, our families are dying, our town is a massive pile of fuck, and you want to crack fucking jokes? Are you fucking serious?"

"All right, calm down, princess."

Greg raised his fist and moved towards Warren.

Lee grabbed him by the shoulders. "Let it go, Greg."

"Can I get anyone a drink?" offered Reverend Ellis, trying to defuse things. Arguments and loud voices made him uncomfortable.

David's ears pricked up. "Do you have any gin?"

"No, sorry," said Reverend Ellis.

"Whiskey?" asked Cam.

"There is wine in the back room," offered Reverend Ellis.

"Good enough for me," said Cam. "David?"

"Agreed."

"We also have snacks back there if you're hungry. There should be enough food for a few days. I expected company to show up."

Lee released his hold on Greg. "Are we good?"

Greg nodded. The immediate urge to strike his Warren subsided, but he wanted some air. He turned and walked into the nave. "I'll be back there if anyone wants me. I need a minute."

Amber followed him through the double doors.

Lee looked around the church and noticed the Reverend stood alone. "Are we the first to come here?"

Reverend Ellis nodded. "All I've heard the past few days has been the moaning and an occasional explosion. The noise has been terrible."

"Why didn't you leave?" asked Cam.

"You're my flock. If you can't take refuge in a church when the world is coming to an end, where can you go? It's Revelations 20:5. But the rest of the dead lived not again until the thousand years were finished. This is the first resurrection. Satan is just a little late."

Warren sighed. "So, this is it then."

Reverend Ellis nodded. "All signs are certainly pointing to the end of days. I'd say our clock has expired in this life."

"That sucks," said Warren.

♦ ♦ ♦ ♦

"Your brother's scared," Amber said as she sat on the bench next to Greg.

"And I'm not? Everything I love could be snatched away from me in a moment, and he wants to make jokes. I don't see how any of this is funny."

"It's how some people deal. He's terrified too. You keep a calm head and Warren cracks jokes." She put her head on Greg's shoulder. "You need to clear the air. If things go bad, you don't want to be mad at him."

"We were born fighting, and we'll probably die fighting. When we were kids, we were in sitting in the back of our parent's car, waving goodbye to our grandparents. It started raining, so I put the window up. His head and arm got stuck in them. I swear to this day I didn't know, but he was convinced I tried to kill him."

"And I still get headaches," Warren said from the doorway with a smile. "Are we cool?"

"Are you going to stop making jokes?"

"I doubt it. I still got your back, though."

Greg smiled. "My little brother to the end." He stood up as Warren walked over to him, and he opened his arms.

"I ain't hugging you, snowflake. I heard there's wine." He grinned.

On cue, Cam came from the back room, holding seven bottles. "This is a good start. Anyone have an opener?"

"Is the Pope Irish?" said Warren as he fished an opener from his pocket.

♦ ♦ ♦ ♦

The last few hours of the day passed by without event. The moaning outside steadily increased in volume, and the banging on the door echoed through the church. By the sixth bottle of wine, their laughter and talking muffled the apocalypse.

"We're losing sunlight," said Reverend Ellis as he looked up at the stained-glass windows. "Should we turn the lights on?"

"Is that wise?" said David. "Do we want to bring any more of those things our way?"

"Is it going to make a difference?" said Cam. "They all know we're here anyway. If this is our last night, I'll be damned if I'm spending it in the dark."

David shrugged. She had a point. "All right, light us up."

"There's no more room in hell," said Warren as the lights flickered on one by one.

"Excuse me?" Cam said as she opened the next bottle of wine.

"My Granddaddy used to say it. When there is no more room in hell, the dead shall inherit the Earth."

"No, he didn't," interrupted Greg.

"Yeah, he did," argued Warren.

"No, you heard it on Dawn of the Dead, you idiot."

"You saw Dawn of the Dead?"

"Everybody did. And since when did you call him Granddaddy?"

Warren shrugged his shoulders.

"And it's *the dead shall walk the Earth*', not inherit. The meek shall inherit the Earth. The dead shall walk it. If you're going to quote a movie, do it right."

"Man, I had a good monologue going, and you ruined it."

"At least you're not doing another Star Wars one," said Ashley with a grin.

"What's wrong with my Star Wars monologues?"

"Nothing, the first twenty times." Ashley smiled.

"You're killing me, Smalls."

"Make yourself useful and hand me the chips," said Ashley laughing as she held a hand.

"Ash?" said Warren as he passed her the bag.

"What?"

"I'm sorry." Warren wore an unusually serious look on his face. One that could almost be considered genuine.

"Excuse me?" said Ashley.

"I'm sorry."

"What for?"

"Everything."

Ashley rolled her eyes. "Stop trying to get in my pants."

"I'm not. I haven't been very good to you, and I'm sorry." For once, he was truthful.

"Warren, you're drunk."

"Yes, but I mean it. I wish I'd treated you better. You deserve that." He paused. "Would this get me in your pants?"

"I wouldn't fuck you again if you were the last man alive. I'd screw Cam before I screwed you."

"I'm okay with that too. At least I'd go out on a high note," Warren said with an ear-to-ear smile.

Cam held up her glass of wine. "Cheers to that."

Warren continued to grin at the potential scenario unraveling before him. There was finally an upside to the zombie-demon apocalypse. He opened his mouth to speak.

"Whatever you're thinking, just stop," said Ashley.

♦ ♦ ♦ ♦

As the night wrapped its arms around the town, the moaning outside increased as one-by-one, the group fell asleep.

Greg was the last man standing and lay staring at the ceiling. He eventually gave up trying to sleep and sat up.

Amber stirred and noticed his restlessness. "What's wrong?"

"I'm going upstairs to the tower," said Greg. "I want to see how many of them are out there. I'll be right back." He leaned over and kissed her on the forehead. He stood up and walked over to the bell tower door.

Seventy-five steps later, he walked out into the chilly night air and drew a heavy breath. The moon glowed bright, allowing him to see more than he expected and far more than he wanted. Every inch of concrete as far as he could see teemed with the undead. His jaw fell as his buzz wore off, and the gravity of the situation set in. He gave the wrecked town another glance before he disappeared inside and returned to Amber.

Greg curled up next to Amber and let out a heavy sigh.

"How many are out there?"

"All of them."

"Fuck."

"Yeah." Greg closed his eyes, and the fingers of sleep finally crept through his body, tormenting him with dreams of death and loss.

"Greg. Greg. Greg." said Warren, raising the volume with each successive mention of his brother's name. "Wake up, man."

Greg finally succumbed to sleep a little after three and was in a deep slumber when he felt a hand against his shoulder, nudging him awake. He slowly opened his eyes and saw Warren standing over him with a concerned look on his face.

"What's going on?" he said quietly, trying to avoid waking Amber.

"Something's wrong."

"Huh?" Greg sat up and rubbed his eyes.

"Something's wrong. Listen."

Greg stopped massaging his eyes and cocked his head to one side. "What am I listening for?"

"Just listen."

"I don't hear anything."

"Exactly."

Greg shook his head, trying to wake up and make sense of Warren.

"The moaning has stopped."

Greg's eyes widened. His brother was right.

"I don't get it," said Warren. "Are they sleeping?"

"Unlikely." Greg gently moved Amber's arm off his shoulder and quickly climbed to his feet.

"Did they change back to normal?"

"Maybe. I'm going up the tower to look." Greg stood up and walked to the staircase.

"Wait for me," said Warren.

A minute later, Greg stepped out into the tower and stared out across the town. The early morning sun highlighted an empty town. Everything seemed quiet. He looked at the street below and turned to see the same situation behind him. "What the hell?"

Warren joined him fifteen seconds later. "What the hell?"

"What do you make of this?" asked Greg.

"I don't know. Where did they all go?"

Greg shrugged. He had no answer for his brother. All five thousand, seven hundred, and thirty-nine demons were gone. No bodies, nothing. Plumes of black smoke continued to stab skyward, and the destruction looked as widespread as the day before, but every zombie-demon had vanished.

Warren showed equal confusion. "Is that it? Is it over?"

"I don't know," stammered Greg. "It sure looks like it."

"Did they go somewhere else?"

"Maybe, but this town isn't that big. Where do you hide almost the entire population?"

Warren shrugged. "What do we do now?"

"Head downstairs and put it to vote. I say we pack up our shit and get out of here."

"You mean, go home?"

"If there's even one left. Let's see what everyone says."

Warren turned and headed back inside as Greg gave the decimated town one last glance. He sighed in relief and followed his brother downstairs.

"Everyone up," shouted Warren as he left the stairwell.

A few hungover voices of protest rose from the group.

"Dammit, Warren," croaked Cam. "Go back to sleep. Armageddon isn't going anywhere."

"Armageddon's been canceled."

"What?" said Cam.

"The zombie-demons have gone."

Cam sat up and rubbed her bloodshot eyes. "If this is another one of your lame-ass jokes, it isn't funny."

"He isn't joking," said Greg as he left the stairwell. "The town is empty."

Slowly the group stirred as the news sank in.

"Come on, I'll show you." Greg walked to the back of the church and stopped at the main doors. He pulled the deadbolt back, took a deep breath, and pushed them open.

"What are you doing?" Cam yelled as the door swung open.

The bright morning light that flooded in proved too harsh for the alcohol punished group, and by the time their eyes adjusted to the sun, Greg was outside.

"See," said Greg. "They've gone."

David wasn't convinced. "How do we know they didn't just walk off and go somewhere else?"

"I looked from the bell tower, it has the best view in town," said Greg. "I couldn't see one of them."

"What do we do now?" asked Amber.

"We can still go to Phoenix, or we stay and clean up this mess," said Greg.

"I want my own bed," said Ashley.

The agreements were unanimous.

"I want your bed too," said Warren mischievously

Ashley slugged him on the arm. "No. Knock your shit off."

"Some of our vehicles are at the garage. We may as well head back there," suggested Greg.

◆ ◆ ◆ ◆

For a hung-over bunch, they moved fast and were on the bus within ten minutes. The promise of clean clothes and a warm bed spurred their motivation.

Reverend Ellis stopped as Amber entered the bus.

"Come on, Reverend," said Greg from the driver's seat. "Time to go."

Reverend Ellis shook his head. "I'm sorry, Greg, I can't leave the church. If people come here searching for shelter, I must keep the doors open. This is where I'm supposed to be."

"Are you sure? I don't think there's many of us left."

Ellis nodded. "I need to be here, just in case."

Greg reached down and shook his hand. "We'll come back with more supplies for you." He stepped back inside the bus and closed the door.

Ellis banged on the side of the bus as it pulled away and waved at the departing group.

CHAPTER 39

Death was fifteen minutes late as he walked into his office. He never started the day late. Susan assumed the ordeal at Oceanview had begun to get to him.

"Is everything okay, sir?" she said as Death put his scythe in the umbrella stand.

"I'm ready for this whole thing to be over." The issues in Oceanview showed no sign of ending, and the warm glow of victory had started to wear off. "I'll be in my office."

"A Gary came by to see you."

Death froze and turned back to Susan. "What did he look like?"

"White suit, car salesman grin. Very charming. He said you'd know what it's about."

"Did he leave anything?" asked Death.

Susan shook her head. "No, he wanted to wait in your office for you, but after a few minutes, he upped and left."

"Did he take anything?"

Again, Susan shook her head. "I don't think so. He had a small bag with him, but it didn't look any different when he left. I offered him coffee and a jellybean, but he declined. Who was he?"

"No one important."

"He looked important."

"Susan, drop it."

Death disappeared into his office and closed the door behind him. He glanced around to see if anything seemed out of place. Nothing appeared to be missing. He furrowed his brow as he eyeballed the room, trying to figure out God's endgame.

The phone on his desk chirped. *"Sir? There's a Luke on the phone. He sounds pretty upset."*

"Oh, this keeps getting better and better." He thumbed the call button. "Put him through."

Death sat down behind his desk. Aside from some occasional handwritten notes on the reaping lists, he never spoke to Lucifer, but there was little doubt who Susan meant. Lucifer almost certainly wanted to discuss the events in Oceanview, although Death could not determine how he became involved as his lists were correct.

The phone chirped, and Susan forwarded the call. "Luc, what can I do for you?"

"What the fuck, Steve?"

"Uh—"

"Don't play coy with me. You know damn well why I'm calling."

Death sighed. It would be one of those phone calls. "I promise you, I have no idea."

"Don't shit a bullshitter, Steve."

Death started to get flustered. He could spin bullshit with the best of them, *'you don't deserve this'*, *'I'm sorry this happened to you'*, *'you're going to a better place'*. He was no stranger to the art of bullshit, but he hated getting called out on bullshit he was not spinning.

"This has your name stamped all over it," said Lucifer. *"Meet me in an hour,"* he demanded.

"Where?" asked Death.

"Pick a place. I don't care."

♦ ♦ ♦ ♦

Death sat in a booth sipping coffee as Lucifer entered the diner. There was no reason for Death to flag him down. Both stood out like sore thumbs, decked head to toe in black. Although, Lucifer's costume of choice consisted of a crisply tailored suit with a black shirt and tie. It was no coincidence that Lucifer was considered to be God's most beautiful angel. He was quite simply stunning to look at.

"Damn, who died?" shouted the jovial prick in the booth next to them.

"You, if you don't focus those squinty little eyes back on your waffles, you fat fuck." Lucifer was not a happy man.

The fat fuck lowered his eyes and returned to ravaging his breakfast.

"Denny's?" said Lucifer as he sat down across from Death. "Don't you deal with enough misery and despair?"

"I kill people for a living. It's exhausting. I need a place to decompress and eat pancakes."

"You always were a cheap bastard. How old is your robe?"

Death looked at his threads. "What's wrong with my robe?"

"Sorry, not judging. I suck at this small talk chit-chat bullshit. You know it's weird finally meeting you. How long have we been working together?"

"I lost count after two thousand years."

"Has it been that long? Feels like yesterday." Lucifer looked around the restaurant. "How come they can see you? I thought you were invisible."

"If the hood is down, I'm visible. It's the only way I can order breakfast."

"A cloak with a cloaking device, I like it. Where's the scythe?"

"I'm not reaping. I don't need it. So, what's going on? We can cut the filler and get to the point."

"Yes. Sorry for yelling on the phone earlier. I tend to get a little wound up when I'm stressed, and I fly off the handle. Anyway, I digress. I get up this morning, I grab my Bloody Mary, and head to my office. But my office isn't empty like it normally is. I have five thousand, seven hundred and thirty-nine people lined up in the hallway waiting for me."

"Okay," said Death, unsure what the correct response should be. "Don't you get hundreds of times that every day?"

"Yes, but this is different. They weren't on my lists. None of these people were scheduled to come to me."

Death put down his coffee. "Okay, you have my attention."

"I have Born Again's down there, Steve. I never have those fuckers there. I fucking hate them. They're hypocrites. They sin their entire lives, find God, and suddenly, they are the moral authority. They don't belong with me."

Death grimaced.

"Oh, it gets worse. I have Jehovah's Witnesses and Mormon's here too. The place is a mess. I don't want people like that. I finally have all the riffraff sorted out, and we're all having a wonderful time. It's like Dick Clark's New Year's Rocking Eve, but with more strippers and coke."

"Wait. How many did you say?"

"Five thousand, seven hundred, and thirty-nine."

And then an alarm rang in Death's head. "That dirty mother fucker."

"Excuse me?" said Lucifer, a little shocked by the outburst.

"I think I know what happened. Can you give me two minutes?"

Lucifer nodded. "Sure, take your time. I want bacon and French toast anyway."

Death closed his eyes and disappeared.

◆ ◆ ◆ ◆

He reappeared in the middle of Oceanview. The town still looked like a bomb went off, but it was quiet, almost too quiet. Wrecked cars lined the street, and dozens of houses burned in the distance. But there were no demons or screaming people running down the sidewalks. The dead bodies were gone, and apart from the mess, there were no signs of an undead outbreak ever occurring. He disappeared and reappeared on the east side of the town. It was the same story, as were the Downtown Park and west side shopping strip. He closed his eyes and disappeared again.

◆ ◆ ◆ ◆

Death reappeared at his office. He stormed in and walked past Susan to his desk. He opened the bottom drawer, pulled out a wooden box, and flipped open the lid. The box was half full of Blood Cards.

"SON OF A BITCH!"

In a flash, he teleported once again.

◆ ◆ ◆ ◆

Death reappeared in front of Lucifer.

"Blood Cards," said Death.

"What?"

"The dirty bastard stole the fucking Blood Cards from my office."

"Who did?" asked Lucifer.

"Gary."

"Gary? I don't get it. Why would he do that?"

"He used my Blood Cards to clean up his mess."

"Why were you sitting on five thousand, seven hundred, and thirty-nine Blood Cards? You only get ten a month."

"I have way more than that. I've been saving them."

"For what?"

Death leaned back in his chair. "Not this."

"Then what?"

"I honestly don't know. As the years passed by, it became harder and harder to decide who deserved them."

"Who deserved them? There is no shortage of assholes in this world. Throw a dart at a newspaper. It ain't difficult." He glanced around the restaurant. "Hell, I could find ten here without even trying."

"That isn't why I have the cards."

"Sure it is. We have an agreement that each month, you get to take out ten scumbags who are poisoning this planet."

"It doesn't say scumbags. It says person or persons of my choice."

"Well, scumbag is implied."

"There is so much more to it than that. I used to feel the same way. And you're right, there is no shortage of assholes, but why should I give them the easy way out? There are people, good people, who are far more deserving of these cards. These cards aren't an excuse to simply wipe the douche of this planet. They can be used to stop suffering. I can actually do something humane with them."

Lucifer pondered the alternative use for a moment. "I didn't think of it like that." He grinned. "Look at you being all caring and shit. I guess it makes sense. It also makes it clearer as to why I never saw any unscheduled dill-holes show up."

"Gary loves the dill-holes."

Lucifer laughed. "Of course he does."

"Anyone who has even stepped one foot in a church is good in his eyes. I never understood it personally. He believes everyone can be saved."

"Yeah, fuck that," Lucifer added. "And people think Hell is such a bad place to be. They have no idea."

"If only you saw some of the names who show up on my good list." He quoted 'good' with his fingers. "Some of the people who go up could shock Hitler."

"Speaking of which, he didn't come my way," said Lucifer.

"Nope. Apparently, genocide can be forgiven if he went to church at least once in his life."

"Or repents like hell on his death bed."

"Yeah, that too."

"Seriously, fuck that," repeated Lucifer. "You can give me the top ten list of the world's biggest ass-clowns, and I guarantee none of them came my way."

"I'll never forget this time about two hundred years ago, a serial pedophile popped up on my list. In his last days in prison, he found God, and he went upstairs. That's when I figured the entire system is broken. I gave up trying to understand it."

"I figured as much. I keep track of the major league douchebags, and if they are part of a church, I don't see them."

The two men stayed silent for a moment. Neither one tried to dwell on the system too often. I made no sense and just gave them a headache.

Lucifer decided to change the subject. "So, how are we going to fix this?"

Death rubbed his chin. "I am going to need you to email me a list."

♦ ♦ ♦ ♦

Death appeared at his office and entered the front door.

Susan stood in his way, clutching a printed email, and wearing a scowl. "You know that Gary, who stopped by?"

Death nodded his head cautiously.

"The Gary I offered coffee and a jellybean to?"

Death knew the direction the discussion was headed.

"The black jellybeans that no one likes?"

A Susan eruption was imminent. In three.

"Gary O'Donnell?" she asked.

Death slowly nodded his head again.

Two.

"Gary O'Donnell, or God as he is known to the rest of us, came here, and I offered him black jellybeans?"

One.

She turned a shade of red Death had not seen before. "My Lord and Savior came here, and I offered him a jellybean? The licorice ones that get left at the bottom of the jar as they suck?"

Death grimaced.

"I OFFERED MY LORD AND SAVIOR A BLACK FUCKING JELLYBEAN! WHO THE FUCK LIKES LICORICE JELLYBEANS? NO ONE, THAT'S WHO."

She threw her hands up in the air in a combination of resignation and disgust. "I'm going to Hell for this. There is a special place in the pits of the underworld reserved for people who pass off bottom-of-the-barrel candy to deities. Did you know he was coming?"

"I—"

"DID YOU KNOW HE WAS COMING?"

"Susan—" Death started.

"Don't fucking Susan me, you fucking asshole."

Susan never cursed, and Death found it a little disconcerting. "No. I promise you, I—"

"Bullshit. You knew I went to church every Sunday when I was mortal. You knew I worshipped the ground he walks on. How could you keep this from me? This is worse than the time I won backstage passes to meet Mick Jagger."

"But you love The Rolling Stones."

"I do. Only it wasn't The Rolling Stones. It was Guns N' Roses. I HATE GUNS N' FUCKING ROSES."

Death tried to speak.

"Don't say a word. There is nothing you can say to make this okay. You don't offer someone black jellybeans, knowing full well they are the dregs of the candy world, and expect an afterlife of haloes and tranquility. I am going to be cast into the fiery pits of Hades to spend my afterlife with pedophiles and reality TV stars."

"Susan, I can fix this. He screwed Luc and—"

"I don't want to hear it." She stood up and picked up her purse from her desk. "I quit."

"Wait, you can't quit on me. Not now."

"Watch me."

"But I need to log into the Blood Cards program and reverse some applications."

"I'm sure you're smart enough to figure out the application," said Susan as she pushed her chair towards the desk.

"Susan, please. I don't have the password."

She sighed. "There's a manual on my desk."

"We're in a hurry. I really need your help."

"No."

"You can save the universe."

Susan stared at Death for a moment. She sighed again and put her purse back down on the desk. "Fine, but you owe me greatly for this."

"Anything. Just name it."

"I'm going to hold you to that, but I'll have to contemplate my demands."

"Take all the time you need."

"Good, because right now, we have a universe to save."

Death smiled and stood behind her as she logged into the Blood Card application.

"So what do you need?"

"We need to remove five thousand, seven hundred, and thirty-nine names from the database."

Susan lowered her glasses and scowled at Death. "This is really going to cost you."

◆ ◆ ◆ ◆

The three-mile drive down Port Road passed by with no drama. Each clear intersection gave Greg more hope that the crisis may indeed be over.

"Five more blocks," he said cheerfully as Amber came up beside him.

"I can't believe it's over," she said as she leaned forward into the windshield. Greg swerved around another car wreck.

Amber's eyes squinted to see something on the horizon. "What's that?" she said, pointing to a gray mass at the end of the street.

"I don't know," said Greg.

He lifted his foot off the gas, and the bus started to lose speed. "What *is* that?"

Slowly the mass came into focus.

"Fuck me," he proclaimed and slammed on the brakes.

"What the shit?" yelled Warren as he fell off his seat. "A little warning next time." He stood up and rubbed his forehead. "What's wrong?" He followed Greg's gaze out of the windshield. "Fuck me sideways."

"There must be a thousand of them," said Greg. He missed by four thousand, seven hundred, and thirty-nine.

Every last demon from Lucifer's waiting room had returned to Oceanview and was sprinting along Port Road towards the bus.

"Back to the church," yelled David.

"For once, I agree with you," said Warren.

"Hurry," shouted Amber.

Greg turned the bus around, and within seconds, the horde slammed into the side of the vehicle and poured around them.

"Now what?" screamed Ashley.

"Go through them," said Warren. "It's the only way."

"Let him drive, Warren," shouted Ashley.

"He's right," said Greg as he pumped the accelerator. "The only way is through."

The undead banged against the sides of the bus, desperate to get in and devour the survivors. The engine groaned as Greg pumped the gas, pushing the bus forward through the heaving tangle of limbs.

"Come on," yelled Greg as the engine spluttered, threatening to stall.

Amber squeezed Greg's shoulder in part encouragement, part pure unadulterated terror.

Greg looked up at the rear-view mirror. Warren stared at him and nodded slowly, and Greg returned the gesture. The action was subtle but clear. The brothers made peace with each other, and if the situation turned bad, they would not die at war.

The bus inched forward and pulled free of the crowd. Greg floored it and headed towards the church. Each street they passed teemed with the undead. Five minutes later, the bus screeched to a stop in front of the church, throwing the passengers around roughly.

"Hurry," yelled Greg.

Amber opened the rear door as the group flooded to the back of the bus and jumped out of the back door. They scrambled from the bus and sprinted the short distance to the church.

Greg ripped the door open and checked everyone as they entered. As Warren ran past, he closed the heavy oak door behind them and locked it. Seconds later, the horde arrived and crashed against the barricade.

"That was too close," said Warren between long, drawn-out breaths.

Greg looked around frantically. "Did anyone grab the food and guns?"

All eyes in the room darted back and forth, hoping someone else confirmed they grabbed them.

"Fuck," yelled Greg.

"We need to go get them," said Warren.

"No way," said Greg. "All of our exits are blocked. Until they leave, we ain't going anywhere."

CHAPTER 40

God watched the numbers increase as the elevator rose through Heaven. He rocked back and forth on his heels, barely able to contain his excitement. The elevator pinged cheerfully as it stopped on the twelfth floor, and Eric from the Jehovah's Witnesses department stepped in.

"Good morning, Eric," said God with a broad smile. "Lovely day, isn't it?"

Eric looked a little surprised at his good mood. "Good morning, sir. It is indeed. Can I give you a pamphlet?"

"What the hell, why not."

Eric's eyes widened in shock. Without skipping a beat, he reached into his satchel, pulled out the latest issue of Watch Tower, and handed it to God with a giant smile on his face. "In this issue, we talk about curing homosexuality."

"There's a cure now?"

"Of course there is a cure. Anything which is an abomination in the Lord's eyes is curable."

"Now hold on," said God. "I never called it an abomination. I happen to find their outlook on life quite endearing. They add so much color to an otherwise dreary palette. Besides, didn't we all experiment in college?"

Eric's smile faded. "It's written in Leviticus 18:22. Thou shalt not lie with mankind, as with womankind. It is an abomination. You said it yourself."

"No. They took it completely out of context. I said a man should not lie *to* his male friends as he would *to* his female friends. Bros before hoes, dude." God held out his hand and feigned dropping an imaginary microphone. "Boom, mic drop."

Eric stammered to find a response. Mercifully, the doors opened, and he made his escape. God grinned to himself as the doors closed. A few floors later, the elevator stopped again, and Spencer the Baptist pranced inside.

"Good morning, sir, "said Spencer. "What a stellar day we're having."

"Oh, Spencer, you have no fucking idea."

"Say, the team and I are planning a barbecue this week. It sure would be swell if you could join us."

"You know what, Spencer, I'd love to. Get in touch with my secretary and send me a calendar invite."

Spencer beamed in both surprise and delight. His years of persistence were finally paying off. "Wow, I'll get my team on it right away. This is wonderful. Do you prefer hot dogs or burgers?"

"Surprise me."

"I'll do both! Do you like potato salad?"

"Do I have a pulse?" asked God.

Spencer had unsuccessfully tried to invite God to the weekly barbecues for decades and did not expect him to finally say yes. "Can you bring chips?"

"Ridged or barbecue? Oh, what the hell. I'll bring both. Will there be Bundt cake? Tell me there's going to be Bundt cake."

Spencer lost his tongue. It was the single greatest day of his afterlife. The elevator door opened, and he stepped out.

"I'll see you next weekend," lied God as the doors closed.

God continued to smile as the elevator passed the last few floors. He stepped out and headed down the hallway towards his office.

◆ ◆ ◆ ◆

"Good morning, Nancy," God said in a sing-songy voice as he passed by his receptionist.

"Sir, you have visitors."

"Tell them I'm busy. I have a long-overdue date with a golf course."

Nancy rose from her seat as he strode by. "Sir?"

God pushed his door open, and the grin on his face promptly disappeared. Lucifer and Death were seated at his desk.

"Gentlemen, to what do I owe?" he said as he quickly composed himself.

"Sit. Now," ordered Lucifer.

God walked behind his desk and sat down in his chair.

Lucifer stared at God for a moment. "Anything you want to share with us?"

"I'm going to a barbecue with Spencer next week, and there's a cure for homosexuality," said God in a lame effort of levity.

"That's not what I meant, and you know it. Anything else?"

God shook his head.

Lucifer looked at God in dismay. "Did you think for a second that we'd not notice?"

"I was hoping," said God.

Lucifer laughed. "Come on, Gary, you dropped off five thousand, seven hundred and thirty-nine unprocessed people in my waiting room. How could you think I wouldn't notice? How did you do it?"

"New hire field trip. Look, I solved the problem, didn't I? Balance is restored, and everything is as it should be."

"No, you just made your problem my problem," said Lucifer. "I don't want your problem."

"How many people do you get a day?" asked God. "What's a few thousand more?"

"So why didn't you take them then?" asked Lucifer.

"Have you seen how they look?" asked God. "They're all kinds of fucked up. They'd scare the natives. I can't have this kind of mass hysteria in Heaven."

"I thought you guys cleaned up the bodies before you allowed them entry?" asked Lucifer. "You know, everybody being in their Sunday best and all that nonsense."

God shook his head. "Not demon zombie things. There's nothing I can do about that. Figured you'd be okay with them as you like all that horror shit."

"Are you listening to yourself? You killed some of them personally. Mr. and Mrs. O'Grady were devout Catholics their entire lives, for fuck's sake," said Lucifer.

"Who?"

"The couple you exploded at the post office. How are they going to feel when they find out they've been sent to Hell because of you? You sent their son there too."

"I'm sure we can find something they've done to be damned for all eternity. She shot at me. That's a solid starting point."

"That isn't how it works, Gary," said Lucifer.

"Fine, you can send them up here."

Death shook his head and finally spoke. "It's not that simple. The Council is involved now."

"What?"

"You circumvented the system, Gary. What outcome did you expect?"

"I—"

"You broke into my office—"

"Your secretary let me in."

"—and stole Blood Cards. Do you know how many people on Earth get Blood Cards? One. Me."

"You weren't using them. I didn't realize you were keeping count."

"Of course I keep count. I'm immortal. What else do I have to do when I get off work?"

"So what does the Council want?" asked God.

"A trade," said Death.

"What kind of trade?"

"You need to trade Mrs. Jenkins for a living soul. One life for another."

"What?"

"You need to talk a human into trading their life for the one of Mrs. Jenkins."

God frowned and shook his head. "They won't agree to that. I'll have to do a mind trick."

"No, magic," said Death. "This has to be on a strict volunteer basis."

"Impossible."

"Patient Zero is dead. This is the only way."

"You saw the mess I made last time I went down there. I won't do it." He spun his chair and turned his back to the two men.

"Then you forfeit your seat on the Council."

God's chair promptly rotated to face lucifer again. "WHAT?"

"The Council has determined if you can't resolve this issue, then your seat opens."

"Then my next in line gets it."

Death nodded.

"And that's you," God said, looking at Lucifer.

"Yeah, and I don't fucking want it," said Lucifer. "Now you see why I want this fixed. The Council is way too much drama and politics for my tastes."

"Then help me keep my seat."

"We can't help you. The Council forbids it," said Lucifer. "You're on your own this time."

"Fine. I'm sure I can persuade them."

"No mind tricks. You will be monitored," Death added.

"This is impossible. The entire town has been wiped out," said God. "How am I supposed to fix that?"

Lucifer shrugged. "Find someone to trade."

"There's no way they will go along with it."

Death smiled at God.

"You're enjoying this, aren't you?" asked God in frustration.

"Oh, you have no idea," said Death. "This might be the greatest day of my life."

CHAPTER 41

The inside of the church fell silent as the group listened to the roar from outside, their hopes of survival slipped away by the minute.

"They're going to get in," said Ashley to no one in particular.

"No way," said Cam. "The door's solid."

"She's right. It won't hold," said David. "Everything breaks eventually."

"Thank you, Captain Chipper," said Warren.

"What are we going to do?" Amber said to Greg softly.

Greg shook his head. "I shouldn't have come back here. I should have found another way out."

"There wasn't another way out. You did the only thing you could. At least we're safe," she said.

"Until we starve, or they find a way in," added David.

"I vote we eat David," said Warren.

"Should I say a prayer?" Reverend Ellis tried to change the subject. "Maybe that will help with our nerves."

"We're probably past praying," said David.

"We're never past the point of praying, my son. In fact, prayer is always the last tool when all other tools have shattered and failed. Prayer is all we have left."

"That's depressing," said David.

"Yeah, David. Pray," added Warren.

"Is this where I'm supposed to repent on my deathbed?"

Warren nodded. "Bingo."

"Not happening."

Greg ignored the bickering. "I should have done something else. There had to be another way."

"Yep, you doomed us all, dipshit," Warren chimed in. "Well done."

"Warren, you know this was the only option," said Amber as she squeezed Greg's hand.

"So you're saying he simply prolonged the inevitable?"

"I didn't see you offering an alternative," said Ashley in Greg's defense.

"You're welcome to go outside," David offered.

"No way, it's too cold," dismissed Warren.

"We have almost no food and no water," said Lee. "Who has ammo left?"

"I have one bullet," said Warren. "That's my way out. What about you guys?"

"I've seen how you shoot," said Ashley. "I wouldn't bother."

Cam sighed. "We need a miracle."

No one else spoke. The gravity of the situation hit the group like a freight train. The end had come.

A whoosh of air cut through the church.

"Did someone say a miracle?" said a voice from the back of the church

The group turned around. God and Raphael stood in front of the doors.

Warren instinctively raised his gun and fired. His last bullet hit God in the shoulder.

God looked at the hole in his jacket. "Ow! What the hell, man? You shot me."

"Sorry," said Warren as he cringed at his action.

"Sorry? You shot me," protested God.

"And I said sorry."

"You don't apologize to someone when you shoot them."

"What should I have done then?"

"Not shoot me."

"I thought you were a zombie-demon."

"Do I look like a zombie-demon to you?"

"No," said Warren hanging his head.

God looked down as he damaged jacket. "This is my favorite suit."

"It looks a little dated," said David.

"I'll have you know that this is an Oscar De La Renta original. He isn't exactly making new ones." God turned back to Warren. "Who shoots someone they just met?"

"You haven't met my brother before, have you?" said Greg.

"I come here to help you, and you shoot me. What is wrong with you?"

Greg laughed at the loaded question. "That list could take a while. How long have you got?"

David was far more interested in the appearance of God than the numerous issues with Warren. "You're here to help us?"

"Yes, we'll get to that in a minute. To everyone else who hasn't shot me, hello," said God cheerfully as he stepped forward and looked around the church. "And can someone take his gun away, please?"

"It doesn't matter. I'm out of bullets anyway," said Warren. "That was my last one."

"Who the fuck are you, anyway?" asked Greg. "And how did you get in?"

"Are you ready to have your minds blown?" asked God.

Greg rolled his eyes. "Just get to the point."

"I'm God."

Greg and David laughed at his ridiculous claim.

God frowned. He expected a much different response.

"Sure you are. And I'm Frankenstein," said Greg as he turned to the group. "Look, everyone, the end of the world is upon us, and God has decided to come down here and help us." He looked back at God. "I'm having a hard enough time with demons. Do you expect me to believe you're God?"

"Raphael, tell him."

"He's telling the truth. He's God."

David needed more convincing. "Which one?"

"What do you mean which one?" said God.

"Which god are you? Are you a god or the God?"

"I'm God."

"There are dozens of active religions not counting Nordic or any of the other gods, goddesses, or spirits of the Greco-Roman pantheon. Then you have the damned polytheistic followers who can't decide who they want to serve," said David matter-of-factly.

"I didn't think you believed in God," said Warren.

"I don't," said David.

"Then why do you know so much about religion?"

"Just because I don't believe, it doesn't mean I haven't read up on it. My decision to not believe is because of the readings I've done. I know my way around a Bible. I just choose not to follow it. My atheism isn't based on not knowing. It's based on knowing."

"Is he Thor?" said Ashley.

"Nah, he's way too scrawny to be Thor," said Amber.

"I am not scrawny," complained God.

"What's his little brother called?" asked Ashley.

"I don't remember," said Amber.

"Loki?" said Greg.

"Yeah, that's him," agreed Ashley.

"Can't be Loki. He doesn't have those horn things on his head," said Amber.

"Then he can't be Toth then either," said Warren.

Greg looked surprised. "You know Egyptian mythology?"

Warren shrugged. "They mentioned it in The Mummy."

"Figures," said Greg.

"So how do we know you're God?" asked David, getting the discussion back on topic.

"Well, how do you think I came in?"

"Through the skylight?" offered Warren.

"Do you see a skylight?" asked God.

Warren looked up at the high ceiling. "No."

"You look younger than I thought you'd be," added Cam.

"Thank you."

"Can I have an autograph?" asked Warren.

"No," said God flatly.

"Aw, come on. I'd get a ton for it on eBay. You could sign a Bible or something."

"No."

"I thought you'd have a beard," added Warren.

"Why would I have a beard?" asked God.

"Don't all wise old men have beards?"

"You're thinking of Jedi," said Cam.

"Oh, yeah." Warren turned to God. "Can you do mind tricks?"

God looked at Raphael eagerly, but Raphael shook his head.

"No," said God with a genuine look of disappointment on his face.

"Wait a minute," said Warren. "How come David can see you? He's an atheist."

"Atheists can see me," said God. "I'm not invisible."

Warren felt genuinely excited to meet God, despite shooting him. "So why don't you come down here more often? People are scrambling to get a glimpse of you. Hell, they keep seeing your son in cornflakes and toast."

"I'm very busy. Heaven doesn't run itself, you know." He turned to Reverend Ellis. "Surely you, a man of the cloth, believes me?"

Even as a man of devout faith, Reverend Ellis admitted to being a little suspicious of the newcomer. "I am open to all outcomes and scenarios. The lord works in mysterious ways."

"See, I knew you were going to say that. If I wasn't God, how come I'd know you were going to say I work in mysterious ways?"

"It's not exactly an uncommon saying," said David. "It offers little proof of who you claim to be."

God pointed to a painting on the wall behind Warren. "I have to ask, who's the hippy?"

Reverend Ellis followed his finger to a picture of Jesus. "It's our Lord and Savior. Surely you recognize him?"

"Are you serious?"

"Your son, if you're who you say you are."

"My son?"

"Jesus Christ Almighty," said Reverend Ellis.

"I know who my son is."

"Then why don't you recognize him?" asked Warren.

"I've never seen that picture before. Why does he look like a dirty pot-smoking rock star?"

"What do you mean?" Reverend Ellis raised an eyebrow. "This is how he's always looked."

"He looks like he smells of patchouli," said God. "Is this what you think he looked like?"

The Reverend nodded. "Yes. It's what biblical historians have told us."

God points to a painting of *'The Last Supper'*. "Who are the old men sitting with him at the barbecue?"

Reverend Ellis was unable to mask his confusion. "Those are his twelve disciples."

"Why are they a bunch of white men?"

"Because his disciples were white men."

"You do realize he was born in Bethlehem, right?" asked God.

"Yes, we know."

"Bethlehem, Israel?"

"Yes, we know."

"Not Pennsylvania."

"Yes."

"And are you aware Bethlehem was and is a predominantly Arab area?"

"Yes, of course."

"And you do know the odds of finding thirteen white guys two thousand years ago in that part of the world were pretty slim, right?"

Reverend Ellis fell silent.

"I mean, it's okay if you want to believe he was white, but he wasn't."

"You're white," said the Reverend.

"Yes, I am, but he got it from his mother."

"Oh."

God watched Reverend Ellis squirming. "Oh, I'm just fucking with you. I actually never met him."

Reverend Ellis sighed as relief swept over him. His Lord and Savior was making him terribly uncomfortable.

"You killed him before we were introduced."

"Oh, Christ." Reverend Ellis put his hand to his mouth in shock.

"I'm fucking with you again. You really need to lighten up a bit."

Reverend Ellis muttered a prayer for forgiveness under his breath.

"I wouldn't waste your time," said God.

Raphael gave him the look of '*stop talking*'. He wanted Heaven's deepest secret to remain private.

"Why are you here?" asked David, trying to ease the burden of guilt from the Reverend. "If you are who you claim to be, there is a reason you are here, and it's likely a damned good one."

"It's about the apocalypse, isn't it?" Greg wasn't asking.

"Yes, it's quite the mess you have here," said God.

"This isn't our fault," said Cam. "This is biblical, end of the world type shit."

"Someone who likely isn't from around here has made a colossal mess of things," said David. "Does that about sum things up?"

God nodded.

"It's no coincidence you're here, is it?" asked David. "Are you responsible for this?"

"Technically, Death is responsible for this."

"You mean the Grim Reaper?" said Amber.

"Yeah. I wouldn't call him that if I were you, he gets really grumpy."

David wasn't interested in names. "So, you're saying Heaven has nothing to do with it?"

"Not directly."

"So if this is Death's mess, why isn't he down here fixing it? Why did he send you?"

God frowned in contempt. "Death doesn't send me anywhere. I'm the one who does the sending, thank you very much. I don't even have to be here at all. You've already made me break twenty percent of my ten commandments."

"If you didn't cause this, there is no reason for you to be here. Unless, of course, this is your doing." David presented a sound argument.

"Okay, fine. I may have had a slight hand in this."

"You started the zombie apocalypse?" asked David.

"Zombie-demons, David," corrected Warren.

David shrugged. "My question still stands."

"Yeah, sorry about that," said God, shrugging. "It was an accident."

Warren did not appreciate God's response. "Well, you're a prick, aren't you? You decimated our town."

"What did you expect, Warren? This is the same guy who threw the ten plagues at us," said David.

"Hey, in my defense, I just sent one."

"No, I distinctly remember there being ten," said David.

"For an atheist, you're a bit of a know it all, aren't you?"

"Let's say I'm curious."

"Well, I know there were ten, but I'm not guilty for nine of them. The red river thing was a parlor trick. I tossed a bunch of berries in the Nile and dyed it. The frogs freaked out and left en masse, and it all went downhill from there. Besides, that happened a long time ago."

"And you're still spreading plagues." David had no intention of letting God off easily. "This demon thing has wiped out half of our town."

"Actually, it's more like ninety-nine percent. You're the last ones left."

Raphael leaned into God. "That's probably not helping."

"We experienced some minor clerical issues," said God, trying a new tactic.

David rolled his eyes in disgust. "Minor clerical issues? You killed most of Oceanview because of a spelling mistake?"

"Actually, more of a database issue," said God.

"And on what level is this considered to be minor?" asked Greg.

"There are lots of planets out there. So yes, in the grand scheme of things, this is minor."

"Well, it's pretty damned major to us," added David. "I thought you were supposed to be all-knowing and all-powerful."

God looked around the group. "Okay, I can see you're not going to be an easy audience to sway. Let's start over. Let's play a game. Tell me a name, and I'll you how they died."

"My cousin Brian," asked Cam.

"Drive-by," said God.

Cam nodded. He was right.

"Where's my Uncle Randall," said Warren.

"Hell," said God. This time he told the truth.

"Why Hell? He was a good man."

"Wasn't there that time when he hopped the turnstiles in the subway?" asked God.

"Yes," admitted Warren.

"And bragged about it at Christmas?"

"Yes."

"I never saw him repenting at church, and bragging about it on Christmas Day of all days, is pretty shitty."

"It's a funny story. I hardly think he deserved Hell," complained Warren, upset about his uncle's fate.

David chimed in again. "What about Hitler?"

"Heaven."

"WHAT?" yelled Warren. "How is that possible?"

"He repented on his death bed."

"Didn't he commit suicide?" added David.

God shrugged. "No one knows."

David rolled his eyes. "Figures," he said as he dismissed the ridiculous response with a wave of his hand.

However, Warren would not let it drop. " Jumping a turnstile is worse than genocide?"

"Jumping a turnstile *and* bragging on Christmas Day. Asking for forgiveness goes a long way," said God.

Warren shook his head in disgust. "You're saying my Uncle Randall is worse than Hitler? Then what the fuck is the criteria for Hell?"

"Not going to church," said God.

"That's it?" asked Warren.

"Yeah, pretty much."

"How many times do I need to go to church to get into Heaven?"

"At least once is a good start."

Warren frowned. "I thought the whole concept of Heaven is be good, do good, and spend an eternity of happiness? As much as be bad, do bad, sends you to Hell. You're saying I only need to repent on my death bed, and it's worth as much as going to church every Sunday of my life?"

"It sounds bad when you put it like that."

"It is fucking bad," said David.

"All those days I wasted," griped Warren. "I even went with hangovers."

"We kind of figured this would be a hard sell, so we brought a flip chart."

"A flip chart?" said David, clearly unimpressed.

"Yeah. Raph, if you please?" Raphael handed God a brass easel.

The group looked at each other in bewilderment as God fumbled with the contraption.

"Do you need help, Gary?" Raphael cringed as soon as he said God's real name.

David's eyes widened. "Your name is Gary?"

God stopped assembling the easel and looked at David. "What's wrong with my name?"

"It's not exactly epic, is it?"

"What were you expecting?" said God, a little hurt that David mocked his name.

"I don't know. Just something other than Gary. It doesn't pack that biblical punch you'd expect. Look, everyone, here comes the arrival of our Lord and Savior, Gary."

"You do kind of sound like an insurance salesman," said Greg.

"Do you want to see the chart or not?"

"Would it have killed him to prepare?" Greg whispered to Warren.

Warren agreed. "Why didn't he use PowerPoint or something?"

"I heard that," said God as he finished his battle with the easel. "We're a Mac environment."

"Why doesn't that surprise me?" said David.

God flipped the chart cover over to reveal a map of the world. "This map was last week. As you can see, things are normal." He turned the sheet over. The new map had a red dot on the north end of Arizona. "This is today." He flipped the page, and the following graphic showed the world completely covered in red. "This is next week."

"That doesn't make any sense at all," said David. "How do you go from minor outbreak to worldwide pandemic in less than a week? Nothing spreads that fast."

"Yeah, it's a little pessimistic, isn't it?" said Cam.

Lee watched the discussion from the back of the group and finally spoke. "Why are you still wearing sunglasses?"

God finally noticed Lee. "Ah, a police officer. A voice of reason. Maybe you can talk some sense into some of these people."

"I don't trust a man whose eyes I can't see."

"Or not."

"The only people who wear sunglasses inside are the blind, the deceitful, and Bono. You don't seem to have trouble seeing, and your accent isn't from Dublin, so where does that leave us?"

"Trust me, you don't want me to take off my glasses," said God. "It would be bad."

"How bad?"

"Awfully."

"He's right," confirmed Reverend Ellis. "Exodus 33:20. And he said, thou canst not see my face, for there shall no man see me, and live."

"Thank you," said God, grateful someone else understood the rule book. "He gets it."

"What'll happen?" asked Warren.

"You'd most likely spontaneously combust," said Reverend Ellis.

"That's quite the small print," said David.

God turned to Raphael. "How come he knows I can't look at humans, and you didn't?"

Raphael shrugged as God rolled his eyes in frustration. "Oversight, I guess."

God turned back to the group. "Look, I know things are scary right now, but I have good news. There is a way we can fix this."

David did not buy God's sales pitch. "You can end the zombie apocalypse?"

"Zombie-demon apocalypse, David," said Warren.

"Zip it, moron." He turned back to face God. "Well?"

God nodded.

"What's it going to cost us?"

"Why would it cost anything?"

"Heaven wouldn't send you if they didn't have to sugar coat it."

God scowled. "There's no fooling you, is there? Fine. The Council of Deities has determined a trade can be made in exchange for patient zero."

"Who?" asked David.

"You've never heard of the Council of Deities?" asked God. "So, there is something you don't know."

The group replied in the negative.

"Oh, you humans are so small and insignificant. There is an entire universe out there, and you have no idea."

"You know insulting us isn't helping, right?" said Lee.

"The Council is made up of Gods, prophets, spiritual leaders, scientists, and all kinds of intelligent and omniscient beings."

David rolled his eyes. "The universe is run by a committee? There's a shock."

Warren wanted to know more. "So you know all the other gods then?"

God nodded. "Some of them."

"What's Buddha like?"

"He's a lovely fellow and has the patience of a saint. We take turns rubbing his belly for good luck, and he doesn't even flinch. The man is a trooper."

David wanted in on the discussion. "What about Muhammad?"

"We don't talk about him."

"I thought he—"

"I said we don't talk about him."

Cam raised her hand. "What's patient zero?"

God opened his mouth to speak, but David was faster.

"Patient zero is the concept that every disease has a single point of origin. If you can find out how it started, you can start working on a cure. Does that about sum it up?" said David.

God nodded his head. "You stole my moment."

"What happened to patient zero?" asked Cam.

"She's dead." said God as he pointed at Greg and Warren. "I had it all under control until Tweedle-dee, and Tweedle-dumb-fuck over here swooped in and doomed you all."

Warren glanced over at his brother. "Which one am I?"

Greg did not pause for thought. "You are definitely Tweedle-dumb-fuck."

"What did I do?" said Warren.

"Were you the one driving the bus?" asked God.

"Yeah."

"Did you run over a demon?"

"I've run over a lot of demons."

"The one you killed at Paradise Bay?"

Warren shrugged.

"Mrs. Jenkins?"

"You killed Mrs. Jenkins?" accused David. "I liked her."

"I didn't know," said Warren in his defense.

"Well, you did," said God. "And guess what? By killing her, you screwed the universe. So that makes you Tweedle-dumb-fuck."

"Come on, that's a bit melodramatic, isn't it?" said Warren.

"Good going, Warren," said David. "Most people are content to screw the pooch. You have to screw the entire universe."

"I didn't mean to," said Warren in his defense.

"But, yet here we are," said God.

"What do you mean by a trade?" David already anticipated the answer. He just wanted to hear it from God's mouth.

"A life in trade for the one lost when you killed patient zero," said God.

The room fell silent as the audience took in what they heard.

"So, you're saying you need a sacrifice?" said David. "Wow, how biblical."

"At what point did I say sacrifice?" said God in his defense. "We need a volunteer to offset the loss of patient zero. Only then will the universe fall back into balance."

"Giving up one's life to save others sounds an awful lot like a sacrifice to me," said David.

Warren raised his hand. "Does the sacrifice have to be a virgin?"

"This is not a sacrifice," said God. "And no."

"It's a sacrifice," said David.

"It's not a sacrifice, but technically it is your fault. You killed patient zero."

"Oh, that's ripe," said David. "The owner of the most misquoted and cherry-picked book on the planet busts us on a technicality. I should have seen that coming. We wouldn't need a patient zero if you hadn't started the zombie apocalypse."

"Zombie-demons," Warren corrected once more.

"One more fucking time," replied David as he stabbed a finger at Warren.

"Hey, I didn't write it," replied God. "It's all on humanity's shoulders."

"I'll do it," Warren blurted out.

"You'll what?" said Greg in disbelief.

"I'll do it."

"Have you lost your fucking mind? You have volunteered to be his human sacrifice," Greg said as he pointed at God.

God started to get flustered. "It isn't a sacrifice."

"Whatever," said Greg as he turned back to Warren. "You don't have to do this, man. We'll figure out another way."

"There is no other way. You saw his ghetto-ass flip chart, Greg. You saw how bad things are going to get if someone doesn't stop it. Obviously, Heaven is fucking worthless."

"Heaven can hear you, you know," said God.

Warren turns to face God. "And you're fucking worthless. This is your mess, and you've left it up to us mere mortals to clean it up." He turned his attention back to his brother. "Greg, my life can finally mean something. Let me do this."

"Your life means something now."

"How many times have you told me I'm a fuck up? Ashley can't even stand me."

"Don't put this on me," said Ashley. "I'm mad at you, but I don't want you to die for me."

Warren turned to God. "So, what do you need? An altar, a knife?"

"Why would I need a knife?"

"I'm a sacrifice," said Warren. "Don't all sacrifices need knives?"

God threw up his hands in resignation. "Fine, it's a sacrifice, but that is so dark ages. We haven't used a knife and altar in hundreds of years. It's quick and painless now. You just need to get on your knees."

"Oh, well, in that case." Warren smiled and knelt in front of God.

"Warren?" pleaded Greg. "Don't do this, man. There must be another way."

"It's okay, Greg."

"Please don't. We'll find another way."

God looked down at Warren. "Do you have any last words?"

"Nope."

God reached into his pocket and pulled out a white glove.

"Are you seriously putting on a glove?" asked Warren.

"Uh, yeah, humans are gross. I don't want my hands all over you. Who knows what I might catch."

"That's rude."

God shrugged as Warren looked up at him. He raised his hand and brought it down upon his sacrifice's head. Warren frantically scrambled out of the way, holding up his hands. God swiped the air Warren's head occupied moments before.

"Whoa, whoa, whoa, what the fuck are you doing?" yelled Warren.

God looked confused. "Taking your life. I thought we were clear on that?"

"You're serious? You were going to fucking kill me?"

"Why wouldn't I be serious?" asked God. "That's the whole point of a sacrifice."

"Oh, I don't know. How about Genesis 22?"

God shrugged.

"You know, Genesis 22. The sacrifice of Isaac."

Another shrug. "I'm sorry, I'm unfamiliar with that one."

"It's in your Bible," said Warren.

"Do you know how many damn books and psalms are in it?" asked God. "I can't keep track."

"It's your job. It's like your employee handbook," said David.

"I've lost count of how often it has been translated and rewritten."

"What are you talking about?" said Warren. "There's just the Bible."

"Actually," started David, "They wrote the original version in Biblical Hebrew, with some portions most notably Daniel and Ezra, in Biblical Aramaic."

"Biblical Hebrew?"

God sighed. The humans were wasting precious time, but David was just getting started.

"Biblical Hebrew, or Classical Hebrew, is an archaic form of the Hebrew language. The first translation of the Hebrew Bible was in Greek. Even if you skip the foreign language editions, just in English, there is the King James Bible, the Geneva Bible, the New Life version—"

"Are you done?" interrupted God.

"Not even close."

"Yes, you are." God held up an index finger to silence him.

David grinned. He had never crawled under a god's skin before and rather enjoyed himself.

"So, as you can see from our smart-ass friend over here, there are hundreds of versions. You'll have to enlighten me."

"You wanted Abraham to prove his loyalty to you and sacrifice his only son as a burned offering," said Warren.

"You said that?" said Cam as her eyes widened.

God pondered the question for a moment. "It sounds vaguely familiar."

"That is fucked up."

"Right?" agreed Warren. "And when he's about to kill his kid, you sent down angels and told him he's being tested," continued Warren.

"Yeah, it does sound familiar now that you mention it."

"This shit right here." David made a circle gesture with his finger. "This is why I'm an atheist. What kind of god keeps his flock in line by telling them to kill their children? Better yet, why does a person want to follow a god who behaves that way?"

"Oh, come on, it was a joke. I thought it was funny," said God.

"Fucked up." David reiterated.

Warren scrambled to prevent his death. "I figured this was the same deal. I'm about to offer myself, and you tell me it's just a test to see how dedicated I am to you."

"I can see why you'd think that," said God.

"So, I'm right?"

"No."

"How is this any different?" asked Warren.

"Genesis 22 didn't have zombie-demons in it, and even if it did, Abraham didn't kill patient zero."

"I said I was sorry."

"Sorry doesn't bring back patient zero now, does it?" said God.

"This is because I shot you, isn't it?"

"No. The Council requires a soul for soul trade. You having just shot me makes this more enjoyable."

"I've changed my mind. I don't want to go."

Warren stood and stepped back to the group.

"Well, here is a way around this," said God.

"There is?" Warren's eyes widened at the hope of being able to survive. "One where I wouldn't have to be sacrificed?"

"Of course, there is always a way around things." God turned to the rest of the group. "Who wants to take his place?"

Warren looked around the group as they lowered their eyes in shame.

"No one?" said God as he looked at the audience.

The silence continued.

"You all fucking suck." He turned to his brother. "Greg?"

Greg opened his mouth to speak.

"Warren, don't you dare do that to your brother," Ashley said, stepping forward. "I'll do it."

"What?" Amber, Greg, and Warren all said in unison.

"I'll do it."

"No, you won't," said Warren. "I will. God's right. This is my fault. I need to be the one to fix it."

Greg stepped up to his brother. "I don't know what to say. I never wanted this to happen. We were supposed to grow old playing pool together and laughing about how much of a fuck-up you are."

"Don't you cry on me, Greg," said Warren.

"Yeah," Greg replied through watery eyes.

Warren's face suddenly turned serious. "I need to tell you something."

"No, man, it's okay. There's nothing left to say," said Greg as he sniffed back a tear.

"No, I can't leave with this out there."

"Look, I know what you're going to say."

"Please."

"I know you were skimming off the books. It's okay. I'm not at you, I docked your pay in small increments and you didn't notice."

"I slept with Amber."

"What?" asked Greg.

"He did not!" protested Amber.

Warren smiled and winked at Greg. "Love you, bro." He looked up at God. "Okay, do it."

Warren closed his eyes tight, and his breathing became heavy and erratic. His journey had reached its end. Were he to have been quizzed on how he expected to check out, being personally killed by God would not have been anywhere near the top of his list. He wanted it to be more sexual in nature and was disappointed boobs and strippers were not involved. Time slowed to a crawl, and the cries and protests from the group became muffled. A bright flash pierced through his closed eyes, and the moaning outside suddenly stopped. Was it over? Unsure of what to expect, Warren slowly opened one eye and saw God standing in front of him. Heaven looked an awful lot like Earth.

"You can stand up," said Ashley from behind him.

Warren opened his other eye and looked around. He was indeed alive. "What happened? Did he change his mind?"

Ashley shook her head and looked down beside Warren. He followed her gaze to see David sprawled on the flood. "What the hell happened? Did God miss?"

"He took your place," said Ashley.

"He WHAT?"

Ashley slowly nodded. "He stepped in last second. He's gone."

Warren struggled to find the right words. Sure, he hated David, but he never expected the guy to sacrifice himself for him. He looked back at God. "I didn't want him to do that. Where did he go?"

"Upstairs, where he belongs," said God.

"Impossible," said Warren.

"David sacrificed himself. It's an instant one-way pass to Heaven," said God as he started to dismantle the easel.

"Where are you going?" asked Warren.

"We're done here," said God. "Mission accomplished. I'm going home to play golf. This whole apocalypse thing has really ruined my green time."

"Did you forget about him being an atheist?" asked Warren.

God paused and blinked. He had indeed overlooked that tiny detail. He turned to Raphael. "We have to go."

Raphael's eyes widened. "Gary, what have you done?"

"We need to leave. Now," said God.

"There can't be an atheist in Heaven," said Raphael. "The Council won't allow it."

"I know. Grab the fucking easel." God shooed him towards the flip chart as he turned back to the group. "Okay, well, this has been fantastic and all, but it's time for me to get back upstairs. I do have a universe to oversee."

Greg stepped forward. "Where are you going? What about the rest of the town? Where are they?"

"They're all dead," said God matter-of-factly.

"All of them?"

God nodded. "It's what happens after the apocalypse."

"Can't you bring them back to life?" asked Cam. "I mean, you are God."

"No."

"Wait a minute," said Lee. "You've wrecked our town, and all the people are dead because of you. We knew those people. I thought patient zero was supposed to reset all of this. You can't leave it this way."

"What do I look like, maintenance? We needed a replacement for patient zero. Therefore, it didn't come with the same privileges as the real patient zero. Different person, different rules. Besides, Death started all this. Take it up with him. I've stayed here longer than I wanted to anyway."

"You claim to be divine. Wiggle your finger and make all of this go away," said Greg.

"Sorry, I don't do parlor tricks."

"When the outside world hears what happened here, there will be questions," said Amber.

"And who is going to believe you? Demons? God? I saw it with my own eyes, and I don't believe it."

"You're supposed to work miracles," said Cam. "Help us fix our town,

339

you owe us that."

"This is supposed to be your forte," said Reverend Ellis. "Your flock needs you."

God sighed in frustration. He had reached his wit's end with Oceanview and just wanted to get back to Heaven. "Fine, I'll fix your damn town and resurrect everyone, then I'm leaving."

"Thank you," said Reverend Ellis.

God nodded a curt acknowledgment and twirled his finger. A second bright light flashed from outside. "There, all fixed."

Raphael tucked the easel under his arm. Seconds later, Earth's Lord and Savior and his right-hand man disappeared as fast as they arrived.

The group looked at each other expectantly. Was it really over?

"Is that it?' asked Amber.

"I guess so. Should we go home," said Greg as he put his arm around Amber and kissed her on the cheek.

Lee walked to the door and pushed it open. Sunlight flooded into the church as the group walked outside. The demons were indeed gone, but the town still looked like a bomb had gone off. There were no signs of the resurrected or any other Oceanview survivors.

"That lying bastard," Warren blurted out. "Our town, it's fucked."

"Son of a bitch," echoed Ashley. "What the hell is this crap?"

Cam shook her head in disgust. "What a shit-hole."

"I don't even know how I am going to call this in," said Lee as he stared at the decimated street. "No one is going to believe any of this."

Warren looked at the chaos. "So now what do we do?"

"I don't know," said Greg.

Lee shrugged his shoulders. "We're Oceanview. We rebuild. That's what we do. What other choice do we have?"

"Fuck that shit, I'm moving," said Cam with a smile. "I'm not cleaning this up." She reached into her pocket, pulled out Donald's check, and smiled sadly. "Time to start over."

"I'm with Cam," said Ashley. "I'm leaving."

"She's right," said Amber. "There's nothing left." She leaned into Greg's ear and smiled. "It looks like you get out of telling Warren we're moving."

Warren grabbed his brother's arm from behind. "Greg?"

"Yeah?"

"We forgot Bob."

EPILOGUE

The rhythmic beat of the wall clock in God's office had pushed him into a light sleep. He drifted peacefully in his chair when a light tapping echoed from the office door. He rolled onto his other side and tried to claw his way back to the peaceful undertones of slumber.

The light tapping rang out again. "Hello?" Nancy's soft voice asked from outside. "Are you awake?"

"I guess I am now," he muttered to himself with a loud yawn. He rubbed his face and tried to caress the sleepiness from his system. "Yes, I'm up," he said.

The door pushed open, and Nancy poked her head through in her usual timid manner. "Someone is here to see you."

"My first appointment isn't for three more hours. Tell them to schedule and come back later. Processes, Nancy."

"He said it's important."

"Tell this mystery guest to make an appointment like everyone else."

"He's very insistent."

"Well, tell him I'm busy."

"I can't he's—"

The door swung open as Death stormed into the office and pushed his way past Nancy. He crossed the room and stopped in front of God. He looked pissed, more pissed than God had ever seen him.

"Sorry, sir." Nancy apologized. "I tried to stop him."

God waved her away. "Don't worry, Nancy, I'll take care of this."

She backed out of the office and carefully closed the door behind her.

341

"Steve, to what do I owe this pleasure?" God remained seated.

Death ignored the question. "How long, Gary?"

God looked genuinely confused. "How long? What do you mean? How long what?"

"How long has it been since you damn near fucked the universe, or have you let it slip from your feeble little mind?"

"Hey, the keyword being near, and isn't it a bit early in the day for insults?"

"How long?"

"About two months. I thought you were better with dates than that."

"So, two months is all it takes for you to forget?"

God started to get irritated. "Forget what?"

Death rolled his eyes in contempt.

"I've been busy dealing with an atheist issue. Can you get to the point?" God had tired of the guessing game.

Death dropped a manila folder on God's desk and stared at it. "Here," he said gruffly.

"What's this?" asked God.

Death clenched his teeth together, frustrated at the need to respond. "We've been here before. You know exactly what this is. Open the damn thing."

God reached over and flipped the folder open. It contained the reaping lists his office had sent to Death earlier in the day. God opened his mouth to speak. He was genuinely confused. "I—"

"Don't say a fucking word, Gary," said Death as he rudely interrupted God.

God cringed. Death seldom cursed, and the few times he did, people needed to pay attention, as he was likely to be rather upset.

"You promised me," said Death. "You swore on your son's life that you took care of things. ON YOUR SON'S LIFE."

God tried to speak up in his defense, but Death had so much more to say.

"You swore to me that your database issues were resolved and that this would never happen again. You gave your word, Gary. You showed me receipts."

"I did. I fixed it," God protested. "I wouldn't lie to you about that. I know how you get." He mumbled the last sentence in the hopes Death did not hear him.

"You're a liar," accused Death. "You fucking lied to me. Again."

342

"I promise you, I really don't know why you're here."

"Then why the fuck did I just have a failed reaping in Brisbane?"

"I love Australians. Their accent is so cute—"

"STAY ON FUCKING TOPIC!" screamed Death. "We're done here. There is nothing you can say or do that will make this right. Do you remember that little soiree in Oceanview? Well, it ain't shit compared to what you've just unleashed on the planet. I'm done reaping. You and Earth, you're on your own. I'm scrubbing my hands of the whole damn lot of you."

God stood up from his chair. "Steve."

"You will call me Death."

"Death, I fixed this. I promise you, we repaired the database. I have no reason to lie to you about that."

"No? And yet here we are with you lying about it." Death no longer cared to listen to God's pathetic excuses. "There aren't enough blood cards in the universe for you to bail your ass out this time, so don't even contemplate it." He turned and headed to the door, slamming it closed behind him.

God picked up the folder and flipped through the pages. He scowled as he reviewed the contents. He reached for the phone on desk and called out into the front desk. "Nancy, don't let him leave."

♦ ♦ ♦ ♦

Death moved quickly towards the elevators. His robes swirled around his as his fury carried him forward. God entered the hallway behind him and waved his arms. "Steve, wait," God yelled.

Death kept moving. He held no intentions of speaking with the idiot. Nothing good would come from it.

"Stop," God pleaded a second time to no avail. "DEATH, WILL YOU FUCKING STOP," he shouted.

Death stopped but refused to turn around. He clenched his teeth and fists in anger, seconds away from punching God in the face. "There is nothing left for you to say, Gary. You fucked the pooch royally this time. You are not going to be weaseling your way out of it with charm and quick wit."

"You think I'm charming?" asked God. He cringed as he caught himself from speaking further. It was not the type of question he should be asking. "Can we please talk about this?" he asked as Death reached the elevators and stopped.

"I'm through talking to you. Nothing changes. Nothing ever changes. Now you can go back to your pompous deity committee and explain how your prize creation destroyed itself."

"Steve, let me say one more thing, and I'll let the matter drop. You'll never hear another word from me."

Death sighed and turned to face God. "One thing and I'm done," he said, holding up a single finger. "Then I never want to see you ever again. Do I make myself clear?"

"Perfectly."

God handed the folder to Death. "This is Lucifer's list."

♦ ♦ ♦ ♦

To Be Continued
in

LUCiFER JUST WaNTEO to PET KiTTENS

♦ ♦ ♦ ♦

www.ingramcontent.com/pod-product-compliance
Lightning Source LLC
Chambersburg PA
CBHW070639180626
46817CB00006B/2173